To Everything a Season

Books by Lauraine Snelling

Song of Blessing

To Everything a Season

An Untamed Heart

Red River of the North

An Untamed Land
A New Day Rising
A Land to Call Home
The Reapers' Song
Tender Mercies
Blessing in Disguise

Return to Red River

A Dream to Follow
Believing the Dream
More Than a Dream

Daughters of Blessing

A Promise for Ellie
Sophie's Dilemma
A Touch of Grace
Rebecca's Reward

Home to Blessing

A Measure of Mercy
No Distance Too Far
A Heart for Home

Wild West Wind

Valley of Dreams
Whispers in the Wind
A Place to Belong

Dakotah Treasures

Ruby
Pearl
Opal
Amethyst

Secret Refuge

Daughter of Twin Oaks
Sisters of the Confederacy
The Long Way Home
A Secret Refuge 3-in-1

To Everything a Season

LAURAINE SNELLING

Published by Bethany House Publishers
11400 Hampshire Avenue South
Bloomington, Minnesota 55438
www.bethanyhouse.com

Bethany House Publishers is a division of
Baker Publishing Group, Grand Rapids, Michigan

Printed in the United States of America

Library of Congress Cataloging-in-Publication Data
Snelling, Lauraine.
To everything a season / Lauraine Snelling.
pages cm. — (Song of Blessing ; Book 1)
Summary: "Miriam Hastings is determined not to let anything get in the way of her plans to leave Blessing, North Dakota, and become an accredited nurse—even love"— Provided by publisher.
ISBN 978-0-7642-1218-5 (cloth : alk. paper) — ISBN 978-0-7642-1104-1 (pbk.) — ISBN 978-0-7642-1219-2 (large-print pbk.)
1. Christian fiction. 2. Love stories. I. Title.
PS3569.N39T6 2014
813′.54—dc23 2014006602

Scripture quotations are from the King James Version of the Bible

Cover design by Jennifer Parker

Author is represented by Books & Such Literary Agency.

14 15 16 17 18 19 20 7 6 5 4 3 2 1

To Sandy and Woodeene,

extraordinary friends,

who always help me far more than they realize.

Two of God's many gifts to me.

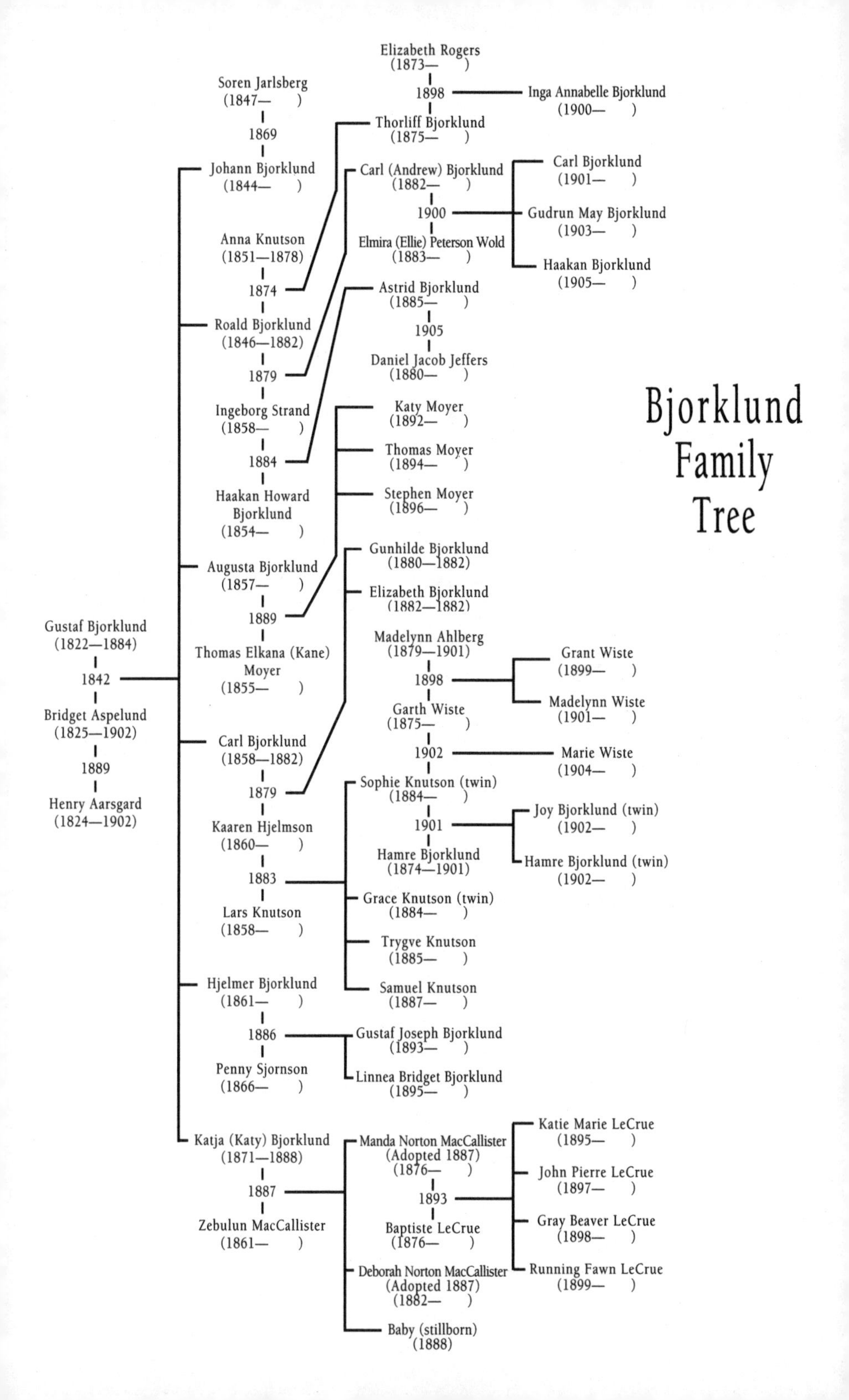

Bjorklund Family Tree
Gustaf Bjorklund (1822—1884)
1842
Bridget Aspelund (1825—1902)
1889
Henry Aarsgard (1824—1902)
Soren Jarlsberg (1847—)
1869
Johann Bjorklund (1844—)
Anna Knutson (1851—1878)
1874
Roald Bjorklund (1846—1882)
1879
Ingeborg Strand (1858—)
1884
Haakan Howard Bjorklund (1854—)
Augusta Bjorklund (1857—)
1889
Thomas Elkana (Kane) Moyer (1855—)
Carl Bjorklund (1858—1882)
1879
Kaaren Hjelmson (1860—)
1883
Lars Knutson (1858—)
Hjelmer Bjorklund (1861—)
1886
Penny Sjornson (1866—)
Katja (Katy) Bjorklund (1871—1888)
1887
Zebulun MacCallister (1861—)
Elizabeth Rogers (1873—)
1898
Thorliff Bjorklund (1875—)
Inga Annabelle Bjorklund (1900—)
Carl (Andrew) Bjorklund (1882—)
1900
Elmira (Ellie) Peterson Wold (1883—)
Carl Bjorklund (1901—)
Gudrun May Bjorklund (1903—)
Haakan Bjorklund (1905—)
Astrid Bjorklund (1885—)
1905
Daniel Jacob Jeffers (1880—)
Katy Moyer (1892—)
Thomas Moyer (1894—)
Stephen Moyer (1896—)
Gunhilde Bjorklund (1880—1882)
Elizabeth Bjorklund (1882—1882)
Madelynn Ahlberg (1879—1901)
1898
Garth Wiste (1875—)
1902
Grant Wiste (1899—)
Madelynn Wiste (1901—)
Marie Wiste (1904—)
Sophie Knutson (twin) (1884—)
1901
Hamre Bjorklund (1874—1901)
Joy Bjorklund (twin) (1902—)
Hamre Bjorklund (twin) (1902—)
Grace Knutson (twin) (1884—)
Trygve Knutson (1885—)
Samuel Knutson (1887—)
Gustaf Joseph Bjorklund (1893—)
Linnea Bridget Bjorklund (1895—)
Manda Norton MacCallister (Adopted 1887) (1876—)
1893
Baptiste LeCrue (1876—)
Katie Marie LeCrue (1895—)
John Pierre LeCrue (1897—)
Gray Beaver LeCrue (1898—)
Running Fawn LeCrue (1899—)
Deborah Norton MacCallister (Adopted 1887) (1882—)
Baby (stillborn) (1888)

Chapter 1

Blessing, North Dakota
May 1905

"I fear something is seriously wrong."

Dr. Astrid Bjorklund Jeffers stared at her mother. Mor never said things like this. She always said God was in control and He knew best. Astrid forced herself to step out of her daughter role and into her doctor role. Forced, because raging through her mind was *Far, my far. What is happening to you?* "Mor, can you tell me what you see that is different?"

Sitting in her rocking chair, her hands quiet in her lap, something so rare that Astrid caught that too, Ingeborg let the song of the rockers fill the quiet room. She slowly wagged her head. "There is nothing specific, like his speech or the shaking. Just a sense I have. One cannot be married for all these years and not sense when something is changing or amiss."

Astrid heaved a sigh, remembering the stroke Far had suffered two years ago. As far as she could tell, he had recovered completely, other than getting tired more easily, but then, he was getting older too. Someone else had mentioned one day after church that Haakan had aged in the last couple of years. But wasn't that to be expected? He worked hard, and always had. Farmers did that. Norwegian farmers maybe even more so. The farm was his life. It provided for them, and he believed God gave them the land to husband and make flourish. Mentally she catalogued the scenes she remembered from the other episode, searching for more knowledge.

"He will resent it if I ask him to see me or Elizabeth for a checkup."

Ingeborg nodded. "He is a man, after all."

"And I am his daughter and Elizabeth his daughter-in-law. Women always see male doctors without qualms, but the reverse . . ." She shook her head, sharing a smile with her mor.

"He respects what you do and admires you for it."

"I know, but letting me help him is something else." Even though both daughter and daughter-in-law were fully accredited physicians, she and Elizabeth still fought the stigma of being women in a man's field. Astrid tucked a strand of aged-honey hair back in the chignon she wore at the base of her head. She'd never gotten into the habit of wearing braids pinned into a coronet like her mother wore.

"I know I must turn this over to God and not fret." Mor stared out the window to the burgeoning greens of spring. Sparrows argued in the branches of the cottonwood tree she had planted at the corner of the house so many years ago. The liquid notes of a meadowlark out in the field floated through the open window. A cow bellowed, adding to the chorus that sang of new life after the long, hard winter. "In my reading this morning, Paul says, 'Be anxious for nothing.' Such an easy thing to read and yet so hard at times."

"After all these years, I would hope it has become easier." *If it hasn't for you, my dear mor who walks so closely with our Lord, how can there be hope for the rest of us?*

Mor's voice was soft, sad. "Ja, until it concerns your husband or your children. To not fret or be anxious takes more trust. God keeps giving me lessons in trusting Him, and about the time I think I understand it, something new comes up. . . ." She sighed. "Easy to do for myself and for all the others around me, but not when it comes to Haakan."

Astrid turned at the sound of a harness jingling. Surely it wasn't time for dinner already. She glanced at their carved walnut clock. The oak box on the wall, with the mouthpiece in black and the receiver on the hook at the side, started its call to attention. One, two, three rings. The call for Tante Kaaren over at the deaf school.

"Answer that, will you?" came from the front porch.

Astrid stood and hustled to pick it up. "Yes?"

"Oh, it's you, Astrid. This is for Kaaren."

"I know. She's just coming in the door. Please hold for a second." She held the receiver out to her tante Kaaren, whose once-golden hair was silvering even more than Ingeborg's.

When Kaaren took the receiver with a smile, Astrid headed for the shiny black cookstove with polished chrome trim and pulled the coffeepot closer to the heat. Lifting the front lid, she inserted a couple of sticks of firewood from the woodbox, grateful that someone had refilled it since early morning. Adjusting the damper, she moved the coffeepot all the way to the hottest section.

"The ginger cookies are in the cookie jar, and we have some corn bread left from last night that we can pour syrup over if you want." The creak of the rocking chair announced that Mor was on her way to the kitchen.

Kaaren replaced the earpiece in its metal hook and turned to Astrid with a smile. "What a treat to find you here. I'm on my way to town and wondered if you want anything at the store." She smiled at Mor, who was retying her apron as she came under the arch from the parlor to the kitchen.

"Let me think. You will stay for coffee?"

"Ja, especially since you said corn bread and syrup. I've not made corn bread lately. No idea why." She nodded to the telephone. "The last of the students just got on the train." She heaved a sigh. "Another year done."

Kaaren Knutson had started the Blessing School for the Deaf years earlier after she'd learned sign language to help her daughter Grace, who was born deaf. Since then the school had become so well-known, they had to turn students away for lack of housing.

The lack of housing in town was becoming more and more of a problem, for Blessing was growing from a farmers' village into a real town, thanks to the hospital, the flour mill, Ingeborg's cheese house, and various other businesses. All were supported by the farms in the Red River Valley, an expanse so flat that wagons never even needed brakes.

"You sit down, Mor, and let me serve you for a change." Astrid smiled at her mother.

Mor rolled her eyes but joined Kaaren at the well-worn kitchen table.

While the coffee was heating, Astrid dipped some hot water from the reservoir into a bowl and set the syrup pitcher in it to warm, slid the pan of corn bread into the oven, and after arranging some cookies on a plate, brought that to the table.

"Use the flowered plates, if you will."

"Oh, we are having a party?" Astrid put the plain white plates back in the cupboard and fetched the hand-painted dishes from the glass-fronted china cabinet that her father had made for her mother last Christmas.

"Of course, to celebrate another year of Kaaren's school and anything else we can think of to celebrate." Ingeborg patted Kaaren's hand on the table. "Whoever would have dreamed of all the changes that are going on. So many people blessed by coming to Blessing."

"We named our town well." The two women shared a memory look of all those years ago when the folks had voted on a name for their town. The men had suggested various names, but when Pastor Solberg decreed, much to the dismay of the males, that the women could indeed vote, the name Blessing carried. Women were still allowed to vote in church matters, but like women everywhere, they were not permitted to vote in general elections, including school elections.

When all was set on the table, Mor took their hands and bowed her head. "Thank you, Lord, for this day and these treasured moments with my sister and daughter. Amen."

Astrid cut into her piece of corn bread smothered in syrup and smiled around the treat. "I've not made this for Daniel yet. I wonder if he will appreciate it like we do."

"There's only one way to find out," Kaaren said after wiping a spot of syrup from her mouth with one of the embroidered napkins Astrid had set at the places. "Although how you find time to do any cooking, what with the hospital and your medical practice, I'll never know."

"Same as you two always have—Mor with the cheese house, and you with a school full of students who board there. Deaf students, no less."

"Well, we certainly do not have a noise problem." They paused as the telephone started to ring again and they counted the rings of the party line. Four rings meant the call was for Penny Bjorklund at the mercantile.

Kaaren paused a moment, looking daydreamy as she savored the corn bread. "I know I could call my order in and Penny would have it ready when I get there, but somehow that seems rude."

Astrid shook her head. "It certainly is convenient." Ever since she and Daniel had moved into their own house, the men having finished the interior during the winter, she'd been juggling the demanding tasks of creating a home while running the hospital and going out to birth babies. It seemed that every young pregnant woman in the area had either delivered already or would be soon. She and Elizabeth took turns with the deliveries, with only two having complications enough to use the hospital. Due to all that, she'd taken advantage of the new service Penny had dreamed up—her helpers brought the orders out to the customers. The service was working so well that the Garrisons, who owned the grocery store, were teaming up with Penny.

Mor set her cup back down. "I've been thinking of something."

"Uh-oh." Kaaren grinned at Astrid. "Now we're in trouble."

"Oh, you." Ingeborg waved off her comment. "Andrew thinks this is a good idea too."

"What about Far?"

A shadow passed over Ingeborg's face. "That's one of the strange things. He has come up with all kinds of objections."

Astrid leaned forward on her elbows. "That's not like Far." Usually her father encouraged new ideas, no matter who they came from, but especially if his beloved came up with the idea.

"I know."

Mor moved her spoon around, then glanced from Astrid to Kaaren. "My idea is to provide milk service to the people in town that do not own a cow. We could bottle it here, or probably at

Andrew's, and deliver once or twice a week. I would be sure to leave plenty of milk for the cheese house and yet help some of those struggling to create a home. I thought of having them come here to pick it up, but delivery seems like a good idea. I know they do things like this in the cities, even in Grand Forks. It's something to think about."

Astrid could only shake her head. Leave it to her mother to come up with another brilliant idea.

The phone rang again, this time for her. "I'm here, Gerald. What is it? Tell her I'll be there as soon as I can get there. Thank you." She turned to the others. "Tante Kaaren, can you give me a ride to town? Gerald says the baby that has dawdled so long has decided to come, and fast."

Kaaren and Astrid were out the door, Kaaren's thank-you sailing over her shoulder.

"I'll call my order in," Ingeborg called from the door as both Astrid and Kaaren climbed up into the buggy.

Turning the buggy, Kaaren set the horse to a fast trot, kicking up twin spirals of dust down the lane. "Do you anticipate trouble?"

"No. Most likely, she won't even really need me, but better safe than sorry."

Kaaren glanced down at the black bag at their feet. "You carried that out to Ingeborg's?"

"It's not heavy—well, not much anyway. Guess I never go anywhere without it."

Kaaren wagged her head, but she was grinning. "Astrid, you are hopeless."

Ingeborg plopped down on the settee on the porch and watched the women go until the buggy was nothing more than a small hazy dust cloud beyond the trees. And who was this coming? She recognized the bonnet immediately—Grace. And the child's face looked disturbed. Child? No. A bride to be, no longer a child.

Ingeborg sighed. She and Haakan were getting old, but somehow she avoided thinking about that. For sure, she still felt as though she were thirty. But here were grandchildren, nieces and nephews, even grandnieces and grandnephews, Grace among them, and still she did not really feel old.

Grace trotted up onto the porch and sat down on the settee at Ingeborg's invitation.

"Tante Ingeborg, I . . . I . . ." Grace looked to be squeezing the life from her hands.

Ingeborg took the hands of this young woman beside her and signed *I love you* into her palm. "All will be well."

All is well already, dear child, Ingeborg thought. What a wonder this young woman was. Grace, deaf since birth, was already a well-known teacher of sign language, and thanks to her mother, she had learned to speak with words as well. It was exactly like knowing two languages. Kaaren had learned to sign so she could help her daughter, and thus was born the Blessing School for the Deaf.

Grace clung to Ingeborg's hands and spoke in her monotone, halting way. "You always say that."

"I know, because it is true. Our Father has proven himself over and over all our lives. I remember when you were born—Sophie first and then you. Sophie was such a squally, noisy baby, and you were so quiet. When we learned you couldn't hear, your mor and I prayed so hard that you would be healed. But God didn't see it that way. And now look how He has blessed so many people through you and your mother!"

Grace leaned her head briefly against her aunt's shoulder. "I am so thankful for you, Tante Ingeborg."

"I will guess here about what's bothering you. You are troubled about your wedding. Uncertain."

"Uncertain. Exactly. Ja, and troubled."

Ingeborg continued to stroke Grace's hands, but was careful to make sure Grace could see her mouth to be able to read her lips. That was another skill Grace had perfected through the years. "You need not doubt your decision to marry Jonathan. I assure you, having the jitters is very normal. Almost everyone gets them."

Grace forced a smile that wasn't really there. "I was ready. But his mother . . ." She sighed.

That was certainly understandable. His mother, who never did like Grace, had done all she could to forestall the wedding and had succeeded in delaying it.

"You have worked so hard, Grace, and done so well. You can do this too. And possibly win her over. In any case, you have won Jonathan. And what does Jonathan want?"

"To be married as soon and as easily as possible. He wants to come here immediately after his graduation and get married that very weekend. Then he plans to farm with my father and Onkel Haakan."

Ingeborg nodded. "We all want that too. When will Jonathan's family be here?"

"They'll be coming for his graduation but plan to stay in Fargo until the day before the wedding on the following Saturday. We will leave for our honeymoon on Sunday. His mother is not happy that I refused to be married in New York. Jonathan did not want to be married in New York either, but she . . ." Grace shrugged and tipped her head to the side. "As you said, all will be well."

"Ja, it will be."

"We *will* go to New York after the wedding for some celebrations with Jonathan's family and friends. But I think Mrs. Gould is also angry because we declined her offer for a wedding trip to Europe. We asked, instead, if they would put the money into the building fund for the addition to the deaf school instead."

Ingeborg had heard all this from Kaaren, but that didn't dim her delight in Grace telling her. Knowing what little she knew of Jonathan's mother, Ingeborg had a pretty fair idea of where Grace fit or didn't fit in with the family. But her own memories of Jonathan's father, the man Ingeborg had met as a new immigrant in New York City, were always treasured in her heart. He had remained a friend all these years. So many years since he had come west, and now he was coming for a wedding of which she was sure his wife did not approve. Life takes strange turns.

Ingeborg had another thought. "Tell me, Grace, are you afraid a child of yours might be deaf? Cannot hear, like you?"

"Ja, sometimes. In the middle of the night if I cannot sleep."

"I have read what I could find about this, and there is no evidence that will always happen. But our God is in charge. Never forget that. And your family is here to gather around you."

Their silence stretched before Grace answered. "I am glad I do not have to live in New York." She fluttered a little wave and stood up, so Ingeborg stood also. Together they walked down the steps and out the lane to the path leading across the small field to the deaf school. The men had built stiles across the fences to make it easier for the visitors, and now that they no longer kept the bull in that pasture, the path was used often.

"Soon the wedding will be here, and you and Jonathan can get settled. And honeymoon, of course." Ingeborg hugged Grace again. "Now, is there anything that I can do for you?"

"Just pray for us and come to the ceremony. I want to keep this as simple as possible."

"Of course I will!"

Grace heaved a sigh and gave a little wave. "Takk. Tusen takk."

Two hours later, Astrid walked back to the surgery, a two-story residence with gables and gingerbread that housed not only the doctors' office and examining rooms but also Thorliff, Elizabeth, and five-year-old Inga. The two doctors had talked of moving to the hospital but so far hadn't made the effort. Besides, they needed the rooms there more for hospital staff and training. Astrid had checked on their six patients at the hospital earlier in the morning.

"My, that was quick," Elizabeth said when Astrid joined her on the back porch.

"The mother was right. That baby boy was not wasting any more time. He came in a rush, and I'm sure I heard him hollering before he emerged. Mother and baby are doing fine. I was mostly a spectator." Astrid smiled up at Thelma, Elizabeth's housekeeper, cook, and whatever else she needed to be. "Ja, I would love a cup of coffee, and no, I've not had dinner."

Thelma believed her main mission in life was to take care of her two doctors, along with all the other things she accomplished. Both doctors had given up on trying to keep up with Thelma, a wiry, whirling wonder of doing and caring with no thought for herself. Even her hair could not keep up with her. Instead of a sedate bun, it flew in all directions, causing her to threaten it with scissors on a daily basis.

By the time Astrid had given the briefest report on their patients, Thelma had set a bowl of thick chicken-and-dumpling soup in front of her, as well as a steaming cup of coffee and fresh muffins, butter, and jam alongside. Just the way Astrid liked it.

"Mange takk."

"Anything else?" Thelma also conserved words like water in a drought.

"I think not. You could bring a cup of coffee out here and sit with us."

The look made Astrid and Elizabeth roll their eyes and share a smile. "I'll keep trying," Astrid called toward the slamming screen door. The first spoon of the meal-in-a-bowl made her sigh with pleasure, a normal reaction to Thelma's cooking.

Elizabeth blew on her spoonful of soup. "We have no patients scheduled for this afternoon, so I suggest you go home, not back to the hospital, at least not yet, and—"

"I guess I can write letters to Chicago from home as well as here or at the hospital."

"I was going to say to take the rest of the afternoon off."

Astrid looked up from her dinner. "Why?"

"Why not?"

"I took time off to go visit Mor."

Elizabeth started to say something, then stared at Astrid. "Something about that visit is bothering you."

"You are too perceptive for your own good." Astrid went on to describe her mother's concern for Haakan. "She can't put a finger on it either, but you and I have both noticed something is different. What do you see?"

"He's been somewhat withdrawn at church. Talking with the men some but more listening."

"Or just being there. Is he listening or . . . ?"

"How should I know? I'm not part of that circle." Elizabeth put her feet up on the hassock.

"I shall ask Thorliff."

"Or Daniel. He's pretty observant, and Haakan is not his father. That makes a difference. Also Reverend Solberg. But what can we do anyway?"

"Knowledge is our first line of defense." Astrid sipped her coffee, elbows propped on the round table. "I've been wracking my brain to pinpoint when the change began, what might have precipitated it."

"He never returned to full robustness after his stroke. No matter how he's tried to think so. Men can be so stubborn."

"I take offense at that comment." Thorliff, husband to Elizabeth, Astrid's brother, and the eldest of the Bjorklund children, did not take the three steps as one, like usual.

"The newspaper is finished." Astrid stated more than asked.

"Yes, thank goodness." He sank down on the chair across the table from Astrid and reached for his wife's hand. "Good to see you out here."

"I know. This is the first day really warm enough to enjoy being outside." An argument started in the tree that hovered over the porch roof and ended when one bird flew off. The cat settled back in her basket and Inga's dog, Scooter, laid his head back on his front paws after greeting Thorliff.

Thelma brought the coffeepot out, poured a cup for him, and refilled Astrid's cup. "Soup or sandwich?" she asked.

"Soup is faster."

Elizabeth's brows arched. "And what is the hurry after finishing the paper? A brief rest would not be amiss."

Thorliff half smiled. "I need to check on the crews."

"Your foremen have all quit?" That arched eyebrow took the slight sting from her words.

Astrid rolled her lips together. Yes, Thorliff was working long and hard hours, but that seemed to be a family trait from both sides of the family. Andrew too. Work hard and long but live the pace of the land.

The jangle of the phone and two rings brought Astrid to her feet.

"You are wanted at the schoolhouse," Thelma told her a moment later. "Something has happened."

"Did they say what for?" she asked as she grabbed her black bag.

Thelma shook her head. "You need a bicycle."

"Good idea." Astrid knew she could walk there faster than she could hitch up a horse. "Call Mor and ask her to start praying."

"She always starts to pray when our telephones ring," Thorliff called as, with one hand clapped on her straw hat to keep it from flying off, Astrid jogged away toward the schoolhouse on the other side of town.

Chapter 2

Inga fell out of the tree!" shouted one of the older boys, running to meet her.

"Is she bleeding?" Astrid kept up her jog, more a running walk.

The boy took her bag and kept pace. "No. Mr. Nyquist said she had to lay still. I mean, *lie* still."

"Good. Thank you. Is school out yet?"

"No, ma'am. Final recess."

Astrid could see a circle of children under a cottonwood tree and the teacher ordering them all back into the schoolhouse. They stepped back when she set her bag down beside her niece, whose head was cradled in Emmy's lap. Inga and the little Indian girl were inseparable. "What were you doing up in the tree?" Astrid knew there would be a good story behind all this, while at the same time she knew instantly what was wrong. Inga's right arm was already swelling midway between wrist and elbow.

"Melissa's kitty was up there, and none of the boys would go get it down, so I did. And she scratched me and bit me and I sort of dropped her, and we both fell out of the tree. I was almost down, but I slipped and fell." Her sniff indicated how hard she was fighting against crying. Tear traces said she'd lost the battle earlier.

"Do you hurt anywhere other than your arm?" While questioning the girl, Astrid felt the back of her head and checked her eyes and extremities.

"I scraped my leg some." She held up her other arm. "And here."

Astrid glanced up to see that the other children had obeyed the teacher and returned to their classroom, other than one of the older girls, who waited to help if need be. "Linnea, will you please go call Dr. Bjorklund's house and tell them we need a wagon or buggy here to take Inga to the office? Emmy, you stay here with us."

"My arm hurts bad, Tante Astrid."

"I know it does. I'm going to wrap it so it won't hurt so bad." While she talked, Astrid removed a dish-towel-sized piece of sheeting from her bag and folded it into a triangle. She slipped it under the arm as gently as possible, but even so, Inga whimpered. "I'm sorry, Inga. Be brave." Helping her sit up, Astrid tied the sling around the back of her neck. "Now, you don't move it. All right?"

After a major sniff and clearing possible tears with the fingers on her other hand, Inga whispered, "Ma is going to be mad at me."

"Why?"

"'Cause I climbed up in the tree. I did that at home, and she was really mad. She said girls do not climb trees. Tante Astrid, if I can't do so many things, why do I have to be a girl? Boys can do anything."

Astrid concentrated on putting things back in her bag. *How do I answer that one?*

"Huh?" Inga pressed.

"Well, I asked my mor the same thing a long time ago, and she said someday I would understand."

"Do you?"

Be honest. "Yes and no. Girls aren't supposed to be doctors either, but—"

"But both you and ma are."

"I know, but it has not been easy." She sat down, putting one arm around Inga and drawing Emmy close with the other. "Mor said that God made me to be a girl for a reason, and that He always knows best."

"Bestamor is really smart."

"She is the wisest person I know, and she listens to what God has to say."

"God talks to her?"

"He talks to all of us. Only we don't always know how to hear Him. She does." The jingle of a harness made her look up. Thorliff and Elizabeth were both in the approaching buggy. Thorliff called "Whoa" to the single horse and stepped down to help his wife alight.

Inga leaned into Astrid, her sturdy little body shaking. A whimper slid out between her tightly clenched teeth.

"I'm sure it's just a broken arm. It feels like a greenstick fracture," Astrid said in place of a greeting. "She's being very brave."

"You sure that is all?" Elizabeth asked as she rushed to kneel down by Astrid. "You fell out of the tree?"

"The kitty bit and scratched me and I dropped her. Then I fell and the kitty ran away, and . . . and I didn't mean to fall."

"Of course. People who climb trees never mean to fall, but if you had not climbed the tree, you wouldn't have broken your arm."

"But no one else would get it down, and she was mewing and crying and . . ."

Thorliff knelt beside his daughter and scooped her up in his arms. "Let's get you home so we can take care of that arm." Standing, he headed for the buggy. "Astrid, you get in back and I'll hand her in to you. Elizabeth, you take the front again. Emmy, you can ride in back too."

Once they were all situated, Elizabeth turned and reached over the seat back for her daughter's hand. "Looks like you got scraped some too."

"There's blood in my shoe. It ran down my leg, but it stopped."

"That Oscar!" Emmy snarled. "He dared Inga to climb the tree, but he was too scared to do it himself."

"Emmy," Inga whispered in warning.

"Did your teacher know you climbed the tree?"

Inga stared at her mother. "He did when I fell out. Someone ran and told him. He said I would have to stay after school when I got better, and I couldn't go on recess forever."

"Serves you right." Thorliff clucked the horse to a trot.

"Pa."

"Well, you disobeyed the rules."

"There wasn't a rule! Teacher never said I could not climb the tree. The boys climb the tree."

Astrid kept her chuckle to herself. Inga was too smart for her own good, an old saying of her mother's. The buggy hit a bump and Inga yelped.

Elizabeth squeezed her hand. "We'll splint it and it won't hurt like that." Astrid could see that Elizabeth had slipped from mother to doctor role now that she knew the accident wasn't so terrible.

Splinting the arm went quickly, although the shortest piece in their supply of wooden slats was still a bit too long. They left Emmy sitting in the chair beside Inga to watch over her, even though Inga had slipped into a sound sleep from the pain medication Astrid supplied. The three adults gathered on the back porch.

"She will heal just fine," Astrid reminded her sister-in-law.

Thorliff grimaced. "Knowing Inga, this probably won't be the last injury she has. In fact, we are probably lucky she's not done something like this before." He picked up the paper and showed them the headline. The large type screamed out at them *BANK ROBBED IN GRAFTON*. "Came in on the telegraph just before I printed the front page. I redid it to include the story. At least no one was injured, other than pride and feelings."

Astrid scanned the story. "But the robbers got away."

"I doubt they'll get far. The sheriff there took a posse after them. Almost like old times with bank robberies and chasing crooks on horseback. The Old West." Thorliff tapped the story with his finger. "Sure made me question what we would do if something like that happened here. We have no law enforcement of any kind. Someone would have to come from Grafton or Grand Forks." He studied the paper, head nodding slightly.

Astrid smiled up at Thelma, who arrived with the coffeepot without being asked.

"Inga is sleeping fine," Thelma announced. "The cookies will be out of the oven in a few minutes. We must not forget to take some in to Emmy." She turned to Thorliff. "Will there be anyone else for supper tonight?"

He looked up at her. "Not that I know of, but I have a meeting with the crew in a few minutes. It shouldn't go late."

"Are you meeting here?"

"At my office."

"I will bring the coffee and cookies over in half an hour or so."

"Takk." He grinned at her, shaking his head. "You spoil us horribly, you know."

A slight tip of her head was her only response as Thelma returned to the kitchen.

Astrid, coffee cup in both hands, sat back against the padded chair. "Nothing like a little excitement to get our hearts pumping. I need to walk like that more often. Taking a buggy makes me lazy."

"I'm thinking of buying a motor car. A Duryea, maybe, or an Olds." Thorliff dropped that bomb in the conversation and watched from under his brows for his wife's reaction.

Elizabeth left her note taking and picked up her coffee cup, well laced with cream, as she liked it. "Should I say something like 'over my dead body' or would you prefer that I ignore you?" The twinkle in her eyes mitigated the bite of the words.

"You and Astrid could use it to get to your patients more quickly."

"Don't get me involved. I already told Daniel my views on the subject. Horses are far more dependable at this point. Especially in emergencies." Astrid gave her brother a patient-sister look. "Remember when Hjelmer brought that monstrosity to town? Scared most of the horses into straight-out flight and then ran into the boardwalk. Nearly took out a citizen or two."

"They have improved the automobiles greatly since then. You'll find lots of them in the cities, even in Grand Forks."

"Fine, but there are suitable roads there. Not here."

Thelma appeared and clunked a plate of frosted chocolate cookies down on the table. "Those newfangled machines are a waste of time and money."

"It's good of you all to support progress. Whatever happened to the man makes the decisions like this?" He stuffed a whole cookie into his mouth.

Three snorts were his only answer.

"Hey, how's your little one?" Daniel Jeffers pushed open the gate and climbed the steps.

"Word does get around. She is sleeping, due to the pain meds," Elizabeth answered. "Broken arm is all, and she is disgusted that she will have to miss recess and stay after school. Teacher's edict."

"Well, it's only a week until school is out anyway." Daniel took a cookie from the plate offered.

The smile he sent his wife made her heart skip. Had anyone told her love could be like this, she'd have scoffed. Astrid moved over on the settee and motioned for Daniel to join her. "I'll be home after I do evening rounds."

"Mother sent me to tell you she has supper all prepared." Daniel had brought his mother to Blessing after his father died, and they had lived at Sophie's boardinghouse until their house was ready.

"She didn't have to do that."

"You know that and I know that, but we also know how much pressure her help takes off you. And"—he reached for another cookie—"Thelma ought to go into the cookie-making business, like Ingeborg could supply us all with bread and cheese."

"And what?"

"Oh, you know how much she needs to be needed. She can't sit still any more than you can."

"Humph" came from the kitchen, making them all share smiles. There were no secrets in the Bjorklund households.

"Here comes Hjelmer. We better get at it. Toby and Joshua should be along any minute." Thorliff stood and stretched. "I'll really appreciate bed tonight. You'd think with all the new equipment I have, getting the paper out wouldn't be so wearing."

"You're not as young as you used to be either. Besides, you

put out more papers now that Blessing has grown so." Elizabeth laid down her paper and pencil as Thorliff went down the walk. "If you'd like, Astrid, I could do rounds this evening. You did them this morning."

"You could, but I will." She thought a moment, then waved at Hjelmer's greeting as he passed. Hjelmer Bjorklund might be her uncle, but he was not all that much older than Thorliff—fifteen years? Something like that. And yet Thorliff seemed so much wiser. "I think we can discharge Mr. Morris in the morning. He has found someone to come in and help him."

"He can walk well with the crutches now?"

"I'll have him walk again tonight. The stump has healed well enough now that infection is no longer a problem. I wish we could find someone who would carve him a prosthesis. Maybe Far could carve something like that. I should ask him."

Elizabeth nodded. "You know, one of the immigrants—oh, I can't think of his name. I'll ask Thorliff. I heard he is a master carver. Better not to put more pressure on Haakan at the moment. They're out seeding anyway."

"True, but they're nearly finished. With the early spring, they were able to get out in the fields faster." Astrid stood. "I'll check on Inga and take some cookies to Emmy. Do you want her to stay here tonight?"

"That is a good idea. Takk. I'll take the calls tonight and do rounds in the morning."

"Do you realize how blessed we are to have telephones now? If you are in the middle of a birthing, you can call me and make new arrangements." She put several cookies on a napkin. "Thanks for the ideas."

After collecting a glass of milk and a plate from Thelma, Astrid took the treats down the hall to the bedroom that was still set up for patients to stay if needed. The family bedrooms were on the second floor, up the curved and carved oak stairway.

"I brought you something." She smiled at Emmy, who was taking her assignment even more seriously than usual, and set the plate with glass and cookies on the bedside table. "Has she stirred at all?"

"Her eyes moved, but she didn't wake up."

"Good. That means she is not in pain enough to waken. Broken bones can hurt really bad."

"Can she go to school tomorrow?"

"I don't know yet. Would you like to stay here tonight?"

"And take care of Inga?"

"Ja."

"I will. You call Grandma?"

"Dr. Elizabeth will. I'm on my way to the hospital. Do you need anything from home?" When Emmy shook her head, Astrid headed for the door. "Enjoy the cookies. There are plenty more when Inga wakes up." She knew Emmy had a habit of saving food, which was not surprising, considering what her life was like before Haakan found the little girl sleeping in the haymow where her uncle had left her, hoping they would take her in. Last summer the uncle came for her but brought her back in the fall in time for school. Astrid was pretty sure it would be the same this year, if the old man was still alive.

On a whim, she stopped by Thorliff's office, where a discussion was going on.

"Come on in," Thorliff called. "What can we do for you?"

"Can you give me the name of that immigrant who is such a good wood carver? I want to ask him to carve Mr. Morris a comfortable prosthesis. The ones in the catalogue can be used as a pattern."

"Ah, that would be Andrei Belin, the Russian. Thanks to Daniel's mother, you can communicate with him somewhat. He's on the crew adding to the boardinghouse." Thorliff glanced at Toby Valders for confirmation. "What kind of wood do you think?"

Astrid shrugged. "Oak or walnut probably. Something tough. Check with Far. He has some large enough pieces stored in the machine shed, I think."

"If he can do it out of one piece, it would be stronger."

"Mange takk. I knew you gentlemen would have the answers for me." Astrid waved good-bye and set off up the block to the boardinghouse, owned by her cousin Sophie. How does one explain a need like this to a man who doesn't have a good grasp of the English language? Maybe instead of asking him, first she should talk it over with her mother-in-law, who was the man's instructor. One more day surely would not make a big difference. Hospital first, then home.

Since she didn't have to make supper, Astrid settled into the office at the hospital. She would write the letter she'd planned on getting to for the last three days, her response to the supervising nurse at the Chicago hospital.

Dear Mrs. Korsheski,

Thank you for your letter of April 30, inquiring about when we will be ready for the first of the student nurses. You said that you would have three young women to send to us in August, and I believe that is a very workable plan. There is also the possibility that Dr. Red Hawk will be sending two students from the reservation. As I mentioned in the past, housing is a problem here in Blessing. I am not complaining about the exciting growth going on here, but housing remains a challenge.

Our medical program is growing, as Dr. Deming, an accredited dentist, has opened his office in the north wing of the hospital building, where our classroom is and future other offices will be located. As my brother Thorliff has pointed out, we should have designed a larger building.

I appreciate your offer to provide specialty teachers for the nurses on a rotating basis. When we dreamed of a hospital, the teaching side of medical care was not in our hopes and plans. But nurses are so needed in less populated areas, as are doctors, as you well know, and we are delighted to be able to provide training for medical persons in rural circumstances.

We are honored by your trust in us to help prepare for the future.

Sincerely,
Dr. Astrid Bjorklund Jeffers

Astrid reread the letter, sealed and addressed the envelope, and placed it in the mail basket. One more thing to cross off her list. Taking up the charts of her patients, she headed for the nurses' station to start there.

"Dr. Bjorklund, I fear we have a situation developing with Mr. Lyme. He refused to eat his evening meal. Even his daughter cannot get him to eat. What else can we do?"

Astrid wished she had some other advice to offer. No one would be happy with what she wanted to say.

But she would say what must be said. Since when had she not said what she felt she should?

Ever since her dear father took up his stubborn fight against age and disability. And she had no idea how to deal with that.

Chapter 3

Artesian?"

"Perhaps." Trygve Knutson nodded as he watched the windmill blades turning in the west wind. "We sure didn't have to go down far." They had dug this well in a damp spot that sported one cattail plant and a clump of water grass.

"I tried digging there, but it kept caving in so I filled it back in." The farmer rocked back on his heels, took off his hat, and swiped his hand across the top of a shiny dome. "Water right here for the asking. Missus won't need to spare every drop, and I won't have to haul barrels from the river. Lord be praised." He stared up at the spinning blades with a tail that pointed west. "Maybe we're gonna make it here after all."

"Pa, can I pump it?" His younger son was jigging in place with excitement.

"You don't have to. See that tank filling? When the wind is blowing, the water will pump itself."

The line of cows watching from behind the fence shoved and shifted around the gate, several announcing their displeasure at being kept from the water. Their plaintive moos and bellows floated on the wind.

Trygve studied the motion of the rotors to make sure all the mechanics were properly placed. Gilbert Brunderson and Gus Baard were loading their tools and gear back onto the wagons they traveled with—one covered, with stove and bunk beds for their living quarters, the other a buckboard they used to pick up the ironwork and other supplies at the nearest railroad drop.

"One more thing, Mr. Knutson. How about you show me how to grease this?"

"Good, because if you don't keep those gears greased, this'll freeze up on you faster than you can milk a cow."

"Let me, Pa." The oldest son, who'd been working right along with them since they'd unloaded the wagon, offered and, without waiting for a response, scampered up the ladder.

Trygve smiled. "You have a fine son there, sir. If he ever wants a job, I'd hire him."

"I was beginning to think we were all going to be looking for jobs, along with a new place to live." The man laid a hand on his younger son's shoulder. "You go over and let those cows out before they tear down the fence."

Trygve kept his eye on the young man on the platform greasing the gears. He learned quickly, seemed to have a natural bent for machines. "Good job. Just make sure that grease pot is always supplied."

The clanging of the dinner bell caught their attention.

"The missus has dinner ready. We want you leaving on full stomachs."

"We appreciate that, sir. Your wife is a good cook."

That hadn't been the case at the last place they'd been to. The three men had taken turns with the cooking after just one meal at that farmhouse. It had been the fastest setup they'd done. Anything to get out of there.

The farmer clapped him on the shoulder. "That boss of yours

owes you a bonus for the fine job you do. Missus will pack you food for tonight too. You know you're welcome to stay on and leave in the morning."

"Thank you, but we have one more well to drill before heading back to Blessing. Be good to get home." Even though they'd only been on the road since the ground thawed, Trygve was ready for a break.

Onkel Hjelmer kept them plenty busy. This was Trygve's second season drilling wells and building windmills. While he got great satisfaction out of seeing those blades begin to turn and the water flow, he felt an urge to get home. Last year he had looked forward to new horizons, new people, and new challenges to face, but this year . . . So far they had had only one dry well. It was a good thing Hjelmer did not guarantee water.

They arrived at the next farm at dusk, introduced themselves, and after supper around a campfire, fell into their beds in the wagon. The woman at the other farm had provided them well with food.

In the morning, even before the sun burst over the horizon, Trygve was out walking the land. This farmer claimed he had paid someone to witch the farm. Trygve had never taken much stock in water witching. A fellow who claims to be able to identify the best location for a well walks about gripping a forked branch, and the branch points him to water? Maybe. Trygve trusted his own ability to read the land more than a hazel stick.

Where the witcher had driven a stake, Trygve saw nothing that indicated water below. But toward the east, he found a tree that had been struck by lightning. A new shoot had sprouted from the burnt stump, green against the black. He nodded and surveyed the land around it. This tree could only have grown this large right here because it tapped water. He stared back toward the house and barn. Not close.

The owner had assured him that the man said that where he had pounded in the stake was the best place to dig the well.

Trygve could hear Onkel Hjelmer reminding him that it was his job to dig wherever the farmer said, not to argue. But he'd dug enough wells now that he had a sense when one might be easy or not. He had a feeling this was going to fall in the *not* category.

Back at the barn, the farmer was watching him. "Whatcha doing out there?"

"Just checking the area." Trygve waved an arm. "I think water is much closer to the surface out by those cottonwoods."

The farmer scowled. "No. I paid the man good money to locate the best place, and we're gonna dig there." He paused. "And, you know, you're running late. That Bjorklund fellow said you'd be here over a week ago."

Trygve sighed. He did not explain that they could not put up a windmill during lightning storms and they'd had at least two of those plus heavy winds. He wasn't sending his men up or going up himself when the weather went against them. But when they built a windmill, it did not blow over. They'd seen one lying flat and the farm abandoned. He fought to ignore his feeling and just do what he was told. After all, the customer was always right. Or so he'd been told.

"We'll dig where you say, but I'm reminding you that if we come up dry, we'll have to charge extra for another drill."

"Maybe I should just get someone else in here."

"Up to you." But Trygve knew there were few drillers in the region, and a couple of them were more shyster than dependable. He waited. Finally he turned and started back to the wagon, where Gilbert and Gus were watching for the order to unload.

"Wait," the farmer called to his back. "No. You go ahead."

"Okay, men, unload."

By the third day of drilling with no water emerging and running out of pipe, Trygve called a halt.

"It's drier 'n a bone," Gus said. "This is a waste of time."

Trygve brushed away a persistent blackfly, out early this year. Sure, they were south of Blessing, but not that far south. Sometimes he hated being right.

"Why you stopping?" The owner stomped his way up to the wagon, strutting up to the site like a banty rooster they'd had one time. That little rooster had taken on the reigning rooster one time too many.

Trygve swallowed his irritation. "It's a dry bore. We've about run out of pipe and—"

"But I paid that man good money, and he said there would be water here." He stabbed at the ground with a gnarly and filthy finger.

"I can't help that." Pointing toward the drill, Trygve said, "Go see for yourself."

As he stomped over there, the man muttered something about lazy workers that couldn't be trusted.

Fists clenched, Gus started after him, glanced at Trygve, stopped.

A soft answer turneth away wrath. Was it his mother's voice or a trick of the breeze? "Let it lie." Trygve nodded to the site. "Pull it out." He looked over to the cottonwood stump barely visible above the green grass. Shame. It was a shame.

"What are they doin'?"

"Pulling the drill. We're done."

"But that Bjorklund, he promised me water, well water. Right here."

Trygve shook his head. "Be right back," he said and headed for the wagon, where he pulled the contract out of the box. Sure enough, the man had signed with an X. Hjelmer had printed in the man's name next to it. Great, the man could not even read.

Returning to the fray, he handed the farmer the paper. "I'm sure you have a copy of this, since Mr. Bjorklund always makes certain the customer gets a contract. That is your name, right?"

The man peered at the line where Trygve was pointing. "A man's word is a man's word. Don't need no fancy paper."

"Then let me read this to you." Finishing the reading, Trygve said. "You can see there is no promise of water. We do our best, but no guarantees."

"How do I know you read it all?"

"So you are calling me a liar?" He was using a soft answer all right, but this time it was laced with steel.

"No, no. Don't get all het up. What you gonna charge to drill again?"

"Half what you paid for the first drill, sir."

"That's highway robbery. You can't do that."

"Sorry." This time Trygve omitted the *sir*. "We'll be on our way, then." He motioned for the loading to continue.

"But I need this well. I was counting on it."

Trygve looked toward the pipe being drawn out of the ground. He counted to ten. And twenty. "Tell you what. You pay me now and we'll move over to the stump out there and drill again."

"But that's too far from the house."

"Better'n hauling water in barrels. You could probably move your house over there." The barn didn't even look strong enough to be moved. Surprising that a bad windstorm hadn't already blown it over. *Lord, give me patience. I've never struck a man, but . . .*

"You promise me water?"

"No, sorry. We never do that. But since those cottonwood trees out there found some, I'm pretty sure we will too."

"You dig and I'll send Bjorklund the money."

"Can't do that. Has to be cash on the nose." Trygve knew this wasn't exactly the way Hjelmer did things, but didn't want to gamble on this man not paying up.

But Hjelmer always told him to use his own judgment. For some reason, Trygve waited. Finally he shook his head. "We'll load our supplies and be on our way." Surely they could get loaded and on the road before dark. He did not want to spend another night there.

"Look, I don't have cash money to pay you, but I got a yearling steer I can trade."

Trygve stared down at this boots, then into the man's eyes. "Show it to me."

They found water fifty feet down, put up the windmill, and were on their way two days later, a very unhappy steer walking along behind the wagon, a rope around his horns leading to the rear of the wagon.

"What's Hjelmer gonna do with this here steer?" Gus asked when they stopped to eat and sleep. "He doesn't even have a pasture."

"Oh, I'm sure he'll turn it out with our cattle. He can either sell it or butcher it when the time comes."

"I was surprised you gave in." Gilbert stirred the contents of the kettle hung over the campfire.

"Guess I just wanted to see if I was right. Cottonwood trees don't lie. Besides, I felt sorry for him. Ignorance can be corrected. Bullheadedness, no."

"Why you s'pose that other man told him wrong?"

"I bet he didn't pay no other man. He just figured he knew and wanted a well close to the house."

Gus added some more wood to the fire. "I felt sorry for his children, a pa like that."

Trygve nodded. "Me too."

The next day they found a town on the railroad, and Trygve made arrangements for them to load up in a boxcar the next day and get back to Blessing faster.

Even though he'd been right about the water, the whole scene had left a bad taste in his mouth. Had he made the right decision? Was taking the steer the best choice? He slept under the wagon that night, like the others, since it didn't look like rain. Good thing they were taking the train. The rims on the wagon wheels all needed to be reset, and sleeping in a real bed, eating his mother's cooking, and scrubbing until he was actually clean all sounded real good.

Besides, they'd not had any news of Blessing in too long. What might have gone on at home by now? Trygve was more than ready to live for something besides water.

Ingeborg caught herself studying Haakan.

"Mange takk," he said, pushing back from the breakfast table and standing.

He didn't look any different. Surely she was worrying for nothing. *Lord, I know you don't want your children worrying, and I know better . . . but . . . but this is Haakan.* Peace trickled into her heart like cool water on a hot day. She sucked in and exhaled, letting the worry float away on the peace.

"We'll be done with the seeding today, a good two weeks early. Thank God for spring. I was beginning to think winter was going to hang on forever. Then it was like a door opening and closing."

Ingeborg nodded. "Andrew is not here yet. Would you like another cup of coffee?"

"Takk, but I think not. Are you going to town to see how Inga is faring?"

"You know me too well." She stepped into his arms instead of around him. "I know a simple break like that is not life threatening, but it sure tugs on this heart of mine."

He rested his chin on the top of her head. "I liked having more time with our grandchildren this winter. With Inga in school, Carl . . ." He paused and did an oh-so-familiar soft sound somewhere between a chuckle and a snort. Inga called it Grandpa's snuckle. She loved coming up with new words. And many of them were so appropriate.

"I will put the dinner in the oven first and then go. Andrew went home after milking, and Freda is over helping Kaaren today, since they are deep cleaning all the dormitory rooms. You know how the young men are talking about calling or writing for more help from Norway? Women need to be included in that." She paused, then looked up at Haakan so she could watch his face. "What if I wrote to my family and asked if anyone wants to come to North Dakota? I've not heard from anyone for so long. But then, I have been remiss in writing too."

He cocked his head to the side just a bit, then nodded. "We've pretty much brought over all the Bjorklunds. Maybe it's time to include your family, the Strands, and anyone they might know of. We have so much to share, and when I read the paper, I can see times are still hard there." He looked off into the distance. "We need to talk with Thorliff and the others so we are all thinking along the same line." He paused and listened to the dog bark his I-know-you welcome. "Ah. Andrew is back at the barn." He hugged Ingeborg close. "I like it being just the two of us for a change."

"Me too." She hugged him back and walked him to the door, where he lifted his hat from the peg on the wall and slid his arms into a light jacket.

He stopped. "You are getting over that Emmy will be leaving again when her uncle comes for her? I know you miss having her here."

"I am. Inga does not like her grandma to have sad eyes. But Inga misses her too. They have become so close."

"Uff da. That child." This time a true chuckle floated over his shoulder as he strode down the steps. Not a snuckle.

Ingeborg watched him go. *Keep him safe, O Lord.* Her prayer joined the twittering of the nesting birds rising on the slight breeze. A perfect spring day. She should be out in the garden instead of thinking of going to see Inga. Several of the deaf students had come over and helped with the planting so that all but the most tender plants were already planted and some were showing bits of green pushing through the rich black soil. They had planted what they could at the huge garden at the deaf school too. Two students had remained to help over the summer. They were good workers, those students.

"A snuckle indeed. Thank you, Lord, for my family." She watched through the screen door as Andrew and his far hooked up the two teams to the drills and drove out of the yard. "Ja, and uff da too. Get yourself going."

At least she had baked bread the day before, and Freda had butchered one of the old hens, so making chicken and dumplings would be easy. She set the pot on the stove, filled it halfway with hot water from the reservoir, and fetched the hen from the icebox to add to the stewpot. Then after chopping the few remaining onions and potatoes, she added sage and salt and pepper and put it all in the kettle. Once it came to a boil on the top of the stove, she slid the deep pot into the oven to slow cook all morning.

She beat two eggs, added salt and dried parsley, wild onion and thyme, along with flour to make a stiff dough for the dumplings. Putting the bowl in the icebox, she headed for the cellar to fetch canned beans, both green and hulled beans, corn, and tomatoes to add when she returned home. With dinner all set, she hung up her apron and picked up the basket she had filled earlier with cookies and dried apple slices—Inga's favorite things. Not that Thelma didn't have similar, but she knew how much Inga would enjoy a basket of Grandma makings.

Her straw hat had replaced her winter one, but she left it hanging on the peg. She was not ready for sunbonnets yet. She wanted the sun on her face and on the rest of her. In the winter she so craved the sunshine that when spring arrived, she could never get enough warm sun to make up for the brief, cold sun that made the snow glitter in the winter.

Ah, what a day! A crow announced to the world that someone was coming through, the meadowlarks and song sparrows serenaded her, and a spider web sported dewdrops that rainbowed the sun. Up ahead, the wheat elevator and the flour mill stood taller than the trees growing back along the river. They had planted trees in Blessing too—cottonwoods, elm, oak, and maples—and all now sprouted their spring green finery. The two-story boardinghouse was growing a new wing, and the old granary had been expanded to house the machinery plant they built for manufacturing the additions to the seed drills, along with a line of new drills that incorporated the invention of Daniel Jeffers' deceased father. Whoever dreamed Blessing would grow like this?

Scooter, Inga's small dog, announced Ingeborg's arrival before she reached the gate to the fenced yard of the Bjorklund house.

"Grandma, you came to see me," Inga shouted from the back porch, where she and her mother were having breakfast.

"Oh, Ingeborg, welcome." Elizabeth rose from her chair and joined her daughter at the top step of the wide, roofed back porch. She kept a hand on Inga's shoulder, reminding her that jumping down the steps might not be a good idea.

"I broke my arm." Inga pointed to the white sling that was now not only tied around her neck but to her body with another strip of sheeting.

"I see that." Ingeborg handed Elizabeth the basket and cupped both hands around Inga's face. She kissed the little girl's nose before making her way to the white wicker settee, where she sat and waited for Inga to climb one-handed up beside her.

"Uff da, this thing is not good." Inga leaned against her grandmother and looked up at her. "What did you bring?"

Elizabeth barked, "Inga! That is not polite."

Inga sighed dramatically. "Takk, Grandma, for the basket."

"How do you know it is for you?"

"Because you know how I love baskets, and I am sure there are cookies in there and dried apples and maybe some cheese. Am I right?"

"Mostly." Ingeborg picked the basket off the table beside her and set it on her granddaughter's lap. Scooter leaped up beside her and stuck his nose into the basket too.

"Go away, Scooter. This is mine."

He sat down beside her, one ear up and one down, which always gave him a questioning look.

"Thank you." Inga lifted out the plate of gingerbread men with raisins for eyes, nose, smile, and three buttons down the front. "You know these are my favoritest in all the world." She bit a leg off one, eating the cookie the way Astrid had taught her.

"Inga?" Her mother's tone was obviously of the reminder sort.

Inga scrunched up her face then heaved a sigh. "Would you like one of my cookies, Mor? Grandma?" Her face brightened. "And coffee?" She started to scoot forward, then flinched and stopped. She shook her head. "This thing hurts!"

"I'm sure it does." Ingeborg wrapped an arm around the girl's shoulder and hugged her gently. "Did Emmy go to school?"

"Ja, but Ma wouldn't let me go."

"Good idea. You can go back in tomorrow, most likely."

"But I won't get any recess, and I'll have to stay after school." The glower on her brow told her feelings on that matter. She chomped down on the other cookie leg.

Thelma brought a tray out and set it on the table with the coffee things and a plate of dried-apple kuchen. "I tried a new recipe, or rather, I altered an old one. I hope you like it."

"No doubt as to that."

Ingeborg looked to Elizabeth. "I take it Astrid is at the hospital?"

"Yes. I was supposed to take morning rounds, but she insisted I stay home with the princess here."

Inga was picking the raisins off her gingerbread man and gave her mother a questioning look. "A broken princess?"

Both women rolled their eyes.

"Do you know what time it is?" Ingeborg asked.

"No. The clock is in the kitchen. Why?"

"I best not dawdle all day. I need to do some things at home." She had started to lean back when a voice seemed to speak clearly: *Go home now*.

"Ingeborg, what is it?"

"I don't know. A voice is saying, 'Go home now.'" She started to stand but sat back down. The command came more urgently.

Ingeborg stood up. Should she call Kaaren to see if she could see if anything was wrong at her house?

"Do you want Thorliff to bring up the horse and buggy?"

"No. I can walk it almost as fast." She picked up her bag.

"Grandma, don't leave." Inga's lower lip stuck out.

"I'm sorry, little one. I have to go home."

"Call me," Elizabeth called to her back.

"I will." Ingeborg set out for home, walking as fast as she could. *Home. What was wrong? Was it Haakan? Andrew? Lord God, keep them safe. Whatever is happening, you are there.*

If that was your command, I am obeying as fast as I can. Her prayers matched her hurrying feet. She could hear a horse coming up behind her.

"Ingeborg, get in," Pastor Solberg said as he stopped his buggy.

"Thank you, Lord. How did you know?" She climbed in, and as soon as she was seated, he set the horse into a fast trot.

"A voice telling me."

"Me too. I was at Thorliff's to visit Inga." She hung on to the arm of the seat, her feet braced against the floorboards as he turned the horse into the lane.

Ingeborg scanned the fields. She could see Andrew still seeding but no Haakan. They'd been in separate fields.

As soon as they trotted into the yard, they saw Haakan's team by the barn. Haakan, still in the seat of his seeder, was slumped forward. Pastor Solberg halted his horse a bit away to keep from startling the team. Ingeborg leaped out before the buggy had fully stopped and darted toward the man, seeing his arm crooked around the lever that closed the seed doors, the only thing keeping him on the seat. At the same moment, she realized with a jolt that if he weren't stuck there, he might've fallen and the seeder could have run over him.

Lord God, what is it? Is he dead? Please don't let him be dead. He's breathing. Thank you, Lord, he's breathing. "He's unconscious," she called to Pastor Solberg.

"I'm coming."

She stood beside her husband, one hand checking the pulse in his neck, the other hand on his back. "No. Go ring the triangle so Andrew can come help."

Solberg did as she said and, with the clanging still echoing across the field, ran back to Ingeborg.

"Can we get him off and lay him on the ground?"

"Haakan, can you hear me?" The *Lord God* litany rolled and rerolled in her mind all the while as she laid her cheek against his back to listen for his heart. Rapid beat but strong. So it wasn't his heart.

"I'm going to try to sit him up so we can unhook his arm."

She could hear horses galloping. Andrew, astride one of his team, stopped them and leaped to the ground. "What is it?"

"We don't know."

"With the two of us we can sit him up, unhook his arm, and get him off the seeder."

"Unhitch the team. If they move . . ."

Ingeborg stood at the horses' noses, gripping the lines as Pastor Solberg unhitched one horse and Andrew the other. With the seeder tongue on the ground, they were better able to help Haakan.

"There are horse blankets in the barn on the wall."

Ingeborg ran to get those. "We can lay him on one and carry him to the house that way." She slid open the main door, retrieved two of the canvas blankets, and ran back outside.

With three of them working together they finally got Haakan stretched out on the blanket on the ground. Ingeborg knelt beside him, gently calling his name and feeling his arm to see if it was broken. No response.

Andrew looked very grim. "Let's get him to the house for now, and I'll have Gerald find Astrid."

They grabbed the corners and sides of the blanket and, on the count of three, lifted with sounds of effort.

"Haakan might be getting older, but he is still a mighty big man," Pastor Solberg grunted out. They had to stop and set their burden down once to catch their breaths, but as they heaved him up again, Lars ran into the yard.

"Let me help." He grabbed a corner, and they carried their

burden up the stairs to the porch. Ingeborg released her grip on the blanket to hold the screen door open. Then she ran ahead to pull the covers back on the bed.

"Just lay him, blanket and all, right here."

"Kaaren called the doctors."

"Good."

As Pastor Solberg started untying Haakan's boots, Ingeborg yanked open her black bag. She unbuttoned his shirt and laid the stethoscope against his chest. His heartbeat was fast but steady. She lifted an eyelid but could see nothing amiss there. He was breathing heavily, but he was not responding. She felt his head and neck for any swelling, but other than some rigidity in his jaw, nothing.

Astrid and Elizabeth came in together. Ingeborg gave them a fast report on what they had done and knew, little that it was.

"It has to be a stroke again. There is no evidence of any injuries, other than that poor shoulder that has been severely strained. We can chip off some ice and ice it. Would an ice pack under his head help?" Astrid asked, turning to Elizabeth.

"It can't hurt. Let's apply the ice packs and get him cleaned up. Then watch him. Can he swallow?"

"I don't know." Ingeborg went into the kitchen to find Reverend Solberg chipping ice off the block in the icebox. "We can get more from the icehouse as we need it." She made two separate packs rolled in dish towels, and while the good Reverend Solberg carried those into the bedroom, she prepared a basin of warm water with soap, and grabbed a washcloth and a towel. All the while she moved through the familiar actions, her mind continued the same "Help us, Lord" litany. "Dear God, wisdom, please. Your wisdom, not just ours."

Chapter 5

"No changes," Astrid said when her mother relieved her in the predawn dark.

"Were you able to get him to swallow any of that broth?"

"Not enough to do much good." The two women, so alike in stature and wearing the same neck-to-ankle-length aprons, stood looking down at the man in the bed. "I talked to him and read his Bible aloud. You've always said patients can hear, even though they cannot respond. He's not even twitching."

"You go on up and sleep for a few hours. Elizabeth said she would take care of things at the hospital."

"I will. Can I get you anything first?" When Ingeborg shook her head, Astrid tucked her arm through her mor's and leaned her head against her shoulder. "I'll call Dr. Morganstein after I sleep and ask if they've learned anything new about patients like this."

Ingeborg nodded and laid her cheek against her daughter's head. "Thank you for staying."

"You know that any of us would. You watch. There will be a steady stream of visitors today, most of them bringing food, since they want to help so bad and care so much."

"All any of us can do is pray, and I know we all are. Yesterday morning Haakan and I had breakfast by ourselves for a change. He commented on how he appreciated that. I can still feel his arms around me and his chin on the top of my head. Please, dear Lord God, let me, let us, have times like that again." She stared up at the ceiling to try to outsmart the tears, but ended up drying her cheeks on the edge of her apron anyway.

"I feel so helpless. After all my training . . ."

"And mine."

"I know you will say to leave it in God's mighty hands."

"It's easier to say and believe when it is someone other than Haakan or one of my children. Or grandchildren. You go on and sleep. Takk for being here. I'm going to sit here and read to him. He loves to be read to."

"All right."

Ingeborg settled herself in the chair and, picking up her Bible, flipped to the Psalms and began reading.

As Astrid had predicted, a steady stream of visitors took turns sitting beside Haakan, some reading to him, some telling him of the events of the last couple of days. Andrew finished seeding the wheat and moved on to disking the oat field. When Thorliff brought Inga out, she sat on the bed beside Haakan and told him all about her broken arm. When she couldn't think of anything more to say, she sang to him—songs she knew and some she made up.

Astrid told Ingeborg about how she and Elizabeth pored over their books, consulted with wise Dr. Morganstein, and took turns going about their regular duties. The earth kept spinning on its axis while the man slept on.

They started exercising his arms and legs. They rolled him from side to side to keep him from getting bed sores. They put very small amounts of water in his mouth. He usually swallowed.

Astrid commented that he was getting dehydrated nonetheless. Ingeborg chose to sleep beside him and let the others go about their lives without round-the-clock supervision.

On Sunday some of the musicians brought their instruments over and played for him. Ingeborg knitted a sweater for three-and-a-half-year-old Carl, starting her Christmas gifts early. Others weeded her garden . . . and life went on. Three calves were born and a foal, and Ingeborg described them to the silent man if Inga didn't do it.

A glad change: He started swallowing the water that they offered him, a scant teaspoon at a time. Ingeborg prepared a rich broth and he swallowed that as well. "Still, he is dehydrated," Astrid commented. The diaper pad beneath him remained dry, not a good sign.

School let out for the summer, so that the children could help on their farms. Inga came by the house that afternoon, sitting on Haakan's bed and explaining with many words about how she had to stay in from recess because she had climbed the tree at school one day. The boys could climb the tree but not the girls. It wasn't fair, she'd decided. She laid her head on his shoulder and stroked his hand as she had seen the others do.

Ingeborg went out to peel the potatoes for dinner, but she could still hear Inga clearly. "You got to wake up, Grandpa. Me and Carl need to go fishing. Emmy's uncle came and got her again. Her cousin, Two Shells, too. Grandma has sad eyes all the time and with Emmy gone, I lost my best friend. But Mor reminds me that Emmy will come back in the fall for school again." Suddenly Inga shouted, "Grandma, come quick! Grandpa is smiling!"

Ingeborg flew in through the open door and dropped down to sit on the edge of the bed. "Oh, Haakan, you *are* smiling. Please, dear Lord, let this be a sign to us, a sign of hope." She took his hand in hers and squeezed gently.

The return pressure was weak but real nonetheless. "Thank you, God. Oh, thank you." She slipped into Norwegian and kept on thanking and praising God.

"Grandma, I don't know what you are saying." Inga sat cross-legged on the bed, one elbow propped on one knee, her chin in her hand.

"Ja, I will talk English, but you little ones need to learn Norwegian too. Thank you for the reminder." She stood. "I will let the others know so we can all rejoice." Her steps light, she hurried to the telephone and lifted the earpiece. "Gerald, could you please let everyone know that Haakan is smiling, and he squeezed my hand back. Inga saw it first."

"Oh, Ingeborg, I am so glad. I will tell all of Blessing, indeed."

"Thank you. I know this is only the beginning, but he is responding." She set the earpiece back on the side prong that held it and stared out the window. These last days had been the longest in her life, or so they felt at the moment. "Lord, only you know what is ahead, but I am so thankful that you are holding us both tight in the palm of your hand. I trust you no matter what. Thank you for your patience with me and my fears."

She knew He heard whispers as well as He knew her thoughts. She went to the icebox and pulled out a jar of broth to heat. Lars had brought her a new block of ice. There had been talk of installing one of those machines that made ice at the hospital, but so far cutting ice from the river and storing it in the icehouse with sawdust to pack around it worked well for the whole town.

The jangling of the phone caught her in midpouring. She set the jar down and returned to the oak box on the wall.

"Mor, that is such wonderful news." Astrid fairly bubbled with joy. "I'll be right out. You tell Inga to take good care of her grandpa."

"Oh, she is. She saw the smile and hollered for me. Astrid,

I know there is a lot ahead, but right now I am weak with joy and relief. I'm afraid I was beginning to lose hope."

"Me too. Sometimes one's knowledge can be a hindrance instead of a help. Do you need anything from town?"

"Only the mail."

"I'll get it."

Ingeborg set the jar in a pan of hot water from the reservoir and left it on the back part of the stove. She went to the bedroom door. "Would you like tea or something else to drink?"

"Milk." Inga smiled at her grandmother. "And cookies?"

"Of course."

"In here or outside?"

"In here. We'll sit by the window." She watched as Inga scooted off the bed, her arm still bound to her body. Another week and Astrid said they would remove the sling and check the arm, although Inga was getting pretty adept at using one arm. The amazing adaptability of a child. Would Haakan recover also? He did not seem to have any paralysis, but once he began moving on his own again, they'd know more.

Later that evening, after Elizabeth had come to check on their patient and taken the protesting Inga home, Ingeborg sat in the darkening bedroom, the breeze lifting the curtains at the window. A sound from the bed caught her attention. "Haakan?" She slipped over to sit on the edge of the bed. His eyelids fluttered and a frown creased his forehead. "Can you hear me? If so, squeeze my hand." This time the squeeze was certain and stronger. "Oh, Haakan, my dear, welcome back from wherever you have been."

The side of his mouth twitched, and a smile curved the dimple in his right cheek.

"Can I get you anything?" She smoothed the hair back off his forehead. He'd lost so much weight, she could feel the bones. "If I bring the broth again, will you take some?"

The nod was so slight she almost missed it, but he was responding. *Finally! Oh, Lord be praised!* "I'll be right back."

This time he swallowed half a cup of spooned-in broth and then he clamped his lips. Ingeborg felt like whirling around the room like Inga. She watched her husband relax, visibly this time, as if he'd been working hard. Which she knew he had. After lying so still in bed, any response would take effort. She remembered back to when she had fainted, or whatever they called it, after she had saved baby Goodie's life. She never knew she could run so fast. God must have given her wings.

And now Andrew and Ellie's little Gudrun May was such a delight. With little Haakan, their newborn boy now three weeks old, Andrew and Ellie had three children, and Ellie was hoping for more.

Resisting the urge to shake her sleeping husband to make sure his activity had not been a dream, she got ready for bed before dusk had darkened into night. The narrow yellow band on the western horizon had shrunk to a thin line when she propped Haakan up on the side facing her and crawled into bed. She took his hand in hers and softly recited the Lord's Prayer in Norwegian, as they did every night. This time he squeezed her hand twice at the amen.

Lord, wake me if he needs me was her slipping-away thought, and when she woke, the rooster was doing his best to get the sun out of bed. Ingeborg had not moved all night. That never happened. Haakan was breathing softly and easily, the breeze fluttered the white lace curtains, and a sleepy bird tried out his morning chirp in a raspy voice. In her light summer robe and bare feet, she strolled to the outhouse, glorying in the lightening sky, with the sickle moon hanging in the west, and the eastern sky giving way to the new day. The rooster crowed again, making her smile. The dew felt chilly on her feet and dampened the edge of her gown. A new day. A glorious new day. Haakan was improving. What more could she ask?

When she returned, Haakan had rolled onto his back. By himself. Another feat that sent her dancing to start the fire in the cookstove, pour out the little remaining coffee, make new, and dip water still warm in the reservoir to wash her face. In all the ordinary daily actions, she kept singing praises. So many things to be thankful for. After checking on Haakan, she took her Bible out on the back porch, where she could watch the sun paint the sky and revel in that perfect moment when the rim of the sun crested the horizon and the trees lining the river shimmered in the glory.

She searched out the psalms of praise and sang them along with the birds.

"Good morning," Freda said as she stepped up on the porch after the brief walk from her house. She had taken over much of the heavy work, including running the cheese house.

"Coffee's hot."

"You had breakfast yet?"

"No, but Haakan is sleeping peacefully, and now I will go get dressed. If Kaaren needs you, we are fine here."

"Is there any bacon left?" At Ingeborg's nod, Freda continued, "Good. Scrambled eggs with bacon and cheese, toast and jam. Then we'll discuss the day."

Ingeborg smiled and tipped her head. "You are such a dear."

Freda shook her head. "Maybe in heaven I will be."

"Then bring a cup of coffee out here and sit with me for a moment." She knew Freda rarely sat down once her day got going.

"If you insist, and then you'll tell me how Haakan truly is doing."

Freda brought the pot out, refilled Ingeborg's cup, and poured her own. "Now."

Ingeborg brought her up to the moment and leaned her head against the cushion. "I was losing hope."

"You and all the rest of us. God sure is never in a hurry to answer our prayers. And believe you me, the whole town is praying."

"I know. We are so blessed. Oh, and instead of toast, we have cinnamon rolls that need to be eaten. Warmed in the oven would be good." She started to get up but Freda waved her back down.

"You just sit for a while. It won't kill you."

Ingeborg gestured to her nightwear.

"No one else is around. Just sit and enjoy the spring around you."

For a change Ingeborg did what she was told, and after they ate, she returned to the bedroom to get dressed for the day. Humming, she sat down to brush out her hair and heard a noise behind her. "Haakan." He was rolling to his side and actually smiled at her.

"Ja. Good." His voice sounded gravely for lack of use.

She sat on the edge of the bed and smiled into his eyes, grateful for a slightly lopsided but returned smile. "I was so afraid this would not be again."

"It . . . was a . . . long . . . way." So raspy. So beautiful to hear.

"Let me get you some warm water and honey. That will soothe your throat." She swiftly twisted her hair and pinned it on top of her head. "I'll be right back. Don't go away." His smile made her float out to the kitchen.

"They are done with the milking." Freda set a crock with a handle up on the counter. "I knew we needed to churn butter, so I brought the cream in to warm. From the look on your face I can tell you have good news."

"Haakan is talking. Warm water with honey will help his scratchy throat."

She poured a blob of honey into a cup of warm water and grabbed a spoon, stirring as she returned to the bedroom. "Do you think you can sit up if I prop you with pillows?"

He nodded but was too weak to do anything to help her. So half sitting, he sipped from the cup, then motioned for her to use the spoon. When Ingeborg set the empty cup aside, his smile was not so lopsided—not a normal wide Haakan smile either, but an improvement.

"You didn't appear to have trouble swallowing."

He shook his head, but not much.

"You need fluids, but if I brought you some cheese, do you think you could eat that?"

"Ja, good."

She picked up his hand and laid her cheek against the back of it. "Ja. Good is right. Thank you, Lord God, Haakan is back."

"I . . . never . . . left." The words came slowly, not much more than a whisper, but she could understand him.

She rolled her eyes, but a tear leaked out anyway. "You could hear us, even when you did not, could not, respond?"

"Ja." He squeezed her hand. "Lie down."

Nodding again, she stood to remove the pillows. When he lay against only one, he sighed, and with a smile, his eyes fluttered closed and he slept.

Ingeborg watched his chest rise and fall, evenly and gently. He was having no trouble breathing. Had he really had another stroke, and if so, how could there be so little apparent damage? If not a stroke, what? Especially since he had been in a coma for so long. Her own husband was a medical mystery to her. She headed to the icebox for cheese, then gently closed the door. He could eat the cheese later.

She could hear the thump of the butter churn on the back porch. Even that sounded joyous. But when she cranked the telephone and picked up the earpiece, tears rained like the sky had opened to deluge the land. Instead, she hung the earpiece back on the prongs and sobbed into her apron-covered hands. The screen door banged against Freda as she flew across the room and wrapped her arms around Ingeborg's shoulders, guiding her to the chair. They sat and she let Ingeborg cry as she gently stroked her arm and shoulder.

Chapter 6

The week passed like a breeze blowing through the window. Astrid and Elizabeth sat behind those attending the meeting called by what was beginning to be known as the city council, unofficially anyway. Penny Bjorklund slipped in to sit beside them.

Astrid knew her mor would be there too, although she hated to leave Haakan, especially in the evening, even though he'd told her to go.

Sophie poked Astrid's arm. "Trygve is back!"

Astrid craned her neck to see. The young man, grinning and shaking hands, was joining the fellows in the corner. He looked tanned and healthy.

Thorliff stepped to the front of the group of about twenty men, and the growing group of women, all of whom owned businesses in Blessing. Rebecca joined them just as Thorliff started talking.

"Glad you could all make it, since the announcement just went out this afternoon. Before we begin the business, Reverend Solberg, will you lead us in prayer?"

John Solberg stood and bowed his head, waiting for the

shuffling to cease before he began. He waited a bit more and then his voice came gently. "Our heavenly Father, who gives us life and livelihood, family and friends, homes and farms, and all of our businesses, we thank you for your presence here among us and within us. Thank you for the myriad ways you have blessed this town and all of us individually. We cannot begin to count the ways and times you have come to us in our needs. Thank you that Haakan is responding so well. Near as I can tell, that fits in the miracle category." A whisper of agreement and nods drew them all even closer. "So Father, now we ask you to bless this meeting, to give us good ideas that can benefit our town and help us to always grow closer to you. We thank you and praise you for hearing us and for always answering. In Jesus' name we pray, amen."

Thorliff stood again. "There are several reasons we believe we needed to get together, and number one on our agenda is the robbery in Grafton. I am sure all of you read the article I printed a while back in the paper. I figured they'd catch the thieves in short order and all would be well. But they are still on the loose, and they robbed the grocery store in Pembina. That was done by only one man, but I've heard tell, the others were nearby."

"Makes no sense. Where could those varmints hide for almost two weeks?"

"I know, Anner, and your safety is part of the reason we are here. Let's face it, we have both a bank and a thriving grocery store. We could be on their list."

"If they are not caught."

"So what do you suggest we do?" Dr. Deming, the dentist, asked, glancing around as if to apologize for a newcomer speaking up.

"Glad you asked," Thorliff said. "Daniel, you're the one who talked with the law in both Grand Forks and Grafton. Would you please tell us what you learned?"

Daniel Jeffers nodded and stood. "I spoke first with the sheriff in Grafton. He is frustrated and furious. The folks of Grafton are hollering for his hide, as if this were his fault. He said we better get together a plan to protect Blessing, but he also reiterated that the band could be discovered any day."

"Right." The sarcasm came from someone else.

"I talked with Grand Forks, and they suggested we hire one of their deputies to patrol the bank and the town at night, since both of the robberies were at night. They said that lawbreakers usually use the same tactics each time."

"Why hire someone when we could take turns?" Hjelmer Bjorklund leaned forward. "We all know how to use guns."

"True, but—"

"How would we pay an outsider?"

"Why not close the bank and make it known that there is no money here any longer? You know, take away the prize."

"Nah, that wouldn't work."

The women glanced at one another. Who said that last? Astrid wished she could see more of the group, but from the back it was hard to tell some of them. Talk about frustrating, being only an observer. Perhaps . . . no, there was no sense in riling the waters.

Trygve stood. "What will it take to hire someone, and do we really want to do that? Would only one man be enough?"

"Three questions?"

"I couldn't get a word in edgewise until this moment."

Everyone chuckled.

Lars Knutson spoke up with a shrug. "Besides, Thorliff, Haakan would have asked one of the questions."

Astrid mentally finished the comment: . . . *if he were here*. But while Haakan wanted to come, he needed too much help getting around yet. He was getting stronger each day. Still, both of his doctors had overruled him. The amazing thing was, he let them. That was not at all like him, to allow their pleading to indeed overrule his desires.

Sophie nudged her with an elbow and leaned close to whisper, "My tongue is bleeding."

Astrid rolled her lips together to keep from laughing out loud. "All of us *females,* I know." She shook her head the slightest bit, indicating they should be paying attention. But her own mind did not want to pay attention. The idea of someone armed and patrolling the streets of Blessing made her stomach sour. One of their own would be bad enough, but the thought of people shooting, bullets flying, and blood pouring . . . Her mind kicked into doctor mode. How would they handle a crisis like that at the hospital? Especially if more than one person were severely wounded. True, they had two doctors, but they lacked nursing staff and sufficient supplies. How could they remedy that in the shortest amount of time?

She jerked her mind back to the discussion in time to hear Mr. Valders move that they hire help from Grand Forks. It looked like the group was divided fairly evenly. Wouldn't waiting until tomorrow for the decision be a better idea?

Thorliff raised his hands to calm the heating discussion. "I know we have a motion on the table, but since we are not an organized governing body, it seems to me that we need to postpone a decision like this until we talk with others in the town."

"Like their wives," Penny whispered, especially since Hjelmer seemed to be siding with the hiring-help faction.

Pastor Solberg stood up and waited for the turmoil to quiet. "I know I have no more say than the others, but I do want to suggest that this is something that needs to be prayed about, diligently. We all know the verse that a soft answer turns away wrath. I am not saying either way here, but the wisdom of sitting quietly before our God and listening for His voice makes a lot of sense to me. We have seen God's miracles so many times in our little town. Let's expect another."

The temperature in the room had cooled considerably, even while he spoke.

"Almost a hangin' mob here," Sophie said from behind the fan she had taken from her bag.

That's what was happening, all right. Astrid gave her cousin a wide-eyed look. "How did you recognize that?"

"Saw it happen one time. Not something I ever want to see again." She looked over her fan to where her husband was sitting. Garth Wiste gave her a slight nod. "You think we can go home now?" she asked Astrid.

"I think they have more business or at least some announcements."

Thorliff stood beside Reverend Solberg. "Thank you, Reverend. As always, you are the voice of wisdom." He turned to the others. "While we have a couple of other things to bring up, I suggest we meet back here tomorrow night after the praying and discussion we need. A show of hands please."

When most of the hands went up, some halfheartedly at best, he nodded again. "Good. Now I have some other news. We have heard from more job seekers, including several who are married. Some of those women agreed they would like work too, so perhaps this will help."

"Where are we going to house them?" Sophie asked. "Two rooms at my boardinghouse already have four bunks in them. I can't handle any more boarders."

"Hjelmer suggested we order army tents. We can build a frame for each rather quickly and erect them out south of the tracks. That would give us until winter to get more housing up."

"What about a couple of apartment houses? We can do two-story, like the boardinghouse. And that new wing on the boardinghouse could be rushed into occupancy more quickly." Toby Valders glanced at the others. "I know our construction teams are being pushed to the maximum, but we will have more help soon."

"And here I was hoping to get my well-drilling team back on the road." Hjelmer said his piece so mournfully that the others laughed, helping to lighten the tension in the room.

Sophie stood and waited until Thorliff nodded to her. "I hate to add fuel to the fire, but many of these new families may have children, so we can count on needing an addition to this school building too . . . before school starts." She gave a slight bow. "And thank you, gentlemen, for the promise that the new wing at the boardinghouse will be usable more quickly."

Garth rolled his eyes, and Thorliff slid into the look he sometimes gave Inga when she had been especially outrageous.

"And on that cheery note, I am now closing this meeting." He smacked his hand on the table. "Done."

"Good thing, before all the women take it upon themselves to . . ."

Astrid didn't hear the rest of the comment due to the hum of conversation fast growing louder than a hum as the group disbanded.

Small groups visited outside in the deepening dusk, and others left immediately.

"You did well, Thorliff," Mr. Valders offered on his way past. "I thought it was going to go worse than that."

"Thank you. And thanks too for being a voice of reason, especially since you manage our bank."

"No money is worth getting shot over." Anner tipped his hat and headed toward home, leaving Astrid with a sense of growing admiration. It was a shame his wife had not been there. The idea of Mrs. Valders sitting still through a meeting like that made Astrid chuckle on the inside. Actually, she was surprised Hildegunn had not come, but then women were not invited. Those that showed up did so without an invitation, and the men were too polite to run them out.

She hooked her arm through her husband's, and they accompanied Elizabeth and Thorliff back toward the Bjorklund House, as theirs was on the way. "I'm glad that's over," Astrid said to no one in particular.

"Me too." Daniel gave her arm a quick squeeze. "When you four ladies showed up, I thought there might be trouble, but those disgruntled hid it well. Thorliff, I'll bet you'll get several letters to the editor over this."

"Possibly. Then I won't have to write an editorial, unless they all agree, of course. Dissension is good for the soul."

"And that is in what Scripture?" Elizabeth asked.

Astrid knew Elizabeth's right eyebrow had arched, even though she couldn't see it in the deepening gloaming.

"I'm sure it must be somewhere." Thorliff stopped, so the others did too. "I sure would love to have Far at the meeting tomorrow night. We could—"

Elizabeth and Astrid both groaned. "Thorliff." They even said his name in unison.

"No one ever brought up a way to pay for help, should we go that route," Daniel said. "The talk of money usually cools any hotheads, not that I really saw that going on tonight. The people of Blessing seem more level-headed than other places I've been to."

"But things they are a-changing." Thorliff shook his head. "We need to make sure newer people feel they are a part of this decision."

"You men better talk with your wives too."

"Or invite them along," Astrid added to Elizabeth's comment.

"We might not have a vote, but we do have opinions and valid ones, at that."

"Astrid, I think we better hurry home before this turns into a suffragette rally."

"'Night," Astrid called over her shoulder as Daniel steered them down the street to their house, where candles waited in the windows on either side of the front door. Daniel's mother insisted that candles always welcome those coming home, winter or summer.

Tonight, Astrid did indeed feel welcome as she climbed the steps to their front porch. What did her husband really believe in regard to permitting everyone to vote—either sex and any color? The thought made her realize there were many areas of life they had not discussed before their wedding.

Not that that would have changed anything.

CHAPTER 7

Anner Valders carefully lifted the front door latch and stepped inside. Had Hildegunn gone to bed yet? Apparently not. A light shone from the kitchen. He crossed the front room and paused in the kitchen doorway.

"So how did the meeting go?" Hildegunn was toweling a large bowl dry.

"Well, I think. We're all aware of the possibility of a robbery. Forewarned is forearmed. They're talking of hiring police protection, or at least a presence."

"Did you stop by Toby's for the molasses?"

Molasses! Of course. He scowled, not just because he had forgotten all about it, but because hers was a rather silly question. He wasn't carrying anything, was he? "I'll go get it. If they're not up, can it wait until morning?"

"Not if you want sticky buns for breakfast. I've set the sponge."

Mustn't waste good flour and eggs. With a sigh, he headed back out the front door and up the street. If Toby was not still up, he would pound on their door until he was. After all, they would not hesitate to pound on his door if the need arose.

Someone's dog barked as he passed the bank alley, which set someone else's dog to barking in the distance. The air hung humid, dark, gloomy. In a way he felt dark and gloomy. What if no one caught those robbers? His bank was vulnerable. In the distance a horse sneezed.

Anner stopped, listening. The sneeze seemed to come from behind the bank. There were no horses stabled near there. Was a horse really back there, or were his ears deceiving him? His hearing was certainly not nearly as sharp as it used to be. He often had trouble discerning directions.

He would check, though, just to make sure. He crossed to the bank and slipped into its shadow. Cautiously he moved to the back alley, remembering just in time about the rain barrel against the wall. He groped until he found it, stepped out around it, continued to the back. He peeked around the corner.

There stood four horses near the back door of the bank. It was so dark, Anner could barely make out a small man sitting on one of them with his back to Anner. He held the other three horses' reins. The horses seemed nervous. They moved about, their hind legs sidestepping, their ears going every which way.

They were here! Those robbers! Right now! Anner needed a gun! He needed Toby! He needed others! What to do? His mind charged off in six directions at once.

What could he do? By the time he ran to someone's house to fetch help, those men might well be done with their thieving business and escaping on their horses. Even if the townsmen could be aroused, by the time they got their horses saddled, the fellows would be long gone. Why, oh why was he not carrying a gun?

Anner was suddenly struck by a horrific, paralyzing thought: Big-city banks insured their holdings. Blessing's bank could not afford to. Any money lost was Anner's responsibility, not some insurance company's.

On impulse, because he couldn't think, Anner slipped out of his jacket. Then he bolted forward toward those horses at a dead run, waving his coat frantically like a brakeman's flag and shrieking at the top of his lungs.

All four horses flung their heads in the air, and as one they wheeled away from him, yanking the reins out of the rider's hand. The rider's horse squealed, reared high, and dumped the fellow off its back and down its rump before galloping away after its companions.

Anner was just reaching the back door as a large man came bursting out of it. The man let out a surprised cry, more a scream, and lashed at Anner with a huge fist, then swung a large and heavy carpetbag at him. Both connected, and Anner went tumbling to the dirt.

He lay there with no breath in him, listening to the boots running away after the horses. He desperately wanted to shout *"Stop! Thief!"* He desperately wanted to breathe. None of that was happening.

From out on the street, Trygve's voice called, "What's going on? Who's there?"

Someone else shouted from what sounded like an upstairs window. Yet another voice called out.

Anner managed a feeble "Help!" The second "Help!" was stronger.

Here came Trygve. The sound of his voice told Anner he was in the alley. "Who's there?"

"Help!" Anner was finally getting his breath back, sort of.

Now Thorliff was there and someone else, and the men were lifting Anner to his feet. His neck hurt mightily, and his ribs felt like they were broken. Maybe they were. The pain was intense all over.

"The robbers . . ." he gasped.

Now several others had arrived. "The door is standing open!" someone yelled. "They were here and they're getting away!"

The pain was so bad, Anner dropped down onto his hands and knees, which only made his ribs hurt much worse. His hands landed on something like paper. "Bring a light!" he shouted with the little bit of breath he could summon. "There's money here. Bills!"

Someone was running off with a hurried "I'll get horses!"

Trygve came out of the bank with a coal-oil lamp. "Who has a match?"

Someone found a match. In the tiny flare and then the lamplight, Anner saw money lying all over the ground.

And Lars shouted, "There! There's one of them right there!"

The lamplight revealed the robber who had been thrown from his horse. He had been trying to crawl away. Now he rolled to his back with his hands out. "I give up." Instantly, two men were grabbing him and hauling him to his feet. He cried out in pain as his leg collapsed. Then he sank between them and fainted dead away.

"Hjelmer's bringing us some horses," Lars said.

"No moon. It's too dark," Trygve said. "We'll never catch them. Let's gather this money that got spilled, and someone tell Astrid and Elizabeth. That fellow and Anner here will both need attention."

Ever since those two women set themselves up as doctors, Anner had been fervently hoping he would never get sick. The very thought of women, young women, at that, tending to him . . . Cheeky women with no qualms about speaking out of turn. No, he wanted to go home, let Hildegunn take care of him. He said so. He protested. They took him over to the hospital anyway, against his wishes.

They laid him out on a bed, and he found it was easiest to simply give up. If he closed his eyes and lay very, very still, his ribs hurt less. Footsteps entered the room. He turned his head to look. Elizabeth Bjorklund and Thorliff. People he did not particularly want to see just now. He closed his eyes again.

In an accusing voice, Thorliff asked, "Why didn't you go for help?"

Anner did not sigh. That would have caused more pain. "I really have no answer for that."

"Oh good! You're here!" Elizabeth's voice. "He is clutching his side. Would you undress the top half of him, please? I'll go make certain Astrid doesn't need me."

Who was there?

Hildegunn's voice. "Of course." He looked at her. Yes, indeed this was Hildegunn, and her face was tear-streaked. She began fumbling with his waistcoat.

Thorliff sounded excited, and he was not an excitable sort. "I just talked to the sheriff. He wants me to get some information from you and call him back. What did they look like?" Another silly question.

"Dark gray shapeless forms. A small one and a large one."

"Only two?"

"Four horses, so probably not."

"What do the horses look like?"

"Dark gray shapeless forms."

Thorliff was beginning to sound impatient. "Were they armed?"

"I've no idea." Anner shuddered. What if they had been? He could be dead now, a bullet in his heart. What could have possessed him to do such a fool thing as to give chase?

"Trygve said he heard someone shriek. Did you wound one? Was one of them slumped over in the saddle or something?"

"The miscreants and their horses departed the scene separately."

"Sep—" Thorliff hooted. "So that was the shrieking! You drove the horses off! Wonderful! Anything else?"

"The large person was carrying a heavy valise or carpetbag. He swung it at me, struck me with it. I would surmise that it was stuffed full of bills, and when he hit me, the clasp gave way and it gaped open, dumping its contents. Or some of its contents."

"And you've no idea how much was taken?"

"If they broke into the till chest, perhaps a hundred, a hundred fifty dollars. It seemed to be mostly small bills on the ground, so that would be the till chest. If they managed to compromise the safe, heaven knows."

Heaven knew. God knew. Or maybe not. Right now, Anner did not know, and the pain and frustration and sorrow weighed him down so horrendously, he doubted God knew or cared.

Astrid stood near the head of the operating table, watching the boy's breathing become slower and deeper. The anesthetic was taking hold.

Annika Nilsson, the only student nurse at the time, stood ready to assist, and over in the corner, Daniel stood with arms folded. "In case you need help," he had said. Help as a doctor or help keeping the boy from attempting to escape? She didn't ask.

A boy. Fourteen at most, certainly not near his full growth. A boy. Robbing banks. She wasn't sure she could deal with this. Any of this. She so wished she were treating Anner instead, but she and Elizabeth had dashed into examining rooms at random, and the men who brought the two in happened to put the boy in here.

He was under far enough. She asked Annika to cut his trousers leg open. It was worse than she'd feared, much worse—a compound fracture that could kill, if the bleeding didn't kill him first. The lower end of his broken right femur was visible. It had pushed through muscle and skin and now protruded over half an inch, and its shattered, bloody end was drying out. If the bone end of a compound fracture dried out, it would die. It would not knit as a normal broken bone would do. It would cause infection, then gangrene, and invariably would be fatal. This child not yet a man faced an agonizing death within the week.

And a horrible thought flashed through her mind. Keep him anesthetized, keep him on heavy morphine, allow him to die comfortably. That would be the most merciful treatment. Medicine is all about mercy, for the patient and for the relatives, assuming there were any.

No. She would amputate the leg. This boy-child would go through life—and probably through jail after jail—with only one leg. But she could do no less. "Get the bone saw ready, please." She wrapped a tourniquet around the thigh above the break and tightened it down.

The amputator's maxim: *Save as much of the leg as possible.* That wasn't much. She poised her scalpel. *Dear Lord, guide my hand.* She paused. Fourteen. Or younger.

Maybe . . . possibly . . . why not? "Daniel? Can you run to the shop, quickly, and grind the head off a six-penny nail? Sharpen both ends. Please?"

He looked puzzled for only a moment and then ran out the door.

Annika looked puzzled too. "You aren't going to nail his leg back together, surely."

"Not exactly." Astrid picked up the scalpel. "While Daniel's gone I want to remove the dried portion of this bone end. It will take some doing, and we're going to have to dig into the flesh here. I will cut; you irrigate."

"I haven't done much in surgery."

"You're here to learn. If my idea fails, you will have learned a way of treating a compound fracture that simply will not work. In any case, you'll learn how to assist a surgeon."

But please, merciful Lord, help this to work!

When Daniel came rushing in with a six-penny nail sharpened at both ends, Astrid was ready. They had exposed the broken bone end down to live, moist bone and sawed off the dry dead part. Annika did a fine job of keeping the whole wound wet with water, then with diluted carbolic acid.

"Now I need that hammer in the bone drawer." Astrid pointed. Annika slapped the hammer into her hand. It was a graceful little hammer—steel, all one piece, and possibly too delicate for the job. With the hammer, Astrid drove one end of the nail up into the femur above the break.

Annika watched, wide-eyed. "Oh, do you really think it might work?"

"If it does, all thanks go to God." She pressed the sawed-off lower part of the femur onto the other sharp nail point. "More carbolic acid."

Annika again irrigated the wound.

"Now we close the wound, splint it, and keep on praying. Suture."

Elizabeth came into the room. "I just taped poor Mr. Valders' ribs— What are you—" She gasped. "Oh, my word!" She watched fascinated as Astrid drew the rectus muscle together above a shiny six-penny nail. Even Daniel was bent low, watching.

"Annika," Astrid explained, "this muscle, the vastus, has three bellies. The bone end tore the lateralis here, so I cut it to get to the bone, since it was damaged anyway. Now we reconnect here and here. Then we put his leg in a traction splint. I'll show you how it's done."

"Will he ever walk again?"

"Not for a long time, but yes, he'll walk. I will advise him against running, though. Who knows what jarring will do to the nail."

"I'm glad. He's such a handsome young man."

Astrid paused, staring at her. "Annika, he's a bank robber."

"A handsome bank robber. Isn't everyone God's child?"

Annika hardly knew Astrid's mor, but she sounded so much like Ingeborg!

"Yes, I agree. He is God's child, the same as we." Astrid smiled to herself. *Well, God, when you deliver a message, you manage to surprise me with it.*

The next morning, Astrid did rounds as quickly as she could, for she wanted to go out to visit her mor and far. Mostly, she simply could not wait to tell Ingeborg about the lesson on judgment that God had sent her.

But her mother beat her to it. Ingeborg showed up at the hospital bright and early. "I heard they caught one of the robbers last night, and he is just a child."

"That's true. Perhaps we can find some coffee and sit for a few minutes. I want to tell you about the—"

"I heard that," came Mrs. Geddick's voice from the kitchen. "Please sit."

They chuckled at each other and sat.

Astrid sobered. "The boy was holding the robbers' horses. Anner spooked them and the boy was thrown. Broke his leg. I don't know if the break became complex immediately or if it happened as they dragged him to the hospital. They were pretty rough with him. I have him in traction. I hope we can save his leg, but we'll probably have to amputate."

Ingeborg wagged her head. "So sad. Imagine how his poor mother must feel. Somewhere."

"She's dead. As the anesthesia was wearing off, he became very talkative. I don't think he realized what he was saying at all. The other three thieves are his brothers. This is how they supported their father until they left home."

Ingeborg's mouth dropped open.

Here came Mrs. Geddick with rolls and coffee and set the tray down. "You received a call while you were on rounds. The sheriff wants to know when he can come arrest your robber."

Astrid sighed. "It will be a while. He won't be able to get up on crutches for several weeks. And that's when the healing will just begin."

Ingeborg frowned. "You'll keep him here in the hospital?"

"I don't know." Astrid wagged her head. "Almost all our beds are full now. What if we need that one? I did learn to curb my tendency to jump to quick judgments. Well, not exactly. God forced the lesson on me."

Astrid smiled at the coffee cup in front of her and just sat for a few moments. "Mor, he doesn't want to be a bank robber. As I said, he was delirious for a while, ranting. To condense half an hour of rambling down to a sentence, he's mad at his brothers, and he knows what they do is wrong, but he doesn't know how to get out of it. Incidentally, he's not quite thirteen yet."

"Twelve years old. No wonder he doesn't know how to free himself. Still a child."

"How well he heals will depend on how persevering he is. It will be a long hard struggle."

"Weeks? Months? How long?" Ingeborg looked so sad that it made Astrid sad.

"At least two months. I don't know. I tried something that hasn't been done. I realize now I should have used two small nails to stabilize the bone so that it can't twist or swivel. I doubt it will ever heal well, and he'll probably end up an amputee despite our efforts, and that will be still another month. Quite possibly the snow will fly before he's ready to go to trial."

"You can't keep him in the hospital that long."

"I know." Perhaps she should have just kept him drowsy on morphine until he died. Heavens, no! What could she be thinking? But the uncertainties of all this weighed her down so heavily.

"He is a child who needs help. We will help him. When he is well enough to leave the hospital, he will stay with your far and me."

"I'm sorry, Sheriff Meeker, but the boy is unconscious. Has been ever since the surgery last night to repair that leg." Astrid stood at the door to the boy's room, one of the few private rooms they had. She didn't mention that they were keeping him sedated to help with the pain.

"I understand, Dr. Bjorklund, but you have to look at my point of view. His brothers might come back for him, you know."

"They don't have any idea if he is dead or alive."

"I'm sure they will be checking. He can give us valuable information about their whereabouts. They aren't stupid, you know." He lifted his hat and scrubbed the palm of his hand over his less-than-abundant hair before settling his hat back.

Astrid wanted nothing more than to go home and sleep for hours. It had been a long night after the surgery, with Reverend Solberg showing up to pray while the rest of them worked to get the boy's leg in the traction splint. When he started to come out of the anesthetic, he had been so restless they were afraid that in spite of the splint, he might make the injury worse. That's when she and Elizabeth had decided to keep him as far under as needed. But what to do now? *Lord, I do need wisdom here.*

I am in over my head, that's for sure. But her first job was to care for her patient. And protect him.

"Sheriff, I do understand, but . . ." She heaved a sigh. "Can you wait for an hour or so? He might be waking by then, and I will permit you to ask him some questions. If he'll be able to answer, I don't know." *Do I tell him what the boy said yesterday under anesthesia or not?* She looked up at the sound of a door.

"Don't worry. That's my deputy. I am going to get some breakfast at the boardinghouse, and he will remain here. Besides catching those crooks, my job is to keep you all safe."

I wish you had thought of that earlier. But what could she say? After all, the people of Blessing had not requested help. Pictures of a big bird with its head in the sand floated through her mind. That had indeed been all of them. "Thank you."

"I'll leave Jason here by the door if you have a chair. I can't cover the outside doors. Another thing. I'll probably deputize some of the men of Blessing to fill in."

Astrid nodded. There was no way she could dredge up a smile at this point. She went to fetch a chair from another room, set it in place, and then joined their head nurse, Deborah MacCallister, at the boy's bedside. "Annika was a great help yesterday. She's a bright student."

"This is a great place to learn the basics. The training was so good, I could complete nursing school in one fall and winter. I've learned that it normally takes at least two years." Deborah checked the boy's pulse. "I think he is starting to come around."

Astrid wrapped her fingers over the boy's toes. They were not turning blue, so the splinting was not too tight, but they were very cold. She wrapped a baby blanket around his foot, for a quilt would have been too heavy.

"Deborah," she asked quietly, "have I made the right decision to try to save his leg like that, or is it just going to cause more infection?"

"We have to trust that God is leading us," Deborah whispered.

"Thanks for the reminder."

"Your mor taught me that when she and Elizabeth were training us. She said you pray, do what you can, and trust God's Word when Jesus promised to never leave us nor forsake us. She reminded me of that just the other day."

"Thank you, I guess." She studied their patient. His eyelids were indeed fluttering. He whimpered and rolled his head from side to side. She laid a hand on his arm and leaned closer. "Take it easy. You are safe here."

"N-no."

The two women exchanged looks over the boy's bed. *What do we do?* Deborah mouthed.

Astrid shrugged. The choices: Keep him sedated and tell the sheriff to come later, or let him question the child, for that was what he was. A child. "Can you hear me?"

A brief nod.

"Good. Then listen carefully. You are in a hospital with a badly broken leg. You will have to stay here for an extended period of time, a long time, to recover from the break and from the surgery we did on your leg. I am Dr. Bjorklund. What is your first name?"

With his eyes still closed, he mumbled something.

"Did you say Manny?"

A tiny nod.

From the other side of his bed, Deborah spoke up. "I am your nurse. You may call me Miss MacCallister, or Nurse MacCallister. If you are hungry, I'll go fix something for you to eat, but you have to lie flat here with your bad leg up in the air. If you understand, please nod. Good. We'll start with a little bread and jam. That should be easy to eat." She started to leave but then stopped at the door. "Do you suppose Manny is short for Manasseh?" Astrid asked. At his slight shudder, she left, nodding.

"Manny. Can you open your eyes?"

The lids fluttered and slowly opened. Fear leaped out at her. His hands clenched in the sheet covering him, grime imbedded so deeply that soap and a washcloth had failed to remove it. His hair hung in strings, and the odor of his body had nothing to do with infection. "The sheriff is coming back to ask you some questions, but he can't hurt you."

He jerked his head up, but when the pain blasted him, he collapsed against the pillow.

"They ran off and left you behind, Manny."

His head quivered more than shook.

"I'm sorry, but that is the truth."

Desolation overrode fear. He closed his eyes again.

"I will stay with you while the sheriff is here."

He clamped his teeth down on his lower lip, the trembling from either the pain or the fear, or both. She wasn't sure.

She recognized the man's voice in the hall and went to the door. Hearing a noise behind her, she turned to see Manny trying to sit up. "Come in," she said as she flew back to stop him. Again he collapsed, this time drenched in sweat. "His name is Manny, and he's in a great deal of pain. Please make this quick so we can give him the pain meds he needs so desperately."

Sheriff Meeker stopped at the foot of the bed. "What is your last name, boy?" Manny shook his head, his jaw tight.

"You're part of the McCrary gang, aren't you. Most likely the youngest brother. Your brothers, if you can call them that, hightailed it out of town, leaving you behind to go to jail. You tell me where they are hiding out, and I'll leave you to the good graces of Dr. Bjorklund here."

"No!" The effort put into the word made him pant.

No matter what Sheriff Meeker said, Manny only answered no, and after a few questions, he just shook his head, eyes closed.

"I'll be back. One more thing. You cooperate with me, and I'll make sure you don't go to jail. You think on that." He turned and walked out, leaving a message with the man at the door.

He's only doing his job, Astrid reminded herself more than once as she prepared a syringe to administer the morphine that would make the boy relax.

Deborah brought in a tray and set it on the stand by the bed. "Can he eat?" At Astrid's nod, she broke off a small piece of bread and held it to his hand. "You can feed yourself, Manny." Slowly his eyes opened and he stuffed the bread into his mouth. Swallowing that, he reached for more. After half the slice and a sip of water, his eyes drifted shut again and he slept.

"I wonder how long it's been since he's eaten. Skinny as he is makes me think food has been scarce."

"Considering how long they've been on the run . . . or probably as the smallest, he is the last to eat and not much is left for him." Astrid checked his pulse. "Do you think those scum will come back for him?"

"Absolutely. If they fear he might give them away."

Astrid shook her head. "I'll look in on Mr. Valders, and then I am going home. You call me if you need me."

Waves of weariness threatened to drown her as she stepped into another room. Anner Valders lay wide awake. He looked toward her and grabbed the ice bag on his head before it slid off. There was no visible sign of his wounds, for painfully broken ribs do not show. Elizabeth had strapped his chest to make breathing less painful. Astrid felt his forehead. No fever to speak of.

"When can I get out of here?"

"I'd suggest you stay overnight, but that is up to you and Hildegunn. Staying here would be easier on her."

He tried to move, but then flinched and grunted. "When do I need to decide?"

"Take your time. Rest some more and then see."

Nodding knocked the ice pack off, and as he scrambled to get it back, he clamped his teeth together.

"Any movements will be pretty painful for a while."

"How long?"

"At least the first few days. Then it will slowly taper off."

"I see."

"Let me know."

She left the room, stopping to leave instructions with Deborah. "When Hildegunn arrives, tell her that Anner is doing well and what he needs most right now is sleep. I left the decision up to them for when he can leave."

On the walk home, even the beauty of the morning failed to revive her much. Had she done the right thing in not amputating immediately? Had the idea to use the nail come from her heavenly Father? Or not? The questions kept plaguing her. Trying to reason took more than she had to offer right now. *Thank you, God, that Elizabeth will be doing evening rounds.* When she reached her bed, she fell across it without even undressing.

That ringing. The telephone. She rolled over and pushed herself to sitting. It stopped. Good.

But one glance out the window and her mind returned full force. If that wasn't early dusk out there, Blessing was under a mighty dark cloud.

"You needn't hurry." Daniel came through the doorway, a cup of something in his raised hand. "Coffee anyone? Coffee?"

Astrid chuckled. Leave it to her husband. How did she ever get so fortunate as to be married to Daniel Jeffers? "Takk."

He handed her the cup and sat down beside her. "Feel better?"

"I do."

"Mother has supper nearly on the table. Looks and smells mighty good."

Astrid inhaled and drank some of her coffee. "I should have been helping her."

"You know, you can't work all night and all day too."

She gave him a false patient look. "Have you heard anything on our patients?"

"Let's see." Daniel counted on his fingers. "Both of your patients are sleeping. The boy is running a temperature. Anner is snoring. He decided to remain one more night. Three of the other patients went home. Mr. Morris is improving. The carved leg is fitting better so he can walk more. He is using a cane too. Anyone else?"

"No new babies?"

"No. Elizabeth said they are all waiting to celebrate the Fourth of July." He leaned over and kissed his wife's cheek. "Umm, you smell good."

"Your nose must be plugged. I am sure I smell like the hospital."

He dropped another kiss on her shoulder and got to his feet. He held out his hand, she took it, and together they strolled down the staircase.

"Thank you," she said at the bottom of the stairs. "That was a nice waking-up."

Amelia Jeffers set the bread plate on the table. "Can you think of anything I missed?" She smiled. "You look better, my dear." She patted Astrid's hand. After Daniel seated them both, she leaned closer to Astrid. "I went out to see Ingeborg and Haakan, and he is looking so much better. Another true miracle, I think. Ingeborg said for you to call if you need her, and she is praying."

"I know, and that is such a comfort. Thank you for this lovely meal." She looked up from dishing up her plate when the telephone jangled. Sure enough, their ring. She motioned for the other two to stay seated and went to answer it.

It was Deborah. "Astrid, Manny is asking for you, but if you are eating, finish your supper first. His temperature is rising."

"Is the deputy still there?"

"A different one is."

"And why are you still there?"

"I'm just finishing up and bringing Annika up to date."

"All right. I'll be over in a bit. You might have Annika put some ice in a wet cloth and place it under Manny's neck. Are there any other signs of infection?" At the negative, she hung up and returned to the dining room, taking her seat again, this time with a sigh.

"Getting worse?"

She nodded. "Hopefully not much." *Please, Lord, take care of this.*

Later a small group of men gathered at the newspaper office, where the discussion, of course, centered around the robbery.

"All that for a measly fifty-five dollars," Thorliff huffed as he shook his head.

"We can thank God it wasn't more," Garth Wiste said quietly.

"I am, but . . ." Thorliff stared out the window. "I think they'll come back tonight. They can't afford to let him talk. Besides, there is no moon tonight."

"But according to the sheriff, their little brother is tough. He's not talking." Trygve tilted his chair back on two legs. "However, we can't leave our people unprotected. Meeker's idea of deputizing tomorrow might just be too late."

"Who's at the hospital now?"

"Annika is the nurse on duty," Daniel answered. "Elizabeth is over there now and the second of the county deputies. The condition of that boy will determine if others take shifts to care for him. I suggest we take turns for the night patrolling the exterior, singly or in teams of two."

"I say at least three." Trygve had been quiet up to now. "Four of us and possibly Toby and Garth."

"Why so many?"

"One of the last wells we drilled before we came home taught me some things. The fellow I bored the well for was both ignorant and stubborn. He was unlettered, which is no crime, but he thought he knew absolutely everything. Adamant about it. If that's what we're dealing with here, willful ignorance and bullheadedness, the brothers will not behave normally. They're unpredictable. We cannot say, 'They will do this,' or 'Surely they wouldn't do that.' We must be ready for anything, and that takes more than just one or two."

The others nodded.

Thorliff looked at Daniel. "You call the others. Okay?"

Daniel nodded.

"Glad we are doing something. The thought of those lowlifes injuring our neighbors and friends . . ." Thorliff wagged his head.

Daniel jotted down a schedule and read it, to the approval of the others. "Good! Then let's get at it. I think we should let Solberg know too. He'll marshal prayer support."

"Good idea." The men rose and headed out the door. This promised to be a long night, but hopefully a productive one.

Thorliff raised his voice. "I'll call Sheriff Meeker and tell him what we are planning."

The others waved. They had much to do. And little time to get started.

Chapter 9

Gabe McCrary was just as noble a leader of men as was Jesse James or Cole Younger. Look how many robberies he and his brothers had pulled off—just as many as any of those others and nary a hitch—well, except for losing Manny, of course. And they were about to take care of that little detail shortly.

They wouldn't have lost him in the first place if it hadn't been so miserable dark in that alley. Why, they ran right past him and never even saw him. Gabe leaned against the side of a big square building of some sort and watched the Blessing hospital across the street.

"You sure that's where he is?" Beside him, Meshach scowled.

"Sure of it, Shack. That little girl was just a gold mine of information. Ask her a question and she'll take off rattling like an empty buckboard for a couple minutes. I thought Pearly Mae would talk your ear off, but this kid's even talkier than Pearly Mae. And she hears everything."

"But kids lie. Well, they tell fibs anyway."

"Pretty certain she weren't lying. Her name's Inga 'cause her grandma's Ingeborg. Says the bank robber is just a young 'un, and he's in the hospital. Broke his leg. So he ain't gonna go running for a while. We might even have to carry him out to the horses."

"Well, I ain't carrying him." Shack's scowl deepened.

"Don't fret your britches. I'll carry him." Jedediah leaned just as casually against the wall. "There's the church bell pealing, so folks are mostly gonna be in the church."

"We give 'em a few minutes or so to get settled and sing something," Gabe said. "Then we go in."

"Because some little chatterbox says so." Shack obviously was not convinced.

Gabe sighed. "Look, she knows everything 'cause her ma and aunt Astrid are doctors there. So she hears all about it."

"You mean her pa and uncle are doctors."

"Nope. Women doctors. Shack, this is gonna be the easiest thing. A couple excitable women is all that stands between us and Manny, and maybe one of them is in church. He might even be all alone in there."

"Can't believe they wouldn't put a guard on him." Shack was looking all around, as if some of those churchgoing people were waiting behind a tree to jump out on him or something. "We shoulda gone back home to Kentucky, like Manny wanted. Rob banks in Kentucky, where we know the lay of the land and there's hills to hide in."

"No banks in Kentucky got money," Jedediah opined.

Shack snorted. "They got a darn sight more than fifty-five dollars in them!"

Jedediah lurched himself upright. "About time to work our way around to there, eh?"

Gabe nodded and stepped back.

As they led their horses back a ways, crossed the street, and headed up the alley, Gabe rehearsed what went wrong Friday night, because he sure didn't want it to happen again. It took them until first light to finally catch up with their horses, and then to find the satchel practically empty . . . He shuddered.

Here was the back door of the hospital. They tied off their horses to a rail fence across the way and casually sauntered to the door.

Gabe tried it. Wasn't locked. He pushed it open. They were in a big kitchen of some sort, probably where they made the patients' food and things. A woman was stirring a pot with her back to them. Silently, they slipped past her and out into a hallway. She didn't look toward them at all.

Where was he? This was a big building. Real big.

"Listen!" Jedediah hissed.

Someone was saying something, ranting, it sounded like. Yelling. Gabe paused. Yep. It sounded like Manny.

But Jed was pushing past him, muttering, "It's him." Jed led the way up and out into a hall.

They did have a guard, and there he sat on a chair outside a door. Was Manny beyond that door?

"Please help!" called a woman's voice from inside the room.

The guard leaped up and ran into the room. More ranting. Yes, it definitely was Manny.

Gabe and Jed, with Shack trailing behind, hurried to the door and stopped, listening.

The woman's voice: "He's out of his head with fever and pain. We gave him morphine, but it will take a few minutes to gain a hold. Please help us hold him until the morphine quiets him."

Another woman's voice: "I have to finish this procedure, and he's moving so much, I could make a mistake."

The guard, presumably: "All right. I have his leg pinned down. Just a scrawny kid, and I can't believe how strong he is."

Gabe stepped into the room. Jed moved in beside him.

Manny was lying on a bed, his head flailing back and forth. He cried out, "I won't go back with them! I can't! Help me!"

One of the two women, the one facing them, looked up and yelped.

The other, a blonde, twisted to look at them. "You're his brothers! Come help us!" She didn't seem scared of them at all, yet she was frantic in a way.

"I'll help." Jed rushed over. He pinned down Manny's arms. "Imagine how strong this kid's gonna be when he gets his growth." Manny was lifting an arm off the bed even with Jed leaning on it.

The blonde barked, "Elizabeth, fill a syringe with morphine, a *big* dose."

The other woman started to say something, but she closed her mouth into a sort of smirk. She picked up one of those shot needles and filled it from a big vial on a tray.

Gabe stared. "You gonna give him a shot? Don't want shots!"

"He is in intense pain," the blonde said. "We had his leg in a traction splint. He tried to get out of bed and twisted the break severely. Now I must operate to repair it if he's ever going to walk again." She bent over the leg with a tool, blocking Gabe's view.

Jed asked, "Ain't you gonna just cut it off?"

"We may have to, but he's so young, I hate to. We'll save it if we can."

Jed looked at her strangely. Obviously he was thinking something. Gabe could usually tell when his brother was thinking something deep.

The woman called Elizabeth was still holding that huge needle. "I have to get more alcohol from the cabinet."

The blonde nodded.

Elizabeth hurried around to the side of the bed, passing Gabe.

Suddenly she tripped and tipped forward, and he felt that needle go right into his behind! Right through his pants and everything!

He yelped and tried to lurch aside, but he bumped into the blonde. But she was tough! She was braced for it, bumped into him right back. Swift as lightning, that Elizabeth woman ran out the door.

His butt hurt where she'd slammed into him, really hurt. "Shack! Grab her!"

But she was gone before that oaf Meshach could even move.

The guard cried out, "I don't dare let go!"

"No, you don't. Please, just keep holding his leg steady." The blonde continued to work on the leg.

A bloody nail fell to the floor. Well, it looked like a nail, but it didn't have a head. Obviously one of those fancy new medical devices.

Jed said, "He's not fighting as much. He ain't dying, is he?"

"No, he was dosed with morphine. It's finally helping him relax. Thank you for holding him down."

"Welcome. I can see what you're doing there. Never saw a human bone before like that. If you bring them ends together, they're gonna knit?"

"We hope so. Suture. Oh, that's right. Elizabeth left." She stepped over to the tray, picked up a couple pieces of thread, and returned to her work. "I suppose we shouldn't try putting him in traction again. He fights it. I'm just hoping this will heal without complications."

"What complications?"

"When a leg bone breaks, the muscles around it contract. It's not something your brain tells it to do. It just happens. And if the bones are the least bit out of line, the muscles can force the end of a bone right out through the skin. It's called a compound fracture. Traction prevents that from happening."

Jed nodded toward a sort of rope harness thing at the foot of the bed. "That the traction?"

"Yes."

"Then put it back on him. I'll make certain he doesn't fight it anymore."

"The devil you will!" Gabe exploded. "We're supposed to get him out of here. Take a hand. We're gonna do it."

Jed stared straight at Gabe. "This here woman is doing some mighty tough work trying to save our brother's leg when she doesn't have to," he said, his voice raised some, which he never did. "She coulda just cut it off. Lots easier. But she didn't and that's good. You try riding a horse with only one leg. Or running, or anything. If she cares that much to try to save it, so will we. You best get out of here while you can. That Elizabeth woman's probably to the church by now fetching up menfolk."

Shack poked Gabe. "He's right. I'm getting outta here!"

Now Gabe was the leader, the boss, and he should have decided something definite about what they ought to do, right? But he couldn't. His brain was kind of fuzzy, not in an unpleasant way but just . . . well, like he'd just got up before dawn. That kind of fuzzy. At least his butt didn't hurt anymore.

Shack bolted toward the door. "I'm going clear away, clear home to Kentucky." He screeched to a halt out in the hall and came running back in. "They're coming already! A half dozen of them, running down the hall this way, Gabe! Whata we do?"

Gabe figured it out. He had the only gun, so he drew it and pointed it right at the blonde.

When the men appeared in the doorway, he yelled, "Stop right there, the lot of you! Back off!"

"Don't hurt Astrid!" one of them shouted, but they backed off and disappeared from the doorway.

Jed was looking at Gabe kind of funny.

Gabe knew they were just outside, waiting. But he wasn't certain what to do next.

He realized something he ought *not* be doing: He was aiming his .45 at the floor. He swung it back up to aim toward the woman. So long as he was doing that, they wouldn't dare barge in or try to shoot him, for fear she'd get it. So far, so good.

Jed was talking to the blonde. "For a couple little females, you two are pretty sharp. When that Elizabeth lost her balance and tipped into Gabe, she stuck a shot into him, didn't she? With morphine." Jed sounded distant, like he was way down at the end of the hall or somewhere, but he was standing right there. Gabe could see him.

"But I don't know if she delivered the whole dose or only part of it, so I can't say how much he actually got." The blonde sounded distant too, like she was a long way off.

"Gabe, gimme the gun." Jed was looking at him weirdly again.

"Why should I? I'm the boss here."

But Gabe realized he was pointing it at the floor again, so when Jed came around the head of the bed and took the gun out of his hand, he didn't object too loudly.

He was in a different room, not that one. And there were different people here, not Jed or Shack or the blonde or the guard. He felt groggy, like he was drunk, but he couldn't be. And he felt sort of happy too, like everything was just fine. He was sitting in a chair . . . well, not sitting, more like sprawling down in it. He sat up straighter.

A smiling fellow pulled a chair up beside his, facing him. "Why, howdy. My name's Clyde Meeker. What's yours?" He pumped Gabe's right hand in an exuberant handshake.

"Gabe McCrary, pleeztameetcha."

"McCrary! I've heard that name before. Ain't you one of them boys that's been holding up banks and stores? If you are, I'm especially pleased to meet you. You boys are a legend around here. Truly admired."

A legend. Think of that! It pleased Gabe mightily. A legend. And admired. "Thankee, sir. I mean, Clyde. Thankee. Yessir, that we are."

"Don't ever see you boys around town, though. Where do you hang out when you're not doing your work? Know what I mean?"

Gabe grinned. "We came on this old abandoned farm, out beyond those low hills out east. Makes a nice place to settle in, y'know? Just set. Rest up. That sorta thing. Legend, huh?" He really, really felt all fuzzy and comfy inside. He hadn't felt this good since he couldn't remember when.

From somewhere off to his right, a woman's voice asked, "Is there a nice stable on that farm?"

"Stable? Yes, ma'am, a mighty fine stable." He looked over to an old woman with a braid that wrapped clear around her head. "Haymow was even half full. We don't have to turn our horses out to graze unless we wanna. Though they's good fences."

The woman said, "Clyde, I know exactly where he's talking about."

"That's right, Ingeborg, you've been here a long time."

"Hefners'. Remember? Anna and Lester left their farm and moved in closer when their daughter died."

"That was before I took office. Can you show me where it is?"

"I can, ja."

Ingeborg. Where did he hear that name before? Try as he might, Gabe could not bring up where he'd heard the name.

This Clyde fellow asked some other questions that Gabe enjoyed answering, but what he enjoyed most was the lovely, warm, peaceful feeling that settled all through him, skin to bone, and made him comfortable. He wondered where Jed and Shack had got to, and he asked a couple times, but nobody seemed to know. The only one they knew was him, Gabe, and they addressed him as *sir* and were really respectful, and they seemed to enjoy his company. For sure, he enjoyed theirs.

Then Clyde suggested they all ride up to somewhere for a drink. Gabe was in for that.

Jed really kind of admired this blond doctor, even if she was a woman. Good looking—a pretty lady—and tough as nails. Nothing seemed to frighten her. She was single-minded when it came to operating on his little brother. And she was good at giving sensible directions.

This doctor lady had stitched Manny's leg all back together. Now she said, "With your help I want to put him back in traction. Then we'll tie his hips and chest down until he wakes up, so he can't try to get up and damage the break more. I'm afraid he's his own worst enemy right now."

"Ain't we all." His oldest brother, Gabe, was gone with the sheriff now and pretty much out of it. Morphine, huh? Pretty slick. Shack stood near the door with the pistol, keeping watch, but the fellows outside weren't causing trouble so far.

"Hold this, please." And then, "Good. Now lift his heel—perfect." And then other directions. "You see how this is going to work?"

And yeah, he could see what they were doing, how they were rigging a harness of ropes to put just a tiny bit of pull on the leg so it couldn't cramp up. Jed realized he didn't even mind a woman bossing him around, and that was strange. He usually didn't cotton to women ordering him around. Maybe it was because she wasn't cranky or pushy. And she obviously really cared about Manny, the gentle way she worked.

So Gabe liked to believe he was the thinker, the mastermind, eh? Too bad he couldn't think past his nose. Or think at all right now, so Jed would take over the thinking. And do a better job of it, no doubt.

"Shack? How we doing over there?"

"They've moved down the hall a piece. Just waiting. What are we gonna do?"

"Been thinking about that. Can't take Manny with us. We'll hafta—"

"But like Gabe said, he'll blab all about us! We can't leave him here."

Jed held a stick of some sort while the doctor wrapped rope around it. "We'll have to leave Manny behind. So here's what we're gonna do. When Manny's all set up here comfortable, we use the doctor for a shield and walk down to the horses. Those fellers won't shoot at us with the doctor right there. Ride out to the edge of town and turn the doctor loose."

"No! We need her for protection!"

"If we take her along, they'll come after us. Not only that, she'll know where we're hiding. We leave her and ride to the river. We'll stay in the river, down in the river bottom, riding in the water along the edge until we get well away, so they can't track us. Then tomorrow, we can start back to Kentucky."

Shack wagged his head. "We don't have enough money."

"Got twice as much as we had. We won't have to pay for food for Gabe and Manny. You and me can escape easy enough."

Shack was thinking about that. Jed could tell when Shack

was thinking: His forehead got all wrinkled. "Guess there ain't no other way."

"I can't think of any." Jed looked at the doctor, looked her right in the eye. "Ma'am, I truly don't want to see you get hurt. I mean that. You're taking good care of Manny, fine care of him, and that means a lot to me. So if you cooperate, I'll let you go soon's we're clear."

She studied him a moment and nodded. "This is probably foolish, but I believe you."

And then he said something he almost never said to a woman. "You can trust me."

Manny didn't look like he was hearing anything, but Jed put a hand on his arm anyway. "Manny, this here's Jed. Listen to me. You do what the doctor says and get that leg healed up, hear? Shack and I are leaving now." Jed got a sudden sick feeling in his stomach. He was abandoning his baby brother. But maybe Manny would have a better life without them. Or land in jail. Who could say?

He reached out and grabbed the doctor's arm. "Here we go." He led her forcibly to the door and opened it. Shack looked scared stiff. What if he panicked?

Jed took the gun out of Shack's hand and held it steady, pointed in a general sort of way toward the doctor. Now if Shack did something stupid, at least he wouldn't be firing rounds, emptying their only gun.

And then the doctor called out, "Daniel? Let us through. They're promising to turn me loose somewhere by Hoaglunds', and I believe they will. Let us through, please!"

Shack peeked out. "Hit's working! I think it's working!" He stepped out into the hall.

Jed followed. Keeping the doctor between them, they walked

to the end of the hall as the men there backed up. *Just keep walking, Jed. Keep calm, keep walking.*

Then they were pushing out the doors, and there were their horses, right where they left them. The men had fallen back. Cowards or smart? Didn't matter. And away out there was an old lady with a braid wound around her head, just standing there, her head bowed, her hands clasped. Granny McCrary did that when she was praying for Jed and his brothers. When she died, the praying stopped. This woman was probably praying for the doctor here, or the men. Everybody surely knew everybody else in this town.

And oh, how Jed wished she was praying for him!

Take Gabe and Manny's horses or not? Jed didn't care much whether Gabe had his horse. He was probably in jail by now, but Jed hated taking Manny's horse. He left them both tied there.

He untied his gelding and handed the reins to Shack. "Hold his head so's the doctor don't kick him." Jed plopped her up behind the saddle with both her legs off this side. He mounted, swinging his right leg over the horn and neck. He gathered up his reins, and Shack leaped aboard his mare. When they took off, the doctor wrapped her arms around his waist, hanging on for dear life.

Shack twisted to look behind. "They ain't following, Jed! We done it! I never woulda thought, but we done it! You're brilliant."

Near the riverbank, Jed drew to a stop. He reached back and wrapped an arm around her waist so she wouldn't fall. "There you go, ma'am."

She slid to the ground. He expected her to run like blue blazes. Instead she turned to him, and her blue eyes met his. "Thank you." And then she did run like blue blazes, back toward town.

Jed kicked and his horse bolted forward. He led the way to the riverbank and down into the water. They splashed along near the west shore, staying off the soft mud that would leave tracks, staying out where the flowing water would erase any marks they made. When Jed's horse started stumbling—he was so tired—they slowed to a walk.

Shack pointed. "I think our place is about out that way, near them trees. We're going past it."

"That's right. Don't want to lead them right up to it. Besides, this land is so flat they can see us two days away. That's why we're staying down here among the trees in the river bottom. Till we're beyond sight."

Shack nodded. "That's good. Yeah."

They kept going for another hour. When the river did a bend, they stopped and let the horses rest and drink.

Shack was grinning, something he rarely did. "That was so smooth! I didn't think you oughta let our hostage get away, but that was sure the thing to do."

"Yep. By the time they find out our place from Gabe or Manny, we'll be long gone. Gabe might let it slip. Doubt Manny will."

Tonight was an old moon, waning gibbous, so they waited until it was up before leaving the river bottom and returning to their lair.

In the corral, which was very well built, Jed loosened his cinch, but he didn't unsaddle. They might have to leave in a hurry. He forked hay to the horses.

They went inside and Jed laid his gun on the table. "I'll take first watch if you want."

"Suits me." Shack headed for the corner cot.

Jed wandered out to the front porch and settled himself to leaning against a porch post.

This place must have been abandoned a while, but the porch post was still solid, didn't creak. The porch back home had fallen down twice since Jed was a kid; for sure you couldn't lean your full weight against those posts like you could this. It wasn't near as sturdy and well made as this place.

And flat. Je-himiny this country was flat! Except for a couple low hills away out on the horizon to the west, you could see forever . . . well, at least half of forever. If riders approached, he'd see their dust rising five miles away, even in moonlight. So in its own way, this old farm was as safe a place to hole up in as any cabin in the Kentucky hills.

He thought about that doctor. He couldn't quit thinking about her. She wore a wedding ring, so she was married. Probably to whoever that Daniel was that she called to. She was noble—that was the only word for it. She'd said, *"I believe you"* like she meant it. And she was caring, truly caring. What did they call her? One of the men said, "Don't hurt Aster." Something like that. He knew girls named Daisy and Violet and even a Petunia, so why not Aster?

You didn't see many stars in Kentucky. With trees and hills all around, you mostly only could look straight up. But out here in this Dakota country, the stars were half the world, horizon to horizon. Amazing stars. He knew some of the constellations—he knew the Big Dipper. It was higher overhead here than it was in Kentucky, but you could still make it out and that way find the North Pole Star that it pointed to. But he couldn't pick out many of the other constellations he remembered from Kentucky, because there were so many stars up there, and they were all so bright that they obscured the patterns. Even with the moon washing out the faint ones, there were too many. Too many stars. Think of that.

He still got a knot in his stomach thinking about running off from Manny. But what else could they've done?

Manny was a fine kid, a good worker. Once he got out of jail for bank robbery, he'd probably make a pretty good life for himself. Maybe he'd find a girl like that doctor, a really good, true girl. Jed had never found one. Besides, if she was a good girl, she wasn't gonna let herself be courted by no bank robber, that's for sure. Jed probably messed up his own chances forever by taking up his pappy's line of work. Too late now to walk a different road.

Or was it? He thought about that a long while. Maybe they should split up. Let Shack go back to Kentucky, since he wanted to. Jed could go someplace where nobody knew him. Maybe Texas. Get a job on a farm or a ranch. He was a good hand with horses. Start building a decent life and looking for a decent woman. Forget this bank robbery business that only brings trouble.

Granny McCrary prayed for the boys for a long time. Maybe her prayers would finally come to something. Like that woman's prayers in town.

By the time the dipper had swung around and it was time to wake up Shack to keep watch, Jed was pretty happy with his new plan of action. He would become a worthwhile man.

The next morning he woke up around sunrise, did his stuff out back in the outhouse, and left the back door of the house open when he came in, so as to let the air move through. This house did tend to get stuffy. He started searching through the cupboards. They couldn't risk a fire, so they couldn't cook. And there wasn't anything left in these cupboards that didn't need cooking.

"I already looked." Shack came in and plopped into a chair. He left the front door open too. "Not even any coffee."

"If we're ever gonna eat again, I guess we might's well hit the road." Jed plopped down across from him. "Say, I been thinking. We might do better if we split up. Then we wouldn't look suspicious or anything."

Shack nodded. "Interesting. I was thinking the same. They're looking for a gang, not just one feller. Split apart, then meet up at home at Pappy's."

"Wonder who lives there now. Everybody we know is passed, 'cept Pearly."

"And she woulda got married by now. Maybe she lives there."

"Good morning, gentlemen."

Jed snapped to his feet so fast, his chair fell on its back and scooted on the floor.

The fellow who wished them good morning was standing in the back doorway, casually leaning against the jamb. The shotgun he held at ready sure got Jed's attention in a hurry. It was a twelve-gauge side-by-side, and the barrels couldn't be any more than fourteen or fifteen inches long. Load that baby with nails, and you could clear a room by firing just once.

"My name's Trygve. I'd suppose you two are the McCrary gentlemen."

Their gun! Where was their gun? Not on the table here.

Shack was already standing there, his arms held high and waving around. He looked terrified.

Jed wasn't feeling so calm himself. He heard boots on the front porch, and the room darkened a bit. Someone was in the front doorway behind him. "Trig Vee. Who lets themselves be named Trig Vee?"

This fellow looked a lot like that doctor, when you think about it—same eyes, about the same color hair. Mostly though, it was the air of confidence, a total lack of fear. Yes, chances were pretty good he was related to her some way.

The man shrugged. "I like it."

Jed turned to look toward the front door. A jovial, somewhat overweight fellow came in, a broad smile on his pudgy face, and waving a pistol. Jed's pistol! "They left it on the porch rail. Figured I'd bring it in for them."

"Nice of you. It looks pretty heavy to me. Maybe you should just carry it for them as a friendly gesture."

"Good idea." The jolly fellow stuffed Jed's gun into his belt and stepped aside. Two others entered, with handcuffs. And badges. That was something of a relief, actually. A vigilante posse would as soon hang you as look at you. At least official law officers just stick you in a jail.

"How'd you find us? It wasn't Manny, and Gabe was in no condition to chat." Jed's arms got yanked behind him, and a fellow clicked genuine steel handcuffs on him. The only other time someone had arrested him, they'd had to use whipcord.

And now Shack was under lock and key as well.

This Trig Vee was smiling, acting totally at home, as if he arrested bank robbers every day. He had a light touch with that shotgun. Authoritative too. "Just a simple native guide—a lady who knows every inch of this region. She even showed us how to move in from the back without raising dust. And she's been praying for the lot of us this whole time."

Jed's chest did a little tickle. "With a braid? An old lady with a braid?"

Trig Vee looked at him curiously. "Yes."

"Prayed for *all* of us?"

"All of us. Including you two."

And Jed's heart made a happy little leap. So a total stranger had taken up where Granny McCrary had left off shepherding her boys.

There was hope for him yet! "Tell her thank you for me."

Chapter 11

Dr. Bjorklund, please come!" Annika called as soon as she reached the doorway of Astrid's office. "He's starting to wake up, but something is wrong and I cannot tell what."

They hastened down the hall together and entered Manny's room.

"Manny, can you hear me?" Astrid checked his pulse, watching his face. "Time to wake up."

The boy whimpered and shook his head, but his lashes fluttered. Fear pulsed from him in waves, and his entire body went rigid.

"Easy now. You have nothing to be afraid of. Your brothers are in jail and will be transported back to Kentucky, where they will be confined to prison for a long time."

"They'll find me." Confusion battled with fear.

"No they won't. Now, you need to get better. We had to operate again, so that is why you've been sleeping so long."

"Thirsty."

"I'm sure you are." She nodded to Nurse Annika, who was standing on the other side of the bed. Together they raised his head so he could swallow more easily. He drank half a glass of water before pulling away. "Hurts." Now he sounded like the boy he was—sad, alone, and forlorn.

"I know. We'll take care of that again, but you need to drink more. And we need to help you move some. Your leg is back in traction, but we can help you sit up." At his nod, she and the nurse packed some pillows behind him so he was sitting up. "Okay?"

He nodded but was panting from the effort.

"Ask cook for some of that soup she made." Astrid turned back to their patient. "Do you have any questions?"

He half shrugged.

"As soon as you eat some soup, I'll give you another injection." She'd planned on a bath for him but decided to wait until he was out again, to mitigate the pain. "You are doing better, Manny. Your temperature is down, so the infection is lessening, and that's the best news we can have right now." And no sign of gangrene.

"W-why are you . . . doin' this?"

"What? You mean why are we taking care of you?"

He nodded.

"Because you are wounded and need care. Do you have any family that . . ."

When he shook his head, she dropped that subject. She knew the men were from Kentucky, but if this boy didn't want to contact any other family members, so be it. Besides, if the rest were like those brothers of his, he was better off without any of them.

Annika set the bowl on the table and positioned the tray with its legs across his body. "Can you feed yourself?" He nodded, but when the spoon didn't make it to his mouth, she took over.

After a few bites, Astrid gave him the pain-killer, he ate a few more bites, and then they helped him lie back down. He was out again before they turned around.

"Do you think there is hope?" Annika asked.

"There is always hope, and right now this case is looking up. Please take supper to the other patients, and I'll check back on him. Then we will give him a real bath, not just hit and miss."

"Can I use a brush?"

The two shared a grin and a giggle.

They continued to fight the pain and fevers for the next two days, but praise God, both seemed to be lessening.

On Tuesday evening Astrid and Elizabeth met back at the hospital.

"I feel like we live here," Astrid said with a smile.

"Well, we pretty much do. But just think, neither one of us spent the night here last night."

"True. I talked with Mor and she is still planning on Manny moving in with them when he's able. If all continues like right now, we may be able to move him in early July."

"He won't be able to withdraw there like he does here."

Manny did not answer questions about his brothers or parents or anything other than a yes and no to direct questions regarding his needs right then. He had slipped and said thank-you a few times, so they took that as an indication that he'd been taught some manners at some time. He was indeed one tough boy.

"Maybe a visitor would help." Elizabeth chewed her bottom lip.

"I offered to bring him books, but he said he doesn't know how to read."

"Oh, how sad. What kind of family did he come from? That does it. We need to find someone to come and read to him. Maybe he knows how to play cards or dominoes or something."

"Mrs. Jeffers could teach him to read. We can ask kids his own age to help, possibly Linnea or Mark Solberg. You know, when you think about it, we don't have a lot of youngsters in that age range. The older boys are all working, and Linnea helps Penny at the store. Sorry, I'm just thinking out loud." She smiled at Elizabeth. "Of course we could sic Inga on him. She'd have him talking in no time."

"Or talk his ears off." The two shared a chuckle.

Nurse Annika stopped beside them. "We are almost out of ice."

"I'll have Thorliff bring some in tomorrow. I know it's helping a lot. What did we ever do before we used ice?"

"We used wet cloths—and kept changing and changing them. Down on the Indian reservation we put those with fevers right into the creek. That worked too."

Elizabeth shook her head. "You are one creative woman, you know. It's a shame we don't have a creek here. The Red River is too muddy to use like that."

"He'll never know what hit him." Astrid covered a yawn. "Let's go home."

She turned when she heard the outside door opening and broke into a smile when Daniel came striding toward her. "How nice."

"I brought you some mail I forgot to pick up yesterday." He greeted Annika and Elizabeth before handing Astrid a letter. "From Chicago."

"Let's sit over there." She motioned to several chairs lined up at the wall. He handed her his pocket knife to slice it open. "Thank you." Why was it her heart would pick up the pace just because he walked into the room? Unfolding the letter, she sank down on the chair and felt his knee rub against hers when he sat. She scanned the short letter and then read it aloud.

"My dear Doctors Bjorklund,

"How good it was to receive your request. I wasn't sure if you would be ready this soon or not. I have three young

women who have agreed to spend a year in Blessing for further training. I know this is a hard thing, especially for one, since her family is dependent upon her meager pay for the extra jobs she does around here. We are working on making it easier for her to be gone. Miriam Hastings is at the head of the class, and I know she will benefit greatly, as will you. The other two are Vera Wells and Corabell Nester, also fine students.

"If this meets with your approval, we will put them on the train here the last part of July. Hopefully that will give you time to prepare. If you have any questions, please give me a call. I am excited about this new training we can provide for our nurses. Perhaps soon we can set up an intern program there for our doctors in training also.

"May our Lord bless all of our efforts.

"Sincerely,

Mrs. Catherine Klein
Administrator, Alfred
Morganstein Hospital for
Women"

"That soon?" Elizabeth's voice squeaked on the words. "Where will we put them? For housing, I mean. I had no idea this would happen so soon."

"Before August." Astrid sighed. "Too soon. Too soon."

Chapter 12

"Grandma, we are here," Inga shouted as she came around the house, riding on her pa's shoulders.

Ingeborg rose to her feet. "Then I had better get the cookies out. Gracious, Thorliff, did you carry her all the way out here?"

He slid his daughter to the ground so she could charge up the steps and throw her good arm around her grandma. She beamed. "Ma said Grace and Jonathan are getting married very soon, and I get to come to the wedding."

Thorliff added, "Only if you can be quiet for the service."

Inga frowned at her father. "It's a wedding, not a service."

Thorliff rolled his eyes and sank into the rocker across from Ingeborg. "Maybe you should go find the cookie jar."

"Okay, Grandma?"

"Ja. It is on the counter, so you can reach it easily."

"On a plate for everyone?" Inga ran to the doorway and paused.

"Ja."

She disappeared inside.

Thorliff asked, "How is Pa doing?"

"He's sleeping again right now. It doesn't take much to wear him out. Astrid and I have been working his legs and arms to help him get his strength back. The miracle is there seems to be little damage, other than the weakness, but lying in bed like that makes anyone weak, let alone whatever happened. I'm just so grateful."

"We all are."

From the kitchen Inga called, "Coffee too?"

Thorliff sighed and heaved himself back up on his feet. "You sit there. We will take care of this."

"But . . ." When Ingeborg started to rise, Thorliff motioned her back and followed his daughter into the kitchen.

Inga waited for her pa to hold open the door so she could carry the cookie plate out. "This thing sure slows me down."

Ingeborg fought the laughter that bubbled so close to the surface.

"Grandma, can Carl come visit today?"

"Maybe another time."

"But Grandpa needs to see him too." She held out the plate of cookies just the way her mother had instructed her in her efforts to teach her daughter manners. Sometimes it even worked, like now.

Ingeborg watched her, smiling. So Grace was finally marrying. Her mother-in-law to be had succeeded in getting Jonathan and Grace to postpone the wedding a bit, no doubt hoping it wouldn't occur at all. Uff da! This spring and summer were indeed taking different turns than others had. Nothing ever remained the same. That was for sure.

Suddenly the day came when Grace and Kaaren left on the train to go to Jonathan's graduation ceremony. While Ingeborg would love to have gone, she knew there was no leaving home right now. She could not yet leave Haakan for so long. But he was gaining strength daily and had graduated to a cane, so he could move about by himself. Stairs seemed to be a bit daunting yet, but he spent hours on either of the porches, sometimes visiting with those who came to call, other times content to watch the land grow its crops.

"Do you think I'll be able to attend the wedding?" he asked on Thursday evening when the sun was already heading downward.

Ingeborg took his hand. "Squeeze." He did so, then changed hands and let her test the other one. "You are getting stronger, that's for sure, but you have to be able to handle the stairs, both here and at the church."

"You would go without me, right?"

"I don't want to, but Freda will be here in case you need anything."

"Good." He gazed off at nothing for a while. "Grace will be a lovely bride, and Jonathan already seems like a member of the family. They have big plans for the deaf school."

"I know, yet what he dreams about is farming, just as he has every summer. Between you and Lars on the farming and Thorliff's crew on construction, he has received a well-rounded education."

"He doesn't care much for repairing machinery, but he is willing to learn." Haakan sighed. "There is so much more to learn now than when we started out. All that machinery is supposed to make a man's life easier. Instead, we farm more land or different crops, and the pace seems to pick up all the time." He cupped both hands over the handle of his carved maple cane and rested his chin on his hands. "I never tire of looking out over the land. It changes moment by moment."

"God is so good to us."

"That He is. I thought perhaps I was going to go on to heaven this time, but He let me stay here." He laid one hand over hers. "But when He calls me, I am ready to go. John and I talked about heaven the other day when he was here. Beautiful as this is, heaven is even more so." He nodded slowly, pensively. "I do hope there is farming there, for that is what I love the best. Other than you and our families."

The birds twittered overhead, parents bringing meals to their hungry brood.

Love brimmed over and ran down her cheeks. "I hope your time is a long time away." She sniffed. "I'm not ready to say good-bye yet."

He turned to smile at her over his shoulder. "But, my dearest Ingeborg, it is not good-bye, but rather, 'I'll see you soon.'"

"Ja, I believe that, but I'm selfish. I want you here where I can touch you and feed you and laugh with you and enjoy moments such as this."

"Ja. That is how I feel too."

For a man of few words, he had just poured the gift of his thoughts into the reservoir of her heart, for her to take out and remember when she needed them.

The morning of the wedding, Ingeborg cut all the roses she could find, along with the daisies and the lily of the valley growing in the shade. The flowers would add a beautiful touch to make this celebration perfect. She stuck them all in buckets of water and sent them on to the church with Kaaren when she stopped by.

"Don't you worry, we have plenty of help, and it looks like a beautiful day, a perfect day for a wedding—neither too hot nor raining."

Ingeborg looked heavenward. "Thank you, Lord."

"Will Haakan be able to come?"

"He is planning on it, determined man that he is."

Kaaren frowned. "Will you need help?"

"Most likely. We'll go early. Thorliff, Andrew, and Daniel are coming. They said they'd carry him out in a chair, if need be." She gave Kaaren a hug. "Don't let the thought of Mrs. Gould give you any concern. We are not New York and have no plans to be so. If she can't appreciate the life her son has chosen here, she is the one who will be the loser. How's Grace?"

"Remarkably composed, ever since she came over and talked with you. Did I tell you that she asked me to sign the service for our deaf friends who are visiting?"

"That will indeed be beautiful."

Through all the preparations and plans, the wedding had hovered out there somewhere, an event far in the future. Then it was here. Right now. This minute.

Their young men helped Haakan down the steps and into the buggy and out again at the church. They seated their father in the second row from the back, as he'd asked.

"Tusen takk," he whispered and gripped their hands.

Ingeborg settled down beside him but on the aisle so she could see better. And enjoy the fragrances! They floated from the flowers at the windows, at the altar, on the steps up to the altar, and anywhere else a bouquet could sit. *It's a wonder that there are any blossoms left in any garden in town with all the flowers I cut,* she thought with a smile.

So many people stopped on their way to their seats to greet Haakan that he glanced at Ingeborg and shook his head. He leaned close and whispered. "I've not been gone that long."

"You were missed."

He nodded and rested his hands on his cane as the organ came to life when Elizabeth's fingers caressed the keys. Music, flowers, peace—a wonderful way to bless the ceremony. Inga sat next to Haakan, with Thorliff beside her.

The men gathered at the front. Jonathan had asked Trygve to stand up with him, and Sophie almost danced down the aisle to stand up for her twin sister. When the organ moved from Handel into Mendelssohn, everyone stood and turned to see Grace. She and Lars paused in the doorway. Instead of walking, she floated down the aisle, her gaze never leaving that of the man she had loved for so long.

Inga had come to stand right at the edge of the pew and, turning to smile at her grandma, sighed. "They are so beautiful." She sniffed the roses on the end of the pew and snuggled in between the arm of the pew and her grandma.

"Dearly beloved, we are gathered here in the sight of God and this company. . . ." John Solberg's voice carried both authority and blessing as he recited the wedding ceremony.

Kaaren stood off to the side, signing as he spoke, and Elizabeth played the organ so softly that they almost didn't notice it was there. Jonathan and Grace both repeated their vows in firm voices, their eyes pledging more than words ever could.

After the final prayer and blessing, John Solberg lifted his arms. "I now pronounce you man and wife, Mr. and Mrs. Jonathan Gould. You may kiss your bride." After the kiss he turned to the congregation. "The cake and a few other refreshments will be served in the basement, although as lovely as it is today, we could all go outside."

Grace beamed as though the sun had taken up residence behind her eyes. She put her arm through Jonathan's, and together they greeted their guests as they made their way back down the aisle.

Haakan and Ingeborg visited with the guests while they waited for the folks to go ahead of them down the stairs.

"Are you sure you can manage those stairs?" Thorliff asked.

"Perhaps it would be better if we set you up under the cottonwood tree and brought the cake to you."

"That's a good idea." Haakan nodded to his son. "Takk."

Good idea, indeed. It wasn't long before everyone brought their food outside, and the bride and groom came out as well to visit with them.

Ingeborg smiled when Mr. and Mrs. Gould came walking toward them. Mr. Gould looked older, for sure, but more dignified than ever. Age certainly became him.

She held out her hand. "So good to see you again, Mr. Gould. We are glad you could come."

"Mrs. Bjorklund, I want you to meet my wife, Geraldine."

Mrs. Gould nodded, her parasol shading her face. "How do you do. My husband has always spoken highly of you." So this was Jonathan's mother. She was unlike her son in every way. He was robust, she thin and angular yet without looking frail. And sour. And grumpy looking, something Jonathan never was. With a smile that never quite made it to her eyes.

"And Mr. Bjorklund, I am so glad to see you up and about." Gould shook Haakan's hand. But when Haakan made to rise to meet his wife, Gould put his hand out. "Please, we need not stand on formality. My wife and I are happy to be able to celebrate this time with you."

Ingeborg smiled and nodded. Happy? Certainly not Mrs. Gould. Ingeborg wished Mrs. Gould could just relax and enjoy herself, engage in the happiness of this day. "I do hope you'll be able to remain in Blessing a few days at least and—"

"I'm afraid we cannot," both Goulds said simultaneously.

Mr. Gould added, "We have commitments in both Minneapolis and Chicago, so we must leave on the eastbound train tomorrow morning." He glanced around. "Is there by any chance a chair for my wife?"

By Ingeborg's elbow, Thorliff said, "I will bring one right out." He returned in a moment and set a chair, a padded one from the church narthex, in the shade of the tree. "Sir, would you like one too?"

"No, thank you." He seated his wife and whispered something in her ear. She nodded tersely.

"Let me bring you some refreshments." Thorliff hurried off.

What to say? Could Ingeborg dispel the dissatisfaction in the woman's face? Probably not. "You must be very proud of your son, graduating with honors like that."

"Yes. He lived up to his word, to the agreement he made with his father to do well in his studies." She didn't sound particularly pleased.

"Jonathan always lives up to his word. It has been our great pleasure to have him with us in the summers. I'm sure that was hard for you." Ingeborg glanced up to catch something in Mr. Gould's eyes. Gratitude perhaps? Relief?

Haakan cleared his throat. "I think I should go home," he whispered.

She took one look at the exhaustion in his face and nodded. When Thorliff finished serving their guests, she touched his arm and tilted her head toward Haakan.

"I'll bring the buggy around right now," he said.

With as little fuss as possible, within minutes they were on their way back home.

At the door, Thorliff and Ingeborg helped Haakan to the ground and up the steps.

Ingeborg smiled. "You did exceedingly well."

"You could go back with Thorliff, you know."

"I know." If there were any way she could put Geraldine Gould at ease, she would go back. And how she would love to have a real visit with Mr. Gould, to show him the hospital, the deaf school, and the other industries in town. He'd helped them from the very beginning, the latest being finding them immigrant workers. She wasn't sure how many investments he'd made through the years, but Thorliff would know.

Thorliff squeezed her arm. "Call the church if you want me to come back for you. I will, gladly."

"Takk."

He climbed into the buggy, picked up the lines, and drove away.

No, Ingeborg could not help the dissatisfied Mrs. Gould. And with a start, she realized why: That was not dissatisfaction on Mrs. Gould's face, it was an aloofness akin to contempt. Mrs. Gould did not want to mingle with these peasants, these simple farmers, and she was deeply disappointed that her dear son had just married one.

So sad.

What troubled Ingeborg most: What did this woman's haughtiness portend for Grace's marriage?

Chapter 13

I am thinking of staying in Blessing." Trygve watched his mor and far for a response. They had given him their blessing to work for Hjelmer and not stay on the farm, but something inside him said it was time to stay here.

"Tired of living in a wagon?" Samuel, his younger brother, looked up from buttering a slice of bread. With the family gathered around the supper table, some of the conversation was by signing, especially since Ilse's husband, George, was deaf, and while he could read lips, he'd not learned to speak verbally. Ilse was his mother's assistant at the deaf school.

"Something like that."

"What brought about this decision?" Kaaren set the bowl of chicken stew back in the center of the table.

"I'm not sure," Trygve answered. "Just something in me says this is what I need to do. I understand that Onkel Hjelmer is counting on me, but Gus could handle a crew and Gilbert could too, if needed. They are both very competent."

"At drilling and building, but how are they in dealing with the folks who order the windmills?" Lars sipped his water. "And you know you are always welcome here, at least during the summer."

Trygve knew that when the deaf school reopened in September, every room in the house and school was put to use. "Takk. Grace and Jonathan said I could have a room in their house as soon as they move in." They wouldn't return from their trip to New York and further wedding celebrations for another week.

"Right now they are waiting on materials for the interior. They brought in several carpenters who excel in finish work. They ordered all the cabinetry from a company in Minneapolis, and Hans and his men are doing a fine job. It just takes so much time." Lars shook his head.

"They were so hoping they could move in as soon as they returned," Kaaren said, finishing her husband's train of thought.

Trygve saw the look they shared. It reminded him of the way Grace and Jonathan looked at each other sometimes. Grace had always been a lovely woman, but since her engagement, she had grown even more beautiful. Strange to be thinking that about his sister, but Grace was more blond, like their mother, and Sophie was darker haired, like their far. The two girls were twins, but no two were more opposite than they.

Would that love look be possible for him someday too? "Perhaps I should start building a house this summer."

"Put your name on the list. It is long." Lars returned to eating. "I thought you were pleased with your job."

"I am—er was, but maybe I'm like Sophie. I got out of Blessing for a time and now home looks more . . . more necessary."

"Sophie traveled a whole lot farther than you did." Samuel reached for the stew bowl, caught his mother's look, and said, "George, would you please pass the chicken?" He signed it at the same time.

Ilse smiled at him, the glint in her eye saying she'd caught his change of mind and passed the bowl.

Having a meal at home was a far cry from eating supper around the campfire with Gus and Gilbert.

"What will you do for work?" Lars asked.

"With Onkel Haakan still recovering, I figured perhaps you needed more help here."

"We will during haying and harvest, as always."

"You probably forgot how to milk cows." Samuel grinned at his brother. Ilse, sitting beside him, gave him an elbow to the ribs.

"One never forgets how to milk a cow." Trygve looked toward his mor, who was nodding.

"Not that your forever or never is very long at this point." Kaaren smiled, an act that lit her face as if a candle flamed within. Could one miss his mother's smile to the point of desiring to return home and perhaps stay home?

Trygve laid his fork down. "I know there is plenty of work here in Blessing. I also know that I am needed for haying. Now, will someone explain to me what happened with Onkel Haakan?"

"He collapsed on the seeder one day and was unconscious for almost a week, but he finally woke up and is slowly regaining his strength. Other than weakness, we are not seeing other side effects, for which we are so thankful. We pray that soon Ingeborg will be trying to keep him from doing too much."

Lars nodded. "He sees the work that needs to be done and expects that he can get back to doing that. Only God knows if that is possible, so having you here might ease his worry. I think you should go talk with him. If nothing else, he probably needs the company."

The next morning, Trygve joined the others at the barn, where the cows were all lined up in the stanchions, waiting patiently to get milked. Tails swished, as heads down, they devoured the grain poured before them.

"You start over there." Lars pointed to a black-and-white cow with a fully distended udder.

"She's new?"

"We bought her last year. She just calved two weeks ago, threw a nice little heifer." Lars unhooked one of the three-legged stools from the post and sat down at an older cow that Trygve recognized. Since all the stanchions were occupied, he knew they were milking twenty-four head.

After wiping the designated cow's udder, he sat down on his stool and placed the bucket between his knees. The familiar odor of warm cow, warm milk, hay, and grain overlaid with fresh manure felt comforting after his time away. With the milk pinging into the bucket, he let his mind wander. Many of life's questions and problems he had worked out with his forehead firmly braced on a cow's flank. With the bucket three-fourths full, he thought of stopping to dump it in the waiting cream can but, instead, decided she must be close to dry.

"Hey, Trygve!" Andrew called.

"Ja?" He turned his head and leaned back to see what his cousin wanted. For some unknown reason, like a lightning strike, the cow planted her right rear foot right in the middle of the bucket, tipping frothy white milk all over Trygve, the floor, and probably part of Blessing. He bit back an expletive as he leaped to his feet, the urge to yell at the cow pounding in his brain while the hoots of the other milkers heated his face.

"Sorry. I forgot to warn you about her. She gets a bit spooky at times."

Two of the barn cats darted over to lap up the milk, both keeping a wary eye on the sputtering man.

"Is she dry yet?" Lars tried to hide his laughter, but Trygve saw through him.

"No." He grabbed another pail, sat back down, and finished the job, only getting one swipe from the restless cow's tail.

"I usually dump the bucket when half done with her," Andrew said as he strolled past on his way to the cream can, where a strainer perched, awaiting the next pour.

"Be a while before you live that one down," Samuel said later as they were walking back home for breakfast.

"Rub it in."

"You jump real quick."

"So she has done that before?"

"Not with a full bucket, but yes."

"Wouldn't kickers be a good idea?"

"We thought she got over it."

Later that day Trygve walked over to the Bjorklund house, whistling as he went. Middle of June and there surely was no more beautiful place on earth than the burgeoning green of the Red River Valley. He could hear the hammering and other construction sounds coming from town, blackbirds singing from the riverbank, and a crow decrying the intrusion of a human in his territory. Nothing smelled better either, not that he'd been that many places, but today he was glad to be home.

Ingeborg held out her arms when she saw her nephew coming from the porch and wrapped him close. "Sit down, sit down. Haakan will be out shortly."

Trygve took the chair she pointed to and studied the lay of the land. Cows and horses out to pasture, the garden growing so fast you could measure it on a stick, and birds gossiping in the cottonwood that shaded the porch. "Takk." He took the coffee cup she handed him, and dropped his voice. "How is Haakan really doing?"

Ingeborg sat across from him. "Better. He is hoping to help with the haying."

"I remember when he had that first attack."

"Ja. He just never seemed to quite get all his strength back, no matter how hard he tried. Now this one's worse."

The screen door squealed. "Well, gud dag, Trygve. Nice to have you visit this morning." Haakan joined Ingeborg on the settee. "I hear you had an accident down at the barn." His Bjorklund blue eyes twinkled even in the shade.

"Not an accident, far as I figure. That old cow did it deliberately."

"Well, don't feel too bad. She got me once too. You just got to watch her."

Ingeborg added, "But she gives as much milk as two of the others, only the cream content is not as good. And we need cream for the cheese."

Trygve tried to study his onkel without appearing to do so. He had aged this year, no doubt of that. His lined face badly needed the sun. His hands were shaking, and even his speech had slowed down. Were his own mor and far growing old like this, or was it from Haakan's being sickly? Perhaps his staying home was indeed what he needed to do. For the sake of the others.

Chapter 14

"All right, ladies, let's get to work on what we came for." After repeating her suggestion twice, Astrid gave up. One had to admit the capture of the robbers was probably the biggest news to hit Blessing, besides perhaps the floods and fires of years gone by. And by such a fluke. This would indeed go down in history. And her own mor playing such an important role in it all! Of course Ingeborg attributed all to the Lord, which was by far the wisest of the many comments. Still, after nearly three weeks, the matter should have been laid to rest. Besides, according to Sheriff Meeker, the three thieves were now griping and complaining on their way to Kentucky, for that was where they had begun their robbery careers.

"Can you believe that the sheriff really told the little brother he was not responsible for the robbery since he only held the horses and was forced to do that?" Hildegunn fairly shook with her intensity. "And my hus—er Mr. Valders agreed with him. Why, that boy has never said a word about his brothers. He refused to give them up to the law. And yet he won't be hauled into court, not even as a witness." Her jaw dropped and she shook her head again. "I never. I just—"

"His name is Manny, and he was very brave. He's only twelve years old, you know. And so sick now. His brothers caused this, and I am glad they will get to learn what life in prison is like." Astrid fought to keep her voice even. A shouting match with Hildegunn was not on her list for the day. Or ever. How that woman had slept through the robbery was beyond imagination. "And besides, they rode off without him." She couldn't resist that last bit of reminder.

"I am so grateful no one else was injured." Penny caught Astrid's gaze. "Things could have been so much worse. Does the boy Manny have any relatives to go to?"

"I have no idea. Right now I just want him to get well. In fact, I need to get back to the hospital, so can we continue with our business to finish planning for the Fourth of July festivities?" She looked around to see heads nodding.

Planning the celebration always took far longer than the event itself did. They had already met twice, and she hoped this meeting would be the final one. After all, they had only a week to go. "Penny, you said you had a report on the governor's coming?"

"I do." She shook her head. "Men!" She stood so she could see all their faces. "Our new governor, Mr. Johnson, had accepted our invitation to speak, but yesterday I received a telephone call saying that he had been unexpectedly called out of town and will not return in time to come to Blessing. He sent his apologies."

"So we don't have a big-name speaker. I don't care much for some of his policies anyway." Hildegunn Valders wore a frown fit to frighten small children. Or recalcitrant politicians. "I was planning on mentioning a few things to him."

"Like providing better law enforcement for small towns?" Elizabeth, who had hurried her rounds at the hospital to join the meeting, quirked her right eyebrow. That robbery had indeed changed the tenor of the town. In spite of horror stories from other towns, somehow they had always felt safe, as if there were a barrier around Blessing to shield them from the realities of the times. While Thorliff's newspaper included highlights—or lowlights, in this case—from around the area, still they had acted as if nothing could touch Blessing. Until too late.

"I've been thinking . . ." Kaaren laid her knitting on her lap, looking at those around her. "What if we did an honoring and thanking program? Maybe it is too late to put a really good one together, but Anner Valders showed real heroism, as did Annika Nilsson, and I think they should be given a public thank-you." She smiled at Hildegunn. "If we do this, I'd like it to be a surprise. Can you keep a secret, Hildegunn?"

"Uh . . ." For Hildegunn to be caught speechless was an event in itself.

Soft chuckles swept the group. Everyone had known for years that "I will ask Mr. Valders about that" was Hildegunn's response to anything that came up.

Astrid reminded herself that putting Hildegunn on the spot was not conducive to building community goodwill. "How about if we decide on this without telling you the particulars? If that would be easier." Astrid caught her mother's nod and smile of approval.

"Thank you." Hildegunn's look of relief made Penny reach over and pat her hand. "Sometimes not knowing is far easier than knowing too much."

When Hildegunn turned her hand over and clasped Penny's, Astrid and Ingeborg shared a look knit of joy and surprise. Someone else cleared her throat, and a sniff or two joined in.

"So, on to the rest of our business. The food is all in order?" Astrid glanced at Sophie, who nodded.

"We are going to roast half a steer over a slow fire like the folks in Texas do. It takes all day, so the men will be putting it on a spit before daylight out beside the ball field, where they will first dig a trench. Mr. Sam followed the diagram my friend from Texas sent me, along with all the instructions. They call it a bar-bee-cue. She said it was really, really good."

"If it's like fishing, you better have another plan, just in case."

"What if it rains?"

"Well, a heavy downpour would cause a problem." Sophie wrinkled her nose. "I'm sure we'll have plenty of food beside the steer in that case. Of course, we'd have to move into the school for the speeches and such. And"— she raised her hands in the air dramatically—"no ball game or races."

"Please, Lord, no rain," Ingeborg said softly.

"Any other news on food?"

"I heard the boardinghouse team is planning on winning again." The year before, the contest for the best and quickest hand-cranked ice cream had gotten quite hot.

"And the baseball teams are practicing?"

"Jonathan Gould is back from his honeymoon and attempting to train his team, if he can get them together at least a couple of times. He said he played some in college, although most of his free time was devoted to the rowing team the year before he came to North Dakota."

The two teams were fairly evenly divided, so the afternoon's entertainment was looking to be exciting. Part of the fun was that so many of the new men in town had turned out for the choosing of the teams. The women planners had decided this Fourth of July celebration was going to include everyone in town and the surrounding area. Thorliff had printed posters that were up everywhere, and everyone was getting excited. A celebration like this could well transcend language barriers. The amazing thing was that even the most recent immigrants knew some form of the game.

"And the prizes for the winning teams in both contests—ice cream and baseball—are set?" Astrid looked to Penny, who had promised to come up with something memorable.

"You know the prizes are not easy with so many people involved. I would welcome any suggestions."

"They get to eat first? That would work for the baseball players. They'll be finished before we serve the food."

"Well, we won't be making ice cream until after the meal."

"That's going to be mighty late. People have to go home to chores."

"I know, but like we decided, folks will return for the dance and fireworks."

"Don't mention fireworks to Thorliff and Daniel. They are sure we'll burn the town down."

"Don't be silly. They're being shot out over the river. Trygve is all in favor of fireworks. He says the men he bought them from assured him they are perfectly safe."

Astrid looked around the room. She saw doubt on other faces too. Were they doing the right or best thing to introduce fireworks into the celebration? Other communities were sponsoring fireworks. "We can cancel that part of the program, you know."

Hildegunn clasped her hands and twisted. "I would not be averse to that. Mr. Valders is against it. He says we've had enough excitement here without a possible fire. I'd die of guilt if that happened, in spite of what those experts say. Accidents do happen, you know. The wind comes up so quick."

For a change Astrid felt swayed to agree with Hildegunn. Looking around the group made her decision. "I suggest we vote on this. Do you want paper or hands?"

"Hands are fine." Sophie sounded a bit impatient. After all, the fireworks were her idea.

"All in favor of not doing fireworks this year—keep in mind

our decision is for this year only—please raise your hand." After counting the votes, she announced, "We will cancel the fireworks for this year. I suggest we follow closely the success or problems other communities have with their fireworks displays." She checked her notes and looked around again. "Anyone have something to add? No? Then we are finished for today."

Sophie wore only a slight frown. "I sure was looking forward to seeing the sparklers over the river. Oh well, maybe—"

Inga and Grant charged into the room at that moment, Grant carrying a huge toad. "We made two toads race like that story Teacher read about a frog race."

"Come see!" He held the toad out to his mother, Sophie, and it immediately released a stream of urine down his arm. "Oh, ugh!"

Astrid saw the look on Sophie's face, and laughter bubbled up and burst, sending the others, at least those who weren't horrified, into spasms too. "You should see your face, Sophie!" Everyone was tittering like schoolgirls.

Ingeborg wiped her eyes. "Maybe next year we should have a toad jumping contest."

"Grant Wiste, take that thing outside right this minute!" Sophie pointed to the door. "And then go scrub yourself."

"But it's not so bad." Inga looked to Astrid for help but only got a laughing face in return.

"Now!"

The children turned and dragged their feet to the door.

"And let that creature go back under the bushes."

"Yes, ma'am," they droned wearily.

Helga Larson appeared in the arched doorway to the dining room. "Coffee is ready in here. I'm setting up a table outside for the children. Can I get you anything else?" Helga was Garth's older sister, who had started helping out a couple of years earlier as a favor, but she now worked for Sophie full time at the Wiste house. Ingeborg envied her speed and efficiency. Helga was already a member of the family, and from the look on her face, she had seen the whole thing.

Astrid motioned the others to make their way to the dining room. The coffee Helga had set out was most likely more of a lunch.

Tittering seemed to be contagious.

"Angie Moen is coming back to Blessing," Ingeborg announced a couple of days later, waving a letter in the air.

"Really?" Astrid looked up from writing in the log she and Elizabeth kept for the hospital. "And gud dag to you too." She blew on the ink on the page so it wouldn't smear. "I thought after her husband died that she was going to remain in Norway with Mr. Moen's family."

Ingeborg nodded. "I thought she and the children maybe would want to stay near his family. But they did spend part of the time here in Blessing too."

"When is she coming back?"

"She said before school starts." Ingeborg squinted her eyes in thought. "I'm trying to think how old Mr. Moen's daughters would be now. I imagine Melissa is close to eight now and how old are the other children? Goodness, I can't even remember their names."

"Well, I think you're right that Melissa is eight, and his two girls were already in school when they married." Astrid closed the leather-bound journal. "I'm done for the day. Let's go have a soda."

"What a marvelous idea. Inga too?"

"Why not." The two walked arm in arm down the street.

What used to be a three-block street now stretched much farther, since all the growth had to go west or south of the railroad tracks. The Red River bordered the east, and the Little Salt River the northern edge of the Bjorklund/Knutson property, which was north of town.

The ring of hammers and the hum of saws kept pace with them. Toby Valders waved from the new wing of the boardinghouse. His crew was painting the exterior at the moment. "Our team is going to win!" Toby shouted, setting his crew to cheering.

"Good luck," Astrid called back.

"Look, Grandma!" Inga shouted and waved her newly freed arm. Swinging on the gate, she shouted again. "Please come see me. I can't leave the yard."

"Uh-oh. She's in trouble again." Ingeborg grimaced.

"So much for inviting her for a soda." Astrid sent her mor a warning look. "If she is being punished, we can't ask her to come."

"I know." Ingeborg raised her voice. "We'll come by later."

"Where you going?" The gate slammed shut, and Inga ran the fence line to be closer to them but still in her prison.

"We have people to talk to," Astrid called back with a wave. "You be good."

"I am." The plaintive cry would wring any grandmother's heart, let alone her tante Astrid's. Scooter, Inga's constant and furry companion, yipped too, as if adding his plea to hers.

As they continued down the street, they waved to some of the house construction crew, and even Joshua waved back. Good. Apparently he had gotten over his desire to marry Astrid, and since then he had fallen in love with Miss Christopherson. Now she was Mrs. Landsverk and still happily managing the dining room at the boardinghouse.

"We will win!" Joshua called, his crew responding the same.

"My lands, I didn't realize everyone was so excited about the ball game."

"Look at all the signs." Astrid pointed to the buildings along the street—Blessing Mercantile, Garrisons' Groceries, the Blessing Bank, the railroad station. Even fence posts and the trunks of trees that lined Main Street sported signs.

"I heard there is a betting pool too."

"Uff da!" Ingeborg snorted. "Must they?"

Astrid let that slide. She didn't think it necessary either, but men would be men. "You know, it is a shame we didn't think to build bleachers for spectators to watch the game. Someday."

"I think a school has to come first."

Astrid chuckled. "My mor, ever practical." She stood aside as they entered so that Ingeborg might go first. "Hi, Rebecca. Do you have time to make a couple of sodas?"

"Of course. Your usual?" Soon the woman who grinned at them would not be able to get as close to the counter as usual. At their nods, she said, "One strawberry, one raspberry coming up." Expertly she built two large sodas. "Let's go out back in the shade."

"Good idea! And you can put your feet up." Astrid led the way.

Sitting in the sprawling shade of the elm tree, Astrid sighed. "Ah, what a way to spend the late afternoon. And please, no discussion of all the past events."

The other two nodded. After a slight pause for sucking on their straws, Rebecca leaned forward. "I decided on prizes for the winning ice cream team." Her eyes sparkled. "They each get a card with numbers on it for five free sodas or dishes of ice cream."

"That's generous."

"Everyone is so excited for the celebration. It'll be the best we've ever had."

"We are certainly in need of one, with all the action going on around here. I hope the newer people can be made to feel welcome. Things seem divisive lately, and that makes me sad."

Astrid studied her mor as unobtrusively as possible. Ingeborg had such a fine sense of such things. Had the robbery introduced a sense of evil into their peaceful town?

Chapter 15

Astrid woke up early on July the fourth, 1905, to the song of waking birds, a rooster crowing, and her husband still asleep beside her. Usually Daniel was up before she was, unless she'd had an emergency during the night. Resisting the urge to snuggle close to him and drift back to sleep, she slid out of bed and tiptoed downstairs to start the stove and the coffee. She'd baked two cakes the night before and had a cast-iron pot of baked beans ready to put in the oven.

She had baked the beans partway the day before. Everyone in town had been cooking and baking, so there would be plenty of food. The men had started the fires in the trench the night before and put the steer on at three in the morning over a deep bed of fiery coals. Daniel had helped with that, so he deserved to sleep a little longer.

Standing at the back screen door barefoot and in her light wrapper, she inhaled the still cool air. So far, there was not a cloud in the sky, and the breeze barely kissed her forehead. How she wished she had shade trees in the backyard. The maple, oak, and cottonwood they had planted could hardly be designated as shade trees yet. Shade saplings, maybe.

She tossed her dishwater on the rosebushes along the front of her house, just like her mor had for all those years. Even though they had a hand pump in the kitchen, she refused to waste the precious water, remembering the days when they had to pump it and haul it in.

Lord, thank you for such a gorgeous day. No rain, no heat. Tiptoeing back upstairs, she gathered her clothes and took them into the bathroom to dress. As she bundled her hair into a snood, to be braided later, she thought about her far. Stubborn, yes. But that stubbornness was what was helping him recover. He was not the kind to give up.

None of them were.

"You're out!"

"Awwww . . ." The groans from the spectators rose as one.

"Onkel Lars won't be very popular by the end of this day." Ellie turned to Ingeborg, seated on the bench beside her. A couple of creative carpenters had fashioned a few benches out of one by tens nailed onto spools of firewood that had been waiting to be split.

"It is all in good fun." Ingeborg held Ellie's baby, little Haakan, on her lap while two-year-old Goodie played with her doll beside them. Carl, Sophie's Linnie, and Inga were looking for bugs and worms in the grass at their feet.

"I don't know. I see some glowering from the west team." She nodded to the team across the field from where they sat.

"Lars hasn't been real popular for the east side either." Ordinarily Haakan would be one of the umpires, usually at first base. Ingeborg knew that Lars didn't mind being behind the plate. Another batter stepped up to the plate, one of the more newly arrived men in town. She couldn't remember his name, but his wife and two children were sitting on benches like theirs over on that side. The batter swung and popped a fly to the shortstop. The "out" rang loud and clear.

"Let's get this over with so we can go eat," Jonathan called to his team out in the field.

Gus Baard swung and missed.

"Strike one." Then a second strike, this one popping backward and not caught.

With a teammate on second base, they could tie the game with a solid hit in this ninth inning with two outs. One run needed to tie, a home run to put the west team ahead.

On the next pitch Gus hit a grounder that bounced by the shortstop. Gus ran to first, sliding in to be safe. They now had runners on both third and first.

The crowd sat back down as Thorliff stepped up to bat.

"Hit it, Pa!" Both Inga and Carl had turned their attention to the game, since they weren't finding many bugs.

A titter swept through both sides of the field and brought grins to the players.

Thorliff swung once and connected on the second pitch with a wicked bounce to left field. The score was tied up, and Johnny Solberg took the bat.

"Just get on base," Ellie muttered, for Andrew was on deck to bat.

Johnny hit a foul, stared down three balls, and then got so excited that he swung at a bad one. The whole east side groaned.

"Take it easy," Jonathan called. "Breathe."

The fifteen-year-old did just that, watched the next ball go by for a walk. The bases were loaded again.

All those rooting for the east side leaped to their feet cheering for him as Andrew, swinging his bat, walked to the batter's box. He swung again.

"Hit it, Pa. Hit it hard!" Carl jumped up and down, Inga and Goodie yelling right along with him. Ingeborg and Ellie were both on their feet. When little Haakan started to cry, Ingeborg patted his back, shushing him but keeping her attention on the batter.

"Strike one!" The west side clapped and cheered.

"Foul ball" canceled out the second pitch.

"Ball one."

"Hit it! Hit it!" The children started the chant, and others picked it up. When Andrew connected with a solid *thunk*, everyone watched the ball make a high arc. Andrew ran to first. Third base tore for home, and the ball dropped straight down toward Dr. Deming's glove. He reached for it and the ball hit him right between the eyes. Only the children screamed and laughed when Andrew crossed the plate. Everyone else had eyes only for the figure flat on his back in the outfield.

Astrid dashed across the field to drop to her knees beside him. The rest of the team gathered around. When Dr. Deming groaned, they all cheered.

"You're going to have a goose egg the size of a melon," Astrid said as she checked him over.

The man nodded, then flinched. "Sorry I dropped the ball."

"You didn't. The ball dropped you." Astrid checked his eyes. "Are you ready to sit up?"

"I think so. This is mortifying."

Two of the men reached down to help him up, and everyone started clapping as he wobbled to his feet. They half carried him over to the benches to sit down.

Lars raised his hands and someone whistled for quiet. "I declare Dr. Deming the hero of our game. He played so hard he stopped the ball with his head." More whistles and cheers. "And the winners of this game will have the honor of being first in the line to eat. Let's give all these players a hand and thank them for playing such a fine game. According to the ladies, our bar-bee-cued beef is ready, and Reverend Solberg will lead us in grace in fifteen minutes. After that the lines form to the east of the tables." He dropped his hands and folks cheered again.

A bit later, Reverend Solberg pushed through the crowd and handed Astrid an ice pack, fighting to get his breath. "I'm getting too old for running like that."

Ice pack held to his forehead, Dr. Deming looked to John Solberg. "You say you are too old to run. Right now I feel ancient. Let a ball get by me like that. Can I blame it on the sun in my eyes?"

"Why not? It could happen to anyone."

"But I played on a really good team in St. Louis ever since school. Disgusting."

"Still, accidents happen. Can I bring you a plate?"

"No, thank you. I can walk fine." But when he stood up, he sat right back down. "Changed my mind. Thanks for the offer."

Astrid and Daniel stood off to the side, surveying the celebration. Blankets were spread on the grass everywhere, some people had brought their chairs, and other folks sat on all the benches and blocks of wood. Children chased each other, a dog barked, and a baby started crying.

"This is the biggest gathering we've ever had." Astrid nodded at someone who called her name, but she broke into a smile when a boy on a flat platform with wheels shouted, "Hey, there's my doc." Benny Valders started to propel his vehicle toward her, but one of the kids grabbed the rope on it and pulled him over to see Astrid. Benny had lost his legs in an accident in Chicago, and since no one knew who his parents were, Astrid had asked Gerald and Rebecca Valders if they might take him in. They had journeyed to the hospital in Chicago to pick him up, and so he came home to Blessing.

"Where've you been lately?" Astrid said as she took his hand.

"I went to stay out on the farm with my family." The pride in his eyes made her blink.

"Marvelous! You had a good time on the farm?"

"I got to ride a horse. Onkel Knute strapped me in the saddle, and I rode all by myself."

"Really?" Astrid smiled up at Daniel. "Can you believe that?"

"I believe anything can happen in Blessing. I've seen too many miracles to doubt it."

Benny said, "They have a big rooster, and he don't like me."

Gerald ambled over to join the conversation. "Show them your badge of courage."

Benny held up his arm. "But I swatted him a good one."

Someone called his name, and he grinned at Astrid again. "I gotta go. Hey, you want to go fishing tomorrow? Me and Pa are going to bring home the supper." He waved, flopped back on his stomach, and using his arms, propelled himself toward the gathering of children. One of them ran over to grab his rope and help him.

Astrid said, "They all do that so naturally."

"I know," Daniel said. "Just like they learn sign language. I guess it's not hard when you're a child. I was so amazed when you told me that when the students from the deaf school first attended the regular school, all the children started learning sign language. And that has continued."

"Tante Astrid, d'you know where Ma is?" Inga tugged at her skirts.

"Most likely at the hospital."

"I don't feel so good." Inga promptly puked up her supper, some on Daniel's shoe. "Euw. Sorry."

"Guess we better take you home."

"Can I just sit by you for a while? I feel better now."

Astrid checked her forehead for heat. It was damp from perspiration after playing with all the younger children, but not from a fever. "Why not." She took Inga's hand, thanked Daniel for cleaning up the mess, and strolled over to a free blanket in the shade of a cottonwood tree. Many people had already left to go home to do their chores, so there were more places to sit now. They had just sat down when Ingeborg brought a plate with cookies and small squares of several cakes to join them.

Ingeborg smiled at Inga. "Mind if I sit with you? Thorliff took Haakan home but he insisted I should stay."

Inga patted the blanket on either side of her. She looked to her grandmother. "I puked on Onkel Daniel's shoe." She laid her head in Ingeborg's lap. "I don't think I want a cookie right now."

Ingeborg stroked the little girl's hair back from her face. "We could go back to your house and—"

"Can't we stay here? I feel better now."

Before long all the blanket space was taken as first Ellie and little Haakan, then Sophie, carrying ten-month-old Marie, sat down. Kaaren came and sat on the edge, making room for Grace and Mrs. Jeffers, who waved away the offer of a chair.

Mrs. Jeffers, who tended to get gossip wrong frequently, said, "Ingeborg, I heard you caught those other two robbers single-handed because they kidnapped Astrid, and you were so angry. That was heroic!"

Kaaren gasped. "Wherever did you hear that? It's not true, any of it."

"But Juney over across the river said it's true."

Ingeborg wagged her head. "It was Elizabeth and Astrid. Their cleverness is what caught the fellows. Elizabeth managed to give one of them a big dose of morphine. While he was still a little scattered, he told the sheriff where they were hiding, out at the Hefner place. I led the sheriff and his men out there, and he arrested them."

"But Astrid—"

"Two of them used Astrid as a shield in order to get out of the hospital, but they turned her loose as soon as they were out in the country. They were actually quite gentlemanly. You see? You should never believe what old Juney says." Ingeborg looked down at her lap to see Inga sound asleep.

"And Haakan is all right?" Amelia asked softly while the others went on to other subjects.

"Just worn out, but he so enjoyed himself today. He lasted a lot longer than I thought he would." Ingeborg caught back a yawn. "It's been a big day."

"Been a big couple of weeks, if you ask me." She swatted at a mosquito. "We need a breeze to keep them away."

The sound of a guitar caught their attention. Sure enough, the musicians were gathering over by the school, where the dirt was packed hard enough to make dancing easier. They watched as several men eased the school piano down the ramp.

"You know something that amazes me about this town?" Amelia had taken a fan from her reticule and used it more as a pointer than for its proper use. "See over there. No one asked for help, but people always step in to do whatever needs to be done. Not just the folks who've been here since the beginning either. Look around." Folks of all ages, sexes, and backgrounds were pitching in to clean up, put things away, move the tables over closer to the school, and set them up again. Knots of people stood or sat around, visiting like those on this blanket.

"I thought for a while that there might be hard words at the ball game, but thanks to Dr. Deming and his forehead, that blew on by too. I think that's why the robbery was such a shock. Life has been hard for so many here that we all treasure the peace we find now."

"Oh, look." Sophie pointed toward the west. As the sun slid down, the few clouds pinked and then burst into a riot of colors, every shade of red, orange, and yellow and fading into purples. The deepening hush turned to an "Aah" when the last rim of gold disappeared. Someone started to clap, and soon everyone was clapping, turning to smile at one another.

Jonathan Gould on the piano and Joshua Landsverk with his guitar started a familiar tune, and without prompting, the song began. "'Blest be the tie that binds . . .'"

In English, German, Norwegian, and Russian, the song rose on the evening breeze.

Another hush and Reverend Solberg raised his hands and his voice. "Let's say this together: 'The Lord bless thee, and keep thee.'"

"'The Lord make His face to shine upon thee.'" Ingeborg took Kaaren's hand, and Karen took Amelia's as she reached out for Sophie's. "'The Lord lift up His countenance upon thee, and give thee peace.'" They all squeezed hands on the amen.

After a gentle silence, the music picked up again, this time singing out an invitation to come dance.

"That was indeed a God visit," Ingeborg said to her family. "Thank you all."

While couples began moving toward the dance area, Ingeborg smiled over her shoulder to see who was leaning up against her. "Why, Sophie, what a good idea. A perfect back rest." She raised her eyes to the horizon's glory that was slowly fading into gentle pinks and purples.

"You know something, Tante Ingeborg?" Sophie turned her face slightly. "I think everyone is going to remember this day.

Years from now people will say, 'You remember that Fourth of July party we had here in 1905? Never seen another one like it.'"

"I think you are right." *Lord, it sure would be dandy if this is the way the rest of the year goes.* She smoothed Inga's hair again, then felt the child's face. Sure enough, she was running a fever.

They all started at the sound of a shot in the distance, rapidly followed by another and another.

"Don't worry, folks," a man called. "That's only firecrackers."

Chapter 16

Chicago, Illinois

But I don't want to leave Chicago.

Miriam Hastings stared at the School of Nursing supervisor. Surely there was some mistake. All she ever wanted was to be a nurse right here in this hospital, where women and children could receive the help they so sorely needed.

"Is there a problem with your assignment? You said you understood that you might be sent out to other locations for practical training." Mrs. Korsheski looked over her round, wire spectacles. "You've done so well that I am grateful we can send you to the brand-new hospital in Blessing, North Dakota. Since it is a small hospital, at least compared to this one, you will be able to learn far more. Dr. Astrid Bjorklund is a protégée of Dr. Morganstein. The hospital there is actually a distant arm of our program. You three will be the first of our student nurses to serve there."

Miriam clamped her teeth together to keep the words she

wanted to say from spilling out. How could she leave her family? The little money she earned was sometimes all that bought food for six other hungry mouths. She usually ate in the hospital cafeteria so she needn't eat at home, the few times she was allowed to leave the premises. The nurses in training were all housed right there with one day off a week.

Miriam cleared her throat. "Have you told the others yet?"

"No. You are the first."

"I see." She could feel the head nurse's eyes drilling right through her starched nurse's cap and into her head. *Say something!* the voice inside her ordered and pleaded. *You can't lose out on this chance*. But then, *What if you are released from the program for insubordination? Then what will happen to your family?* She tried to speak, but the words refused to come.

Mrs. Korsheski studied her, then leaned forward. "Miriam, what is it? I was so sure you'd be overjoyed at an opportunity like this."

Miriam slowly shook her head, forcing the words out. "I am honored that you feel you can trust me with this opportunity, but . . ."

"It's your family, isn't it?"

"Yes." Too broken to be anything but honest, Miriam spoke to her fists clenched in her lap. "They . . . they need every penny I can send to them." Most student nurses did not receive any pay, instead paying for their schooling, but Miriam did extra work to earn money to send home.

"I see." Mrs. Korsheski sat back in her chair. "There has to be a way for us to deal with this. Tell me about your family again. I know I have notes written in your file, but refresh my memory."

"My mother has a chronic illness, so she is weak much of the time. She became a seamstress, and that has pretty much become the family business. I am the eldest of six. A brother of sixteen works anywhere he can find work; my fifteen-year-old sister both sews and has assumed the care of our mother; my brother, who is fourteen, picks up what jobs he can and helps at home; my ten-year-old sister has dropped out of school so she can help with most of the cooking and cleaning; and our youngest sister, who is eight, is still in school. Mother insists that her children have as much education as possible, so she teaches those at home when she can."

"And your father?"

"He was killed in a strike several years ago. That one wasn't as bad as the Teamster strike, but several were killed." Miriam kept her voice to a near monotone, fighting to keep control of her emotions.

"If I remember right, your oldest sister is a very good seamstress. She and your mother did some work for us at one time?"

"Yes, they did."

Mrs. Korsheski wrote some notes on the pad of paper in front of her. "You let me work on this. Surely there is a solution to be found." She looked up, eyes still narrowed in thought. "Tell Miss Wells to come in, please."

"Thank you." Miriam stood. "Uh . . ."

"Yes?"

"Uh . . ." Miriam turned and, fighting to keep some semblance of composure, left the room. She nodded to the first of the two young women sitting on the bench outside the door. "You're next, Vera."

"What did she . . . ?"

But Miriam had fled down the hall to the women's room.

"How can I leave them?" She stared at the tear-streaked face in the mirror. "Pull yourself together. It's not like you are being hauled off to the poor farm or some such. She is trying to help you, and you behave like a flibbertigibbet, with no sense whatsoever. Other people leave home to go for work or school all the time. Or even to travel."

Travel. A snort caught her by surprise. She had always dreamed of boarding a train and going off to see the world. Or on a ship—not traveling in steerage like her mother had when she came from London and her father from Bingham, but as an actual passenger in a stateroom. *Oh girl, such fine dreams you have. Such a foolish waste of time and effort. Pull yourself together. You are a student nurse who has been offered an excellent opportunity. You will not let this pass you by. After all, it is for one year, not for a lifetime.* She tucked one stubborn curl under her cap and then another.

Her dark hair had a mind of its own. Staying confined in a net and cap was difficult, to say the least. She splashed water on her face to wipe away any trace of tears and dried her hands. Smoothing her apron, she started for the door, only to be pushed back by the exuberant Vera.

"We are going on a train to North Dakota. Can you believe it? I am so excited!"

"I never would have guessed." As soon as the words popped out of her mouth, Miriam wanted to bite them back.

"Oh, this is so wonderful." Vera grabbed her around the waist and spun them both.

"Enough!" Miriam could feel some pins slipping from her hair. At least one pinged on the linoleum floor. "Stop!" She planted her feet as the taller young woman slowed.

Vera stopped all right. A dead stop! Her eyes widened, took on a sparkle as a grin spread her rounded cheeks. "Surely there will be plenty of young men out there, men of courting age, who desire marriage—not just wastrels, but like forever." The last word came out on a reverent breath. "And whose God is not the bottle."

Vera wouldn't mind leaving her family. She had basically cut herself adrift from them when she announced she was registering for nursing school. That she had managed to make it through high school was a testament to the girl's determination in the face of her family's derision. *Hoity-toity* was one of the kinder phrases they used to try to dissuade her.

Miriam knew all this, due to confidences shared through the two years they'd been in school together. "We are not going to Blessing, North Dakota, to find a husband. We are going to improve our nursing skills."

Vera nodded, but her eyes said, "*Just watch.*"

Miriam crouched down to locate the hairpins that were no longer in her hair, where they belonged. Locating two, she turned back to the mirror and, after removing the hatpins that secured her cap in place, pulled off the net, sending more pins in flight.

"Now look what you've done." She tried to sound stern but failed. Vera was irrepressible. She knew that, but for some reason had assumed the job of assisting her fellow students to live up to the standards set out by the staff of Morganstein Hospital's nursing program. They all had been reminded of the standards at the fall meeting that started each new year.

"Give it up. You know only braiding can control that wild mop of yours." Vera bent over and retrieved a couple more pins.

The door opened and Corabell Nester, shock blanching her face, stopped just inside and leaned against the wall. "I can't do this. I just can't."

"Why not?" Miriam stared at her in the mirror, at the same time fighting to get the hair net back in place.

"What is it, Corabell? You look like . . . like you've seen a ghost." Vera crossed to her friend and put an arm around her shoulders. "If you think you can't go to Blessing, why, of course you can. I will be with you and Miriam too."

"It's too far. I've never been so far from home. Coming here was bad enough, and now I'm supposed to go halfway around the world to—"

"First off. North Dakota is only a couple of days by train. It is not halfway around the world, and secondly, don't be a goose. Of course you can do it." Miriam almost said a most unladylike and unnurselike word as she fussed with her hair. "Maybe I should just cut all this hair off and be done with it."

Corabell and Vera stared at her in the mirror, their mouths open and eyes round in shock. "You wouldn't." Even their voices matched.

Miriam stuck the hatpins through the muffin-like white cap, fixing it to her hair as firmly as possible. She checked the clock. "We have exactly four minutes to get to class." The others groaned as they all headed for the door. Now was the time to concentrate on the lecture and put all the worries of a possible upcoming trip to bed for a time.

Arm in arm, the three marched down the hall to the classroom, pasted the proper decorum on their faces, and made their way to their assigned seats. At least they weren't the last to enter the room, but still they earned the frown of Professor Gutenheimer.

"Good you could come." With steely eyes, the gray-haired man in the frock coat glared at the two nurses who tried to tiptoe in after the three.

"Uh, yes, sir."

Miriam crushed the sigh that threatened to erupt. This man might be head of his field, but how did he manage to remain an instructor here at the Morganstein Hospital? He quite obviously did not respect the calling of nursing but held them and probably all women in contempt. *Pompous* was far too mild a term to apply to His Honor. What would his comeuppance take?

A sneaky thought slipped through her mind. At least in North Dakota they would not have to endure the snide remarks of Dr. Gutenheimer of Harvard, as he was always introduced, including when he introduced himself.

An hour and a half later, the class filed out, all of them looking as bleary-eyed as Miriam felt. Dr. Gutenheimer had expounded on the benefits and uses of carbolic acid, which he called phenol, as if it were a recent discovery and therefore causing a great deal of excitement in the medical community.

Where had he been for the last fifty years that carbolic acid had been in use? She had been reading some of the American Medical Association publications in the hospital library. If this drug worked as well as those who discovered it said, it would be a wonder drug in the fight against infection, the likes of which they'd not seen before. Hyperbole like that only caused her to raise her eyebrows.

At the supper table, the discussion continued amongst the nurses. But Miriam was forced to leave before they finished, since she had the night shift and needed at least a few hours' sleep before going out on the floor. Sometimes the night shift was easier, depending on the cases.

If only sleep could be easy, but her mind could not or would not leave her family. How would they ever survive without her? They needed not only the money she sent home but the medical help for her mother and the work she was able to send to her siblings when she saw a need they could fill at the hospital. They wouldn't even be able to talk with her—not that they could easily now, but . . . the miles apart seemed impossible.

What if her mother died in one of her attacks and Miriam was too far away to help? She was getting visibly weaker all the time.

And how could Miriam herself go on without her mother's wisdom?

Chapter 17

Blessing, North Dakota

"Onkel Hjelmer, I am having serious doubts about continuing to work on the well-drilling crew. We keep having to travel farther from Blessing, and with Onkel Haakan unable to work the fields now, I need to be here."

Hjelmer shook his head. "Trygve, I understand your feelings, but I have another twenty or so orders, and the farmers are already getting impatient with us taking so long to get to them. If I can't send this crew out, I'll have to cancel, and . . ." He stared down at the kitchen table. Penny had the store open and with Linnea helping her and the younger children out pulling weeds in the garden, the house was strangely silent.

"I thought of that. I hate to leave you in the lurch like this, but Gus Baard could run this crew. We've worked together now for more than a year, and he is as level-headed as they come. You know that."

"I was hoping to start a second crew with him as lead. I've

even ordered the wagon." Hjelmer looked at the book where he kept his notes. "It should be here any day. Then we need to outfit it."

"You need to talk to Mr. Sam about some repairs on the one we have. All the wheel rims should be reset, and that rear axle is wearing."

"What we could do is move all the tools to the new wagon so the crew can head out again without waiting for the repairs."

"True." *Did he not hear me?* Trygve stared at his onkel. "Where are the new wells to be dug?"

"Western North Dakota and eastern Montana. I'm thinking to put everything on a railcar so you can get there more quickly."

"Hjelmer, I cannot go out with this crew. I am needed here."

"Well, Lars said all the seeding was done, so things will be a bit slower until haying starts, and—"

"Haying will start in a week or so. Not time enough for me to go out and come back. I'm sorry, but this is the way it has to be."

"But Jonathan is back now. He'll be helping."

Did the man never think of anyone but himself? Trygve tried to ignore the bubbling and snorting of his awakening anger. "They should pay someone else to help when this able-bodied son will be out drilling wells?" For years he'd heard his mor and far's comments on the younger of the Bjorklund brothers, who would rather be gallivanting around the country than staying home to help with the family store and raising the family, leaving all that up to Penny.

Granted, Hjelmer had a gift for making money. It seemed that whatever he put his mind to prospered, the drilling crew a case in point. He'd even done a stint in the state legislature, but for some reason, chose not to run again. Possibly because his family was so unhappy in Bismarck. When Penny was forced to take the store back from the scalawag who bought it and got run out of town, the family returned to Blessing.

These thoughts railroaded through Trygve's head while he fought to calm himself. Instead of yelling like he wanted, he said softly, deliberately inserting a thread of steel in his voice, "I will do what I can to help you from here, but I will not be going out with this crew. Gus can take over without any problem. He has shared all parts of the job, and he knows the men. We'd need to find one more to go with him. I was thinking of the Geddick sons. Joseph and Heinz are hard workers and dependable."

"True." Hjelmer shook his head. "That is all well and good, but I was counting on you. How about if I give you a raise? You do this trip and—"

"No!" Trygve sucked in a deep breath and unclamped his teeth so he could talk. "You give the raise to Gus, since he'll be running the crew. If you want I will get the wagon repaired and help get another crew on board. If not, give me my paycheck and we will call it good." A smile was beyond what he could do with his reclamped jaw.

"Some gratitude . . ." Hjelmer muttered under his breath.

That's it! Trygve slapped his hands on the table and pushed back his chair.

"Now, don't go getting in a huff. We'll work this out. I'll have your pay this afternoon after the bank opens." He put on a smile. "I don't want this to come between us. You go ahead and do what you said, and if you will get this crew up and going, I'd appreciate it."

"Takk. I'll take care of that immediately. Do you want to talk with Gus or do you want me to?"

"You go ahead and then have him come to see me." Hjelmer stuck out his hand and Trygve shook it.

"Will you be around?"

"Ja, for a few more days."

Trygve stood. "I'll talk with you soon."

Hjelmer looked up from some notes he was writing. There might have been a bit of frost in his eyes, but Trygve chose to ignore that and headed back outside.

Whistling, he stepped out on the porch. He would not be traveling with this crew. The thought both pleased him and left a bit of a pang. Haying was not his favorite job. Samuel loved farming with his father, like his cousin Andrew, but Trygve had really enjoyed traveling in the wagon, putting up a new well, and moving on. Perhaps he had a bit of the wanderlust, like Sophie used to have. Besides, if Jonathan and Grace had their way, they would be building an addition on to the deaf school in this next year.

"How did it go?" his mother asked when Trygve strolled in the door just before dinner.

"Well, Hjelmer tried to keep me running the crew, but when I stood up to leave, he talked business. I will not be going out again, but I will be helping get this crew out, with Gus as foreman." He went on to describe the meeting, taking platters and bowls from Kaaren's hands to set on the table. "Where are Grace and Jonathan?"

"Over at their house. They'll be back when I ring the dinner bell."

"Good. How do you think Onkel Haakan is really doing? I was planning on stopping there again on the way home, but after getting the wagon to Mr. Sam, I ran out of time."

"You probably know as well as I do how he's doing." Hands on her hips, she surveyed the table. "Go ring the bell, will you, please?"

He did as asked and stepped back into the kitchen. "I suppose, but what I want to know is what lies ahead."

"Only God knows that." She greeted Ilse and turned back to Trygve. "My personal opinion is he will not be back out in the fields. He might be able to help with the milking and chores around the barn and house, but I pray he is wise enough not to insist on working machinery and a team again. And I pray Ingeborg is strong enough to dissuade him if he does insist."

"Then I was right in what I told Hjelmer. My restless feet are ready to be back in Blessing again. There is plenty to do around here, that's for sure."

When they all were seated and the meal blessed, Kaaren said, "Astrid has sent out a prayer request. They had two burn victims come into the hospital, one last night and one this morning, both caused by fireworks. One is pretty severe. I'm sure grateful we decided to not do the fireworks over the river this year."

"I don't care if they never do them," Grace said, in her careful way. "We had two people, newly deaf, come to the school because of injuries due to the fireworks. Losing your hearing is a terrible price to pay for a few minutes of pleasure."

Since Trygve had been one of those who grumbled about the change in plans, he wisely kept his mouth shut. He'd seen fireworks one time in Grand Forks and thought them splendid. Especially after talking with the men who traveled the country setting off the displays.

He glanced around the table. Ilse and her husband, George McBride, who had been a student at the deaf school when he was younger; two high school students, who chose to stay and work to earn their tuition for the next year; Samuel, the youngest of the Knutson family, who'd recently turned eighteen; Grace and Jonathan, who were acting like the newlyweds they were;

and his far and mor. Thinking while eating, he studied his far. Lars was indeed looking older and what? Worn? Tired? Haying hadn't even started, and harvesting would follow quickly on that. He was not just needed at Haakan's but here too.

Why had he not noticed this before?

Chapter 18

Manny, I want you to meet my mother, Mrs. Bjorklund. Mor, this is Manny McCrary, the boy you've been praying for." Astrid waved a hand and then stepped back.

"Hello, Manny." Ingeborg held out her hand. With more than a slight hesitation, the boy shook hands with her from the bed, along with a slight nod. Panic showed in his eyes.

"Mrs. Bjorklund is going to be working with you to help get you up and walking with crutches. She has helped many people through the years. I know you get tired of lying here, so I expect you to do what she tells you. I need to go see to other patients, but you can call for me if you need me." Astrid left the hospital room.

Ingeborg watched her leave, and a swell of pride touched her even now. She turned and smiled again at her patient. "I'm going to tell you a bit about what I'll be doing, so if you have any questions, you can ask me. I'll do the best I can to answer them." She paused. "All right?"

His nod was brief, but at least he responded.

"Today we will be working with your arms and good leg. I need to know how strong you are. I heard that you were very strong before this all began, but your body has been through a lot, and muscles get weak quickly when you are lying in bed. Squeeze my hand, please."

She picked up one hand, and he squeezed. "Can you squeeze harder? You needn't worry about hurting me." He did so. "Good. Even harder? Ah, that's better." He was going to need that hand-and-arm strength to manage walking with crutches.

After testing the other hand, she held out her arm. "I'm going to push down on your arm like this and then up. See if you can keep me from moving your arm." His grimace said he was doing all he could, but she was able to make his arm move both up and down. "Now make a fist and bend your elbow." She pulled against his knotted fist, and again he could not keep the elbow bent.

His groan made her smile gently. "You needn't feel bad. Actually you are doing very well." She laid a hand on his chest. "See if you can sit up." He flopped back with another groan. "I know. Frustrating, isn't it?" When she rolled back the sheet and moved to his good leg, he was breathing hard. With a hand on his shin, she said, "Now raise your leg." When he grunted in the effort, she removed her hand. "See how far you can lift it now." When his leg rose, she smiled. "Good. How about raising it to touch my hand ten times?"

By eight, he was shaking and the leg flopped back down as if it weren't connected. "I can't."

"That's why I am here. You'll get your strength back quickly. Bend your leg. That's it, good. Now raise your foot from your knee ten times. Very good." She looked up in time to catch an almost smile. Perhaps she was getting through to him. "Now I'm going to rub some salve into your other leg and foot, but I'll be careful about the incision. This should feel good."

With great care she massaged his foot and up his calf, working even more gently as she neared his knee. With feather lightness she slowly moved her hands up the sides of his thigh to allow the warmth of her hands to penetrate the dressing. All the while she watched for any flinching that would indicate pain. Instead, she saw and felt him relax and exhale in relief.

"Why are you doing this?"

"Simple. We all want you to get better, and this is the best way I know how to help right now. The sooner we get you walking with the crutches, the sooner you can leave the hospital."

"Then what?"

"Then you are going to come to my house, where I can take care of you more easily." Ingeborg pulled the chair over beside the bed. "And there you can have more visitors."

"I don't know nobody here."

"I know, but I have friends who are looking forward to meeting you."

"Why?" He sounded hostile, which was a small step up from being fearful.

"Because they want to. Inga wants to know if you know how to play rock, paper, scissors."

"Who is Inga?"

"My granddaughter." Ingeborg smiled. "She's funny. Do you like music?"

He nodded. "Don't everyone?"

"Possibly. Johnny Solberg asked me to ask if you've ever played an instrument."

"We had a banjo once."

"And you played on that?"

"Sorta."

"Good. He plays the guitar, and he thought perhaps you might like to learn how."

Interest sparked his eyes, making her smile inside too. "Maybe. If I got time."

"Dr. Bjorklund said you don't know how to read. Is that true?"

"I can do sums."

"So you did go to school?"

He shook his head. "Ma taught me to count and add some and subtract, so's I could handle money."

"Well, I have a friend who would like to come to my house and teach you to read."

"Why?"

Exasperation crept into her tone. "Why not?"

He frowned and scratched his head. "Don't none of you know me."

"But you see, this is the way we can get to know you."

"Why? I helped rob your bank. Why do you want to get to know me?"

"Ah, so that is what's troubling you." She nodded and patted his hand. "We have reason to think that your brothers forced you to help them, and you had no choice but to go along with what they told you to do. And now that they are gone and will not be coming back anytime soon, you will need a home for as long as you want to stay. Someday, if you want to go back to Kentucky, you can do that, but for now, you are here in Blessing, and we want you to be part of our family and our town."

He huffed out a sigh. "Don't make no sense."

She waited a minute and then asked, "Do you have any other questions?"

"How come there are two Dr. Bjorklunds? They both your girls?"

"No. Dr. Elizabeth Bjorklund is married to my son Thorliff, and their little girl is Inga. The Dr. Bjorklund here today is my daughter."

"You a doctor too?"

"No, but I do know a lot about medical things. I used to be the midwife for this area and took care of all kinds of injuries because we had no doctors. We live quite a ways from towns big enough to have doctors." Ingeborg reached down into her bag and brought out her knitting. "Did they have doctors where you came from?"

"No. Too far."

"Like us, huh?"

"Not flat like this, though. Mountains."

"Really? I've not seen mountains since I left Norway all those long years ago. Are your mountains tall enough to have snow on them?" Closing her eyes, she could still picture the seter and the true mountains surrounding the mountain farm. White snow flashing against a cobalt sky. The pang that shot through her reminded her why she never allowed herself to think of that home across the ocean.

"Why did you leave there if you like it so?"

Ingeborg smiled gently. "Many Norwegians emigrated so that we could have land to farm. Norway is a small country, with much of it in mountains, so farmland is scarce." Her knitting needles clicked quietly.

"Is it far away?"

"Clear on the other side of the Atlantic Ocean." *I'll bet he doesn't even know what an ocean is.* "Have you ever seen a map?"

"No. Only one that Gabe, my oldest brother, drew so we could find the hideout."

"When you go to school this fall, you'll see maps. We have some in books at our house."

"I ain't goin' to no school." He clamped his arms across his chest.

Ingeborg leaned back in her chair. "Whyever not? All the children here go to school all the way through the twelfth grade. Then some go on to college." The yarn flew through her fingers as she knit in a closed circle.

"What are you making?"

"A hat for you to wear this winter. It gets mighty cold here."

His voice gruff, he muttered, "I don't need no hat."

"We shall see."

Ingeborg put her knitting away. "I must be going now, but you don't need me here to work your arms and leg and belly muscles. The more you do the things I showed you, the stronger you will become and the sooner you will walk again." She patted his hand lying on the sheet. "Dinner will be here soon, and I have a feeling you might have more company this afternoon."

When he started to mutter, "I don't need . . ." she held up her hand. "Yes, you do need our help, and we will make sure you get it." She waved as she left the room in a swirl of skirts.

Astrid met her at the nurses' station. "You did get him talking. I knew you would." Astrid hugged her mother. "He didn't have a chance."

"He's one stubborn boy who likes to think he is a man and can do everything he needs." She patted her daughter's cheek. "I need to get home and get dinner for Haakan. I left the kettle of soup on the back of the stove. He said he'd not let the stove go out. He's moving around the house better all the time and can go up and down the porch steps, so he's not feeling so confined."

"And hates his need to take a nap?"

"Of course. You know your far." She wagged her head. "I'm thinking he and Manny might just be good for each other."

"Mor, you're always thinking. Or perhaps *plotting* is not a bad word to use."

Astrid liked some weeks better than others, and this was not one of them. One of the burn victims was sent home the next day with honey covering the wound, his hand wrapped, and the arm in a sling. The other, though, had burns on his face, but the most severe were on his hand and chest. When he started coughing, the doctors knew they were in trouble. In spite of all the treatment and prayers, they buried him four days later.

"That was so senseless!" Astrid stormed around her house that night, fuming and pounding her feet on the stairs. "All because of fireworks. A whole field burned in Pembina. It could have taken out the town."

Daniel stared from his rampaging wife to his mother and back to his wife. "How can I help you?"

"You can't. Unless you can work miracles and bring him back. His wife has a little boy and a baby girl to raise by herself. She told me the men had been drinking too."

She sank down on the stairs, and Daniel came to sit beside her. He put his arm around her shoulders, and she leaned into his quiet strength, her head on his shoulder. A dry sob slipped out. "I felt so useless. We have to learn better ways to treat burns and the pneumonia that took him. You know what the medical book says, put butter or something greasy on the burn and hot packs. We used ice, and near as I can tell, that's a lot more effective. Why would you put heat on heat?"

Daniel simply hugged her closer.

She could feel herself begin to run down. "I'm sorry, Daniel, for ranting on like this. Such a waste for nothing."

That night she was called out for a birthing and got there just in time to catch a perfect baby boy as he slid out into the world. "In a bit of a hurry, weren't you, young man?" She laid the baby on his mother's chest and went about her duties humming. As her mor would say, "The Lord giveth and the Lord taketh away. Blessed be the name of the Lord."

As she drove the horse and buggy home in the predawn chill, she stopped along the road to watch the sun lemon the sky, the brassy rim peek up bit by bit until the sun leaped up to begin its daily journey. The birds followed the lead of a song sparrow and broke into a chorus of song that lifted on the breeze and heralded the new day. A dog barked as she trotted by and another across a field answered. The horse snorted and tugged at the bit, but Astrid held him steady so she could savor the moment.

According to Thorliff and Hjelmer, they should all have automobiles by now. "That will be the day," she said, setting the horse's ears to twitching. Once home she unhitched the horse and led him into the stall for a bit of grain before turning him loose in the small pasture.

Daniel found her some time later sound asleep on the wicker settee on the back porch. He kissed her, pulled her to her feet, and helped her up the stairs in spite of her protests that she needed to wash and get over to the hospital. He tucked her into bed, saying he'd wake her in an hour.

He didn't. The church bell woke her at noon. Refusing to be disgruntled on such a perfect summer day, she arrived at the hospital just in time to see Manny take his first steps with the crutches that had been waiting for him.

"You keep this up and in two days, I think you can be moved to the Bjorklund farmhouse."

"That's what I told him." Her mor sat near the door watching proudly. She smiled at her daughter. "We have his bed all ready for him."

I sure hope I am making the right decision, Astrid said to herself. *At least he won't be able to run away for some time. I hope. Please, Lord, let it be so.*

But the fire and defiance in his eyes made her question it.

Chapter 19

I think those south fields are ready to be cut." Lars tipped his hat back on his head and wiped his forehead with a handkerchief.

Haakan grunted his assent. "Both mowers are ready?"

He nodded. "I finished sharpening teeth today. Talk about cutting it short."

"Andrew's pretty good with a stone and file."

Lars smiled up at Freda when she handed each of them a glass of strawberry swizzle. "Takk."

The two men lifted their glasses in salute, and Lars drank half of his, Haakan only sipping.

"Sure turned hot this week." Lars mopped the back of his neck too. "Good sitting here in the shade, though."

Haakan grunted again, and it was not assent. "I'd rather be out replacing mower teeth."

"I know. I set George to cleaning out the haymows on both places. Weather holds like this, and we'll be hauling by Friday."

"I had the rakes all greased before I went down, so those are ready."

"Did you ever get the lift ropes replaced in your haymow?"

"Andrew and I did it last winter." Haakan took another drink.

"Where's Ingeborg?"

"Working with that boy at the hospital. She and Astrid decided to bring him out here soon as he can manage crutches. He can't even read."

"Didn't seem reading was high in the minds of those wasters. All that and they only got fifty-five dollars." Lars drained his glass. "You sure you want that boy out here? Might steal you blind."

"How could he when he can't even walk?" Haakan glanced up in the tree, where a couple of birds got into an argument. "Poor, dumb kid, growing up in a family like that."

"Might be we can turn him into a farmer."

"We can try. I'm thinking I might be able to drive one of the hay wagons."

"We'll see." Lars got to his feet with a low groan. "Better get to milking. Tell Ingeborg we've got plenty of cream ready for the cheese house."

"I will. Guess she should be home anytime now." Haakan sipped. "Freda pretty much runs that now, you know. We should be hearing one of these days if any of her relatives from Norway want to come over and help."

"Forgot about that. Ja, that's true. Both Kaaren and Ingeborg sent letters." Lars settled his hat back square on his head. "Later." And he headed for the barn and the milking stanchions.

When Ingeborg drove her buggy into the yard, Haakan was rocking on the front porch. Good. She had noticed coming in that the hay was ready to cut. Haakan, the farmer, seemed content to sit and watch others farm, though. She knew it had to be difficult for him.

But when she joined him on the porch, Haakan casually mentioned his idea that he'd suggested to Lars—driving the hay wagon.

She turned real quiet, then said gently, "I wish you wouldn't. That's taking a big chance."

"No it's not. We can tie me to the hayrick if need be."

Ingeborg's eyebrows arched a bit. Then she closed her eyes. *Please, Lord, show him how dangerous an idea that is.*

Friday night Thorliff had supper with his parents. After they were done and Ingeborg was cleaning up, Andrew joined them, and then before long Trygve and Lars arrived too.

"Why, what a surprise." Ingeborg welcomed them, slid the coffeepot back to the front hot part of the stove, and fed the fire. "I'd have baked a cake had I known you were coming." She looked from face to face, catching the idea they weren't there on a social call. *O Lord, now what?* While she dished the cookies onto a plate, she watched as one by one they pulled out a chair at the table.

Haakan made his way in from the back porch. "Well, how good to see all of you."

"Far, we need to talk." Thorliff pulled out his father's chair.

"About what?" Haakan sat down and leaned against the chair back.

With everyone seated, Thorliff started the meeting. "We heard that you are planning on driving one of the hay wagons."

"Ja, I think I can do that. Once I get up there, I should be fine. Can tie myself to the hayrick if need be." He smiled like that was a joke. Andrew shook his head.

"What if you collapse and fall off?"

"I said we can tie me up." His voice took on an edge.

Thorliff leaned forward. "What's your rush? All that heat out there. Could get sunstroke mighty easy."

"We don't want you to try it yet, Far."

Haakan sat up straighter and leaned forward. "Are you trying to tell me I can't go out and work my own land?"

"No, we're telling you that you need to take more time off until you are stronger."

"I'm not an invalid."

Thorliff was keeping his voice quiet. "No one said you are. But you've been very ill, and it wasn't long ago we weren't sure if you were going to live or die. Have you talked with Mor about it? Astrid or Elizabeth?"

"I mentioned it to Ingeborg the other night."

She brought the cups to the table and returned for the coffeepot, all without a word. Going around the table, she filled Haakan's cup last, squeezing his shoulder gently as she poured. "Cream and sugar anyone?"

All of the men studied their coffee as if seeking wisdom in the darkness.

Thorliff dunked his cookie and, after taking a bite, followed with a swallow of coffee. "What if you went down out in the field and were to slide off the rack and under the wagon?"

"Or the wheels? Or the team panicked and took off?"

"Or this sets you back and you never fully recover?"

"Onkel Haakan, we want you to be around for a long time. Please, can't you see the wisdom in this?" This last was from Trygve.

"You gave up a good job with the well drilling to stay home and help, all because of me?"

"No, there were many reasons. I know I made the right decision."

"Hjelmer is still pretty upset." Haakan still had an edge in his voice.

"I know and I'm sorry, but he'll get over it when he sees the other men doing as good a job or even better."

"That's beside the point." Thorliff passed the cookie plate on around the table. "We are asking you to please give up this idea for now."

"I can't."

"Can't or won't?"

"How are you going to get up on the rack?"

"I'll get a ladder!" Haakan pushed back from the table. "I will see you at the barn in the morning." He walked straight to his bedroom and closed the door.

"So now what?" Andrew asked, looking at his mother. "He's too weak to even drag a ladder. Look at him walk."

"I swear, I . . ." Thorliff slammed the palm of his hand on the table. "Stubborn! What else can you say? Stubborn, bullheaded, pigheaded. Mor, he cannot handle this. Look at him. He's not even walking like he used to yet."

"Then you all better spend time praying that God will make it clear to him tonight."

"You talk to him."

"I'll give him my opinion if he asks. But otherwise it won't work." She gave a tiny smile. "It took me a while to learn, but . . ." She paused and looked around the room. "I have a feeling we have a whole room of really stubborn Norwegian men. So, someday I'll tell your wives how to handle you."

They all rolled their eyes as if choreographed.

"I have plenty more cookies. God is going to work this out. Why would He fail us now?"

"But what if He lets Haakan go out there and collapse?"

Ingeborg rolled her lips together. "If that's what needs to

be, then that's what will happen." *But please, Lord God, keep that from happening.*

That night she found herself repeatedly waking up to make sure he was all right, but Haakan slept through the night as if the meeting had never occurred. Every time she woke, she prayed for him to be wise in the morning.

He awoke early, at first light. "Pretty soon I am going back to the barn in the mornings to milk cows again." He said his piece firmly, letting her know his mind was made up. Was there anything more stubborn than a Norwegian whose mind was made up?

Ingeborg clenched her teeth, got up, and dressed without a word and without looking him in the eye. She did not offer to help him in any way and even her stride said what she thought. She rattled the grate with extra gusto, started the fire, and took the empty coffeepot to the sink to fill. Pumping water with a vengeance, she caught a reflection of herself in the window. She filled the pot with water and set it on the quickly heating stove. That too got an extra clang. All the while her mind kept pace. *Stubborn. Stubborn. Stubborn.* Now she understood it was a pride issue also. He would show those young sprouts!

She added the coffee grounds to the water and shoved more wood in the firebox. The frying pan clanged. The floor shook under her feet, and even the cat stayed away, watching her from behind the stove. Saved fat sizzled in the pan waiting for the slices of cornmeal mush she had cooked and left to set up overnight.

When Haakan sat down at the table, he was dressed for work, including his boots, the first time he'd worn them since the collapse. The coffee nearly sloshed over the rim of the cup when she set it down before him.

Ingeborg Bjorklund, talk about him being stubborn. Look at the way you're acting. Ignoring the voice was difficult, but she managed. Breakfast was a strangely silent affair, since Freda had spent the night at Kaaren's so they could continue to scrub down all the dorm rooms. In fact, the entire school building. Kaaren always had the building all fresh and clean for the new and returning students.

She bowed her head, Haakan said grace, and they ate. Without talking.

Finally Haakan said, "Are you so angry you cannot even speak?"

She nodded.

"But you never get angry like this, not for years and years. Is my wanting to help with the haying such a terrible thing? Ingeborg, I have to be able to work again, or what is the sense of living?"

Her eyes welled up and one overflowed. "Haakan, I do not believe you are strong enough for this—not yet. I fear you are taking your life in your hands and all because you are too proud to admit you just might possibly have made a mistake last night. All those men were here because they love you and respect you and want you here with all of us for a long time yet."

"You know I have said that if it is my time to go home to heaven, I am ready."

"I understand that and I am too, but that does not give one permission to take foolish chances."

"So now I am a fool too?"

"No! But you are doing a foolish thing. And I don't want you to have a setback, serious or otherwise." She laid her hand over his. "Please, Haakan, please."

He stared down at their hands. "I have to try, my Inge. I have to try. If I feel weak or dizzy, I will return to the house. All right?"

"What can I say? You know my mind. All right." She went to the door with him and watched as he walked to the barn. The milkers were finished, so the cows were gathered around the water tank, drinking their fill. Then they followed the lead bossy, single file, out to the far pasture. Coffee cup in hand, she leaned against the porch post, letting God's creation soothe her angry spirit.

"Now I have to confess that anger, don't I?" A twittering bird seemed to look right at her and give instructions. "And, Lord, this shows that I am not trusting you in all things." *Be not afraid* tiptoed through her mind. "Fear not. That's what this is, isn't it? Lord, I do want to trust you, but sometimes it is so hard. I know you are bigger than a man's pride, and you can be more stubborn than anyone. I give him back to you. My anger only made noise, and it gave me an upset stomach. I am sorry. Thank you for the way you send peace. I can feel it seeping into my skin and surrounding my heart. Your peace and joy, O Lord. I will sing praises to your holy name."

A meadowlark sat on one of the fence posts to the garden and, beak wide, sang to her. The aria made her smile and whisper more words of thanks. The cat wound around her ankles, and when she picked the old girl up, the purring motor rumbled in her hands.

A snuggling cat, birds singing, the leaves of the cottonwood whispering secrets, a horse nickering, a calf bawling—all the sounds of a summer morning. *God, you are in your heavens, and all is right with my world.* Humming, she went inside to start the bread dough.

"Ingeborg, can you get the door?" Lars called a while later.

She ran to push the screen open to see Lars and Andrew half walking, half carrying Haakan to the steps of the porch.

"Okay, Haakan, you have to step up now. Can you hear me?"

"Ja. I will step up." Haakan did so, raising first one foot and then the other as the two men stepped with him.

"Haakan, do you want to lie in bed or out here?" Ingeborg spoke slowly and distinctly.

"Out here, please. I just need to rest, not sleep." His voice was faint, but he spoke clearly.

"Let me get some pillows." She hurried back into the house and brought pillows to cushion the wicker arms. Together they sat him down on the cushioned settee, and Andrew lifted his father's legs so he could recline against the pillows.

"There, Far. Better?"

"Ja. This is good."

"What happened?" Ingeborg's heart pounded as if she had carried him.

"I promised you, Inge, that if I felt faint I would ask for help. I did and they did and no one is hurt, including me."

"Thank you, Lord."

"Ja, thank you, Lord God." His eyes began drifting closed. "Takk for the help, Andrew, Lars. Tell the others I am all right. I'll see you all at dinner."

She followed the two men to the gate. "All is well?"

"Ja. We will tell you later. The sun has dried the dew so now we can get out there and start bringing the hay in." Andrew took her hand. "It was a good thing, Mor. God did a good thing."

"Good thing? He collapsed!"

"Ja. Now he knows he's not ready to work in the fields. It took this to convince him."

Ja. Ingeborg could not do that, so God did. Why did she not depend upon Him first instead of later?

She watched them stride back to the hayracks and horses, anxious to be about their work. "Thank you, Lord, for taking good care of my Haakan. And all of us. Now please protect them all."

Chapter 20

Chicago, Illinois

Miriam counted her few remaining coins. Yes, she had to use some for the trolley. She wouldn't have time tomorrow to walk clear home and back. But she had to see her family to say good-bye.

Just the thought brought a monstrous lump to her throat. A year. It would be a year before she could return to Chicago. A year stretched to eternity. Her common sense chided her. *It is only a year. Other people are gone from their families for years on end. You can write letters, and you know the mail comes to Blessing, not just from it.*

Common sense was not a comfort, not by any means.

Right after breakfast the next morning, she tucked the extra bread, cheese, roast chicken, and a jar of soup into her bag. Cook was so generous to send food like this to her family. If only she were bringing better news too. She'd waited, hoping

Mrs. Korsheski would have found ways to help like she said she would, but there had been no mention of anything so far.

Their train tickets were for Friday afternoon and it was already Sunday.

A knock at her door raised her hopes, but they were dashed again when it was Corabell standing there, wringing her hands, sniffing back tears.

Miriam put on a welcoming face. "Come in." She stepped back. "How can I help you?" She wanted to scream, "*What are you bawling about now, for heaven's sake?*" But she refrained. That would bring on a crying jag that would flood the room.

"I *c-can't* go to Blessing, Miriam. I just can't." The *can't* came out on a wail.

Miriam guided her to the edge of the bed and sat her down. "Of course you can. No one ever died of homesickness. And look, you've not even left Chicago yet. Go see your family today and enjoy yourself." She didn't mention saying good-bye.

Corabell nodded, sniffed, mopped, and heaved a sigh. "Thank you. You are so good to me. I know I am a ninny; after all, this is the chance of a lifetime."

"Right." She was glad to see that this young nurse had indeed been listening to her counsel in former bouts like this. "Corabell, I hate to rush you, but I need to catch the trolley. I will see you this evening at supper."

"Oh, I am so sorry. I'm taking up precious time with your family." She rose to her feet. At least no more tears flowed. Smiling even though her lips quivered, she thanked Miriam again and left.

Miriam sagged against the closed door. What a worrier that woman was. How she ever had the courage to enroll in nursing school was beyond what she could imagine. Yet she was a good nurse in her caring for patients. For some reason ill women found comfort in Corabell, and she often could be found at the bedside of a patient. Especially those in extremis or comatose. Why could she be so compassionate in helping patients and yet such a soggy mess of tears when it came to leaving Chicago? Quickly, before she had any more interruptions, Miriam pinned her hat on her nest of hair and, basket on arm, headed for the outside door. The trolley would not wait.

But once she hopped on, it sure was slow. Or perhaps she was too impatient. That thought almost made her smile. Her? Impatient? She smiled at the dowager sitting across from her, but all she received in return was a slight nodding of the head. A dip, you might call it.

When the trolley finally reached her stop, she stepped down and, ignoring strictures to be more ladylike, walk-trotted the three blocks to the tenement where they lived. By the time she stepped onto the fourth floor, she needed to stop and catch her breath. But the need to see her family was greater, so she strode down the hall, ignoring the smells of filth, despair, and stale booze. She knocked the three, pause, one signal and waited for someone to unlock the door.

Her sister, Mercy, the one closest to her in age, threw wide the door and, along with the others, piled around Miriam as she hugged each one.

"I was beginning to think you were never coming." Eight-year-old Truth, whose dark hair hung in one long braid, hugged her again.

"I've come every time I said I would." She kissed her finger and tapped it on the girl's turned-up nose.

"No, one time you had a 'mergency and couldn't come." Her eyes darkened reproachfully.

"Oh, that's right." Truth never forgot anything. She hugged her little sister once more and asked, "Where is Tonio?"

"He got a job for two whole weeks." Joy, the quiet one, loved school but gave it up to stay with their mother. So the others taught her whatever they could when they were home. Miriam brought her books from the hospital library to read whenever she could.

"And maybe longer." Este, at fourteen, worked as many places as he could and, when not working, picked up coal along the train tracks for them to heat with in the winter. He brought wood when he could scavenge that too. He helped with the sewing business by picking up and delivering orders.

She lowered her voice. "How is Mama?"

"Waiting for you. She said if she was sleeping, you were to wake her." Mercy picked up the basket Miriam had set on the floor. "Thank you. Anything will be a treat after a rather steady diet of porridge. Este found some potatoes and carrots in the dump at the market that were so good. He is a master at finding things we might use. Mama was talking about the gardens they grew in England. Wouldn't a garden be a wondrous thing?"

Miriam dug in her bag and pulled out her remaining coins. She would walk back to the hospital. Handing them to Mercy, she whispered, "I just wish it were more." Should she tell them about Mrs. Korsheski's possibly sending work their way? *Holy Father, let it be so*. She caught herself. Such a habit and yet so futile.

The others followed her as she opened the door to their mother's room, where the figure in the bed barely raised the covers.

Her eyes fluttered open and she extended a thin hand. "Oh, you have come. You have finally come."

Miriam sank down on the edge of the bed, and the others found places to sit, both Joy and Truth perching at the foot. The heat in the room nearly captured her breath. Summer in Chicago could be punishing. Heat in the summer, bone-freezing wind and cold in the winter. She kissed the back of her mother's hand. If only there were something more that could be done for her. Possibly another visit to the hospital. Last time it had helped build her strength.

"When will you be on your way to North Dakota?"

"We leave Friday afternoon." Her fingers on her mother's wrist told of an ever weakening heart. "Mercy said you were talking about your gardens in the old country. I heard that the ground is so fertile where I am going that whatever you put in the ground comes up tenfold. They plant cottonwood trees by just sticking a green branch in the ground and watering it."

"Ah, the gardens we used to have in England. Oh yes. When you get to Dakota, go walking among the fields and gardens for me, please. What do they grow?"

"I don't know. I hear the winters are much colder than in England or here in Chicago, and with lots of snow."

"Ah, the goat cheese I used to make." Her smile made her whole face brighten. "We had a herd of goats, so we had plenty of milk, and—" But a cough cut her off. When she could breathe again, she asked, "How is your school going?"

"Very well." She went on to describe the two nurses who would be going with her. "If Corabell can get over her fears of being so far away from home. And Vera? All she dreams of is a husband. But they are both good nurses."

"What if you meet the man of your dreams out there?" Mercy poked her sister on a shoulder blade. "You could, you know."

"Don't you fear. I will be back. Mrs. Korsheski has promised me a position at the hospital in the surgical ward if I prove my skills well in that area. She feels we will come back with far more experience than we would gain here." She watched her mother's eyes close in spite of her efforts to stay awake. Turning, she caught Mercy's nod. "All the time?"

"No, but today is worse. She was so excited you were coming that I think it wore her out." She motioned to the door, and they all filed into the other room.

"So tell me what has been happening."

"With Mother or . . . ?" Mercy picked up a pillowcase she was embroidering.

"With everything."

For the next two hours, her siblings shared what had been happening and asked Miriam questions about life at the hospital. When the shadows lengthened across the room, she went in to say good-bye to her mother. "You will write to me, won't you?" she pleaded, the ache in her heart almost unbearable.

"I will. I just hope you can read it."

"Oh, I will read it. Mother, I am going to ask Mrs. Korsheski if they will admit you to the hospital again to see if there is anything more they can do. Are you eating?"

"Yes, some." She clung to her daughter's hand. "I know the others save out the best bits for me, and that is unfair. They all work so hard, they need every bit of food we can find."

"Cook sent some soup for you. She said to be of good courage and asked if there is any way you can get out in the sun, at least for a bit every day. You do sit in front of the window in the morning, don't you?"

Her mother nodded. "When I can." She smiled with her eyes more than her mouth. "You go with God, and I pray He will bring you back to us."

"He will." *If not God, I will make sure I come back.* He'd not answered any of her prayers for so long she had pretty much given up on the love He said He had for them. Or at least the priest had said. That thought brought up another. "Has a priest been here to visit you?"

"Not since Father Mulganey grew too old to serve. The

younger priests don't seem to take care of their flock the way he did."

Not surprising, Miriam thought. *You no longer have anything to put in the offering box*. But if God was serious about taking care of the poor and the widows, why had He not sent help?

"It is not our place to question the almighty God. I will pray for you, my Miriam, not that I have ever quit. That He will keep you safe and bring you home again."

"Well, in the meantime, I will ask Mrs. Korsheski if you can be admitted again." She leaned over and kissed her mother's pale cheek. "You eat that soup and you will feel better." *For that is all I have to offer you*. She shook her head. No, she couldn't go. She could not leave her family like this. She would tell Mrs. Korsheski in the morning.

Her mother clasped her hand. "Listen to me." Her voice took on a semblance of authority. "You will not cancel your plans to stay here for us. God has provided for us so far. We have a roof over our heads, and we have not starved to death. You will go."

Miriam nodded, anything to pacify the agitated woman in the bed. "I have to leave now. I will write." She kissed her mother's hand again. "Thank you for praying." Knowing what she'd just said bordered on a lie, she left the room, hugged her sisters and brothers too, since Tonio had come home, and started out the door.

"I will walk partway with you." Tonio stood from his place by the window, where an evening breeze was blowing off the lake and breathing coolness into the room.

"You needn't do that." She wanted to lie and tell him she was taking the trolley, but . . . "Only to the trolley, then."

"You have the nickel for that?"

"She gave all her money to me." Mercy ducked when she caught Miriam's glare.

"Give the nickel back to her. She will take the trolley." Tonio cocked an eyebrow at his older sister. "I will be paid this week. The trolley is safer for a woman alone on the streets in the evening."

Miriam tried to not accept it, but when Tonio took the coin from Mercy and laid it in her palm, she gave up. She hugged everyone again and followed Tonio out the door and down the stairs. He swung her basket as they walked, after tucking her hand around his crooked elbow.

"Uh, I have a question. When did you become this man I see?"

"Over the last months. I could no longer be a boy. My family needs me too desperately. Men are more likely to be hired than a boy."

"I see." But she didn't. "Do you think this job might last longer?"

He nodded. "I work harder than two of the others put together. The foreman has noticed."

"What are you doing?"

"Loading railroad cars."

The trolley was only half a block away when they reached the stop. She took her basket back after hugging him tight. "Please take care of yourself so you can take care of the others." He nodded. "And write to me. I need to see home through your eyes."

"I cannot promise that, but I will try."

She stepped up and dropped her nickel in the coin box. She should have walked instead.

"I saved you a plate," Cook said when Miriam arrived in the dining room after all the others had left. "How is your mother?"

"More frail all the time, if that is possible. But she said she has good days and bad days, and today happened to be a bad one."

"And you believed her?"

"The others said the same."

"I'll be right back." When Cook returned, she handed her a warm plate of mashed potatoes, gravy, roasted chicken, and a mixture of canned vegetables. "We have gingerbread for dessert. You can have it with applesauce or hard sauce."

"I'll take the hard sauce. I'm not sure I've ever had that." Miriam picked up her plate and set it on a white-clothed table, then retrieved her utensils and the square of gingerbread. "Thank you. I feel guilty for eating so wonderfully when my family is getting by on so little."

"That's life, all right. Now, you enjoy your supper and leave the worrying to God. He's much better at it than we are."

There it was. God again. Should she tell Cook of her new certainty? That God was sitting up in His heaven and maybe shaking His head over what was going on down on earth but not lifting a finger? She knew what she had to do. Go tell Mrs. Korsheski that she absolutely refused to go. No, that wasn't the best way. But her family could not survive without her help. If she had to, she'd go to Mrs. Shaunnessy, head of the nursing school, and explain the situation.

But what if they do not allow you to stay in school if you don't accept their plan? Kick you right out for insubordination? Then what will you do? Would the voice of torment never cease?

CHAPTER 21

BLESSING, NORTH DAKOTA

"What are we going to do for housing for our nurses? They arrive Sunday!" Astrid paced the floor of her living room. "They need to be near the hospital."

"And there definitely is no room at the boardinghouse?" Daniel asked.

"No. Sophie says not. She's sorry, but the new addition isn't open yet, and that is where we planned for them to stay."

"We tried, Astrid, we really did. Give us two more weeks." Thorliff shrugged and shook his head. "If the materials had all been delivered like promised, we'd have made it. We'll get those three rooms or that one big one ready by then. They are putting up the interior walls now. Then it is plaster and paint, and then Sophie can move the furniture in. Might be sooner than two weeks, if all goes well."

"Thank you. They can't stay at Mor's. It's too far to walk in for the night shift. We could house them in the one ward at the hospital temporarily, but if something happens and we need those beds . . ."

Mrs. Jeffers chimed in. "Cannot two of them, at least, stay here?"

"I thought of that," Astrid said, "but that would be a lot of extra work for you."

Mrs. Jeffers shook her head. "It won't be forever, you know."

"The other could stay at our house," Thorliff added. "It's a shame the deaf school is also too far out of town for people who work the night shift. I take it they will take turns on the shifts."

"Yes. That's part of their training." Astrid went to stand at the window, looking out but seeing nothing. Why did everything have to be a problem? She'd much rather be concerned with sick people than housing for the nurses and all the others coming to town.

"What about the two Indian women Red Hawk is sending up?"

"We have more than a month until they get here, and Kaaren said they could stay out there."

Astrid spun around. "That's it for now, then. By the way, you better ask Thelma and Elizabeth if a student boarder is a good idea. I'll be at the hospital if you need me." She kissed Daniel on the cheek, picked up her black bag, and headed out the door. By the time she reached the hospital, sweat was already trickling down her back, and she had to mop her face and neck. Good haying and garden growing weather, good for the wheat too, but fans were needed for humans.

Today Elizabeth had their office open, but it sure would be good when they could move that out here. Plans for the next wing were already dreamed and drawn. As she walked by the larger of the two wards, her mind switched gears. What if they were to put movable walls in that long room so that, until it was needed for more patients, they could use the space for examining rooms and an office? The same could apply for housing for the students. They would be cubicles more than rooms, but they ate in the dining room and there was a bathroom. She smiled to herself. Indoor plumbing was a boon beyond measure. She'd have to talk with Thorliff and Daniel. How difficult would that be?

Pausing in the hallway outside Manny's room, she heard her mother's voice.

"You're doing well."

"Ain't neither. I hate these sticks."

"Would you rather stay in bed?"

"No. I'd rather walk." Manny came clumping to the door and saw Astrid. "How long?" He nodded to his crutches. Astrid walked beside him as he swung out and maneuvered clumsily down the hall.

"You had a terrible bad break. The surgical wound is healing well, but when bones are separated like that, they take longer to heal. And if you rush it, you might make it worse and be flat back in traction."

"Might?" They turned at the outside door and made their way back.

"Look, Manny, you are lucky or, as my mother would say, blessed to have a right leg at all. Most doctors would have taken the leg off and been done with it." She could feel him staring at her.

"Why din't you?" His voice lost the belligerent tone.

"Because even though that leg will be shorter than the other, if we have no complications, you should be able to walk again. And ride a horse. I believe a good boot maker could help that by putting an inch- or two-inch thick sole on the right boot."

"I—I din't know." His voice cracked.

"Or you could have died from gangrene. That is why we are

being so careful to avoid infection." Might as well lay it all out. "The traction helped keep the bones straight. When you are in bed, we will put a mild traction on it again, just to be safe."

Manny entered his room and turned, his back to the bed. He hoisted himself backward onto the bed, using only his arms. Good. He pretty much had his upper body strength back. He would need it.

Astrid smiled at her mother, who sat knitting away.

"It will sure be good when those trees outside grow tall enough to give some shade." Ingeborg nodded to the window. She had been the one who'd insisted they plant the trees last fall, and as usual she had been right. The cottonwood trees outstripped any other tree in rapid growth, but the maples would be useful too in a few years.

"That it will. Manny is walking better all the time. We'll put some fleece on the handgrips and the underarm part. Padding should help. But for now and tomorrow, back in traction. I sure wish we had one of those new x-ray machines that can make the bones visible. Another one of those 'someday' things."

Ingeborg nodded. "Manny, your room is ready at my house as soon as you are released. The big problem is going to be the four steps up to the porches. As you get stronger, you'll make it fine, but for now I suspect we'll need to get you some help."

They all three looked up as a voice came from the window, "Grandma, we came to see you."

"You and who else? And what are you standing on?"

"Benny's wheels. He's here too. Can Manny come to the window? We want to meet him."

"Who is she?" Manny asked Astrid.

"My niece Inga. I told her she can't come in here to see you and bring germs."

"Uff da!" The little girl's head disappeared.

"She's a girl. Who is Benny?"

"You can walk over there." She handed him his crutches and helped him off the bed.

"Do I have to?"

"It would be polite."

The head appeared again. "Sorry. I slipped."

"Don't go pushing." A boy's voice came from below.

"I won't. Are you coming to see us, Manny?"

"I guess." He did better getting balanced this time and sticked over to the window.

"Hi. I'm Inga and this is my friend Benny. He lives at the soda shop. I live at the doctor's house." She pointed over her shoulder. The cart shifted and she grabbed the windowsill. "Whew, that was close."

"You got crutches, Manny. You are so lucky." Benny grinned up.

"What happened to your legs?" Manny's eyes grew round.

"My Doc had to cut them off 'cause a big dray wagon ran over me and mashed 'em up."

Astrid watched from over Manny's shoulder. Benny's grin had to be the most contagious anywhere.

"Who you talkin' about?"

"My Doc? Why, she is standing right there. Hi, Doc." He gave her a whole-arm wave. Benny lived in superlatives.

"So when do you get to go to Grandma's? She makes the best cookies anywhere. I help her make gingerbread men, with raisins." Inga cocked her head. "How come you talk so funny?"

Manny's eyebrows flattened. "I don't talk funny, but you sure do."

Uh-oh, Astrid thought. *Here we go.*

Inga's eyes narrowed, but when she went to plant her hands on her hips, she fell backward off the cart and sat down with an *oomph*. "Now see what you did!"

"I din't do nothin'."

Benny grinned at his friend. "You want me to help you up?"

She batted away his hand and stood, then dusted off the back of her skirt. "Now Ma will be after me again. She says I get dirty on purpose. But this was an accident. Right, Tante Astrid?"

Manny turned to look at Astrid. "Tante?"

"That means *aunt*. She is using some Norwegian words." At his confused look, Astrid added, "Many people here in Blessing, Mrs. Bjorklund included"—she nodded over her shoulder to Ingeborg, who was carefully knitting her stitches off the needles—"came from Norway and spoke Norwegian before they learned English. Some of us grew up here and learned to talk in Norwegian also." *Should I tell him about the deaf school or will that add more confusion to the conversation?*

Inga sat down on Benny's cart with him. "We will come to see you when you get to Grandma's. Do you know how to play checkers?"

Manny nodded. "I used to play with Papaw."

"Papaw?"

"My ma's father."

"Oh, good. Benny taught some of us to play checkers. We play rock, scissor, paper too. And we read books from the school library."

Astrid interrupted their conversation. "I think Manny needs to get back to bed so I can put the traction back on before I leave."

"Okay." Inga and Benny waved. "Maybe tomorrow Grandma will bring you a gingerbread man."

"And maybe not," Ingeborg said softly. "I have beans to can."

"You should have brought them and had Manny help snap them."

Manny shot her a disgusted look, and he sticked back to bed. This time when he lay down, he exhaled a sigh of relief.

"Hurting?"

"Some."

Astrid unwrapped the traction cord. "Manny, you have to be honest with me—no trying to be a man and tough it out. I can help you best when you tell me the truth. Now, is the pain okay or is it getting worse?" She waited, watching the emotions chase across his face.

"Bad and getting worse. Started out only a bit, like when the dog scratches you. Now it's like the dog bit you."

Astrid smiled at his description. "Thank you. That helps me. I'll have the nurse bring something, along with water. You need to drink a lot."

"But then I'll have to—"

"I know, but you've been doing fine." She looked to her mother, who held up the stocking cap. "I like that blue stripe. Try the hat on Manny. See how it fits."

Manny looked rather doubtful but pulled the hat down over his ears. His eyes widened. "That's warm." He took it off and handed it back to Ingeborg. "That really is for me?"

"Ja, and it looks good on you. I'll keep it safe until winter."

"What if I'm not here for winter?"

Ingeborg put the hat away and brought the lotion out of her bag. She spread it on her hands and started gently working on his bad leg. "Why, I'll send it with you. It's yours. Just you don't go running off in the middle of the night or some such." She stopped her stroking and stared at him. "Promise me?"

"Well, uh . . . you would let me go?"

"If you can walk and you know where you are going, yes. We would send a pack with you with food and your things in it. You are not a prisoner here, Manny, but we do hope you will be so happy here you want to stay." She paused. "Oh, and Haakan said to tell you that your horse is waiting for you out in our pasture."

"Why you are doin' all this makes no more sense'n a dog chasin' his tail. Dumb dog never catches it."

"Sense or not, that's just the way it is here. And besides, that dumb dog is having a good time, and that's important too."

The next afternoon Trygve arrived with a wagon, a pallet of quilts in back, and Ingeborg perched beside him on the seat. He helped her down and together they went inside the hospital.

When they stepped into Manny's room, he was sitting on the bed, all dressed in the shirt and pants Kaaren had dug out of the box of clothing she kept at the deaf school. The right leg of the pants had been slit open up past the knee, so they were easy to put on. His boots were in a pack on the chair, and he was wearing moccasins that Metiz had made years earlier. Ingeborg had always known that someone was going to need them sometime.

"Well, look at you." Ingeborg smiled. "Why, Manny, you clean up real good."

He fingered his shirt. "I never had no clothes fine as these." He looked up at her. "Why?" His head wagged from side to side, as if of its own accord. "Makes no sense. And someone done patched my shirt and pants so I got two of each." More doubtful wags.

"Why not, Manny? You needed help and here you will receive it."

"I know. 'That's the way you do things here.'" He parodied her, not unkindly. "But it don't make no sense."

"One of these days you and I will have a real talk about why we do these things. For now, I want you to meet another nephew of mine: Trygve Knutson. He has come to help you out to the wagon and will help you up the stairs into my house."

Manny nodded and mumbled, "Pleasedtameetcha."

"Glad to be able to help," Trygve said. "Are you ready?"

"He is," Dr. Elizabeth said from the doorway. "I have some medicine and dressings to send with you." She held out a packet. "Thanks, Trygve, for taking time off the haying."

"Feels kind of good, actually. No hayseed down the back here. Besides, we're about done. You ever done any haying, Manny?" When the boy shook his head, he half shrugged. "We get the grass mowed and dried and haul the hay to the barns and haystacks close by to feed our cattle during the winter."

Manny looked from Ingeborg to Trygve and back to Ingeborg. "Winter's that bad?"

"Oh yes. We can have snowdrifts clear to the roofs of the barns. You wait and see. Winter here is different from where you grew up. Sometime I hope you'll tell us more about Kentucky. None of us have ever been there."

Shutters snapped shut over Manny's face, and he stared down at his hands. When Ingeborg handed him his crutches, he swung his legs over the edge of the bed and, once his good foot was on the floor, put the now-padded sticks, as he called them, under his arms and rose to his feet.

"Thankee," he said to Dr. Elizabeth and Nurse MacCallister.

"You are welcome."

"I will pay you somehow, someday."

"No rush. But thank you for offering. I'll see you one day soon."

With Ingeborg and Trygve pacing beside him, he made it to the door without stopping. When Trygve held open the door, he went through and paused, inhaling the fragrances of the summer day. "Aah." He shut his eyes and breathed deep again.

Trygve put his bag in the back and waited for him beside the wagon.

Ingeborg watched the boy, rejoicing in his appreciation of the beauty around them. He had been so sorry and withdrawn. Perhaps he was at last emerging from that shell.

The sun drew the smell of green grass, dry dirt road, flowers, and trees out from the source so that the breeze could waft around them, to be appreciated by those who took time to savor the summer day. The dog sitting in the wagon bed was one of the appreciators. With one ear flopped and the other cocked, he thumped his tail and, standing at the downed tailgate, wagged some more. His tail beat a tattoo against the sideboard.

Manny's gaze zeroed in on the scraggly gray dog, and a smile widened his face. He turned to Ingeborg. "Your dog?"

"Well, yes. One of our farm dogs. A stray, he just showed up one day. He herds the cattle, announces company, and whatever else he is needed to do. You had a dog?"

Manny nodded as he sticked to the dog and held out a hand, which Patches gave a cursory sniff, three licks, and a wagging whine. "Good boy." He sat down and twisted enough so that Trygve could help him swing his legs up. Patches immediately settled in next to Manny.

"Do you want to lie down?"

"Can't I sit here?"

"Sure. Here, I'll pad the wagon side and you can lean against that." Trygve folded up a blanket and did the fixing, then slammed the tailgate shut. After helping Ingeborg up, he climbed up into the box, and within moments they were driving down the street toward the boardinghouse.

Ingeborg identified all the buildings as they passed them. The boardinghouse on the left, businesses up ahead, the houses they passed after they turned onto the street that became the road to the Bjorklund and Knutson farms. "That's Dr. Elizabeth's house on the right, along with the newspaper office. Dr. Astrid's is across that field. We have a lot of building going on here in Blessing."

When they turned into the Bjorklund lane, Patches leaped up and out over the tailgate to run yipping beside the wagon.

"You can see the hay wagons out in the field and the haystacks they are building beside the barn. That means the haymow is full," Trygve explained. "Soon, you'll know this land like the back of your hand. That's the Red River ahead of us to the east. It flows near the hospital too. You probably smelled it at times." He turned in the seat. "You know how to milk a cow?"

Manny nodded.

"You like fishing?"

"We used to fish a lot."

When the wagon stopped by the house, Manny stared. Once out of the wagon, he sticked his way to the porch steps.

Ingeborg smiled at the awe on his face. "My husband Haakan is waiting for you on the porch. You can see him there. He has been ill or he would be out in the fields with the others."

"You ready?" Trygve asked.

Manny nodded. Trygve scooped an arm around his waist and hoisted him up the steps.

Ingeborg readily recognized the white band around the boy's mouth and the sweat on his forehead. They should have given him the pain medicine before they left the hospital. Right now he looked about to faint.

"Let's get him down on the settee so he can lie down if he needs to."

Trygve picked Manny up again, this time not setting him down until they reached the settee. "Can you manage the rest?"

"Umm." The boy's jaw was clenched to fight off the pain. He

turned and Trygve lowered him to the seat. Manny collapsed against the cushions on the back with a groan. He tried to lift his legs, but Trygve helped him swing them up on the seat, then helped him scoot to a cushioned arm.

"Pain's bad?" he whispered.

Manny nodded, his eyes already closed. His shallow breathing and now white face told Ingeborg more than if he'd said words.

She brought morphine with a glass of water. When he'd downed them both, she laid a wet cloth on his forehead and another behind his neck. His pulse was strong and his breathing had returned to normal. "You sleep as long as you need, and when you wake up, I'll get you something more to drink and to eat. You are home, Manny." She stroked the hair back from his forehead. "You are home."

Please, dear God, bring healing to this boy's leg but even more to his soul and spirit. Please help him to learn what love is, and why we do what we do.

CHAPTER 22

CHICAGO, ILLINOIS

You have ducked this ever since Monday and it's already Wednesday, so get yourself in there to talk to Mrs. Korsheski."

Miriam glared at the face in the mirror. "You will go do this now!" She closed her eyes, sucked in a deep breath, and grabbed her apron from the hook on the wall. Then she pinned her starched cap in place, thought to try to tame her wild mane, but gave up on that idea and headed for the door. Stomped her way might be a better description. She inhaled deep and exhaled, then reached for the doorknob.

A knock on the door made her jump back, her hand flat on her chest. "Y-yes?"

"Message for you from Mrs. Korsheski."

Puffing out another breath, Miriam reached for the doorknob, and this time opened it. Expecting a note, the young woman announced, "Mrs. Korsheski wants to see you in her office immediately."

Land sakes, what have I done now? "Of course. I am on my way." She shut the door behind her, all thoughts of her own demand left behind as she fretted over *What now?* all the way down the two staircases to the main floor. Outside the closed door she sucked in another breath, along with what she hoped was the courage to accept whatever she was to hear. She knocked.

"Come in." Mrs. Korsheski looked up with a smile. "Oh good, Miriam. I'm glad you could come so quickly." She pointed at the chair in front of the desk. "Sit down, please."

Miriam took a deep breath and remained standing. "Ma'am. Mrs. Korsheski . . . I, uh . . ." One more deep breath. "I am convinced that I cannot go to North Dakota after all. I would love to travel there. I've always wanted to, but I'm needed more here. I have family responsibilities thrust upon me, and until Truth is older . . . I mean . . . No. I simply cannot do it." She sat down, totally deflated. "I'm sorry. I know you were counting on me, but no. I'm sorry." And she added another no just for good measure.

Mrs. Korsheski's smile had faded, but she did not seem angry. "Your family depends upon you for your income, right?"

"Yes, ma'am. Also, Joy is ten and already dropped out of school. I am hoping eventually to help her to go back. Truth is eight and I want to save her from having to abandon her education like her sister did, and . . . well, you see how it is." Miriam perched on the edge of the chair, her hands woven together in her lap. And waited.

"Yes, I see." Mrs. Korsheski still did not look angry. Perhaps Miriam would be able to stay on here even though she had disobeyed their wishes.

"Also, there's my mother. She is becoming increasingly frail and needs medical attention now. My nursing experience could mean the difference between her living and dying."

Mrs. Korsheski nodded slowly. Quietly, deliberately, she signed another paper on her desk and set the pen back in the inkwell. She gathered her papers and danced them on end to straighten them, then laid them aside. "We chose you carefully. I'm disappointed that you feel you cannot do this."

"I am disappointed as well. I truly am. I recognize that it's a wonderful opportunity and I would love to, but . . ." She shrugged mightily. Well, the woman had just said she had disappointed them. She was as good as out the door now.

"And this is your final decision?"

Miriam meant to say, "Yes, ma'am," out loud, but it ended up a whisper. Miriam had just sealed her fate. How did she feel? Terrified. That was how. What would happen to them all now?

Mrs. Korsheski clasped her hands on the now cleared wooden desktop. "This took longer to put together than I had hoped, but I want to inform you of some decisions." She leaned forward. "First, we want to admit your mother for observation to see if we have something new that might help. Her heart insufficiency is the root of the problem, as you well know. We may be able to ameliorate that."

Miriam's heart leaped. "Oh, I'm so grateful. She is declining."

"Good. Now, we have a position in housekeeping that Mercy—she is fifteen now, right?—will fill nicely. If Tonio is willing to learn about furnaces and plumbing and all the myriad things that can break down in a building like this, our maintenance man, Mr. Ruger, would appreciate an assistant. You know Mr. Ruger. This old building is getting to be far too much for one man to handle, and he is not young anymore."

Miriam's eyes were getting hot. She'd break down in tears if she wasn't careful.

"While I too believe that Joy should return to school, someone has to be there when we send your mother home again. Unless we can get her functioning independently, of course. Now, as for Este."

Even Este? Undersized fourteen-year-old Este!

"If Este would be willing to work in both the kitchen part time, doing whatever Cook tells him to do, and with the gardener part time, we can have full-time work for him too." She paused, studying Miriam closely.

"I-I cannot believe this."

"One of the responsibilities of the housekeeping department is mending. Perhaps Mercy can work here part of the day and take the mending home to be with your mother so that Joy can return to school. We'll have to work on that."

"You've thought of everything!"

"The one thing I'd like to do most, and only God can do that, is to restore your mother's health. I admire her. She raised six fine young people, people willing to work, people who put responsibility for others ahead of themselves. I'm not talking about just you but about all your mother's children. We will do what we can. Perhaps not being so concerned about a place to live and food to eat will make it easier for her too."

What could she say? Miriam stuttered, started a word, quit, groped for another. She leaped to her feet because Mrs. Korsheski stood up.

"I'm sure you realize your protests about being unable to go to Dakota have fallen on deaf ears. You will go. Do you know what I am hoping?"

"No, ma'am. What?"

"That Mercy might decide she wants to be a nurse as well. She is a talented and caring young woman from what little I've seen of her. Much like you."

"Have you told my family all this yet?"

"No. I wanted to tell you first. I'm of a mind that we will send you out tomorrow with the hospital's carriage. That way both you and your mother will have a way to get back here. I suspect you would like to get her settled in before you leave. And with the others working here, they can visit her more easily."

Miriam tried to hold back the tears, but the stubborn things trickled down her cheeks nevertheless. She dug around in her pocket for a handkerchief but came up empty-handed. Mrs. Korsheski pulled a square of muslin from her drawer and handed it across the desk. "Crying is not a mortal sin, you know."

Sniff. "I know, but it is a sign of weakness." Sniff and blow.

"Or great feelings. I choose to believe the latter. Plan to leave here about ten tomorrow morning, after morning rounds, and you should be able to be back by dinner. Oh, and bring Este and your sisters. You said Tonio has a job right now?"

Miriam nodded.

"Tell him to come see me when he is let go. And should miracles happen and he finds a solid job, then I believe we will ask Este to train with Mr. Ruger."

"Este does have a knack for fixing things." *And scavenging food for his family.* "Our mother often mentions the gardens when she and Da were first married. I think Este would really like to work in the garden too."

"I will keep that in mind." Mrs. Korsheski penciled in a note, nodded, and kept on nodding as she wore a contemplative look. Then she slapped her hands on the desk. "Now you must get on with your duties. And you need to pack for the trip."

While Vera and Corabell each had a steamer trunk, Miriam did not have such a thing—not even a small trunk. She could pack nearly all she owned in one suitcase. Two dresses, a gored serge skirt in dark gray wool, two waists, and her nurse's aprons.

Her schoolbooks would go in a separate box. She could pack her winter undergarments in another box and ask to have it sent to her later.

That afternoon she flew about her duties, stopped briefly for supper, tucked the children in, and packed her things in half an hour. Tomorrow she was bringing her mother to the hospital! What joy, what relief. And what if they could indeed help her, at least to improve her lot?

Miriam retired that night so full of gratitude she floated above the bed, sure she would never sleep a wink.

Even though Dr. Gutenheimer was abrupt with the nurses during rounds in the morning when he discovered a mistake that was made, this time she did not let that bother her. While she knew who had made the error, she understood he was trying to make clear to all of them the seriousness of the infraction.

"You must check and recheck the medications that are ordered and do the treatments just as I say. Falling asleep on the night shift is cause for dismissal in most hospitals—immediate dismissal—for there are no excuses. Should this happen again the entire class will be on probation. Do you understand?"

They all answered as one voice. "Yes, Doctor."

Our last day. For a whole year. At the end of their term in Blessing, they would have one month back at the hospital before their final examination and graduation. It seemed incomprehensible.

Poor Corabell had a bad case of the mopes that day. While she did her nursing duties as well as ever, tears had dripped during breakfast. Several classmates commented that if Corabell did not want to go, they would be glad to take her place.

The class had started out with twenty, but some had dropped

out for various reasons. Often the hard work was the real reason. So now there were twelve left and three of them going off to spend a year at the hospital in Blessing. Two of the third-year group were planning on going to the mission field, two were interning at hospitals outside the city, and the others would spend time at various clinics in the city, most of which were there to bring medical help to the poor, of which there were many in Chicago and the surrounding area.

Miriam waited by the front door for the driver with the carriage. She smiled when Mrs. Korsheski stepped up beside her.

"I decided to go with you, if that is all right."

"Of course. I can get my mother ready while you tell the others what you have in mind." *Telling your supervisor what to do, are you? Please, Miriam, do not be so bossy.* She flinched at the instructions that flew through her mind. "Please pardon me for my effrontery."

"No. That is one of the many things I like about you. You are forthright and well organized. You see how things should be done, and you are not afraid to step out and do them."

"I . . . uh . . . uh . . ." Miriam blinked, trying to accept what Mrs. Korsheski had said. For a woman who was usually so chary with her commendations to lay out a list of good attributes was almost beyond believing. "Thank you," she croaked around the blockage in her throat.

"That is one of the major reasons I want you to go to Blessing. You will be a real help for the doctors Bjorklund, and I am sure you will help in the training of the two Indian women who will be joining as students in September. Astrid, Elizabeth, and Ingeborg trained two Indian women last year to assist Dr. Red Hawk. Do you remember him?"

"Of course. He was so looking forward to returning to help his people." She had a memory of the young doctor encouraging a child to try harder. "This hospital has a wide circle of influence, doesn't it? I didn't realize how much was happening."

The lovely black landau pulled in close to the curb.

"Ready, Nurses?" The driver hopped down and held open the door for them. What luxury!

The driver helped them down and glared at a couple of little boys who were edging too close to the horses, one of which stamped a front hoof and snorted. "Stay back a'fore you get hurt."

They drew considerable attention when the carriage entered the tenements. People stopped on the trash-strewn sidewalks to look, and children chased them down the street. Embarrassment crept heat up Miriam's neck as they mounted the four flights of stairs. She was used to the stench, the filth, but having Mrs. Korsheski with her heightened her awareness of the squalor. If only she could get her family out of there. That was one reason she had gone into nurses' training—to make enough money to move her family to someplace better. She rapped the signal on the door and heard someone approaching.

"Who is it?" Joy's voice.

"Miriam, along with Mrs. Korsheski." The door flew open, and Joy threw her arms around her sister.

"You are back so soon!" She raised her voice. "Ma, Miriam is here!" Then she eased backward so they could enter. At least the flat was in order and clean as always, such a reprieve from the hallway.

"Mother wants to know if you are all right." Mercy came through the bedroom door. "Oh, we have company." In her fluster, she failed to greet Mrs. Korsheski.

"Hello, Mercy. I decided to come because we have some good news for all of you." Mrs. Korsheski didn't seem to mind any of their confusion.

Miriam led the way into her mother's bedroom. "Is today better?" she whispered to Mercy as she passed by her.

"Yes, much." She leaned over the bed. "Mother, Mrs. Korsheski is here from the hospital with Miriam. Would you like me to help you sit up with pillows?"

"Aye, please." She struggled and scooted as Mercy arranged her pillows. "Oh, Miriam, we get to see you again before you leave." She clasped her daughter's hand. "And welcome to our home, Mrs. Korsheski. I am sorry we have nothing to offer you. We're out of tea, but Mercy planned to get some tomorrow."

"No, thank you. We need nothing. We have good news for you and the children. We want to admit you to the hospital again for observation, to see if there is any way we can help you. There may be some new treatments to try. Are you willing?"

"Oh yes. Aye!" And Miriam's mother, so careful to use American English, slipped into her brogue. "'Twould be . . . aye. Treatments. Do ye really think?"

"We'll see. Miriam, you prepare her. Children, all of you come out here with me." And Mrs. Korsheski left the bedroom.

"Eh, Miriam, I am so flustered, I canna think. I must dress."

"Is your wrapper in the clothespress?"

"Aye."

Miriam studied her a moment. Her mother was paler than ever, her skin cool to the touch, her fingers cold. "Then we will take you like this." She pawed through the clothespress. Everyone's clothing was in this one wardrobe.

"That Mrs. Korsheski, such a lovely lady."

"She is indeed." Miriam pulled out the old threadbare robe and brought it to the bed. "She has jobs for Este and Mercy and even Tonio, if his present work ends. There will be more money coming to you. She saw to it. We have so much to be grateful for."

"Jobs! Eh, Miriam, do you not hear angels singing?"

No, Miriam did not. As she tucked her mother into the wrapper, her despair silenced any angels up there. Her mother had lost so much weight. Thin arms, weak legs. Miriam should definitely not be leaving her. But with all Mrs. Korsheski had arranged, Miriam dare not stay here. She helped her mother to her feet and supported her as they shuffled out into the living room.

Mrs. Korsheski was already explaining to the others all that she had arranged. The surprise and joy on their faces was evident.

"Shall I send the children down for the driver to come get her?" Mrs. Korsheski asked when they were all ready to leave.

"Mercy and I can manage, I think. She is so thin she weighs nothing."

Mrs. Korsheski pointed to Este. "Bring some blankets."

He ran back to the bedroom.

Mercy and Miriam supported their mother so much, they were practically carrying her. They were forced to stop on each landing to regroup, but they got her to the ground floor without any mishaps. The driver lifted her up into the buggy without even a puff of exertion. Este handed up the blankets and they wrapped her up, for in spite of the warm sun, she was shivering.

"Need I go get another blanket?" Mercy asked.

Mother's voice was so weak, and she was back to her careful American English. "No, thank you, Mercy. I will be very comfortable in a moment. I must get my breath is all."

Miriam sat on one side of their mother and Mercy on the other, both of them rubbing her arms and shoulders. Mrs. Korsheski shared the other seat with Este and the two girls, whose eyes were round and smiles stretching their faces.

Miriam almost smiled. Never had any of them ridden through the streets in such splendor. No wonder her family was so excited. Mother laid her head back on the seat and closed her eyes, but at least she had stopped shivering. That feeling of doom pressed in again, the ache of knowing that as of tomorrow afternoon, Miriam would not see any of them again for an entire year.

At the hospital, two of the aides brought out a stretcher, which made Mama's trip inside far easier. Once she was settled in a bed, the two younger girls sat on either side of her bed and rubbed her hands.

"You go to sleep, Mama," cooed Joy. "You can rest well here, and you are not to worry about us. Why, Mrs. Korsheski even gave us money to take the trolley home. Mercy is meeting with her now. Este is talking to the man who takes care of the garden, and then he will talk with the cook. After that we will go home to tell Tonio all the good news. Won't he be happy too?"

"He will. And to think I will see at least some of you every day. What a gift that is. At church on Sunday, you remember to thank our Father for all this He has given us."

"We will."

"But you are not to tell people I am not at home."

"If you want." They had only one neighbor who would even care, but Mama was always very careful ever since Papa had been killed. Life had taken a terrible turn after that.

Miriam hugged them all a bit later as they were ready to leave and she'd changed back into her apron and cap. "You be careful now," she reminded them. "And make sure you write. I will send you my address right away."

"A year is so long," Truth said with a sigh. "Our home is not the same with you gone. And now Mama too. I wish I could go with you. They probably have a school in that town you are going to."

"I'm sure they do, but I do not know where I will be living. The year will go by fast, and then I will be back again. You mark the days on the calendar." She hugged Mercy again and whispered in her ear. "Tell me how Mama is doing. I want to hear all the news."

"I will." She stepped back, tears sliding down her face. "Thank you for getting Mama in here."

"I didn't even get a chance to ask. Mrs. Korsheski is as close to sainthood as anyone I know."

"And you used to complain about her!" A smile danced behind the tears.

"I will like working here." Este hugged her last. "The garden is huge."

Miriam watched them go down the steps and turn up the street to the trolley stop. *"God, if you really care, please watch out for my family."*

The next afternoon, after many good-byes and well-wishes from the staff and a trolley ride to the train station, the three young women boarded the westbound train, Corabell with a kerchief to her eyes, Vera with eyes dancing in delight, and Miriam climbing the steps feeling the load heavier than she could bear. She took the window seat and watched as they pulled out of the station. The hot air blowing in through the partially opened windows bore coal smoke and even tiny cinders. The urge to scrub the window felt nearly irresistible.

Her future was beyond imagination. One year. A year that appeared to stretch forever. She tried to swallow the lump in her throat. They did not need two crybabies in this group. One was bad enough.

What terrors lay ahead?

BLESSING, NORTH DAKOTA

"Trygve, could you please bring a wagon to the station this afternoon to meet our nurses?" Astrid asked after church that Sunday morning.

"Of course. I'll be helping put up the tents for the immigrant workers from New York. Interesting they are all coming in on the same train."

"I know. That surprised me too."

"Are you going to Tante Ingeborg's for dinner?"

Astrid half shrugged. "Mor is so pleased to have all of us back out there, I couldn't say no."

Now that Haakan was feeling so much better, Ingeborg and Haakan had left directly after the service to finish preparing. They used to get together there all the time, but more recently the families had pretty much been having Sunday dinner at their own houses. Astrid seemed to spend half of her life at the hospital.

"The train arrives at three o'clock, right?"

"Ja. I will be there too. And after delivering their luggage to our house and Thorliff's, I will take them on a tour of the hospital."

"Won't they be tired from the journey?"

"It won't take long. We have our first class tomorrow morning."

She glanced down to see Inga shifting from one foot to the other beside her. "What is it, Inga?"

"Pa said I was not to interrupt you, so I didn't, did I?"

"No. I spoke to you first." Astrid rolled her lips together. How could one ignore a girl with Inga's energy shifting beside them?

"Can I—er, *may* I go out to Grandma's house with you? Pa said he had to go put up tents, and I know the other men do too, but I don't want to wait."

"Wait for what?" Elizabeth stopped beside them.

"I better get going so we can all get out there." Trygve grinned at Inga. "See you later, and remember, Manny doesn't talk funny."

"I know. Just different." The disgust leaped from her face.

Elizabeth tried to force a sort of smile, but she didn't succeed. "I think before I go out to Grandma's, I am going to go lie down for a bit."

"You are not feeling well?"

"Not really. Perhaps I have a touch of whatever is going around."

Astrid's smile worked better. "Let us walk with you. I'll stop and pick up my basket, and then Inga and I can walk on out to Mor's."

"I'll ask Thorliff to bring me in the buggy later."

Reverend Solberg joined them. "I'm going to help with the tents for the newcomers too, so we will be out later. I'm glad they set the time at one thirty. With all the hands helping we should have those tents up in an hour or so. Good thing we did the frames earlier."

"I'll tell her. Glad you are all coming too." It felt like forever since they'd all gathered for Sunday dinner at Mor's.

Once they were on their way to the farm, Inga swung Astrid's hand as she hopped along. Inga did nothing in a straight line, so she soon dropped Astrid's hand but kept on chattering. Astrid listened to tales of her and Benny, of their trial by window at the hospital, of how strange Manny talked, of her dog, and the kittens that were now nearly grown.

"I still have Emmy's cat, but I don't think she is going to want to leave her family when Emmy comes home." She paused for a moment. "We are almost to August and then September comes after that, so Emmy will be home soon."

"Good for you on the calendar. Have you asked Grandma if it is all right for Emmy to have another cat at her house? Grandma's cat might not like a rival."

"What's a rival?"

"Someone or something that . . ." Astrid paused, searching for a good definition. "Something that is competing for the same thing another one wants. Like two dogs and one bone. They are rivals for the bone."

"Oh. So if Benny and I want the same gingerbread man, we would be rivals?" She nodded. "That is why it is always good to have two of everything."

"Would that life were like that," Astrid said under her breath.

"Why?"

"So people wouldn't fight so much. That's what starts wars—two countries wanting the same thing—more land usually."

"Oh."

"Do you have rivals?"

"Not that I know of."

"I don't think I do either."

"No, probably not."

Scraggy gray Patches, the new dog at home, came barking down the lane to greet them, jumping up to quickly lick Inga's cheek, running around them, up the lane, back, another quick kiss, and finally slowing to a trot beside Inga, where her hand rested on his head as they walked.

A trestle table was set up under the cottonwood tree in the shade with tablecloths already spread on it and enough plates and cups to keep the breeze from flicking the tablecloths off and dancing them away. Benches and chairs were scattered around, including the wicker furniture from the porch. Haakan was sitting in one chair and Manny on the settee so he could keep his leg up.

Inga ran ahead and threw herself into her grandpa's hug. At his invitation she perched on his knee and breathlessly caught Haakan up on the news.

Astrid greeted both males and set her basket on the table before going on into the house, where Freda and Ingeborg were busy getting ready.

"Do you want to chip ice for the swizzle?" Ingeborg asked after the greeting.

"Of course." Astrid took an ice pick out of the drawer and, after opening the icebox, started stabbing the halfway melted block of ice.

The chatter level rose in the kitchen as others arrived. Carl and Grant ran outside to play with Inga. Ellie gave the baby to Haakan to hold so she could help in the kitchen. Astrid glanced out the window to see her far and Manny talking as if they were old friends.

"Is that some kind of miracle going on out there? The boy talks to you two and no one else?"

"I guess he trusts us."

"I saw how you were with him at the hospital, but Far? He's not usually a big talker either."

"I think he decided that helping that boy get well was something he could do right now. He's felt so useless, but now he has a purpose." Ingeborg put an arm around her daughter's shoulders. "I think we are seeing God at work."

Astrid heaved a sigh. "Did you hear the muttering at church about you and Far taking that heathen bank-robbing boy in?"

"No. Whoever would say something like that? He's a wounded boy who has never had family like we all have. Perhaps we can help him learn how to be a member of a real family."

Astrid smiled. "Finish your sentence."

Ingeborg's eyebrows lifted. "And that is?"

"Why, show him God's love and forgiveness, of course."

"Ja, that too." Her eyes narrowed. "So who is at the root of the muttering?"

"Well, I'd guess Anner Valders. And Hildegunn goes right along with whatever he decrees." Astrid turned from the window. "I used to think she told him what to think and say, but now I know differently."

"How do you know that?"

"His stay in the hospital. He can be a bit of a tyrant. Not bad, but a bit. He is out for vengeance toward those McCrary men. If he had his way, I think he would have them hanged. I wished for a gun when they were holding me hostage, but they never really injured anyone. I know one thing: I was fighting mad more so than frightened."

"Daniel and Thorliff could have shot them with pleasure at that point. It's a good thing God prevented that. I would think that the guilt of knowing you killed someone would be terribly hard to get rid of."

Astrid grimaced. "It's bad enough on the operating table."

"Or the man who died from burns?"

Astrid nodded. "I have to keep putting those things back in God's hands, or I wouldn't be able to keep going." She turned at Inga's bursting through the screen door, Carl hot on her heels. "A calf was just borned down at the barn!"

"Oh good."

"Did you tell Grandpa?" Astrid asked.

"He's sleeping, and Manny is too."

"Not anymore, I'd guess," Ingeborg said under her breath.

Astrid held out her hand. "Come on. I'll go back down with you."

"We watched from the stall door."

"She shook her head at us, so we didn't go in," Carl said, standing solid while Inga danced around.

"That's wise." Astrid shared a grin with her mor and Ellie, and then she and the children trooped down to the barn.

Astrid leaned on the stall's half wall. "Well, old girl, you are doing just all right." The calf was up and nursing already, the cow glaring at the humans in warning. Inga and Carl looked through the slats in the gate.

"Is it a boy calf or a girl calf?" Inga asked.

"We'll find out later. Leave them alone for now." She checked the water pail in the corner, and it was still full.

When the tent erectors arrived at the farm, the women and older children carried the food outside. Reverend Solberg said the blessing, and everyone took plates to fill at the table.

Astrid went over to Manny to ask what he wanted, but ten-year-old Linnea was already there.

"If you want I will bring a plate over to you." When he nodded, she asked, "What would you like?"

"Anything is good."

"Then I'll give you a bit of everything."

He never raised his eyes to look at her. "All right."

"Didn't your mother teach you to say please?" Linnea asked.

He nodded and muttered please so quietly she could barely hear him.

When she brought him a plate brimming with roast beef, small new potatoes, gravy, lettuce salad, and a buttered slice of bread, he did have the grace to say thank-you.

"You're welcome." She started to leave and then threw over her shoulder, "I like the way you talk."

Astrid and Penny shared a covert smile. "Did you prompt her to do that?"

Penny shook her head. "No. Never thought about it. That's Linnea though, always watching out for the underdog." They went to fill their plates. "Did you know Linnea and Johnny have been practicing together? She picks up the chords naturally. Elizabeth says she has a good ear and is learning more of the music for sing-a-longs and even some of the dances."

Astrid wagged her head. "All this has been going on, and I never knew about it."

"Well, it's not exactly like you've been out looking for things to do. Joshua is a good teacher too. He plays with them when they get together in the evening. Makes me wonder if any of our immigrant workers are musicians."

Trygve stopped by the bench where Penny and Astrid were sitting on his way back to the table. "We need to get to the station in half an hour."

Astrid gasped. "Oh mercy. I forgot to watch the time."

Penny shrugged. "Well, he didn't, so all is well."

"Guess I got to enjoying myself too much." Astrid finished mopping her gravy with the last of her bread. She glanced over at Manny, who was talking, or at least listening, to Johnny

Solberg. "I'd forgotten, but Manny mentioned they had a banjo at their house at one time, so perhaps we have another musician there." She rose and took her plate into the kitchen, where Ellie was setting up the dishpans with soapy water on the cooler part of the stove.

Ellie grinned. "Thank you."

"What did you do? Beat Freda off with a stick?"

"No, I just mentioned she should go sit down and relax with the others for a while. My mor taught me how to do dishes long, long ago, and I felt it was only fair she share the work through me around here."

Ingeborg grinned. "Good for you, Ellie."

"Wagon's leaving," Trygve called from in front of the house.

"Can I stay with Grandma? Please, Pa, please?" Inga never did anything low key.

Astrid walked out the front door to hear Thorliff saying, "Did Grandma say it is all right?"

"She said I could spend the night if I wanted, and I do. And if you said I could. And since Ma didn't come, I can't ask her too."

"Tell Grandma fine for now, and I will phone her later."

"About staying all night?"

"Ja." Thorliff walked over to the buggy and untied the horse from the hitching rail. "You can ride with me, Astrid. Easier than the wagon." He tipped his hat at Trygve. "See you in town."

Once they were trotting down the lane, she turned to Thorliff. "Why did Elizabeth not come?"

"She was sleeping, and I didn't want to wake her. She didn't sleep well last night, and this whatever has made her tired. She was up coughing during the night. Thelma said she'd tell her."

"She seems to catch everything that comes around. Not good for a doctor."

"I know. I was hoping she would move more into administration so she didn't have so much contact with sick patients, at least for a while."

"I tried, but she kept leaving that for me. I know we are going to have to find someone to run the hospital business, but . . ."

"You could write to Mrs. Korsheski and see if they know of someone."

"I could, but the hospital cannot afford to pay someone like that. You know that Elizabeth and I do not take out wages. We've got to get it on its feet before that can happen."

"And get more paying patients?" He gave her a big brother look, a big brother who probably did know best in this situation, but Astrid had no answers for him.

"Just drive."

Thorliff chuckled. They could hear the whistle to the east on the tracks when they stopped at the train station. "Elizabeth was planning to be here to help welcome them, but I doubt she will be."

"That's fine. You're greeting your workers, right?"

"I'll walk them out to their tents. Sophie has agreed to serve them supper out in the backyard until we see how healthy these men are. I hope we do not have any sick ones like last time."

"Me too." Together they walked to the center of the wooden platform, where Daniel was waiting with a handcart.

"How did you get here so quick?" she asked.

"I left a while ago, but you and Penny were visiting so happily that Mother and I came on in. She wanted to make sure there was lemonade ready."

Astrid tucked her arm around his. "You are the best husband ever. How come I am so lucky?"

"Thank you, but you are easy to love."

The train hissed and screeched to a halt, steam billowing

out. The conductor waved, jumped down, and turned to bring out the step. Three young women stood waiting on the inside steps.

"This must be them." Astrid stepped forward and smiled. One by one, the conductor helped them down. The first resembled a frightened rabbit, timid with a red nose that she held a handkerchief to. The second wore a grin as wide as her face. Her eyes locked on Trygve. And the third, the smallest of the three, with wild black hair that was supposedly confined in a net with a hat perching like a bird in a nest, descended with a firm step.

"I am Dr. Astrid Bjorklund Jeffers, and this is my husband, Daniel." She extended her hand to the timid one. "And you are . . . ?"

"Corabell Nester." Even her handshake was weak.

"I am Vera Wells, and I am delighted to be here." This one shook hands with Astrid firmly and smiled brightly at Trygve, who seemed to have eyes only for the third.

"I am Nurse Miriam Hastings, and I am pleased to meet you. I have heard so much about the doctors Bjorklund."

Her gaze snagged on that of Trygve's, and she raised her chin slightly before looking back to Astrid. "Our luggage is in the car behind the passenger cars."

"Yes. Mr. Knutson and Mr. Jeffers will see to that. I do hope your train ride was satisfactory."

"It was. Thank you."

She had a lovely lilt to her voice, and they all spoke English well. What a relief that was.

"Since we have a very small town, I will show you where you are to stay until your boardinghouse rooms are ready. Then we will go to the hospital for a tour. Unless you are all too weary."

When they all murmured that they were all right, she motioned them to head east on Main Street.

Glancing over her shoulder, she saw two men helping a third off the train. *Oh please, Lord, don't let this be a repeat of the last group of men that arrived.*

Chapter 24

And that concludes our tour of the hospital. Easy, wasn't it?"

"Dr. Bjorklund, everything looks so new." Miriam stared around her.

"Well, yes, the hospital has not been open very long. Your hospital in Chicago is quite old in comparison. We are still trying to bring in needed supplies, but we learned years ago to make do with what we had, which wasn't much. Tomorrow we'll show you our offices at Dr. Bjorklund's house." When someone snickered, Astrid continued. "Perhaps I should start using my married name, Jeffers, but everyone is used to me being Bjorklund, so it can be confusing."

"How many staff are on each shift?" Corabell asked.

"Well, much of it depends on how many patients we have here. We always have one nurse, and what you might call an orderly on duty. Here each of us just does whatever needs to be done—not laundry but sometimes cleaning. We have someone come in during the day to do the laundry. The drying lines are behind the hospital. I know we need a regular cleaner too, but we don't have one right now."

"Are we to understand that money is a problem here?" Miriam questioned.

"Yes and no. We are not totally self-supporting, by any means. We are a part of the hospital in Chicago, and they help support us. We are praying we will grow to meet all of our dreams. The need is here, but—"

The bang of the front door against the wall snapped their attention around. Two men were carrying or rather dragging a man by his shoulders. Thorliff had held the door open for them.

"We have a problem, Dr. Bjorklund. A serious one."

Astrid and Deborah MacCallister got to the patient at the same time.

"Let's get him into the examining room."

Nurse Deborah ran down the hall and opened a door. "Bring him in here."

"Does he speak English?" She looked to the two men helping him. "To start, do you speak English?"

One man nodded. "He does but with a heavy accent. He understands more than he can speak."

"What nationality?"

"Irish. I've worked with him before. He's a good carpenter."

Together they hoisted him up on the padded table.

"Can you open his shirt so I can listen to his chest?" The men did as she asked and then stepped back. She moved the stethoscope around, then said to the men, "We will keep him here, but could you tell us what you know before you leave?"

"His name is Seamus O'Flaherty. He's had a cough ever since I knew him, maybe two, three months. We had a job repairing a building down on the piers in New York, and when that was done, we couldn't find no more work. Then we heard of a man looking for workers to go to North Dakota. We signed right up."

Astrid looked over. Miriam had picked up some paper and

was writing down what the man said. Looking to the other new nurses, she said, "Would you two please go scrub in case I need more help here? Thank you, Miriam." She turned back to the man. "Sir, what is your name?"

"Harvey, ma'am. Harvey Jessup."

"Does he have a family?"

"Yes. We all do. But we had to get work and so we came."

"I see." She looked to Thorliff, who was leaning against the doorjamb. "Could you help them undress Mr. O'Flaherty and move him into the room we are going to go get ready?"

"Of course."

She turned to the two new men. "Please, before you leave here, scrub at our sink, just in case we are dealing with something contagious. And then thank you very much. We appreciate your help. I know supper will be served at the boardinghouse, and you must be famished."

"Thank you, Doctor."

Astrid laid a gown on the table and left the room, beckoning to her three new nurses. "There are aprons hanging in the nurses' room. Please put one on and scrub. We need to get the private room ready. We're going to isolate him."

"May we ask what your probable diagnosis is?" Miriam looked up from her notes. "Pneumonia?"

"I hope so." Astrid shook her head. "I know that sounds cruel, but the possible alternatives are . . ." She looked to the nurses for answers.

"Uh, influenza? Uh, what did his lungs sound like?" Corabell Nester stammered but was trying.

"Please don't say consumption," Vera Wells added.

"When we have him settled, we will give him a bath. Since we do not have a male orderly, we will have to bathe him . . . uh . . . discreetly. Then you will each take his temperature and listen to his lungs. Nurse Hastings, please continue with the record keeping. We have to have accurate records, but make sure you listen too." Record keeping was one of the things that too often fell through the not-enough-workers cracks. And one of the duties she often found herself catching up on late at night.

Deborah fixed two buckets of soap and carbolic acid, to be ready for them to wash the bed frame, the table beside the bed, and finally to mop the floor. "This is going to be one fast room preparation. Come on, ladies."

Astrid returned to the examining room and knocked on the door. "How are you doing?"

"Nearly finished," Thorliff answered.

"He will be more comfortable with his head higher, so take that padded V frame there in the corner and get him braced against it for now. The room isn't quite ready." She paused a moment. "Gentlemen, I have another question. Have you seen him cough up any blood?"

"Not that we know of."

"Thank you."

She fetched a stretcher and leaned it against the wall by the door. When it opened and the two men came out, she pointed to it and asked, "Can you please stay long enough to help carry him into the other room? Has he regained consciousness yet?"

"Don't think he was ever out, just too weak or something to answer. That train ride was mighty tiring. 'Specially when you are sick."

"Was he sick when you left New York?"

"Not like this," the other man added.

Good. He can speak English too. Possibly German. But unsure of what accent she was dealing with, she just asked, "What country did you come from?"

"Holland. I have been in this country almost a year. My

brother wrote and told me to learn English, so we did as much as we could before we came."

"You were very wise. Life here will be much easier without a language barrier."

When the room was ready, she brought her nurses in. "While they hold the stretcher, we are going to lift him over. You know how, correct?"

They nodded and lined up along the table opposite of the stretcher. "Now we will lift and you men slide that under him." The four women slipped their hands underneath the sheet he was lying on and lifted on the count of three. Even at that, the strain on Corabell's face was not good.

In the room they repeated the drill, only this time Thorliff helped too, and once their patient was on the bed, she excused the men and thanked them again. Then they set a V frame under the mattress to raise the head and spread a sheet over their patient.

When she saw him trying to say something, Astrid leaned closer.

"Th-thankee," he strained to say.

"You are welcome. I'm going to make something for you to drink that will soothe your throat. Are you more comfortable?"

He nodded, closing his eyes again.

After all three nurses finished the observation and had him drink the honey, lemon, and whiskey in hot water, they left the room.

"All right, what did you observe?" She nodded to Corabell first.

"His lungs are congested, rattling like pneumonia, but he is not running a high temperature."

"Anyone notice anything else?"

"His skin color is gray, and his nails are on the blue side. He is not getting enough air."

"Good. Anything else?"

"No, but the V frame should help relieve his breathing. We could do percussion on his back to loosen up the congestion in his lungs." Miriam turned at the sound of the man coughing. "Do you have squares of muslin he can use and possibly a spittoon? That way we could see if there was any blood."

"And you could ask him about that when he is awake enough."

"The more fluid he drinks, the more his lungs will loosen too."

Astrid smiled and nodded at the same time. "Very good. I know you are used to having a doctor who lays down the law, but we do things a bit differently here. Because we are so short-staffed, we work as a team. So you will be called on to help with diagnoses, charting, and treatments of all kinds. There are many old-time treatments that are very effective, and since my mother is an expert in those, we learn from her also. Observation and paying attention to what you sense are critically important.

"For right now, the treatment plan is to force fluids, give him good food to help rebuild his system, and keep him comfortable so he can get well. Any questions?"

The three shook their heads. "Then we will return to my house, where Mrs. Jeffers will most likely have supper ready. And I am sure you are weary enough to drop, so a good night's sleep will be appreciated. You will not be on call tonight. I was hoping to introduce you to the other Dr. Bjorklund, but we will wait until tomorrow for that."

I sure hope she feels well enough to help with the classes. The thought of all she had to do made Astrid feel as if she were sinking into a mud pit. In just over a month the two Indian women would be here, and Kaaren would be starting school, so she would not have time to help, as she did with the others.

Thank God Far was doing better, so maybe Mor could help. But she had already taken Manny in and was continuing to work with getting him stronger. There was a limit to Mor's time and energy.

The other men they had isolated at the school. She would ask Elizabeth to read up on consumption. Perhaps there were some new things that could help more. If that was indeed what they were dealing with.

Amelia Jeffers did have a supper of sliced cheese, bread, salads from the garden, and a dessert of raspberry pie ready for them.

"I made sure we had lots of hot water, so if any of you would like to take a bath, you may. I remember feeling so grimy when I came out here on the train. We are hoping your rooms at the boardinghouse will be ready in a couple of weeks. For the moment one of you will board at the other doctor's house, but for tonight, perhaps we can make you comfortable here. No doubt you will be the first guests in the new wing."

The next morning after rounds, Astrid assigned different jobs to the three at the hospital and at midmorning returned to talk with Elizabeth, who was sitting on the back porch drinking tea with some toast on a plate beside her. Astrid sank into a chair.

"I take it Inga stayed with Grandma last night?"

"Yes, to her delight and my relief. I felt so much better last night, and now here I am again."

"The nausea is back?" A cup of coffee appeared at her side, along with toast and jam. "Thank you, Thelma."

"You know, I was ready for one of them to stay here, but . . ." She glanced at Elizabeth. "We do have plenty of room." She shrugged "Maybe. . ."

"Thank you, but I figured you had enough going on here, and Mrs. Jeffers is delighted to have the young ladies there. She absolutely endeared herself to them last night when she said they could have baths."

"I just wish I would get over this . . . this malaise. I am sick and tired of feeling sick and tired."

"It will go away soon." Thelma picked up some dishes.

Astrid turned to look at the older woman. "How do you know?"

"Why, she's pregnant."

"I am not!" Elizabeth set her cup down with a rattle. "Whatever makes you think that?"

"Classic morning sickness, and you probably missed one of your cycles."

"No I didn't—umm, I don't think so."

Thelma shrugged and returned to the kitchen.

"Could she be right?" Astrid felt she'd been dealt a severe blow to her diaphragm.

"No, we've been so careful. Impossible."

Abstinence is the only sure way, my friend, and you just admitted to not following that path. "Any other symptoms? Sore breasts? Tired? Well, we know about that one. Think, Elizabeth. She could be right. And if she is, we have some serious planning to do." *She's lost what? Three babies? And each time she has taken longer to recover. Dear God, what are we going to do? I warned them she might not make it through another pregnancy. Oh, Thorliff, I am not going to be the one to tell you.*

"When is your next cycle due?"

Elizabeth closed her eyes, the better to figure. "Two weeks, and I am always on time."

Astrid sipped her coffee and nibbled on her toast. "Then we will know for sure. And if you are pregnant, you will be off your feet. You can lead classes from your settee. You can take charge of the medical records, ordering supplies, and all the other things you can do without getting up."

Shaking her head, Elizabeth stared into her teacup. "I'm not going to mention this to Thorliff until we know for certain. I'm still not sure Thelma is correct, so I refuse to worry about it until I know."

If only we knew what goes on in her body that she has such a terrible time carrying babies to term. "I must get back to the hospital. If you have anyone needing a doctor, send them over there."

And you can start your own study program by reading all you can about women who lose babies.

Chapter 25

He could not get her out of his mind.

"Trygve? Hello, Trygve." Ingeborg leaned over and tapped him on the arm. "Woolgathering? This isn't like you."

"Oh, sorry." He blinked and mentally shook himself. This was not like him at all. No female had ever taken up residence in his head like this. She had stepped off that train, and she was all he could see. Or hear, for that matter. She didn't really have an accent but did have a lovely lilt to her voice. Tiny, but he had a feeling she packed a wallop, not to be underestimated at any point.

Ingeborg patted his arm. "I heard about you at the train station. Astrid said you looked like someone had whacked you one. You couldn't take your eyes off her."

"Was it that obvious?"

"Probably only to those who have known and loved you for a long time. One of the other nurses, Vera, I believe it was, tried to get your attention, but it sounds like you never even saw her."

"Who?" He was trying to think who she meant. He had met all three nurses, but for the life of him, he couldn't remember either of the others. He'd hauled their baggage to Astrid's house, but they had insisted he not drag the trunks upstairs, since they would be moving to the boardinghouse as soon as it was ready.

"See what I mean?" His aunt arched an eyebrow and turned to see Haakan come out on the porch. "Good morning again."

Haakan yawned and stretched his arms above his head, tapping his fingers on the tongue-and-groove ceiling. "How can I sleep so much? This is outrageous."

"Making up for all those years you never got enough sleep, perhaps?" Trygve studied his onkel. He certainly looked far better than he had, but this whole sick thing had aged him—a lot. "You ready to walk to town with me?"

"Can I have a cup of coffee first?"

"I imagine. Where's Manny?"

"Down at the barn. He and Inga are playing with the calf that was born on Sunday. He tries to act like she's a little kid and not to bother him, but you know Inga. She'll get through to him better than anyone. She and Benny. He is still amazed at all that Benny does."

"Aren't we all?"

"True." He accepted the coffee Ingeborg poured for him and leaned against a porch post, looking out over the wheat fields starting to turn in some spots. "Harvest will be starting right on time. The wheat's losing color." He looked toward Trygve. "You going with the harvest crew this year?"

"No. Far and I talked about it. Samuel and Jonathan will go, but I will remain here. Andrew too, right?"

"Someone has to do all the chores here. I am hoping I'll be able to milk again one of these days. That shouldn't endanger anyone, other than me if I get kicked or something."

"Freda and I have not lost our ability to milk cows, you know. Are they taking any of the immigrants along? I know that Jessup fellow misses farming. He said so at church on Sunday."

"Really?" That caught Haakan's attention. "Perhaps I should talk with him." He turned back to Ingeborg. "You know, I'm surprised we've not gotten any responses to our letters to Valdres. Do you suppose the mail got thrown overboard?"

"I seriously doubt that. Perhaps they are trying to decide who will come, if anyone. It's not easy to make such a decision."

Trygve watched her face take on a faraway look, but only for a moment. He knew thoughts of her life growing up in Norway sometimes intruded. His tante had confided once that for all these years in Dakota she had refused to dwell on memories of home. In fact, had refused to even let them out of the trunk where they were stored, for fear they would leap out and make her homesick. What must it be like to leave so much behind?

"You ready?" Trygve asked Haakan when he had set his cup down.

"Let's go."

Trygve smiled inside but didn't let it show. Had Haakan caught on to the fact that every day someone different appeared to walk with him? If not to town, out in the fields. The other night, he'd gone fishing with Ingeborg, Inga, and Carl. He'd come back crowing that this little grandson of his was quite a fisherman. Not that Inga and Ingeborg were not, he hastened to add, but Carl seemed to have a knack for bringing home the most fish. But Inga caught the biggest.

And then Inga tattled that Haakan was having such a good time watching the others that he didn't pay a lot of attention to his own pole. Inga kept it from being towed down the river and landed his fish. "You got to pay attention, Grandpa," she had reminded him. Inga and Carl took fishing seriously.

Haakan vowed he'd not had so much fun fishing in a long time.

Trygve joined the fish fry that night—fresh fish, along with new potatoes that Inga and Carl had learned how to dig out properly. Ingeborg dug under the plants with her fingers, rather than pulling the plants out. That way the plant could keep on producing. The children acted like they were on a treasure hunt, which was not far from the truth. New potatoes, many the size of a walnut, were such a summer treat. That and fresh string beans, and Ingeborg's famous lettuce salad with her dressing made of sugar, cream, and vinegar didn't need dessert to top it off. It had been a lovely evening to cherish. He figured he appreciated these things more now that he'd been gone so long.

"Going to be hot again," Haakan said as they walked.

"'Fraid so. I have to have another talk with Hjelmer. He's still mad that I backed out of the well-drilling crew."

"But you got the team off, right?"

"And got the old wagon all ready for a second crew, but he is having trouble finding men to go."

Haakan chuckled. "He might be forced to offer more pay."

Hjelmer was famous for holding his money tight to his chest, rather than paying top dollar.

"Or use some of the immigrants. But speaking English is necessary, at least for the foreman. He needs to be able to talk with his crew."

"So he wants you to go out with this wagon and train a new crew?"

"Right."

"Are you going to?"

"No. I feel I'm needed here." *And besides, I want to get to know Miss Miriam Hastings. I wonder if she has a man in Chicago waiting for her.*

As they walked into town, Haakan turned to go to Thorliff's house. "I promised Elizabeth I would stop here for her to listen to my heart after the walk in." They both stopped and looked ahead to see a stranger leading a horse into town. Coming from the east.

Haakan watched. "Wonder who that guy is."

"His horse is limping mighty bad. Probably why he is leading it."

"There's Pastor Solberg. Looks like he's going to talk to the fellow."

Trygve watched as Haakan opened the gate and then mounted the steps to the back porch. Then, hands in his pockets, Trygve strode on up to Main Street. Seemed strange to call it that. They'd just platted out the town and named some streets earlier this spring. Somehow saying Main Street sounded puffed up, like they thought they were bigger than they were. Not wanting to eavesdrop, he waved and turned to go to the post office.

Hjelmer said to meet him for coffee at the house at ten and it was nearly that now. He'd rather have met him at the office at Thorliff's, so he'd have backup if necessary. But then, when did he ever get his rathers?

~

Blessing.

Lovely name for a village.

So, Father Devlin ruminated, *does the name bestow blessing upon its denizens, or do the denizens bless the town?* Most likely it was mutual. At any rate, perhaps they would have a livery stable here. And that would indeed bless Father Devlin.

He walked slower than usual, leading his lame horse. The horse stumbled, even though there was not a stone in sight, so Devlin slowed more.

The snail's pace as they entered town enabled the father to admire it better. Houses and outbuildings appeared tidy and in uniformly good repair, unlike those in so many prairie frontier towns. Most had pretty picket fences. From behind one of the fences, a small towheaded girl grinned and waved enthusiastically, so he waved back enthusiastically too, grinning.

He walked on.

Ah, now this is hopeful. Very hopeful. There seemed to be quite a bit of new construction. Hammering, shouting, and there was a large building attached to a building with a sign saying it was a boardinghouse. He was an excellent carpenter and woodcarver, so perhaps he could fatten up his purse before moving on. It was mighty flat now.

A tent city sprouted out in the distance beyond the railroad. Could that be where the workers lived? Devlin knew he could fit into that quite easily.

He dropped a rein over a hitching post in front of the boardinghouse, the only tying necessary to hold this old nag, and started toward the tents.

Down the boardinghouse steps came a cheerful fellow in a clerical collar that looked similar to Devlin's collar, except that his was clean. Blessing was looking better all the time.

The man extended a hand. "Welcome to Blessing. My name is John Solberg."

"Me name be Thomas Devlin. Delighted to meet ye, Father."

This John Solberg with the clerical collar chuckled. "Locally, they refer to me as Reverend or Pastor, not Father."

"Eh, then so shall I, Reverend Solberg. I was looking mayhap for a livery stable or stockyard. Me horse went lame, and I'd like the advice of someone who is a good hand with horses."

"Perhaps I can help, or I know someone who can." He led the way toward the street, so Devlin fell in beside him. "Just about everyone in this area is a good hand with horses."

"Everyone in this area save meself, Reverend. I be a complete ninny with horses. I grew up in Dublin and Philadelphia, transported by cabs and trolleys, and left the matter of horses to others."

Reverend Solberg lifted the rein off the hitching post and led the horse two steps. He stopped, dropped the rein, and picked up its left front foot. "Mm." He let the foot down gently and snapped his pocket knife open.

"Eh, I'd not dreamt surgery would be required." Father Devlin bent over to watch as the man lifted the horse's foot again and braced it on his knee.

The fellow chuckled as he pointed with the knife blade. "A loose bolt."

"The shoe be *bolted* on? I thought—"

"No, your gelding picked up the bolt walking on the road. It wedged in the hoof here at the shoe. You see? The more he walks on it, the worse it digs in." He wielded his knife blade purposefully. "I am trying to pry it loose and get it out of there."

The horse threw its head up and jerked back, pulling its foot off his knee.

A very pleasant young man appeared beside them. "Trouble?"

"Daniel, would you hold the horse, please? This may be uncomfortable for him."

"Certainly." The young fellow stepped to the horse's head and seized it, not by the bridle but by clamping its head under his arm and grasping an ear and the nostrils. Good hand with horses? These men both were. They knew instantly what to do and did not have to coach each other on the proper next step.

Reverend Solberg worked on his patient a few minutes, released the foot gently, and then stood erect. He handed Devlin a small iron bolt. "If possible, you might let him rest a couple of days. I hate to be the bearer of bad news, but it's not hopeful. There is damage in the hoof wall, and it could become inflamed. That is, laminitis, which can turn into founder. And at his age, if he founders, the most humane thing you can do is put him down."

"'Twould be sad, he being only nine years old."

Both of these gentlemen studied him in an odd way.

Daniel asked, "May I show you something?"

"Of course."

With his thumbs, the young man drew the horse's lips apart. "In a very young horse you can read the age by the number of teeth that have erupted. After age five or six, you look at these front teeth here. See how steeply they slant forward. They slant farther and farther forward as he ages. And do you see the heavy wear on the crowns of these teeth here?"

"Oh my." Devlin frowned. "How old might ye think he be?"

"Fifteen at least, probably years older. Eighteen or twenty."

Reverend Solberg was nodding.

"'Tis a powerful lesson to me, gentlemen. Never take the word of a horse trader at face value. I appreciate yer ministrations immensely. Might I pay ye for yer time?"

"Not at all." The reverend smiled. A warm smile he had. "Anything else we can do for you?"

"Eh, since ye mention it. Be there work for a practiced journeyman carpenter? I am also known as a good woodcarver."

Daniel looked at the reverend and grinned. The reverend returned the favor.

Daniel motioned. "You could not have come at a better time. Come right this way. I'll introduce you to our foreman, Andrei Belin. You can begin work immediately."

Ah, yes indeed. This was surely a blessing town.

"And me horse?"

Reverend Solberg stepped in. "I'll take him down to the livery. They can let him loose in their pasture. After work you might want to go talk to the liveryman, Rayner, and see if there's any treatment you can do for your horse."

"A fine idea. Thankee." Thomas Devlin unhooked a bag of tools and a fat bedroll, along with another bag of personal belongings. "I be ready. Lead on."

Trygve stepped out of the post office as Reverend Solberg was leading the still-limping horse to the livery. "So what was that all about?"

"Well, we have a new carpenter come to town, name of Thomas Devlin, as Irish as they come. Daniel took him over to the boardinghouse to work there. Says he's also a woodcarver. If so, he will be good with finish work."

"How about that?" Trygve shook his head. "Strange."

"Ja, but God doesn't always work according to our specifications."

"True. You might pray this meeting with Hjelmer goes well."

"I will. Don't let yourself get all riled up. You can't hear the still small voice of God when you're shouting."

Trygve grinned at him. "Might be one of those times when one of the Bible verses you made me memorize can come in handy."

"And which might that be?"

"'A soft answer turneth away wrath.' I use it a lot."

Solberg turned away chuckling, and with the sense of peace still surrounding him, Trygve walked around the store and to the house in the back.

Penny and Hjelmer were sitting on their front porch and waved him over.

"You two look mighty comfortable out here. Who's minding the store?"

"Gus and Linnea. They are getting too grown up to play at Sophie's."

"That seems to be the gathering place for the kids."

Penny pointed to a chair. "Sit yourself. I need to get back to the store, and I hear this is a business meeting. I do not need one more business to think on."

"Uh-oh. What do you have in the works now? Are you in cahoots with Sophie or some such?"

"Lord save us," Hjelmer muttered under his breath.

"Now look who's talking." Penny playfully slapped his shoulder. "You just want to come up with all the new ideas yourself."

"There's a new man in town. He just walked in with a lame horse. Daniel sent him over to work on the boardinghouse."

"Really? Do you think he might be interested in drilling wells?"

"I have no idea. Ask Solberg his impression. The man has an Irish accent but speaks good English."

That was getting to be the password lately. Speaks good English. So many of their immigrant workers spoke little English. Mrs. Jeffers' class for learning English was growing all the time.

"See you later." Penny headed for the store and Hjelmer pointed to the coffeepot.

"No, thanks. I need to get back to Thorliff's before Haakan takes it in his head to walk home alone. Ingeborg is trying to keep tabs on him now that he can walk decently again."

"He walked to town?"

"Ja. I walked him here. He has to get his strength back. He so wants to get back to work. Said he'd start milking again soon."

"He could do more woodcarving. Penny's store is carrying some other products made by people in Blessing. Maybe he could do something for that."

"Like what?"

"I have no idea. Just thinking out loud." Hjelmer turned

slightly and looked straight at Trygve. "What would it take to get you to take this new crew out, just for a short run until they really know their jobs?"

Trygve made sure it looked like he was thinking hard when all he wanted to do was shake his head and say, *"Nothing. I won't, that's all."* But a soft answer turneth away wrath.

"Hjelmer, what would it take for you to run for office again?" He'd heard Hjelmer's diatribe against the legislature more than once. How you couldn't get him back into that beehive of rascals for anything.

"Well, I can't think of anything. I just know I will not go back to that."

"Same here. I am more convinced than ever that I am needed right here in Blessing. I will not be going with the threshing crew when they start traveling either. I am staying right here in Blessing." He kept his voice soft and gentle, shaking his head to make his point.

"What if I doubled your wages?"

"No. Onkel Hjelmer, please understand. It is not the money. I was happy running the crew. I enjoyed seeing the country, meeting the people. But now I need to be here."

"But now that you've finished getting the wagon and supplies ready, you don't even have a job."

"There's plenty of work here in Blessing. I'm not concerned about that." He held up a hand, palm out. "Please, can we leave this here? You and I have both been accused of being stubborn. I don't want hard feelings."

Hjelmer tented his fingers in front of his chest, leaning back in his chair. Tapping one forefinger against the other. "It takes a special skill—"

"Drilling a well and building a windmill don't take a genius. Just experience."

"Training."

"Ja, if you want to call it that. Why don't you advertise for a well driller?"

Hjelmer slapped his palms on the table. "I need one now! I have orders to be filled."

Trygve rose to his feet. "You'll think of something." He paused. "Wasn't Zeb, uh, Mac . . . Can't think of his name."

"MacCallister. He headed for Montana after Katie died."

"Right. Wasn't he a well driller? Does Deborah hear from them at all?"

"I don't know, but . . ." Hjelmer quit tapping his fingers.

Trygve left before he could get into an argument in spite of himself. He hoped he'd heard the last of it, but . . .

Chapter 26

"What would you like me to do first?" Miriam asked.

Nurse MacCallister crossed to the nurses' station. "We have six patients in the ward and our man in the private room. He has not been responding much today. We changed his bed, and I've put extra pads under him, since we have to keep cleaning him up. This makes it easier."

"Has he eaten anything?"

"We spooned a little broth in, and he swallowed. Did the same with water. He's dehydrated something fierce. We've been keeping damp cloths on him to help with that."

"Do we know for sure it is consumption?"

"Not for sure. There are several other things it could be, but Dr. Bjorklund thinks it is that. We all expected him to become more alert with enough fluids and easing the coughing."

Nurse MacCallister wrote something on one of the charts. "Once we have everyone settled for the night, there's a list of chores on the wall in the nurses' room. I will go ahead and dispense meds, and you can work with Mr. O'Flaherty. See if you can get him to respond. There is broth in the kitchen. Cook made a new batch today." She paused. "Do you speak Irish?"

"The language is called Gaelic."

"Are you Irish?"

Miriam smiled and slipped into the accent she'd grown up with. "No, my mum sounded more like this. My father was killed several years ago, and his accent was even more cockney. But when I was growing up, we lived in a neighborhood predominantly Irish, so meself, I can speak plenty of Gaelic too. We learn languages so easily as children. Then I studied Latin in school, even some Italian, since my teacher spoke so many languages. I was fortunate." She shrugged. "The languages have been helpful working at the hospital."

Nurse MacCallister looked at her briefly, strangely. "Well, maybe if he hears some Gaelic words he will respond more. If he can respond."

Miriam paused. "He's that bad off?"

Nurse MacCallister shrugged. "Guess we'll find out."

Miriam washed her hands before entering the room. Dusk was dimming the room, so she lit the lamp on the table beside the bed.

"Mr. O'Flaherty, me name be Nurse Miriam Hastings, and I shall be caring for you tonight." She took his hand. "Please squeeze me hand if ye can hear me." She repeated the request in Gaelic.

He immediately squeezed her hand.

"Can ye open yer eyes?" Again in Gaelic. His eyelids fluttered but did not open all the way. Instead, he started to cough. She covered his mouth with one of the squares and waited, stroking his hand. When it eased, she wiped his mouth. No bloody sputum.

"I shall return immediately, sir."

Quickly she set a tray with a cup of broth and a spoon, along with the mixture of honey, lemon, and whiskey, and carried it to his room. She adjusted his pillows so he was sitting up more.

And she used Gaelic. "Here is food for you, Taoiseach." She used the formal word for leader or presider. He almost smiled.

She'd fed him half a cup when the next spoonful trickled out the side of his mouth. Another cough wracked him. When she'd cleaned up the phlegm, she said, "Let us see if this cough medicine will help." She gave him a tablespoon of the syrup and watched him swallow. "I'll leave ye now, but I shall return later, and we shall do this again. Need ye anything more, sir?"

When he shook his head, she doused the lamp and stepped back into the hallway.

A man with a clerical collar stood waiting. "I'd like to see him, if I may."

"Ah, you are Father . . . ?"

"Thomas Devlin, Nurse. I heard of his need from some of the others who live in the tents. I have a cot there now too." His voice carried a hint of the brogue too.

"Well, Father Devlin . . ."

The welcome Irish lilt came forth. "I be going by Thomas here, or if ye must be formal, Mr. Devlin."

Questions bombarded her mind, but she kept her nurse face in place. "Of course ye may see him. Would ye like me to light the lamp again?"

"No, and I thank ye. Does he speak English or only the auld tongue?"

"He responds well to Gaelic, aye. He has not been understanding our orders or requests on how to help him."

"I see." He nodded while talking. "I could translate for you."

"Meself does fine. 'Tis the others."

A broad, happy grin spread across his face. "I see. Thank ye, Nurse, for assisting me." He touched his forehead and slipped into the man's room.

Now, that's a puzzlement, she thought as she went about

her duties. Half an hour later when she returned to check on her patient, Father Devlin was gone, but he had left a note on the nightstand.

His name is Seamus O'Flaherty from Clifden in County Galway. He has been in this country about a year, his family still in Ireland. He has had this cough and feeling ill for over six months now. His mother died of consumption a year ago. I will return tomorrow evening after work.

TD

If he doesn't want to go by Father, why does he wear the collar? What is the story behind this? Miriam knew there had to be a story. There always was. She finished her shift at six in the morning and, along with Nurse MacCallister, briefed the two incoming student nurses and the nurse named Annika Nilsson.

She and Nurse MacCallister walked out into a glorious summer day. The dew still sparkled on the grass and birds sang from the trees growing along Main Street. Other than the birdsong, the early morning quiet made her stop and look around.

"I've never heard such quiet."

Nurse MacCallister stopped too. "What do you mean?" She looked around in confusion.

"I have lived in Chicago all my life, and it is never quiet there. Never. Even in the wee hours of the morning, there are trolleys clanging, conveyances on the streets . . . it is never still. The quietest I've ever known is when the first snow falls. But this"—she swept her arm in an arc—"this sky is so blue it hurts my eyes, birds sing, they really do, and . . ." She paused and inhaled. "The air is clean. No smoke, no grit, no stench of garbage and offal, and . . . and . . ." She raised her face to the sun again. "This is like nothing I've ever dreamed."

"That's just the way it is here. When harvest starts, there will be more dust as farmers bring their grain into the flourmill. You'll smell cow manure out by the Bjorklunds' and other farms that sell cream to the cheese house."

"Cheese house?"

"Ja, Ingeborg Bjorklund has a cheese-making business. They ship to lots of other places, even to New York. She started that soon after they settled here. She is an amazing woman. Most every baby born until Thorliff married Dr. Elizabeth and brought her here came into this world with Ingeborg's help. She was the midwife and pretty much the doctor back then. Dr. Astrid is her daughter."

"You grew up here?"

"I did. On a farm south of town." They'd reached the street in front of Astrid's house. "I'll see you this evening. Hope you can sleep well."

Miriam smiled. "I hate to miss any part of this day sleeping."

"I usually sleep until one o'clock or so. Sometimes I have to put cotton in my ears to keep out the noise." She nodded to the men gathering by the boardinghouse. "Once the construction starts, it is pretty noisy here. They are not only adding to that one, but houses are going up everywhere. That tent town out there?" She pointed to the south. "Those people have to have places to live in by the time the snow flies. You can't live outside in the winter here—it's too cold and windy." She waved as she went up the street.

Miriam looked over the workers getting set to work on the addition. They'd be able to move in in two weeks? But then, she'd not seen the inside. The new section that attached to the main building looked far ahead of the rest.

She made her way up the walk to the front door. Surely she could come in the back way and take her coffee out on the porch there. She let herself in as quietly as possible, but a voice called from the kitchen.

"Good morning, Miriam. Breakfast is ready."

She followed the voice down the hall to the kitchen, where Mrs. Jeffers was slicing bread. "Good morning."

"Oh, it is indeed. I can't wait to get out in the garden." She turned. "Now what would you like?"

"Whatever you are making is fine with me." All of a sudden a wave of weariness rolled right over her and nearly brought her to her knees.

"Good. We have oatmeal if you'd like, or I can make eggs."

"Oatmeal is fine. And a piece of that delicious-looking bread. Is it possible to eat out on the porch?"

"Of course. That is where Daniel and Dr. Astrid are right now. You go join them, and I'll bring your food out. The milk and cream and both honey and sugar are out there." She took a cup down from the cupboard and handed it to her. "Serve yourself coffee, or if you'd rather tea, that can be ready in just a couple of minutes."

"Coffee is fine." She poured her cup and paused at the screen door. It was like another room out there—chairs with cushions, a round table with roses in the center, a settee with a low table in front of it that also had a bouquet of various roses on it. Pink, white, and yellow. Such beauty. These people must be very wealthy to live like this. A vision of the tenements where her family lived made her swallow. They used to live in a house farther out of the city, but after her father died, they were forced to move to the tenement, the only place they could afford.

How her mother would love it here. She looked out the back.

Surely that was the garden beyond the beds of roses. The riot of colors almost made her dizzy.

"Come join us, Miriam. You put in a long day yesterday and the shift last night. You must be exhausted." Dr. Astrid smiled at her.

"I didn't know that until a couple of minutes ago." Miriam walked over, and Mr. Jeffers stood to help her with her chair. "Thank you." She sank down into the cushions with a sigh mixed of both weariness and pleasure.

"How did the night go?" Astrid asked.

"Good. Did you know we have a priest in town?"

"What?" Astrid stared at her. "What do you mean?"

"I mean a Father Thomas Devlin. Apparently they've hired him to work on the boardinghouse, and though he is wearing a clerical collar, he is introducing himself as Thomas Devlin. He came and visited with our consumptive patient. The patient spoke Gaelic with the priest, and he found out more information for us. Mr. O'Flaherty's mother died of consumption less than a year ago." Miriam smiled and thanked Mrs. Jeffers for the oatmeal now in front of her.

"Are you of the Catholic faith?" Astrid asked. "Not that it makes any difference."

"No. I was born Anglican, but the two are similar in many ways." Miriam started to add more and decided to keep her ideas about God to herself.

"But you recognized him as a priest?"

"He is wearing a rather dirty clerical collar."

"I see." She sipped her coffee, elbows propped on the table. "And you speak Gaelic?"

Miriam nodded. "Some. I learned it from the kids in my very Irish neighborhood. But since I've not used it for some time, I don't remember it all."

"Like I learned to speak Norwegian as a child, but we don't use it as much here in Blessing as we used to. Because of that, though, I can understand some German. Mrs. Jeffers holds classes here to help the immigrants learn English. She's very good at it."

"I'm good at what?" Mrs. Jeffers asked as she joined them at the table.

"I was telling Miriam about your classes."

"The hardest one to understand is Mr. Belin. He speaks Russian, but he is trying so hard to learn."

"He is such a good carpenter that we've made him a foreman. He has a good eye to see what has to be done next." Daniel passed the plate of sliced bread to Miriam, and Dr. Astrid moved the butter and jam nearer.

"I've never had breakfast out on a back porch like this. You have no idea how idyllic Blessing is. Just walking from the hospital to here was a feast for the eyes. And ears too. The silence was alive, but oh, the gift of quiet."

"I went to med school in Chicago for my surgical training. I was not impressed with Chicago. I've never been to such a dirty place in my life, but then, I've not been to very many cities. Maybe they are all like that. Coal smoke is pretty dirty."

"I have always lived there, so that is what I know." She smiled at Mrs. Jeffers. "This is so good. Thank you." She turned to Astrid. "I have a favor to ask. I want to write a letter to my mother and family, but I'm afraid I do not have any paper."

"We'll fix that." Mrs. Jeffers set her coffee cup down. "I'll get it right now."

"No, please. I am not going to do that before I sleep. I can feel myself slipping away here."

"I will have supplies ready for you when you wake up. You sleep as long as you can. I hope all the pounding and sawing won't keep you awake."

Miriam snorted. "After what I am used to, this is more like music." She folded her napkin and laid it beside her plate. "If you don't mind, I am going to bed. Thank you for your hospitality." She pushed back her chair and left before Mr. Jeffers had time to rise.

She paused when she heard Dr. Astrid say, "This is sure a strange turn of events, wouldn't you say?"

Mr. Jeffers replied, "I think we should say nothing of the priest. Just a new man. For some reason he is not announcing it, and I want to honor that. Thank you for this lovely break." He went whistling down the steps and out the gate.

Miriam shed her clothes and slipped into bed. The sewing machine sat right under the window, where the curtains billowed in the breeze. Yes, there was construction noise, but no matter.

Her room was in the shade by the time Miriam woke. The temperature had risen but was still not uncomfortable. Miriam could hear voices downstairs. One male and Mrs. Jeffers. What a nice woman she was. They all were. She washed at the basin and slipped into her one other dress, leaving the one she'd worn hanging on a peg along the wall. If only she had enough money to buy some cotton fabric and sew herself something for the summer. Her serge skirt had been hot enough on the train and good for traveling but not for wearing here. She tamed her hair as well as she was able to, confining it to a net at the back of her head and, after making her bed, left the room.

Admiring the furnishings, she made her way back to the kitchen to find Mrs. Jeffers and that young man who had delivered their luggage enjoying a bright red drink on the back porch.

"There you are, dear. I do hope you slept well."

"I did, thank you. What time is it?"

"Three thirty, and you must be famished. Do you remember Trygve Knutson? You met him yesterday at the train."

"Of course. You argued with us about taking the trunks upstairs, and all we were trying to do was save you a backache."

He smiled at her, a brilliant smile that caught her in midbreath. "And here I was trying to be polite, to welcome you to Blessing."

Mrs. Jeffers returned with a plate of bread, cheese, little carrots, and some lovely lettuce. She set down another of the glasses with red liquid and ice. "This should tide you over till supper."

Miriam sat down and stared at her plate.

"Is something wrong?"

"Oh no. It is just that this is so . . . so pretty. Are these things from your garden?"

"Yes, and tonight we are having the last of the peas. Good thing we planted plenty of potatoes, as I keep sneaking out the little ones for us to eat now. At this rate, we won't have enough for winter."

Miriam could feel Trygve's eyes on her. She glanced up, bread with butter and cheese on it and a leaf of lettuce in one hand, and could feel a touch of heat moving up her neck. "Is something wrong?"

"No, not a thing. The drink you have there is called strawberry swizzle. I think you'll like it. But what I really came for—we have a soda shop in town, and I thought perhaps we could go for a soda and walk around town so you can get to know where you live."

"I . . . uh . . . I . . ." She looked to Mrs. Jeffers for help.

"Oh, I think that is a fine idea. Let her finish her meal first, Trygve. You have to be at the hospital at seven?"

"Yes." Go for a soda? Just like that? Were all the people in Blessing as nice and friendly as those she had met? She had never gone with a young man for a soda. She only vaguely knew what a soda was.

He watched her intently as she sipped from her glass. Her smile widened as she set it back down. "That is delicious."

She finished her lunch and rose to take her plate inside, but Mrs. Jeffers stopped her with a *tut-tut*. "You go enjoy yourself. You can help me another time."

So before she knew it, she was walking down the street, with Mr. Knutson pointing out all the buildings, telling her about his sister Sophie, who owned and ran the boardinghouse; Grace, who recently got married; and his younger brother, Samuel; along with Mr. Valders, who ran the bank; and Mrs. Valders, who ran the post office. He pointed to Garrisons' Groceries, the Blessing Mercantile, and right over there, the Soda Shoppe. "Rebecca Valders owns the Soda Shoppe, and she specializes in good syrups, necessary for good sodas, I am told."

"My goodness, but this is really a rather busy little town."

"Yes, and it is growing faster than we can provide housing. All the houses being built are for the workers who have come here."

"Hey, Mr. Trygve, you came to visit us."

"I did." He turned to Miriam. "Miss Hastings, I want you to meet Benny Valders. He came from Chicago too, when Dr. Bjorklund was going to school there."

"Are you a doctor too?" Benny asked with a grin wide enough to break his face.

"No, I am a nurse in training."

"At the big hospital in Chicago?"

"Yes."

"That's where I met My Doc. She had to take off my legs because I got run over by a dray, and it crushed 'em. Then she brought me home with her, and now I have a family here. My ma has a baby that's my little brother. His name is Swen, and he rides on my cart."

Miriam grinned back at him. "You look like a pretty good driver with that cart of yours."

"I am. Come in and have a soda. When I get bigger I am going to learn to make sodas for people."

Trygve held open the door and whispered in her ear as she passed. "Benny is terribly shy, as you may have noticed."

She laughed at him over her shoulder. He was staring at her like that again.

"Welcome," a young woman said from behind the counter. "You must be one of the nursing students. I am Rebecca."

"And I am Miriam Hastings. I have never had a soda before, so this is an adventure."

"Well, Trygve brought you to the right place, especially for your first one. What flavor would you like?" She rattled off a list of six.

"I'll take the strawberry, please." *Here I am in a soda shop with a good-looking young man, and I just arrived. What whirlwind caught me up?*

Chapter 27

Canning never used to wear her out like this. They were only a week into August, so she would still be at it for weeks.

"You go out on the porch and join Haakan and Manny. I'll mix up some gingerbread for supper tonight. The pork chops are ready to put on, and the noodles are drying fine." Freda made shooing motions with her hands.

"I'll take that last pan of beans to snap, then."

"I thought to can them whole and pickle part of them. What do you think?"

"That would be different." Ingeborg stopped before opening the screen door and watched Haakan with Manny.

"You never had a knife before?" Haakan asked.

"Sure I did. But just whittled sticks and such. Didn't never carve nothing. Not like you do."

"Who made the furniture for your house?"

"Papaw used to. But he died. Pa wasn't much for workin' like that. He grew tabaccy to sell for cash money. Din't have too good a luck with it. Nor much of anything, really. He did good with moonshine, till the rev'nooers like to strung him up. Busted up his still and one of his arms."

Haakan kept on working the piece of wood he had rough-shaped into a soup ladle.

What kind of a life has that poor boy led? Ingeborg sat down on the chair Freda set behind her, relishing the breeze cooling her skin. Canning turned the kitchen into a steam bath. But they would most certainly appreciate the results in the winter. The shelves down in the cellar were already lined with canned raspberries and strawberries, jam, syrup, string beans, and some canned shelled beans. The leather britches were drying up in the extra bedrooms. The heat of the sun on the roof could dry most anything.

"So you would teach me how to carve like that?"

Ingeborg knew what great courage it took for the boy to ask that. Haakan did not let on his joy. He'd confided to Ingeborg that he wasn't sure if he was getting through to Manny. But he was.

"First, you need to keep your knife really sharp. I use a whetstone all the time." Haakan picked up the stone, spit on it, and started working his knife around in circles on the gritty surface. "You do first one side then the other. Always in a circle. If you do so often enough, you'll hone a good edge on your knife, then keeping it up is far easier." He reached down in the toolbox beside his chair and handed Manny one of the stones too.

"So where is your knife?"

Manny hung his head. "I . . . I lost it. Or one of my brothers took it. Not sure which."

"First of all, you need a knife." Haakan put his wood and knife down. "I'll go look in a couple places. I'm sure we have another one somewhere. We'll start you out on something easier than the one I'm working on. There are never too many wooden spoons in a kitchen."

Ingeborg scooted her chair back to let Haakan come in.

She mouthed *I told you so* when he went by, making him grin back at her. She felt like they were being conspirators, ganging up on a bruised and broken boy. One who needed all the love and attention they could give him, even though Manny had no idea what he needed or wanted. Right now the way to his heart was not only good food but a man who cared and showed it.

She watched as Manny studied the hand-carved pieces of his crutch. He ran his fingers over the crossbar and studied the holes the bar fit into. When Haakan returned Manny pointed to his crutch.

"Did you make this?"

"Well, me and Lars." Haakan sat down beside him. "See, we started with a strong willow branch that was still green so that it could be bent. I tried using one and splitting it to make the two sides here." He ran his fingers over the parts he wanted Manny to understand. "Then we carved a curved bar for the top, but that didn't turn out strong enough, so we went with two branches and bolted them together, then carved the two crossbars, one for under the arm, one for the hands. That's something about figuring out a project like this. We had to make it sturdy enough to last and smooth enough so you wouldn't get slivers. Next time, I'm going to use seasoned wood like—"

"What is seasoned?"

"Wood that's been dried. We put pieces we think might work for something up in the rafters of the machine shed. Good wood is a treasure. Did your Papaw have a place to store the wood he might use?"

"Don't know. I was too young to learn enough. And then he died and no one else liked to do wood like he did."

"Seems you have an interest in it."

"Maybe."

Ingeborg watched Manny draw back. As if he might have said too much?

"I found you a knife, but it needs a good edge. Been in the drawer too long, I guess." Haakan handed the knife to Manny, whose smile took off without his permission.

"For me?"

Haakan nodded. "It needs to be used. Tools are like people. They need to be used. And useful. So let's start getting edges on both blades. The little blade is good for getting into small places, but you will use the large blade mostly, so let's start sharpening that one." He opened his knife blade, picked up his whetstone, and waited for Manny to do the same. "Now you just do what I do and we'll see how this goes." Manny followed his every move, and within moments, they were both making circles on the grainy stone.

Ingeborg enjoyed just watching them. Seeing life in Manny's eyes was worth any kind of effort, and Haakan made it all look so simple.

"Okay, let's turn that blade over and do the same on the other side. Tilt your knife a hair more. After a while you develop a sixth sense that tells you when the knife is just right. Because yours is so dull, it will take plenty of grinding. Let me work with yours, and you see what a finer edge feels like."

"But what if I mess up your blade?" Manny's eyes widened.

Was he afraid? Ingeborg added a specific prayer to her ongoing list. Someone wounded that boy pretty bad if he didn't do something just right.

"I'll be watching to make sure you keep on track. Manny, this isn't life or death. We're just sharpening our knives."

The boy nodded, but his shoulders looked pinned to his earlobes.

Ingeborg wanted to go out and rub his back, his shoulders, give him a haircut, tease him into a smile or possibly a laugh. The only time she'd heard him laugh was when he was with Inga and Benny and the two calves in the barn.

"Where are you off to?" Haakan asked while keeping an eye on Manny and his circle-making on the whetstone.

Trygve leaned again the porch post, sipping from the glass of strawberry swizzle Freda had brought out immediately when Trygve greeted the others.

"I'm going in to retrieve the mail. You want to walk along?"

Haakan nodded. "Thought I'd wait until it started to cool down a bit, but . . ."

Ingeborg stepped out the door. "How about you help Freda and me for a while, Manny? And I was thinking, Miss Hastings is working the day shift today, so she might enjoy coming out here for supper if you would walk her out?" While she looked to Haakan, she kept an eye on Trygve. If he were a woman, would he be blushing? It was just as she thought. Their Trygve was finally smitten. She and Kaaren had been fairly sure, and they were both delighted. They'd not mentioned it to Haakan and Lars yet. Was this one of the reasons Trygve chose not to go out with the threshing crew? Although Andrew did need more help at home too.

Manny looked up from his careful knife sharpening with a nod. He handed his knife to Haakan. "What do you think?"

Haakan felt the edge with his thumb, then held the knife blade up to the light. "It's coming right along. You'll need to work on the tip more, but were you to cut that small block into slivers, this would work. The finer the edge the sharper, but it takes plenty of practice to feel the difference. Try cutting fine, even slivers off that piece of wood. When you whittled as a boy you weren't trying for perfection. The smoother you shave and cut, the less sanding you will have to do. Keep all your shavings in a basket—makes good fire starter."

"So right now that is my job? To make good fire starter?"

Ingeborg chuckled when Haakan snuckled. She loved that combination of a snort and a chuckle. Manny grinned. She could tell he was pleased to get that reaction from Haakan.

"We all started there." Trygve set his glass on the table. "Thanks, Freda. That hit the spot. I'm ready when you are."

"I'll call and talk with Miss Hastings."

"Takk." When Haakan started down the steps, Trygve reached around the post and handed him his cane. "You better use this. I don't want them coming after me."

Haakan rolled his eyes but took the cane.

Ingeborg thanked Trygve and sent them on their way, being careful to watch Haakan so he did not realize she was doing so. Her "mothering," as he called it, was not appreciated.

Turning back to the kitchen, she picked the earpiece off the oaken box on the wall, asked Gerald to ring the hospital, and smiled to herself both inside and out. Haakan would say she was matchmaking again. So what was wrong with that?

"Hello, Deborah, could I possibly speak with Nurse Hastings if she is available?"

"Of course. She is just getting ready to leave."

"And who is working the next shift?"

"Nurse Wells. I am so thankful for our student nurses. Ah, Ingeborg, we are so blessed."

"Indeed we are." Ingeborg heard the thump of Manny's crutches and the slam of the screen door.

"This is Nurse Hastings. How may I help you?"

"This is Ingeborg Bjorklund, and I have a favor to ask."

"Of course. How can I help you?"

"Trygve is walking in with Haakan to get the mail. I was wondering if you would like to walk back with them and come for supper. I would like your opinion on how Haakan is progressing. You know, we make sure someone is always with him, but he is chafing against that lately, and I asked him to go in for a checkup. . . . Well, you can guess his reaction."

Miriam chuckled. "Thank you. Of course I will do that. Let me tell Dr. Bjorklund what we are planning, since her mother-in-law is so generous to feed us all the time."

"Thank you. I look forward to your observations."

"Is there anything specific you are looking for?"

"Pace, breathing, things like that. I am hoping they will go have a soda. Haakan does love a soda."

"Don't we all?"

Ingeborg hung up and turned to share a secret look with Freda. Plotting could be a pleasure at times. "You want to bet that they will return with Inga swinging her grandpa's hand and making him laugh?"

"Haakan needs to laugh more."

"What is it you wanted me to do?" Manny perched on the tall stool they had moved into the kitchen for him.

"You can scrub the potatoes and peel the eggs I boiled a while ago."

"Women's work again," he mumbled under his breath.

Ingeborg shrugged. "To eat, you have to work, and since you can't milk cows yet or weed the garden or . . ." Her eyebrows went up along with her comment.

Manny smacked an egg on the table in front of him, but she knew he wasn't really pouting. It was as if he needed to make sure he knew better but was being forced to do women's work. And yet he had asked. Ingeborg shook her head slowly. There was never a dull moment, that was for sure. And once Inga got here, dull ran for cover.

"How come some eggs are white and some are brown?"

"Two different breeds of chickens."

"They taste the same."

"Yes. The difference is only on the shell. If you want to scrub the potatoes out back, I'll bring out the bucket."

He scooped the shells into a bowl to dump in the bucket kept for the chickens. "How come you feed the eggshells back to them?"

"Some people say it makes the hens eat the eggs, but we've not found that. They need the calcium to make more shells. I read once that people who live by the sea feed their chickens ground-up oyster shells to help them produce stronger shells."

"What are oysters?"

"A kind of shellfish. You find them attached to the rocks on the seacoast. I think they are best fried. Or smoked."

Freda was finishing up the gravy when they heard Inga calling "Grandma!" and the dog barking a welcome. She pounded up the steps and threw herself into Ingeborg's arms.

"Good thing I am sitting down. Where are the others?"

"They are coming, but I needed to see you." Inga paused and lowered her voice. "Do you know Grandpa goes slower than he used to?"

"I know, but he is getting stronger."

"I sure hope so." She hugged Ingeborg again, her topics changing as fast as her words flew. "Miss Hastings is a nurse, and she came too. She said you invited her."

"I did."

"She has lots of brothers and sisters, but she is the oldest, and they live in a big city called Chicago, and she is learning to be a nurse. But it seems to me she already knows lots about being a nurse because she is at our hospital and taking care of our patients." She paused to suck in a lightning-fast breath. "And—"

Ingeborg laid her finger lightly on Inga's grinning mouth. "And you asked her a million questions?"

The little girl frowned at her. "How else can I learn anything? And besides, she said her littlest sister is only eight, and she goes to school too." She wrinkled her forehead. "I can't remember her name. Joy, Mercy, *humph*. Oh, maybe she is the one called Truth. Aren't those the bestest names?" She hugged Ingeborg tight. "Maybe they could move out here so Miss Hastings wouldn't miss them so much." She threw her grandmother a calculating look. "Your house isn't big enough for all of them, but you would take good care of them like you do Manny and me and Emmy." She threw her arms wide. "And everybody!" With that she tore down the steps again and ran back to the others.

Ingeborg glanced over at Manny, who wore an openmouthed-shock look. He caught Ingeborg's gaze and shook his head. "I never heard anyone talk so fast in my whole life."

Ingeborg's grin swelled to a chuckle, and the two laughed together, bringing Freda to the door. "What am I missing out here? Those potatoes done?"

"Yes, ma'am." He grabbed a small one and handed her the full bowl. "You don't need to cook them, ya know." He bit the crispy new potato in half and crunched away.

Freda shook her head and swapped a shrug with Ingeborg, who really agreed with Manny. New potatoes—well, even older ones—did taste good raw, just like carrots and turnips and rutabagas. Only beets were better cooked than raw.

Inga returned, riding on Trygve's shoulders. He bent over at the steps to let her dismount onto the porch. "You know, you are getting a bit too big for that anymore." He flexed his shoulders, then tweaked her nose.

"I like seeing so far. You're a good horsey." She spun around to confront Haakan, who had folded down into his favorite rocking chair. "You ever thought about getting a pony for your grandchildren?" Hands on hips, she wrinkled her brow. "Or maybe two, so Carl and I can ride together? I saw a picture in a book where kids were riding. They had saddles even. Why would you need a saddle to ride?"

Miriam smiled at Inga. "I saw children riding ponies in a park in Chicago. And grown-ups riding real horses too. They had fancy clothes and hats and boots, and they looked quite grand."

"When Manny gets his leg all better, he can come out to the fields and ride the workhorses in. They like kids."

"How do you know they like you?" Manny asked.

"They snuffle your hair and check your pockets for carrots. They like sugar lumps too."

Manny gave her an I-don't-believe-you-for-one-minute look.

Inga shrugged. "You'll just have to see. Carl and I do that lots."

Freda came to the screen door. "Supper is all set up at the table. Inga, go wash your hands."

"But I didn't play in the dirt, not at all."

Trygve swooped her up and carried her into the kitchen, giggling away. The others followed, with Miriam and Ingeborg at the rear.

Miriam whispered, "Your husband did well, but I think the heat is harder than the walking. You can tell he does not like taking it easy."

"So true."

"But Inga is so good for him. She makes him laugh and forget we are walking slower than normal."

"Thank you." Ingeborg glanced up to catch Trygve watching Miriam, waiting to pull out her chair. Besotted. Definitely beyond smitten. Did he know the difficulty he faced? She only planned on getting through this year in the hinterland and then returning to Chicago. More than once in their few talks, the young woman had spoken with longing of her family and her ailing mother. Obviously, her family tugged at her heart far more than could any swain.

Oh, dear Trygve, you have a hard row ahead.

Chapter 28

Strolling back to town as the sun sank toward the horizon after the delightful meal at Ingeborg's made Miriam miss her family even more. How her mother would have loved visiting there, walking in the garden, probably asking for the recipes, enthralled by the land and the warmth of the sun. Her mother was never warm enough anymore. Even thinking such a far-fetched idea was a terrible waste of time. Her mother would never travel again. It would be a miracle if she ever left her bed, no matter how strong her spirit.

Miriam went from euphoria to despair in one breath.

"Thank you for coming out with us." Trygve's voice sounded richer in the gloaming.

She could feel the warmth of the man's arm as he walked so close beside her. "I am the one to be thankful. Your aunt Ingeborg is one in ten million. It would be impossible to feel like an outsider in her presence."

"Ja, that is true. Everyone becomes part of her family as soon as they meet her. If they . . ."

She waited and, when he didn't continue, asked, "If they what?" Glancing up, she caught the thoughtfulness on his face.

"If they are at all willing, I guess. I've known of some, not many, who resent her, you know?"

"Resent her for what?"

He shrugged and shook his head. "I can't find the words for what flipped through my mind. There is one family in town, the missus particularly, who . . ." He shook his head again. "No, that is gossip, and we all try hard not to engage in that. Reverend Solberg ferrets out and kills off gossip faster than a cat on a mouse. He abhors gossip, yet in a small town like this . . ." He snorted. "Guess people are like that everywhere."

"I don't know what small towns are like, but a rumor can whip through the hospital in seconds." She thought for a moment. "Would it be gossip to fill me in on the story of Manny and the bank robbers?"

"No. As Thorliff would say, that is news, not gossip." He gave her an abbreviated version. "So Astrid and Elizabeth did two surgeries on his leg, absolutely refusing to take the leg off like most doctors would have, and Solberg, Ingeborg, and all the rest prayed him through it all. The boy really does not realize how very blessed he is to have two legs."

The fence to Dr. Astrid's house was just ahead. The frogs had started singing at the river, and with no breeze, the mosquitoes added to the evening music. She slapped another that had landed on her arm.

"How come those horrid things don't seem to bother you?"

"Tante Ingeborg makes a lotion of comfrey and something else that keeps them away. Besides, North Dakota mosquitoes are particular. Lovely young ladies' blood is preferable to hardworking farmers'."

She chuckled. "I'm sure story-telling farmers are even less preferable."

"Must be." He paused at the gate. "What shift are you working tomorrow?"

"Days for two more. Then I am off one and then to nights for three shifts."

"Which do you like the best?"

She looked off to the west, where the sun had painted over the blue with colors she was sure she'd never seen before. "We do not have sunsets like this in Chicago. I think I would never tire of such beauty."

"Me too."

But when she glanced up, he was staring at her, not the flaming sunset. Heat hotter than any sunburn crept up her neck and ears. She jerked her attention back, keeping herself from meeting his gaze. "I . . . uh . . . th-thank you . . ." She moved closer to the gate. "I better get inside before the mosquitoes carry me away."

"I'd never let them do that." He stepped back and opened the gate for her. "I'll be there to walk you over for a soda when your shift is done tomorrow."

"I'm afraid that could get to be a habit." There. She had her voice under control again. "Good night." Without waiting for his response, she hustled up the walk and the porch steps without a backward glance, because she could feel his eyes on her back, and her neck had not cooled off.

"That was some exit." Vera giggled from the other side of the porch. The creaking swing seemed to be laughing too.

Instead of flying up to her room like she wanted, Miriam sucked in a deep breath and forced herself to stroll across the porch and join Mrs. Jeffers and the young nurse.

"Now, don't you be teasing her," Mrs. Jeffers said, a laugh

undergirding her voice. "Trygve is a fine young man and has the best of manners. I'm sure he did not act forward in any way."

Miriam reached up and unpinned her hat. "Ah, that is better." She laid the hat on a narrow table and sank down into the other chair. "Are the mosquitoes not bothering you out here?"

"Not so bad as long as we burn that foul-smelling candle." Mrs. Jeffers pointed to the squat candle that flickered on the table in front of the porch swing for two. "By the way, there was a letter for you at the post office this afternoon. I forgot to give it to you before you went out to the Bjorklunds'."

"He just rushed her off her feet." Vera giggled again. "Shame you had those chaperones along."

"Vera! Mrs. Bjorklund asked me to accompany them because she wanted my opinion on how well her husband is doing after his latest episode."

"Nice of her." She pushed the swing to a creaking. "That little Inga. She reminds me just a bit of what my baby sister used to be like. My mother fought to make her act properly, but she was never absolutely successful."

"She certainly is curious—about everything. And highly entertaining. She was thrilled to get to spend the night at her grandmother's." Miriam ignored the murmured "convenient" and turned to Mrs. Jeffers. "The letter is on the entry table?"

"Yes, dear. And if you have any letters to send, you leave them in that salver, and we'll make sure they get to the post office. I will have breakfast ready for you at six o'clock, so you do not feel rushed."

Miriam stood. "You are so good to us. We will be eternally spoiled. Coming, Vera?"

"In a bit. 'Night."

Up in the room that she shared with a sewing machine and a dressmaker's form, Miriam hung her hat on the peg on the wall. She disliked hats, but she disliked being sunburnt worse. She crossed to the windows to make sure both were open as wide as possible to catch a cross breeze and sank down into the rocking chair beside the lamp on the whatnot table. She lit the lamp, adjusted the wick so the kerosene would not smoke up the chimney, and set the glass chimney back in place.

A letter from home. Her first, although she had sent two. Rather than ripping the envelope open as she was prone to do, she sliced it gently with the letter opener in the basket that shared the space with the lamp. Unfolding the two thin sheets, she rejoiced to see her mother's spidery writing.

My dearest Miriam,

It is with great joy that I have grown strong enough with all this good care at the hospital to be able to write legibly again. I refuse to allow my horrid thoughts of being sent back to the tenement with all the filth there to take up residence in my mind. Instead, I thank all the hosts of heaven for this gift of grace. I just wish you were here to share in my delight. Thank you for your letters. I treasure them so.

I need to write to them more often. Guilt dug in like a mosquito's bite. She'd been here a little over a week now. Surely she could do better than a letter every few days. Especially since they meant so much to her mother.

I try not to worry about my children being left in that horrid place, but they assure me they are doing well. There has been some sewing needed here. Tonio still has his job, and both Mercy and Este are happy to be working here. They work long hours, but at least Joy has been able to stay in school, although I only see her on Sunday. I am so grateful to be able to give you good news for a change.

I know you are doing your best there, and I pray the training is helpful. I count the days until you return. I send you greetings from the others. They have promised to write too.

Your loving mother

Miriam tucked the letter into her case and undressed for bed. She'd thought to have a bath tonight, but her eyes had grown heavier with the weight of unshed tears. Was God really there taking care of them, as their mother always said? Was God even interested in those locked into the squalor of the tenements of Chicago or any other city?

Going for a soda on the way home to the big comfortable house could easily become a habit. "Why can you be here like this every day?" she asked Trygve when he showed up the next afternoon.

"I go home afterward to help with the chores, and I work before I come here, so I look at this as my rest break for the day. Since haying is in full swing now, I will not be able to come tomorrow." He took a swallow from his chocolate mint soda that Rebecca said she was trying out. Holding the glass up, he studied it. "Not as good as some."

"After tomorrow I go on night shifts again."

"I know. I would find that terribly difficult. I like to sleep at night."

"I like the night shift. It is cooler. Many of our patients sleep through the night, and that gives me time to give more care to those who are awake."

"What about the man who was having such a struggle?"

She shook her head. "I feel so sorry for him. Here, he finally has a good job and he is dying."

"For sure?"

"He is so weak and unresponsive much of the time. We do our best to get him to eat or drink, but he takes so very little." She stared up into the branches of the tree that shaded the yard of the Soda Shoppe. Children were laughing inside and other places on the street. Hammers and saws proclaimed the continual building going on. A line of horse-drawn wagons filled with grain waited at the granary.

"Can I get you anything else?" Rebecca asked. "What did you think of that combination, Trygve?"

"It is good, but the berry ones are better."

"Now that we have ice cream again, that is our best seller."

"Can you sit down for a bit?" Ever the nurse, Miriam noted the slightly swollen ankles that seemed to be associated with the heat, as well as the increasing girth of the pregnant woman.

"I will a bit later. As soon as Gerald is done on the switchboard, he will run the shop while I finish up supper. Benny is trying to figure a way he can help more. He is so smart—he can add up the totals without a paper and pencil. He does it all in his head."

Miriam thought back to the conversation she'd had with Mrs. Jeffers, who was always ready to answer questions about the town and the folks of Blessing. She'd said how she admired Rebecca for keeping her business growing while her baby son, Swen, who was born in January, moved into the crawling stage. At seven months old now, they corralled him behind the soda counter or he rode sometimes with Benny on the wagon. The two were inseparable since school had let out. And now here Rebecca was showing again, another baby on the way. Good thing they had family to help at times. Hildegunn had become a doting grandmother, and Rebecca's family helped when needed. She'd also heard that Anji Baard Moen, Rebecca's oldest sister was coming back from living in Norway where her husband died.

Trygve slurped the last from his soda and set the glass down. "Thanks, Rebecca. Some of us are talking about how we might be able to help Benny."

"I'll keep praying for God to give us all the best of ideas."

There it was again. Another one in this town who trusted God would work out something special just for them. Miriam had heard Reverend Solberg praying with some of those in the hospital too. As did Ingeborg. If only she could believe like they did.

Some days were worse than other days. This day was horrible. Since telephone calls had not located Thorliff, Astrid hurried into the house. Oh good! Thorliff was home. He must have been out on one of the building projects. "Thorliff, can you find Father Devlin and bring him to the hospital?"

He looked at her oddly. "Now?"

"Please."

Thorliff got up from the table and grabbed his hat on the way out.

Astrid felt a heaviness, a terrible sadness within her. Their Irishman looked close to dying, and there was nothing she could do about it. She returned to the hospital.

After checking the nurses' station, she found the nurses changing the bedding for one of their incontinent patients. "There you are, Miriam. I just sent Thorliff searching for Father Devlin. Please come."

They both hurried to Mr. O'Flaherty's bedside. "He is comatose, bordering on delirium, and since you were able to help him before . . ." She knew Miriam had come on duty only a short time earlier.

Miriam stepped in close to the man's head and said something.

The most beautiful smile spread across his face, and he opened his eyes. He responded.

She asked a question.

His voice was raspy, shaky, but he responded.

She said a single word.

He responded.

Miriam looked at Astrid. "He's forgotten that Father Devlin visited him before and is so afraid he is going to die alone and unforgiven. Thank you for seeking Father Devlin again." Even though Mr. O'Flaherty's speech was halted and barely discernible, he was more calm with a nurse who could speak not only his home tongue, but was familiar with his religion too.

Thorliff hurried through the door with Thomas Devlin in tow. He might be working as a carpenter, but he still wore the clerical collar, in spite of its badly needing a scrubbing.

Miriam simply nodded toward the patient, and in a heartbeat, the carpenter became a priest. Astrid was astonished at the transformation. He was the same man, and yet . . .

The carpenter-father made the sign of the cross. "God's peace be in this place."

Miriam replied, "And in all who live and work here."

The father hooked a finger in his collar, pulled it away from his neck, and with his other hand drew out a small pouch on a cord. From the pouch he brought a tiny cross and a small vial, like ones used for medicines. He held the cross close to the patient's lips. Mr. O'Flaherty raised his head and drew the cross to his mouth. He kissed it and flopped back on the pillow. His whole face changed, from fearful to peaceful. Tears leaked down his cheeks. Happy tears, it would appear.

The two of them conversed for a few moments, which took longer due to the long pauses on the part of their patient. Astrid was surprised he was able to respond as much as he did. And sad that he no longer remembered the priest's other visits and the hours Miriam had spent with him. But, she reminded herself, he responded at the time. Surely God understood and remembered.

Miriam looked at Astrid. "Does your church have a formal confession?"

"Not like this."

Even Thorliff was watching with rapt attention.

Miriam lowered her voice. "He just blessed this place and asked for the services of a guardian angel. Sure and the service of a guardian angel would not be amiss." She raised her voice. "Amen."

All sorts of questions raced through Astrid's head. The main one? This man was obviously a priest, albeit Anglican, but why was a priest working as a carpenter?

Thorliff moved in closer, watching intently. Astrid glanced at him. She at least had seen Father Devlin working with this man before, so this wasn't such a surprise to her.

Still murmuring in Latin, the priest touched his thumb to each of Mr. Flaherty's eyelids.

Miriam explained, "He is saying, briefly, 'By this holy anointing and by His most tender mercy, may the Lord forgive you all the evil you have done through the power of sight.' And now he'll forgive and bind the evil done by each of Mr. O'Flaherty's other body parts."

Speaking rapidly, the priest touched his thumb to the man's

nostrils, his lips, his hands, his legs, his feet. After each touch, he wiped off the site of the touch with the cotton Miriam had given him.

But Astrid was struck by their patient's face. It had been drawn, terrified, but now she could see an expression of peace. Not joy, for the man was dying. But peace. A pleasant peace. She might not understand all that was going on, but this man was receiving what had been the most important thing in the world to him.

Miriam disappeared and returned with a small basin of water.

The priest recited some prayers and crossed himself. With fingers shaking in weakness, Mr. O'Flaherty drew the sign of the cross on his chest. His body relaxed, seeming to almost melt back into the pillow.

Father Devlin stepped away.

Miriam held the basin and a towel out to him. He carefully washed and dried his hands.

He smiled at her. "I thankee. A bit rough and ready, but quite adequate." He looked at Astrid, held her eye. "And I thank ye, Dr. Bjorklund, for allowing me to serve this fellow. 'Tis a gift. Ye cannot ken the extraordinary value of that gift."

Astrid realized she might not understand the full value, but she saw and understood its effect. Mr. O'Flaherty convulsed in another fit of coughing, and when it stopped, the peace drew back into place. Perhaps for some of the newcomers to Blessing, there were important needs that were not being met. Astrid promised herself she would talk with Reverend Solberg. She'd heard that the two men were becoming friends. An Anglican priest and a Lutheran pastor. Wasn't this the way God wanted His church to be? But deep inside, she had a feeling there was trouble brewing, especially if everyone did not understand the differences and the similarities of the churches.

Chapter 29

"Good evening, Trygve!" Miriam smiled. Smiling came easily when he was around.

"You are on night shift, right?" Trygve watched her.

"I start in an hour or so."

"Would you like to take a walk? We wouldn't go far, of course."

"Yes, I would. Thank you."

They strolled together down the street toward the river.

Saturday night. Miriam understood that in most of the country, especially in the rural areas, Saturday night was when swains took their ladies out to dances, or to soda shops, or just out walking. She'd heard of hayrides and barn dances and shucking bees, where the whole community got together to shuck corn.

Corn. They didn't grow corn in Chicago. So much was different here. But it didn't matter what sort of entertainment was out there. Miriam would be in here, working in this hospital, handling the night shift. She would complete her training, then go back to Chicago. Her mother. Tonio. All her siblings. She missed them.

"What are you thinking about?" Trygve was looking at her intently.

"Chicago. My family. We are very close. I miss them."

"So which do you like best—Chicago or Blessing?"

She thought about this. Chicago? Dirt and squalor, magnificent buildings, pretty parks, the lake, downtown bustle. Mud when it rained, except on the main streets. Blessing? Fresh air, bright new buildings, strange smells that were nevertheless clean, hardly any bustle. Mud, when it rained. "It doesn't matter, really—here or there. It's the people. There are lovely people here, but my family is there."

Trygve was staring off in the distance, no doubt thinking. "My onkel Haakan and tante Ingeborg came here from Norway. Tante Ingeborg started the cheese house, and Onkel Haakan built their farm."

"A marvelous place. Very warm and inviting."

"Ja. Then they invited the rest of the family to come out from Norway. And friends. Land is hard to find in Norway. You can almost never just buy land. It's handed down from generation to generation, always being split into smaller lots. Here, there is almost no end to good farmland."

"Ah. So that is why there are so many Norwegian people around. That is also why there are so many Polish, Italian, and Russian people in Chicago. And Irish. Often the Irish are not well received. But in Chicago they have opportunities."

"You should bring your family out here. Lots of opportunities."

She shook her head. "I often think my mother would love to visit, but she's too frail. And my brothers and sisters are making lives for themselves there."

"And you are determined to go back to Chicago?"

She frowned at him. "Your voice sounds tense, like I'm making a wrong choice. Why? That has been the arrangement all along."

"Have you prayed about it?"

What could she say? She knew all these people prayed at the drop of a hat. "No. I leave prayer for others." She stopped. "We should turn back. I go on duty soon."

"Of course." They started walking back the way they had come. "Arrangements can be changed, you know." And then he was silent.

What was he thinking? What was she thinking? She felt mixed up.

"Miriam? Would you do me an immense favor?"

"I suppose. What is it?"

"Come to church with me tomorrow."

Oh dear. How could she get out of this? "I'll have come right off work, after being up all night. I would fall asleep in the pew."

He smiled. "Sometimes the godliest fall asleep in the pew. I'll poke you now and then. But I would like you to come with me. I really would."

"I, uh . . ."

"And dinner afterwards, of course. As a favor to me, Miriam?"

She could say that nice Anglican girls did not go to Lutheran services, but she was not a nice Anglican girl, and he knew it. On the other hand, she really did want to do him a favor, to please him. It was only an hour. Surely she could survive an hour. "If you wish, yes. I will go."

"Thank you, Miriam!" At the hospital door, he took her hand in his and kissed her knuckles. And walked away.

This surprised her. Dr. Bjorklund had once claimed that in Norway, a man and woman never showed any display of affection in public. Her neck was burning hot as she entered the building.

She waged still another losing battle with this hair of hers, fighting to contain it neatly in her nursing cap. She sat briefly at the station, going through the notes from the day. Apparently

Mr. O'Flaherty was the only patient at the moment whose condition was serious.

She took up her notepad and began at the far end of the hall, visiting each ward, talking softly to those patients still awake. She visited Mr. O'Flaherty last.

Something was wrong. He was not awake, but he was not in peaceful sleep the way she'd hoped. His breathing was heavy, irregular.

"Mr. O'Flaherty?"

Nothing. Wait. He was raising his arm, or trying to. She grasped his hand in hers. He still could barely breathe. She switched to Gaelic and asked if he needed the priest.

Yes.

She ran to the phone and called Dr. Bjorklund.

"I'll send Daniel for Father Devlin immediately." Dr. Bjorklund hung up.

Miriam ran back to the room and took up Mr. O'Flaherty's hand. "They are sending for Father Devlin. He'll be here soon." She repeated the message in Gaelic.

He squeezed her hand slightly. Or did he? It was hard to tell.

Dr. Bjorklund entered the room.

"Oh good," Miriam said. "Mr. O'Flaherty, your doctor is here." Also in Gaelic.

Dr. Bjorklund's hair was not pinned up, but most likely, she had been prepared for bed. Or in bed. Miriam felt bad about calling, but she felt even worse that she did not know what to do for Mr. O'Flaherty.

Dr. Bjorklund stood beside his bed, a rather grim look about her. "Good evening, Mr. O'Flaherty. As you know, Nurse Hastings is a student nurse from Chicago. I would like to use you for a moment. Nurse, please demonstrate three different ways to check his circulation."

Miriam frowned. Why this? Why now? "With a stethoscope I listen to his heart, of course. Uh, and I might press a fingernail like this." She pinched a fingernail on the hand she was holding. It turned white, but it took several long seconds to return to pink. "Also, I might look at the color of the inside of a lower eyelid." Carefully, she pulled downward with a thumb on Mr. O'Flaherty's eye. The eyelid was nearly white.

"Very good, Nurse. Now demonstrate how you might test for responsiveness."

She looked at Dr. Bjorklund. Mr. O'Flaherty was dying. Miriam was pretty sure of that. The tests just now showed very poor circulation. Why was the doctor not letting him go in peace?

She was about to act when Reverend Solberg came hastening in. "Good evening, Astrid. Good evening, Miss Hastings."

"Good evening, sir." Miriam stepped back to give him ample room beside the bed.

"Good evening, Reverend Solberg. Thank you for coming." Dr. Bjorklund bent over to speak to Mr. O'Flaherty. "I asked Reverend Solberg to come by in case Father Devlin was slow to respond. They have to find him in the tent city, and he may have retired for the night."

The reverend took up the hand Miriam had just let go of. "I am John Solberg, Mr. O'Flaherty. We have met."

The door burst open and in came the good father, all out of breath. "Top o' the evening, all. Eh, John. So good of ye to come. Thankee." He continued around the bed to take Mr. O'Flaherty's other hand.

He began in Gaelic, and to Miriam's surprise he recited one of St. Patrick's poems in Gaelic, the one about Jesus around me and above me and all. Mr. O'Flaherty smiled faintly. Father Devlin spoke again, and his voice was upbeat, lilting.

Miriam translated, not so much word for word as meaning for

meaning. "He said there was not a lot of new sin Mr. O'Flaherty could have committed in the hospital bed, so he is administering a sort of blanket absolution for anything they might have missed earlier."

Father Devlin switched to Latin as he pulled out that pouch and opened his little vial of oil, moistening his thumb. He anointed Mr. O'Flaherty's forehead.

"Now he's officially cleansing Mr. O'Flaherty of all sin and guilt. And now he's praying."

Mr. O'Flaherty smiled. That faint smile had turned into a true smile. His mouth moved, but no words came out. Then, a raspy sort of whisper.

"I'm not certain, but I believe Mr. O'Flaherty is praising the name of God and Jesus and the Holy Spirit. Aye, he is."

Father Devlin made the sign of the cross over the patient, tapping the patient's forehead, his shoulders, and his chest.

The patient exhaled. He did not inhale. The belabored breathing had stopped. The smile remained.

Miriam and the father crossed themselves.

Quietly, Astrid drew the bed sheet up over Mr. O'Flaherty's still-smiling face.

Miriam was so overcome that she almost forgot to snatch up a bit of cotton for the father to wipe off his thumb.

"Thankee, lass. Ye need not fetch a basin. This will do." And he popped the thumb into his mouth. Rough and ready, he called it. It was that, but it was also official policy nonetheless, so far as Miriam could remember. The priest could consume the oil if washing was not an immediate option.

Reverend Solberg's head was bowed, his hands clasped. Presently, he stood erect and opened his eyes. "Astrid, Thomas, I have been praying quite a bit about this. This man is not the only person in our midst who is from a different church. There are actually quite a few. Not the least of them is your nurse here, Miss Hastings. Thomas, I see how great the need is, just in this man's dying face. The peace you brought him. I could not have done that."

Father Devlin nodded. "Eh, technically, ye could have done it, but he would not have known ye can. And the knowing, that's what brought him peace. 'Tis all in how we're brought up, of course. And how God directs our paths."

"Thomas, will you come to church with me tomorrow, please? I want to approach the congregation about building a church to serve those who were brought up differently. I think it's high time Blessing was a blessing to everyone, not just some of us."

Dr. Bjorklund frowned. "Remember the grumbling when news got out that we let the father here perform extreme unction? There could be trouble. Resistance."

"I agree. I am also strongly convinced we must serve everyone we can. This man was a Christian, Astrid, as true as anyone in my congregation. The need is there. Besides . . ." There was a twinkle in his eye. "The best defense is a good offense."

The two men left together.

Dr. Bjorklund turned to leave.

"Doctor?" Miriam crossed to her.

She stopped and turned back. "Yes?"

"Why did ye quiz me on a dying man, please? Why not let him go in peace?"

"You know the solace that the father provided him before. I was afraid Mr. O'Flaherty might die before Father Devlin could get here. You are the closest he has to next of kin, you with your Gaelic. If anything could keep his attention, keep him with us, it would be that."

Miriam grinned. "And it worked! I see."

"Since he has no next of kin, would you wash him, please? Prepare the body?"

"Yes, ma'am. I would be honored."

"Do you need help with it?"

"I can manage. I'll call if I need someone."

The doctor nodded. "You did well this evening, Miriam. Thank you. Good night." And she left.

Miriam had nearly the whole shift to think. When she did rounds an hour later, all her patients were resting comfortably. Next she washed the body of a man who had died alone and only by the grace of God received appropriate rites.

In the morning she would go with a nice Norwegian man to visit a church that an Anglican priest would also visit. The world was such a strange place!

During the wee hours of the morning she very nearly fell asleep, despite all the drama and dread. Was she doing the right thing by accepting Trygve's invitation? The priest had accepted the reverend's invitation, but that was for business purposes, you might say, the prospect of building another church. The work of the Lord. Still, he was going. Did that mean she had made the correct choice? By the time she went off duty she was very confused and weary.

She washed, dressed, and fought her hair to a standstill. That took a while. But when Trygve stopped by for her, her hat was perched at a jaunty angle and pinned down with three different sizes of hatpins and hairpins.

As they walked to church and she told him about her night, a startling thought struck her. Was she supposed to make final arrangements, since she was sort of the next of kin, even though she wasn't? What arrangements ought to be made? Her mother had made all their father's arrangements, and the priest did for others in their Chicago church.

Reverend Solberg met her and Trygve at the door. "Good morning to you both."

Trygve was grinning cheerfully. She had just told him a man had died in her presence, but apparently it didn't hit him the way it weighed on her.

"Reverend Solberg, are there arrangements that I must make? I know nothing about this."

"Not at all. Tommy—that is, Father Devlin—put together a service for this afternoon. I will announce it, of course. And thank you for your ministry, Miss Hastings. It was needed and most welcome."

She stuttered just a little. She hadn't been expecting that. "You're welcome." All she did was pop out a cotton bit for the father. And prepare the body. And translate for the reverend and doctor, who did not know Latin and Gaelic.

Here came the Bjorklund wagon, and that Manny McCrary was driving. My goodness, but he was doing well. And look at how proudly he sat there. She suspected the Bjorklund team was well broken, but they responded beautifully as he drew the wagon alongside the church.

They dropped the tailgate in back, and old Mr. Bjorklund, Onkel Haakan, doddered down a set of steps someone had obviously made for just that purpose. Andrew reached up to give him a hand, and there was Father Devlin, stepping up on his other side. They helped him to the ground. They supported Tante Ingeborg too, but she was much sprightlier.

"Good morning, you two!" Ingeborg seized Miriam's hands in hers. "It is so good to see you here! Astrid called this morning and told me about Mr. O'Flaherty and how pleased she was with the way you handled it."

"I'm glad I could be of service."

"She asked me to bring some food for the graveside service

this afternoon. She called others too." Trygve's aunt went on describing a few other items of preparation. Good. It would all be taken care of, and Miriam didn't have to take responsibility for a man related to her only by roots in the old country and a language hardly anyone spoke anymore, not even in Ireland.

As the service began, they all rose to sing a hymn and pray. Then they all sat down again, and she just kept going down to dreamland. And Trygve let her! He let her down. He had said that if she fell asleep he would poke her. He did not.

A harsh voice nearby woke her abruptly. Anner Valders had stood up. "I object to the whole idea, Reverend. We do not need another church in Blessing. If people want to go to church, let them come to this one." And he waved an arm toward Miriam, singling her out! "Like this young lady. See? She wants to come to church, so here she is. And all that Latin mumbo-jumbo. Don't need it. Nobody understands Latin anyway."

Her mouth dropped open and she almost stood up to say, *"I understand Latin perfectly well, thank you. And so do many others."* But she kept her seat and clapped both hands over her mouth. She must not embarrass Trygve.

She really had been asleep. There stood Father Devlin up beside Reverend Solberg, and she had slept through the introduction!

Someone else stood up and said, "I agree with Anner. There aren't that many people in town who would benefit from a second church. It's unwise to build a fine church nobody will use."

"How many people are we talking about, anyway?" someone else asked.

"It doesn't matter how many there are!" Mr. Valders interrupted. "Let them come right here. Good, solid Christian church. Full of believers, the kind of church Jesus prefers."

She gasped. How could he . . . ? He didn't understand at all. Yet, people obviously believed him.

The reverend barked, "Anner, this is a service of worship, not a town meeting. We will discuss a new church later. For now, I just want you all to know that Father Devlin is available for anyone who feels the need for his services. And I trust you all realize that I fully support his ministry. Now let's turn to hymn 247 and sing all four verses."

Anner Valders stood up again, obviously to object. Someone on the other side of him yanked on his arm and sat him down again. It was not Mrs. Valders. She sat on this side of him.

Dr. Bjorklund—the Elizabeth one—flipped rapidly through her hymnal to find the page. She struck the opening chords.

Trygve opened the book and held it so they both could use it, but Miriam did not know the song at all. In Chicago she had rarely gone to church, and then not to services with singing. At her father's funeral a choir had sung strange words to a very familiar old tune that Miriam loved— "The Ash Grove." That was about it for music, so far as she was concerned.

She would be *so* glad when this horrible morning was finally over with.

One last amen, and it was done.

The reverend greeted all as they filed out, smiling, shaking hands. At his side, Father Devlin laughed and talked to people, a cheerful carpenter in holy orders. People laughed and talked to him.

Mr. Valders did not laugh or talk. He glared.

As he marched away, Father Devlin cheerfully called, "The Lord's blessing be upon ye, sir!" Quietly he said, "I thought briefly of blessing him in Latin, but I doubt he'd appreciate it."

Trygve started to escort Miriam toward home.

"Trygve?" Tante Ingeborg trotted to catch up to them. "Please bring Miriam along and come to dinner. I've invited Reverend

Solberg and the Father. I also invited Anner, but he and Hildegunn have other plans."

"Thank you, Tante Ingeborg! We'd love to."

They continued on.

"Oh, we'd love to, eh?" Why did Miriam feel so out of sorts? "When shall I sleep today? Or perhaps I need not."

"Oh, that's right. You're on night duty again tonight." He frowned. "I can bring you home right after dinner. We don't need to sit around. Although it should be very interesting."

Interesting? Trouble! Miriam dreaded what was coming in this town.

And part of it was her fault.

CHAPTER 30

I never dreamed something like this would happen in Blessing."

"*Hmpff*. People are people no matter where they are." Freda slammed the bread dough over and kneaded it as if she were dealing with Anner Valders. "You know better than to think the people of Blessing are perfect." Slam and push. "Besides, it'll all blow over. You watch."

Ingeborg paused in her bean snapping and wiped the perspiration from her forehead with her apron. "You might be right, but Anner carries a lot of weight."

"That's for sure."

Ingeborg shook her head, a grin tugging at her mouth. Their town banker had indeed added some girth over the last couple of years. All the building and the businesses growing had been good for the town and especially for the town bank. More and more, Anner Valders was acting as if he owned the bank rather than just managed it for the community, which really owned it. *Pompous* was getting to be a good word for him.

Ingeborg asked, "So you think we should just ignore it all?"

"Well, I wasn't in church yesterday, but it sounds like Haakan, Lars, and the others handled it very well."

"We've never had dissension like that. John Solberg is the closest to a saint that I know. And that Father Devlin is charming, with his ready smile and, as Kaaren said, his lilting accent." She smiled, thinking of the Sunday dinners here at the farm like they had done for so many years. "I think John is enjoying a growing friendship with Thomas. Tommy. He said not to call him Father, or Priest or Reverend, even." She stared off into the distance while her fingers continued to break the string beans into smaller pieces. "There has to be a story there, you know."

"Mark my words, much as you and I want this to blow ever, there will be—"

Freda paused at the sound of boots on the steps.

"Where's Haakan?" Trygve's voice.

"Come on in. He and Manny are down at the barn."

Freda laid the well-kneaded dough in the crockery bowl and spread a clean towel over it before setting it in a spot of sun to rise. One thing for sure, on August days like this the bread rose quickly.

Trygve kept the screen door from slamming as he entered. "I thought Inga was here."

"She's down at the barn too."

"What's going on?"

"Calf being born. Coffee?" Ingeborg set her finished pan of green beans in the sink.

"No, thanks."

"Are you sick?" Freda added more wood to the fire and pulled the canner full of now-sterile empty jars off to the side to be filled with beans.

"Is Onkel Haakan okay? Far is sure disgusted with *Mr.* Valders." He emphasized the *mister* part.

Ingeborg paused to consider. "I think we all are, if not disgusted, truly disappointed." She opened the oven door with her apron protecting her hand. "Pies are done. Since the haying crew is having dinner at your house, did you by any chance bring a wagon over?"

"Why do you think I really am here? Call me errand boy today."

"The cheese is wrapped there on the table. The pot of ham and beans has been cooking most of the night, and the pies will need to cool for a bit."

"The rolls will be ready in about an hour," Freda added. Since Kaaren had more room and help, she had decreed that she would be feeding the harvest crew at the deaf school this year, rather than taking turns like they had in the past.

"What do you think of putting Manny to work driving the wagon, hauling the grain into town?" Trygve asked. "I thought to take him with me to get used to driving."

"He can't get in and out of the wagon, you know."

"I know, but he is already learning to drive."

"Ask Haakan. He's been working with the boy on woodcarving and says they start milking tomorrow morning."

He headed for the door. "Back in a bit." He paused. "Besides, Haakan had Manny drive to church yesterday, and he did just fine."

Ingeborg glanced at the clock. How could noon be coming so fast? Inga's footsteps pounded up the stairs.

"Grandma, the calf is standing up already and nursing, and we got to see it be borned, and Grandpa said it is a boy calf. How does he know that?"

Ingeborg hugged her granddaughter to her and leaned her cheek down on the hair that refused to stay in the braids she had dutifully put in place earlier in the morning. "I'm glad you got to see the calf born." *So, what will Elizabeth say when Inga goes home and tells her how to tell a boy calf from a girl calf?*

Thank you, Haakan. Sometimes the best offense is to ignore the question. "Did you decide on a name for the calf? That makes four now, right?"

"Five, Grandma. One was borned out in the field, 'member? And Patches found it before Onkel Andrew did, and Grandpa said he should have gone looking earlier, and you said—"

Ingeborg laid a finger over the little mouth. "That's right. I forgot, is all. So what are you going to name it?"

"If it was a heifer"—she said the proper word with a wide grin—"we would call her Daisy, 'cause the daisies are still blooming, but Grandpa said we should call him Thistle, cause he was hard on his ma. What did he mean?"

"You ask him. I have no idea." Ingeborg was sure that was a double snort she heard from Freda, who was sliding another pair of pies into the oven. Earlier they had taken a spice cake out to feed the men at supper. Freda had a knack for never having to answer Inga's questions.

Manny's crutches creaked on the steps. He'd gone to putting both under one arm and hopping up the three steps with the other hand on the railing Haakan had built for him. The chairs groaned as they sank into them. Somehow Inga had not learned to keep the door from slamming as she headed outside, no doubt to ask another barrage of questions. Let Haakan deal with them, although she was certain he'd had an earful in the barn.

"Is this the last of it?" Trygve shoved the hot soup pot into the only corner left in the wagon.

Freda called "Ja" over her shoulder and went back inside. Tante Ingeborg waited by the rail to see him off, holding the horse, which she had untied.

He watched his tante Ingeborg for a few moments. She got

tired once in a while now. He could see it in the way she moved. So? Everyone who works hard gets tired, and no one worked harder than she. But somehow Tante Ingeborg never did. Until Onkel Haakan started to slide.

"Manny? Coming?"

"I'm here." The boy came clomping over to the front wheel. Farm life seemed to be suiting him well. He had a rosy-cheeked look to him, and the shirt he was wearing was a little too small. They said he'd been strong for his size before the whole bank-and-hospital thing. He seemed to be getting his strength back.

"Here." Trygve stepped in behind him. "I'll boost you up into the wagon box."

"I can do it." Manny tossed his crutches into the wagon in front of the box.

Trygve stepped back, glancing at Tante Ingeborg. She was smiling too. Let the boy try and fail. Then Trygve could boost him.

Manny gripped the top of the front wheel with both hands and, with a mighty lunge, straightened his arms. He hung there a moment, then stepped with his good leg on a wheel spoke. Another lunge, and he was gripping the iron rod that served as an arm rest on the wagon seat. One more lurching lunge dragged him into the wagon. He hopped around to sitting on the iron rod, then sort of slid onto the box seat. It was slow and clumsy, but he'd done it. He beamed triumphantly.

Tante Ingeborg clapped her hands.

Trygve climbed in. "Good job, Manny!" He gathered in the lines and handed them to the boy. "You drive."

Manny took the lines. "Ain't like riding a horse, where you use your knees and legs to tell it what to do." He fumbled the lines a little but got them divided out correctly. It took him a minute to position his hands so that the lines were a good length.

Tante Ingeborg let go and stepped back. She was smiling brightly.

So was Manny. He flicked the lines and clucked, bracing his good leg against the dashboard.

The wagon lurched and rattled and they were off.

"Going to the deaf school, right?"

"Right. You're a good hand with horses, Manny."

"That's what Shack says. 'Course that's why I always ended up cleaning out the horse shed. He'd hand me a shovel and say, 'You're good with horses, Manny.'"

"Why is he named Shack?"

"His name's Meshach. You know, Shadrach, Meshach and Abednego? Daniel's buddies? Mine's Manasseh. That was Joseph's son. You know, Joseph, his coat of many colors? What's Trygve? Never heard of no one named Trygve."

"Trygve means true, or trustworthy in Norwegian."

Manny handled the lines well, turning the horses by gently drawing, not tugging. "Ma, she read the Bible. Pa couldn't read a'tall, but he said we had to have Bible names so as God would know us. He'd drop it on the table on its back—"

"Spine?"

"Yeah. So's it would fall open, then put his finger on the page. Ma would start there and read out loud till she came to a man's name, and that's what we'd be called. 'Cept once she reared back and said, 'No son of mine gonna be named Herod!' And Pa had to drop the book again. That was Jed. Jedediah."

Trygve kept his smile from reaching his mouth.

When they reached the school, Trygve didn't even have to leave the wagon box. Lots of eager hayers' hands unloaded their dinner. It did smell good.

Manny asked, "You said to the boardinghouse?"

"Yes. We'll eat there."

"Suits me." And Manny turned the wagon toward town.

A smile leaped to Trygve's mouth when he saw Miriam walking toward the boardinghouse with a basket over her arm.

They pulled up to the door. "Manny, do you think you can unhitch?"

"Sure can! I can get down without your help too." It took him a while to get his bad leg over the side and his good leg on the wheel spoke. What would happen if one of his arms gave out? But he seemed to have that extra strength back. He made it to the ground and got his crutches. "I can take care of it, Mr. Trygve." He tucked the lead line under his arm and hobbled off toward the shed.

Miriam wagged her head. "How can he do that? He's making wonderful progress."

"He is." Trygve took the basket out of her hand and opened the door for her. "After dinner I would like to take you out for a soda."

"After dinner I would enjoy that."

He could hardly wait for dinner to begin—he was quite hungry—and end, so he could take the lovely Miriam Hastings to the soda shop. Finally, finally, they walked out into the bright, hot sunshine and ambled down the street. He ordered and they waited until the sodas were made, then took them out to enjoy under the vine-covered lattice arbor. By this time of the year the arbor was very cool and inviting, the vines so thick with leaves, the sun could not get through.

"You are right, you know." Miriam sipped at her soda. "No matter how good chocolate is, these berry ones are tastier. And they do interesting things inside your mouth. Little bursts of flavor."

"I agree. Miriam, thank you for going with me to church yesterday. I appreciate it. I know you did it as a favor to me."

"I never— How can I say this? I really don't care to go again. That Mr. Valders calling me out like that. It was horrible!"

"I agree. He should not have done that or voiced his opinion during the service. But Reverend Solberg shouldn't have voiced his opinion either, when you come right down to it, and Mr. Valders does have some very good points."

She stopped midspoonful and gaped. "Good points? Didn't you attend the burial?"

"Well, no. I didn't know the fellow well. Besides, I had to return the dinner leavings."

"That Anner Valders after the interment service! He complained that the Father did Mr. O'Flaherty's burial ceremony in Latin and nobody could understand. He said Father Devlin should not be deliberately causing dissension like this—as if any dissension is all the Father's fault—and then to blaspheme poor Father Devlin the way he did, saying if you can't speak English, why, you should just go back where you came from! He said that."

"Yes, but—"

"He called us all foreigners, Trygve! Said this is a Christian nation that speaks English, and we can—" She was so furious her face was red. "Just what do you call someone who thinks Norwegian is just fine but not Gaelic or Russian? Or Latin? He even stated that Mr. O'Flaherty should not be buried in a Christian cemetery because the Irish are not Christians. *He said that*, Trygve!"

"You're overstating it, Miriam. Mr. Valders is really quite a good Christian man, he just—"

"How can you call yourselves Christians and treat a priest like that? A man of God! And why in the world would anyone care where Mr. O'Flaherty is buried? Certainly not his immediate neighbors!"

"You don't understand!"

"Oh, yes I do! I understand far too thoroughly."

"Listen to me. It is just one man. Just one opinion, and—"

"Which he voiced in no uncertain terms, and half the people were nodding, agreeing with him. This is why I don't go to any church, and believe me, from now on that includes yours."

"As I was saying, I mean this Father Devlin is just one man, not Valders. It's not like we have a whole host of people who don't like our church and want to go to some other church. They—"

"There are plenty of unhappy workers. Most of the construction crews out of the East are *not* members of your church. They belong to many churches. You have no idea what they want, what they are saying, or how much they need a church of their own. And certainly that Mr. Valders does not."

"If they want us to know what they're saying, let them come to church speaking English."

She stood up and slapped her napkin on the table. "Thank you for the soda, but I'd rather go back to my room. I have things to do."

He stood up.

Her eyes were blazing. "Don't bother. I can probably find my way home."

She snatched up her reticule and stormed out, that funny little hat perched precariously in her thick mane of hair.

Women! How could she be so cool and in command one moment and so wildly hotheaded and wrong the next? She didn't even listen to what he was really trying to say.

Onkel Hjelmer always said it was no wonder women were denied the vote. A person that irrational can't be trusted to make good choices.

He was about done with women. Any woman.

Especially *that* woman!

Bah!

Chapter 31

"All right, so what is really going on?" Astrid stared at Elizabeth, her tone saying far more than the words.

Elizabeth leaned back on the settee on the porch, her face as pale as winter snow.

Astrid realized immediately that she'd lost more weight too, and the rest she'd prescribed didn't seem to be helping.

Ingeborg moved to the settee and sat on the edge, taking Elizabeth's hand in hers. "We can only help you if we have more than an idea of what the problem is."

"It shouldn't be a problem. We should all be rejoicing."

"Where is Inga?" Astrid asked.

"Playing over at Sophie's." A tear trickled from the edge of Elizabeth's eye, meandering over her cheek.

"Have you told Thorliff yet?"

A shake of the head. "He is already worried and probably has figured it out. But then again, perhaps not. Men don't usually count such things."

"So how many cycles have you missed?"

"Two, for sure. We were so very careful, I should not be pregnant."

"There's only one sure way." Astrid leaned against the back of her chair, eyes closed and weighted down with such dark thoughts, she could hardly breathe. How could she help keep Elizabeth alive this time when they almost lost her last time? Suspecting this, she'd not tried to lay out a plan yet, so intently hoping it wasn't true.

The distant song of a meadowlark, usually soothing, couldn't penetrate the miasma. She glanced over to see her mother, eyes closed and lips moving, doing the thing that always kept her sane. Prayer didn't always work that way with her daughter or her daughter-in-law.

"Do you think I do not carry enough guilt already?" Elizabeth finally asked.

"It takes two." Astrid knew she was being cruel, but— But what? What was she to do? What was Thorliff to do? Ingeborg had her work cut out for her—prayer. *Lord, I am trying to learn to trust you, but preventing a pregnancy would have made this easier for all of us.* Of what use . . . She decided to go no further with that line of thought. But how would she get through the months ahead being the only doctor, running the hospital, training nurses—including the two Indian women soon to arrive—and fighting to keep Elizabeth and her baby alive? The load threatened to cut off her breathing, it sat so heavy.

"When will you tell Thorliff, or do you want me to?"

"I will."

"Does Thelma know?" Ingeborg asked.

"Of course. She's the one who told me what was wrong. Oh, Astrid, Ingeborg, I want the joy that carrying a baby brings, a baby sister or brother for Inga, perhaps a son for Thorliff. A baby to hold in my arms and . . ." Another tear followed the first. "And yes, I do understand the ramifications of this pregnancy. But I will do everything you, we, all of us think best."

"Bed rest with nourishing food, limited but planned exercise, and taking everything we can find to build your strength," Astrid started. "We will move you into one of the patient rooms downstairs—no stairs, no lifting. We will contact the Chicago hospital and any others we can think of to get the latest information on a problem like this." As the instructions flowed like water on a gentle slope, Astrid was surprised. She had no idea Elizabeth had been thinking along these lines, obviously expecting this diagnosis.

"Yes, Doctor. I can at least keep the books and order supplies."

"As long as it doesn't make you tired. You have to stop before you get tired. Oh, and worrying will do that worse than anything."

"I figure the baby was conceived end of May or so."

"So we might be two and a half months along, so sometime in February."

"I so love playing the piano for church." Elizabeth heaved a sigh. "Good thing we have Jonathan back."

"When will you tell Thorliff?" Ingeborg spoke gently, all the time stroking Elizabeth's hand and arm. "I'm thinking we need to bring Reverend Solberg into this immediately, and Kaaren. Any others are up to you, as to when you make an announcement, not that making an announcement is necessary, but you are one of the doctors here, and people will wonder why you are not treating patients."

"I guess we'll wait and see on that. Right now I'm glad that none of the nurses are staying here."

Astrid nodded. "True, but that might be a possibility, if we feel that can help you."

"Thelma will be a combination sergeant, nurse, and town crier."

Ingeborg and Astrid exchanged a look full of questions.

"So we are in agreement, then?" Astrid asked.

"As to actions?"

"Yes. Mor?"

"Then we pray God's will be done. And we pray for strength, but even more for peace and for Him to bathe Elizabeth and Thorliff in His love and protection."

Peace did flow gently on the breeze, settling like butterfly wings. *If only I could hang on to this peace,* Astrid thought. *Peace is not something I've experienced much lately.* Not with all the dissension regarding the Valders and the workmen and the town. Unrest was afoot, not peace. *Why is it that we can't rejoice in the new man in town who has so much to offer?*

"Mor, have you and Reverend Solberg talked about Anner Valders and how to handle the mess he is causing?"

"We are praying for God's will and wisdom and an extra dose of love."

"I really like that Thomas Devlin. He was so good with Mr. O'Flaherty, and I've heard that his sense of humor has spread among the building crews. I hope he will stay here. And no, I am not afraid of another church moving in here. I've not canvassed the workers to see what faith they belong to. Some have come to our church. Maybe we need to make a better effort at inviting the others." Astrid paused to think. "Amelia has quite a large class learning English. They have to meet at the school because the only other places big enough are our church and the dining room at the boardinghouse. The school seems most appropriate, but perhaps we should move it to the church."

"I wouldn't ask Mr. Valders about that." Elizabeth shook her head. "Has anyone heard what Hildegunn has to say?"

"She parrots *Mr.* Valders."

Ingeborg chuckled. "She has always said that, but I really thought she was the one in charge."

"Me too. Guess it goes to show you just never know." Astrid rose. "I need to get back to the hospital. I have asked Deborah to keep good track of what medicines and supplies we need. She'll turn the inventory in to you. Having a manager for the hospital would help, that's for sure. Make sure you pray we have no major crises. I, for one, am grateful you were not in contact with Mr. O'Flaherty. Nor the other immigrant workers."

The nurses were changing shifts when she walked in the door. For a change, Trygve was not waiting to walk Nurse Hastings home or to the Soda Shoppe, as they'd done so often. Come to think of it, she'd not seen him for a few days. She stilled her curiosity with stern instructions to mind her own business and sat down to check through the charts and see what had transpired in the last few hours. Hopefully not much. Some patients they could send home. Here was a new case of pneumonia. That could be bad this early in the season. And Grant Wiste, Sophie's stepson, was here with a broken finger. That child got into more scrapes.

But mostly her mind and her worries went back to Elizabeth. Dear Elizabeth. *O God, why do you do these things to us?*

Manny was napping again.

Haakan watched the boy's breathing and remembered his own sons at Manny's age. He thought at first that they were simply getting lazy when they slept so much, but Ingeborg said differently. *"Please be patient, Haakan. Look how many helpings the boys eat at every meal. They are getting their growth and changing from boys into men. They won't stay 'lazy' long."* And she was right. She was almost always right. Now they were diligent and faithful workers—all his children were.

Today was bright and hot without a cloud in the sky. This

morning the boys were out getting the combine and wagons ready. Except Andrew, who was helping Lars today. They would haul the harvesting equipment to the fields tonight. Tomorrow at first light, wheat harvest would begin, and not a moment too soon.

There was another point of pride. Haakan simply gazed out across the distance over the golden rippling wheat, admiring its sheer beauty. And promise. They would bring in a rich harvest this year. Bumper crop. Thick stand, full heads. A couple days ago, Haakan had walked out to the field to check. The wheat had been on the edge of perfect ripeness then. It was ready now.

Wait. He stood up and strained his eyes. What was that out in the wheat? Something moving. Uff da! That brown cow. She had somehow broken through the fence. The boys were gone. Ingeborg was in town. Manny was still useless. That left Haakan.

He picked up his walking stick beside the door and carefully went down the steps. He found himself almost smiling. For weeks he had watched the work go on without being able to help at all. The few times he'd tried, the boys had to bring him home, as if he were some old invalid. Right now, though, he would make the difference between a full harvest and a lost harvest. Determined, he marched out to the field. If one cow was out, the others would follow within a matter of minutes. A herd the size of theirs would knock the entire field down before he could find help.

If the cows knocked the mature wheat down, the combine could not pick it up. If the combine ran over it and could not pick it up, it was pretty much lost. Scythes couldn't pick it up very good either. People with sickles could save some of the downed wheat, but not much. Anyway, who could afford time to sickle fallen wheat during this, the busiest time of harvest?

He found the break in the fence. And there was another cow picking her way over the fallen fence! Three in the field now! They could ruin the whole field! And a fourth . . . Haakan swung his walking stick and shouted. Startled, the fourth and her followers turned aside and trotted off.

He watched them for a moment, then climbed clumsily across the fallen fence and broke into a sort of trot toward the other three. Look at the mess they were making of his prime wheat!

He was winded by the time he had worked his way around behind the cows. His walking stick was very handy. He tied his handkerchief to the end of it. Now when he waved it, it frightened the cows enough to get them moving back toward the break.

It took him nearly twenty minutes to get all the cows back into the pasture where he wanted them. In his youth, he could have done it in three. *Ah, but Haakan, it's no matter that you are an old man. You did it! See? You did it!* He leaned against a fence post for a few minutes, simply mustering his strength.

He got to work on restacking the rails, mending the fence break as best he could with no tools. It took him a long time. Was his mending job good enough? Possibly not. That brown bossy would only have to lean into it and she'd break it down again. He should put them in the south pasture.

No, since he was headed home anyway, he would drive the cows with him up to the barn. Then the boys could let them out into the other pasture when they returned. That would be a lot easier, and anything easier was good. Haakan was now very weary. His whole body thudded. He was no longer in good shape, but then he knew that. He also knew he'd been getting stronger with all his walking. Right now he might have argued the effort.

The cows had made their way down to the riverbed. Apparently wandering around in a wheat field makes a cow thirsty. He followed them down the steep slope, leaning heavily on his stick. His handkerchief was still tied to the end of it, so he would have no problem driving them home.

He was now absolutely spent. Worn out. Instead of driving the cows back to the barn, he would climb out of the riverbed and go back to the fence break. Protect it, keep the cows away from it. He would sit down and wait there until either Ingeborg or the boys returned. They would see he was gone, come looking, and he would flag them from where he sat. He would not even need to stand up to signal them. He would just wave his walking stick. The handkerchief would be easily seen. And he could shout. That too.

They would mend the break properly and all would be well.

He drove his stick into the dirt and leaned on it heavily, beginning the long climb from the river bottom back up to the field. Another step. Another.

His legs buckled and he landed heavily on his side. They would not see him down here. He must get back up to field level. Could he climb back up on his feet? He made a few useless attempts. No. He would crawl up and out on his hands and knees. That would have to do.

He could not get up onto his hands and knees. He would have to rest a while. If he heard voices, he would shout.

The pain began in his left arm. What had he done to his arm with all his flailing around on the ground? It spread into his neck. And now his chest felt as though one of the cows were sitting on it.

The pain filled his neck and his arm and his chest. Intense pain. Intense pressure. He had never felt this before. Not all this. His ears rang.

Surely he could master this situation. He had always accomplished whatever it was that he absolutely had to do. Ingeborg and the children would be so disappointed in him. He was failing himself and them.

He must rest. He closed his eyes and tried to breathe deeply, to relieve the pressure. Deep breaths would not come.

He might die. His eyes popped open. Where did that thought come from?

From God, no doubt, because the thought grew and filled his mind and heart. He was dying. Apparently this was the moment. Not in a warm, comfortable bed with Ingeborg and the children gathered about. Not in Astrid's lovely new hospital receiving loving care.

Out here alone on a riverbank in the sun and heat, with cows probably even now testing the patch job on the fence, threatening his wheat. *His* wheat.

No. He was not alone. Ingeborg would be the first to tell him God was right there beside him. Haakan did not doubt that God was.

And this, he decided, was quite all right. He was surrounded not by gloom and weeping mourners but by warm and fertile soil, cool grass, dazzling sun. His land rose up and gently wrapped itself around him.

His land.

He thought of his life and opportunities in Norway. He could never ever have built a life there close to the life he had enjoyed here, with Ingeborg at his side. Here he had built not just a fine, productive farm but a heritage, a gift to his children and his children's children, for who knows how long.

Sweat, yes, and many tears. But triumph too.

That soft bed would soon be gone. Even the mourners would eventually disappear. But his lasting heritage, this land around him, would remain. He was leaving behind something infinitely bigger and longer lived, and more beautiful than any one person. And few indeed are the men who can claim that triumph.

Very well. Have your way, God.

I love you, Ingeborg.

CHAPTER 32

Something is wrong, I have to go home."

"I'll get the buggy." Thorliff left before she could answer.

"I can get there faster on foot."

"The horse is already harnessed, so it will only take a couple of minutes." Elizabeth laid a restraining hand on Ingeborg's arm. "Why don't you call and learn what you can that way?"

"Ja, I didn't think of that." She let the phone ring and ring.

"I'm sorry, Ingeborg, there is no answer. You want me to call Knutsons or Andrew?" Gerald paused. "I can do an emergency ring, you know."

"But I don't know that it is an emergency. Just a feeling I have. Takk." She set the earpiece back on the prongs.

"Mor, Thorliff has the buggy at the gate," Elizabeth called from the porch.

"Takk." All the while she rushed to the buggy, *Please, Lord, help* pounded through her mind.

"Hang on!" Thorliff slapped the reins, and the horse broke into a trot. Once beyond the houses, he clucked again, and the buggy rocked from the speed of the cantering horse.

Patches did not greet them when they drove in.

"Where's the dog?"

"He went with Andrew in the wagon to the elevator. You know how he loves to ride in the wagon." Ingeborg leaped to the ground the instant the buggy stopped and ran to the porch steps. "Haakan? Haakan? Where are you?"

Silence. She tore into the house, her heart now thundering. *Where is he, Lord? Help!* She checked the bedroom. No. Where was Manny? She could hear Thorliff calling, and when she reached the gate, an answer came from the barn. Manny and Thorliff were at the barn door.

"I fell asleep and when I woke up, he was gone, so I went looking for him." Manny looked as terror stricken as she felt. "I can't find him anywhere."

"Think, Mor. Where might he have gone? Would he have walked to town alone?"

"I don't think so. Kaaren's? Perhaps." She rubbed her forehead, fighting to get her mind to calm down and think. "If he collapsed somewhere, we would miss him, so we need to cover every inch of the house, the buildings . . ."

Manny stumped beside her. "It's all my fault! I should not have slept. Where could he be?"

Thorliff called from the house. "He is not at Kaaren's or at Andrew's, and I asked Gerald to put out an emergency call. You stay here at the house to answer the calls."

"Manny could do that. We need to check every room in the house, the cheese house, all the buildings. He could have taken one of the horses."

Thorliff climbed the stairs as she searched every room. His hat was not on the peg. She checked the back porch. "Thorliff, his hat and walking stick are not here."

The telephone jangled and she motioned for Manny to answer. "Reverend Solberg has notified the pray-ers."

"Thorliff, check the outhouse and the cheese house. Freda is over at Kaaren's." While he did that, she looked toward Kaaren's, where the men had been putting the final repairs on the harvesting machinery. Harvest was due to start as soon as the dew was off the wheat in the morning. Roiling dust marked the speed of the wagons and the horses of approaching people.

Thorliff leaned against a post to catch his breath, shaking his head at the same time. "Where could he have gone?"

"Did we call Ellie? Maybe he is there."

"When the emergency call went out, she'd have called to say he was there."

"Of course. O Lord God . . ."

Thorliff wrapped his arms around her while she sobbed into his shoulder. "Thorliff, I think he is gone home."

"Nei, do not say that! We will find him. He is sitting resting somewhere, or he is unconscious, but we will find him."

Lars and Jonathan galloped up the lane on harnessed work horses and leaped off before the horses fully stopped. "Have you gone through the barn yet?"

"Not completely." Both men headed for the barn.

Ingeborg took the wet cloth Manny handed her and wiped her face. She sucked in a deep breath, caught it on a sob, coughed, and let all her air out.

"Here, sit down before you faint." Thorliff led her to the settee and sat her down.

"Manny, please stay by the telephone. That's where you can help most." He squatted in front of his mother. "Are you feeling faint?"

"Nei. I am. . . ." She breathed in and out deeply again. "I am in God's arms. Haakan is too."

Kaaren and Freda climbed the stairs, and Kaaren sat down, gathering Ingeborg into her arms. "We'll get through this."

"Ja."

"She says Pa has gone home. She means to heaven. It cannot be!" Thorliff slammed his hand against the post. "No, it cannot be."

Kaaren tipped Ingeborg's chin up and looked into her eyes. "Peace is what I see in you," she whispered.

"Ja. I keep thinking on the verse, 'I will extend peace to her like a river.' It flows through my mind and my soul." She could hear Thorliff giving the arriving people instructions on where to look, planning—it was his gift.

Patches charged up the steps and skidded to a stop in front of her, followed by Andrew. "I should never have taken the dog. Have you combed the house? If he has fallen, it would be so easy to not see him."

Ingeborg petted the dog, ruffling his ears. And then looking into his eyes, she said, "Go find Haakan, Patches. Go find Haakan."

Paws lightly kissed her nose and spun for the steps.

"You better keep up with him."

"He gets cows, not people, Mor."

"He knows what I said. Just follow him."

"You've got cows in the wheat field along the river!" one of the newer arrivals hollered.

"Oh, not now!" Thorliff muttered something else too low for his mother to hear, but she recognized the frustration building in her elder son. Sometimes he was so like Roald. His father had been a man of fewer words than his son, but they both handled anger the same way. Tamp it down, but sometimes words not normally used spouted out.

She found her mind wandering, thinking of Haakan fishing with Carl and Inga. Of his teaching Manny to carve. Of his steadfast love, both for her and for their God. They needed to have another ball game. He made such a good umpire.

"Ingeborg?" John Solberg knelt in front of her. He took her hands and squeezed gently.

"Ja, I am good. Haakan has gone home, and I already miss him more than I can say, but I know."

"I'm not surprised. God has spoken to and through you for many years. Now, remember these words if you forget all else. No guilt! You must not allow guilt to get the barest of footholds. Satan will do that, you know. You were not here, but that too was according to God's plan. He is in charge. He is here, in and around us, holding us close."

"I know. He has not let me go, and He never will, but this is not the way I would have had it. John, he was alone."

"No. No, he wasn't. Haakan was not alone, and I am sure his last thought was of you. But he was not alone. God never leaves His children alone, especially when He is bringing them home." He squeezed her hands again, ever so gently and full of love.

"I do not grieve for Haakan. He was so ready to go home, looking forward to heaven, but I grieve for all of us. We who are left behind." She tipped her head back and let the tears flow.

Astrid climbed the steps and sat down by her mother. They hugged together, their tears mingling. "Inga is staying with her mother. I asked Elizabeth not to come right now, both for her sake and Inga's. Ellie is staying at home with the children too. She said to tell you how much she loves you and is praying they will find him sitting or resting somewhere."

"They will find his body," Ingeborg said gently, "but Haakan has gone home."

"I think that too. Oh, Mor, I am not ready to be without my far yet. I should be, but I am not."

"None of us are ever ready." Ingeborg dropped kisses and tears in her daughter's hair and rested her cheek on the top of her head. *Thank you, Lord, for my children, my family, my friends. O Lord God . . .* She sniffed back more tears, gave up, and picked up one of the muslin squares Freda had set on the table beside her. At least they dried quickly.

Manny sticked along the porch from the front of the house. "They found him. The dog went right—" His voice broke and he swung around and left again.

Preparations. They must be made, Ingeborg thought. She should be up and busy now. She sat. Others must do it. She had no strength. Her mind returned to her memories.

Later, Thorliff came out the door. "I've set up the sawhorses with that door we always use in the parlor. What else can I do?"

"We can cover it with sheets."

"I did. Freda said they will prepare him and asked what you would like them to dress him in."

"His good suit is hanging in the closet."

"I'll get it out."

Sometime later, when all that could be done was finished, Ingeborg smoothed back Haakan's hair. He still looked so peaceful, and that is what the men who found him said. *"He looked so peaceful."* She looked to Reverend Solberg beside her. "Can we have the funeral tomorrow?"

"Of course, but there is ice if you want to postpone it for a day or so."

"Why? He's gone. As far as I'm concerned, we could have it this evening, as soon as they can build the box and dig the hole."

"Andrew and Thorliff, with Lars helping, are building the box now. Several others are at the cemetery digging. The call has gone out, and people are passing on the information. Tomorrow morning at ten at the church we'll have the service. Hildegunn has taken charge of the noon meal."

"Did you tell everyone no black? Haakan hated the black of mourning. One night when we were talking, he said he knew this was not proper, but the Irish have it right. Throw a party. He would be in heaven, celebrating with all the saints and angels, and he hoped we could do the same."

"Leave it to Haakan. What a request, especially at this time of unrest. Have a party. We will do that to the best of our ability."

Lars had told them what he thought happened. The cows got in the wheat. Since no one else was around, Haakan went to chase them out, then fixed the fence as well as he could. He tried to drive the cows up from the river, probably to the barn, but his heart quit on the riverbank.

Ingeborg said, "I am not surprised that he died that way, taking care of his land, his wheat, and his cows."

"Neither am I. Is there anything special you would like me to say tomorrow?" John Solberg had not left her side.

"A mighty man of God has gone home to be with his Lord. And then tell them all what they need to do so they can see Jesus in heaven also. I trust you to keep it simple."

"May I ask if anyone has something to say?"

"If you want. But remind them that Haakan was a simple man who shunned praise. Please do not embarrass him."

Solberg's chuckle barely disturbed the peace in the room. "Do you mind if others come through the night to be with you?"

"If they want, but it is not necessary. I don't care what is proper."

Memories, like reliving their life together, floated through her mind as the hours of darkness flowed by. With the first light of dawn, she rose, stretched, kissed him one last time and, after dipping some warm water from the reservoir, went to her bedroom to wash and dress for the day. The sight of her wearing the daisy-sprigged blue dimity dress always made his eyes light up, and so that was what she put on. She wove a narrow blue ribbon through her braids, wrapped coronet fashion around her head, and mopped her tears again when she caught herself staring at their bed. She would now sleep there alone.

The rattling of the grate said that Freda was up and preparing to set the coffee on.

"You go out and watch the sunrise, see the world come alive." Freda held up a hand when Ingeborg started to say something. "No, please let me do this." Freda ducked her head. "Please."

The rooster crowing heralded the day's beginning. Chirps turned to birdsong as the morning breeze kissed the leaves of the cottonwood, setting in motion another part of the morning song. A cowbell clanged as the cows headed for the barn to be milked, a calf bawled, the rooster continued his announcements of the day. And the aroma of coffee drifted out the door.

When Freda brought out the coffee and cakes from the night before, she set the tray down and sank into the cushioned chair. "Morning comes and the day goes on, as if nothing has changed."

"Joy comes in the morning."

"I know that's what the Bible says, but there will be plenty of weeping today too. I saw Thorliff and Andrew down at the shop. The coffin is ready."

"We will use a couple of the sheets to line it."

They arrived at the church an hour early, but people were already lined up to pay their respects. They filed past the coffin once it was set up on more sawhorses, and often went back outside to wait for the service. Haakan had touched many lives through the years.

When there was no more standing room, let alone sitting room, Reverend Solberg opened all the windows and doors so those outside could hear the service. Ingeborg felt as though she were floating, and while she listened to those who spoke, she found to her relief that the well of tears seemed to have been drained dry. *Thank you, Lord,* rolled over and over in her mind and soul.

When the service ended, many of the people grouped at the graveside while many others set up the tables and benches for the meal Hildegunn had organized. Since everyone came bearing food, there would be plenty to eat.

"Ashes to ashes, dust to dust." Reverend Solberg conducted the burial in the graveyard attached to the church. Another new grave was not far away, but for that burial there had been no crowd. Only a few mourners had attended that service.

One day, she promised the man she'd been married to for over twenty years, *I will be with you again, and we can worship our God together, face-to- face. It might be a long time, so don't get impatient.* She sprinkled the rich black soil on the top of the wooden box, as did her children, and stepped back.

"I want my grandpa to come back. I miss him." Inga's voice rang true. She broke away from her parents and ran to Ingeborg, who hugged her close.

"Me too," she whispered.

Together they stood until the benediction trumpeted out across the prairie. She said it with Reverend Solberg. "'The Lord bless thee, and keep thee: the Lord make his face shine upon thee, and be gracious unto thee: the Lord lift up his countenance upon thee, and give thee peace.' Amen."

Lord God, I will not get through this without your peace. I know the days ahead will be hard.

She turned when Thorliff and Andrew surrounded her. "Takk. Tusen takk," she said to those around her. With Inga clutching her hand, she followed her sons.

"Would you rather go home?" Andrew whispered in her ear.

"No, here is good. All will be well."

Hildegunn Valders stopped her and, to her surprise, put both arms around Ingeborg and hugged her close. "I am so sorry, dearest Ingeborg. So very sorry."

Ingeborg hugged her back. "Tusen takk for all you have done."

"You know our women. They do what needs to be done. And death does not usually warn us to get ready."

"Ah, so true."

Ingeborg moved among the people, thanking them for coming and inviting them to go ahead and eat. She turned with a smile when Joshua Landsverk and Johnny tuned their guitars and started to play. One of the new men stopped to talk with them and then left, soon returning with a fiddle. Another did the same and returned with a concertina, and then a mouth organ joined in. They played hymns and favorite songs and asked for requests.

That night in bed, Ingeborg lay looking up at the ceiling. "Dearest Haakan, I hope you enjoyed your going-away party. I know it was nothing like the welcome-home party you've been enjoying, but we did our best to celebrate your life."

She rolled onto her side and laid her arm across the place where he always slept. And the tears flowed again.

Chapter 33

Ingeborg wiped the flowing drops from her forehead and returned to her churn. *Ka-chunk, ka-chunk.* Somehow, slamming the dasher felt remarkably good. *Lord God, you didn't warn me I would miss him so much. I don't remember it being this bad last time, when Roald died.*

Ka-chunk. She listened to the dasher so she'd hear the difference when the butter was rising. *Ka-chunk.* She slammed it three more times, and the tune changed. She slammed it a couple more times, then took it all to the sink, where she could pour the contents into a sieve over a big bowl so the butter could drain before she washed it. Like kneading bread, churning butter could bring a sense of peace. First the physical exertion and then the beauty of a loaf of bread or a full butter mold.

"Grandma, come quick," Inga hollered through the screen door.

Ingeborg set the dasher down and followed the giggles around the porch.

Jumping up and down, Inga was pointing down the lane.

Tears welled up in Ingeborg's eyes and rolled over the lids. The old Indian man, a little girl at his side, made her heart leap.

"Emmy's coming home. Emmy!" Inga leaped from the porch and ran down the walk, out the fence gate, and down the lane. "Emmy!"

The little girl looked up at the old man and darted past him. The two little girls met and threw their arms around each other.

Ingeborg could hear their giggles on the breeze. Tears so near the surface blurred her vision yet again, but at least this time, they were tears of joy. She waited, delighting in the picture of the reunited friends, who were more like the sisters that neither child had. When they reached the gate, the two darted up to the porch, and Ingeborg instantly had a little girl hugging her on each side.

"See, Grandma? I knew Emmy would come back." Inga looked up at her. "You got tears again."

Ingeborg sniffed and, with an arm around each, hugged them tight. "But good tears this time." She smiled at Wolf Runs, whose face looked more deeply lined than ever, if that were possible. "Thank you for bringing her back."

He nodded and, removing a bundle from his shoulders, set it on the step.

"Please, come sit on the back porch, and I will bring you something to eat."

He nodded again. "Thank you."

Emmy picked up her bundle, and the two girls chattered their way around the house on the porch. Then the back screen door slammed.

"You came early," Ingeborg said. School was still more than a week away. The years before he'd brought her with only a day or two to spare.

"Great Spirit said Grandma needed blessing."

Ingeborg closed her eyes for a moment, her thank-you winging heavenward. "Our Holy Spirit always knows what we need. Thank you for listening."

He stopped and so did she.

"The child can stay with you now?"

Confused, she asked, "Through the school year again?"

"No. I will not be back. Her home with you now."

She turned and looked into his eyes. "Are you ill?"

He half shrugged. "Better this way. I am old." He waited.

"Ja, Emmy will always have a home here, and I thank you."

"Good."

"What about Two Shells? Will she come too?"

"Maybe later, if you want."

"She is always welcome too."

They continued on around to the back porch. "You sit and rest. I will bring you a plate." She paused again. "If you would like to stay here too . . ." Was that a smile she saw?

He settled into a chair and closed his eyes.

She fixed him a sandwich with meat and cheese, and then added a dish of applesauce and some cookies. The girls came thundering down the stairs and ran out the door, but this time Emmy stopped the screen door from slamming.

"Going to see the calves and the kittens in the barn," Inga sang over her shoulder.

Ingeborg brought the plate out to the uncle and set it beside him, then returned to finish washing the butter. She'd dumped the earlier washings into the bucket for the pigs and chickens. When this final wash water ran clear, she salted the golden butter, patted it into the three waiting molds, and set them in the icebox. Once she'd scrubbed the churn, she went outside to set it in the sunshine to dry. Wolf Runs was gone, but by the plate lay a dark feather tipped in white.

Emmy and Inga skipped up the steps.

"Did you tell your uncle good-bye?"

Emmy nodded. "I can stay here?"

"This is your home."

She clutched Ingeborg around the waist. "Someday I will go back." Her sniffs were the only indication of her tears.

"Someday, when you are ready, we will take you back, but this is your home for now."

A child. God had given her another child. For keeps this time?

"Would you two like to have coffee with me?" At their nods, Ingeborg returned to the kitchen, half listening to their chatter.

"Where is Manny?" Inga turned and told Emmy about the boy who had come to live there too.

"He is driving wagon for the harvesters." While the harvesters were at work in their fields now, they'd not moved the noisy separator out by the barn yet. She set the tray down on the table, and the three sat down.

"I told Emmy about Grandpa going home to heaven." Inga stared at her grandmother. "Will you always have sad eyes? I miss him too."

"I hope not." *Please, dear God, bring back the joy, so I no longer have sad eyes.*

"Miriam, there is a call for you." Deborah nodded toward the telephone on the wall in the hospital office.

"For me?" Fear hit her stomach as if driven by a sledgehammer.

"Mrs. Korsheski, from the hospital in Chicago."

"Thank you." Her heart racing triple time, Miriam kept herself from running, either to the office or out the front door. *Breathe!* The voice in her head was not a suggestion but a command. *Breathe.*

Dread cramped her stomach as she picked up the earpiece.

"Miriam Hastings."

"This is Nurse Frasier from Nurse Korsheski's office. Hold please."

Please, please—not my mother.

The familiar voice came back on the line. "Miriam, I hate to be the bearer of bad tidings, but your mother is failing, and we have decided that we should let you know. If you want to see her again this side of heaven, you need to come now. And, yes, she is asking for you."

"I . . . I have no money for a train ticket."

"We know. The hospital there will pay for your ticket. We will talk with Dr. Bjorklund and give her instructions to that effect."

But why are you doing this? That and other questions screamed through her mind. "Of course I want to see her, but—"

"I am afraid we are calling late, and you have missed today's train. But can you be on the next one tomorrow?"

"Yes. Yes, I will."

"One thing we ask is that you will return to Blessing to finish out your year there."

But what about my family? I have no choice—or do I? "Th-thank you."

"Someone will meet you at the station."

Why are they . . . ? How can this be?

She must have muttered some other unintelligible something, but she only knew for sure the earpiece was no longer in her hand, and she was huddled in a chair, trying to cry silently but unable to hold back the sobs. *Not my mother. Please don't take my mother. I need her. We need her. Oh, please . . .* As she quieted and mopped her eyes, she realized someone had been rubbing her shoulders and upper back.

"*Shh*, all will be well. You have family here now too, and you are not alone."

"Dr. Bjorklund?" Miriam blinked away the fog.

"Ja. Mrs. Korsheski telephoned me too." Her hand kept making circular motions, gently, like the kiss of an angel. "You will go and take care of your mother, and when you return, we will be here. Your Blessing family."

But what if I can't come back? Or don't?

"Your shift will be done shortly. Go to the nurses' room and wash your face, and you will feel much better. Do your report and please make sure your notes are clear on the charts and anything else you can think of."

"Wh-why?" She clamped jaw and eyes against another freshet.

"Why what?" Astrid cocked her head to the side.

"Why is everyone being so kind to me?"

"Who is everyone?"

"Mrs. Korsheski, the hospital, you . . ." She shook her head, a frown pushing her starched hat higher.

Astrid smiled. "My mor always says you catch more flies with honey than vinegar, but then I always wondered what to do with the flies. But Reverend Solberg would say to be kind to one another. Kindness is a highly underrated trait."

"There's no kindness where I come from. Other than in my family, and sometimes even that is questionable." *And not everyone in Blessing is kind either*. Some of them had not treated either her or Father Devlin kindly.

Trygve was waiting for her the next morning when she was ready to leave for the train station. "I can carry your bags for you."

"I only have this one suitcase."

"Then I will carry that." He took it from her hand as if she'd volunteered it.

Mrs. Jeffers gave her one last hug at the edge of the porch. "You hurry back now, and please greet your mother from us here." She tucked an envelope into Miriam's hand. "For your mother."

Miriam's eyebrows turned into question marks.

"Never fear, just from one mother to another." She clasped Miriam's shoulders. "You are a fine nurse and a finer daughter."

"Th-thank you."

A breeze teased the tendrils of hair that refused to remain confined in the net atop her head where her hat perched precariously. She paused at the step and looked out over the riotous rose beds and to the garden. How she wished her mother could have seen all this.

"You needn't say good-bye to this place. You will be coming back." Trygve stared up at her. For a change she was a bit higher than he, but not much.

"But if I do, it will not be the same."

"True. There is a sense in the air that fall is coming soon. We always feel that toward the end of harvest." He held out a hand.

She looked from his face to his hand and back. Then laid her hand in his.

Sure enough, it was still there, that strange tremor or something that singed her skin whenever they touched. She should have put her gloves on. It was still there, even though she'd spouted off to him after that miserable church service.

At the station, he made sure she had her ticket. They could hear the whistle announcing the train over the prairie to the west.

As it drew nearer, Trygve took her hand again. The silence lengthened. Silences used to be comfortable between them, but now the tension thrummed like a finely stretched violin string. But the music had gone out of it.

He stared into her eyes. "Miriam, I believe I have loved you ever since I first saw you. The most important thing I have to know is . . . do you love me?" The words rippled out and into her heart like a pebble in a pond. Or in this case, a boulder.

Miriam closed her eyes in fear that he could see into her heart. Did she? Did she really? Could she—so soon?

Yes. Maybe—in spite of being furious? Her heart swelled with love for this man. *But.* That love would have to be stomped on like burning coals until it died. There were no answers to this but for her to leave and for him to stay here. She'd heard broken hearts took a long time to heal. Be that as it may, hers would just have to heal, time or no.

"Trygve, I cannot change my mind."

"Cannot or will not? And besides, you did not answer my question." He took her hands in his. She could hear the train far down the track, the train that would carry her away. He squeezed gently. "Please answer me."

I cannot lie.

You must.

She looked down at their hands, unable to let him see. Slowly she shook her head. "I think I am coming to care for you, Trygve, but I do not think it is the kind of love to bring to a marriage." There. She'd said it.

The train whistle blew, too much closer, too quickly.

"Look at me." Had he shouted, the words could not have penetrated her heart any deeper. The heat from his hands burned into her skin, muscle, and bone, then flew like an arrow straight into her heart.

She raised her gaze, fighting to keep the tears from overflowing.

"Your eyes say one thing and your mouth another. No matter what is going on in this town, this is not the end for us. I will find a way."

The screeching train wheels echoed her heart's cry. Sparks

flew from the iron wheels on the iron track, like the sparks that leaped between them whenever they met.

She tugged her hands loose and stepped back. "Good-bye, Trygve. And thank you for bringing me to the station."

"This is not the end. On my life, I promise you, this is not the end." He picked up her valise and handed it off to the conductor.

"Good-bye." What a dreadful word! And she would have to say it again far too soon, to her dear mother.

Would all of life be nothing but good-byes?

"Remember." He gripped her hands. "I want you to know, and to understand, that if you do not come back, I will come for you."

"I . . . uh . . ." She stuttered to a stop at the look in his eyes. A thousand honeybees buzzed in her mind. Unable to break the lock of his gaze, she swallowed. *Think of something!* "Uh . . ." She started to argue, but that faded away.

"I will." He nodded and glanced toward the steaming behemoth screeching down at them.

She ordered her backbone to do its job, pushed her shoulders back, and retrieved her hand. "Thank you for escorting me, Mr. Knutson."

"My name is Trygve." One eyebrow raised slightly. He leaned forward, a barely visible motion.

He's going to kiss me. She took a step backward and almost stumbled on the stool the conductor banged against the wooden platform.

He passed her suitcase to the conductor, took her hand to assist her onto the stool, and stepped back. He touched a finger to the brim of his hat. "Blessing and I will be waiting." The door sighed closed.

She found a seat at the window.

He was watching. She must wave. It was the least she could do. She raised a hand to the window.

He smiled brightly. Glowed. Waved back.

Her new family? No, Dr. Bjorklund, her family waited in Chicago. By some miracle her mother was still alive and waiting for her.

One of the passengers called to someone through an open window. "We will be back."

No, I will not be back. My place is in Chicago. Mama, please wait for me. She straightened her spine, planted her feet flat on the floor, and stared toward the front of the car, where the conductor was coming through picking up tickets.

Against her determination, she looked out the window again. Sure enough, Trygve waited, waved again, and touched the brim of his hat. She heard him in her mind. *My name is Trygve, and I will come for you.*

He was a determined man, but her family needed her in Chicago. No matter what her heart wanted to do.

If only she knew for certain what her heart wanted: A life in Blessing or a life in Chicago. Was there any possibility of a compromise? Her mother would say that God has a plan. Could she trust that?

Lauraine Snelling is the award-winning author of over 70 books, fiction and nonfiction, for adults and young adults. Her books have sold over 2 million copies. Besides writing books and articles, she teaches at writers' conferences across the country. She and her husband make their home in Tehachapi, California.

More From Lauraine Snelling

To learn more about Lauraine and her books, visit laurainesnelling.com.

Ingeborg Strand dreams more of becoming a midwife than of finding a husband—until she meets university student Nils Aarvidson. Could Nils be the man God intends her to marry, or is He leading her toward an entirely different path?

An Untamed Heart

Astrid Bjorklund loves Blessing, the prairie town settled by her family, and enjoys studying medicine under Dr. Elizabeth Bjorklund's direction. But when she feels God might be calling her to the mission field, will she have to leave her beloved town—and her chance for love—behind?

HOME TO BLESSING: *A Measure of Mercy, No Distance Too Far, A Heart for Home*

More Fiction You May Enjoy

In small-town West Virginia, 1954, one newcomer's special gift with food produces both gratitude and censure. Will she and her daughter find a home in Wise—or leave brokenhearted?

Miracle in a Dry Season by Sarah Loudin Thomas
sarahloudinthomas.com

United in a quest to cure tuberculosis, physician Trevor McDonough and statistician Kate Livingston must overcome past secrets and current threats to find hope for their cause—and their hearts.

With Every Breath by Elizabeth Camden
elizabethcamden.com

On British-occupied Michilimackinac Island, voyageur Pierre Durant and his childhood friend Angelique MacKenzie must decide where their loyalties lie and what they will risk for love.

Captured By Love by Jody Hedlund
jodyhedlund.com